THE CALL

THE CALL

Charlotte Lewis

Copyright © 2021 by Charlotte Lewis.

Library of Congress Control Number:		2021907598
ISBN:	Hardcover	978-1-6641-6850-3
	Softcover	978-1-6641-6849-7
	eBook	978-1-6641-6848-0

All rights reserved. No part of this book may be reproduced or transmitted in any form or by any means, electronic or mechanical, including photocopying, recording, or by any information storage and retrieval system, without permission in writing from the copyright owner.

This is a work of fiction. Names, characters, places and incidents either are the product of the author's imagination or are used fictitiously, and any resemblance to any actual persons, living or dead, events, or locales is entirely coincidental.

Any people depicted in stock imagery provided by Getty Images are models, and such images are being used for illustrative purposes only.
Certain stock imagery © Getty Images.

Print information available on the last page.

Rev. date: 04/28/2021

To order additional copies of this book, contact:
Xlibris
844-714-8691
www.Xlibris.com
Orders@Xlibris.com
828756

For Holly, with thanks.

CHAPTER ONE

The power went out at the same instant a gust of wind rattled the family room doors. I could see the doors from the kitchen counter where I had ingredients laid out to make a cake. The wind gusted again and the doors rattled even harder. I stepped out of the kitchen to get a better view of the backyard. In thirty years, the doors have never shook so heavily. Potted plants on the deck are tipped and rolling about. The trees are in a frenzy; the hedges look tangled. There is a plume of leaves and debris slowly working its way above the yard. It flattened the chairs by the pool and picked up two small tables into its rotation. As soon as it was positioned over the pool, the plume collapsed - dumping itself into the water. The tables are upside down and floating. I hope the wind will ease before they sink into the pool. The trees are trembling but seem to be slowly returning to normal. I ran onto the deck, down the stairs and to the pool. The first table is resting against the rim and I snatched it out of the water. The second table is a few feet further out. The pool net was undisturbed by the wind and I used it to guide the second table to the edge.

My husband made these two wooden tables more than twenty years ago. There's so little I have left of him. I put the tables on the deck under the overhang. They seem no worse for their water bath.

As I came back into the family room, the house phone rang. Impossible, the house phone system depends on electricity. "Hello?" Silence. Perhaps the power triggered just long enough to cause the phone to ring. It has happened before. But I said hello again. Just in case, you know.

"Maddy, is that you?" Tears welled. I haven't heard that voice in fifteen years. It can't be. I couldn't answer. "Maddy?"

"Wes!!?"

"Maddy, I l----" The line went dead. The caller didn't hang up. The line went dead. I yelled into the phone aware it was fruitless. But how? How could this be?

A knock on the front door. "Grams, are you home? Are you okay? The wind took two trees down in our front yard. Your power must still be off. Ours is. I didn't hear your door chime."

My oldest grandson came in through the house. "Are you okay, Grams? Mom sent me over to check. She couldn't get through by phone." He looked at me and the phone I still had in my hand. "Did it ring? It couldn't. Your power is off, I'm sure."

How do I tell a sixteen year old that I just got a call from his grandfather; his grandfather who disappeared fifteen years ago? He looked at me more closely than usual. "You're crying. What happened?" He pulled out his cell phone. "Mom, something's wrong with Grams."... "I don't know. She's holding the telephone and crying."

My daughter and her family live a few blocks from me. Less than half a mile. She was here a few minutes later. She didn't laugh at me. She decided the power must have blinked on just long enough for the phone call but blinked off just as quickly. Why did I think it was her Dad? "Lee, no one other than your father has ever called me Maddy. And, I recognized his voice." She said nothing but I could almost see the wheels turning. I gathered myself together and hung up the phone. What madness is this? That's what it is. Madness. I shook my head. Madness. My grandson is trying to decipher what his Mother and I have said. It makes no sense to him. Of course, it wouldn't.

We went into the kitchen. Trying to act normal, I began measuring ingredients for the cake. There is a slight tremor in my hands. No one else seems to notice. I want desperately to replay those few words. How could the phone ring? How could it be Wes? But my daughter and grandson are watching me. It's been too long for hallucinations like this. I know what I heard.

Deciding, I guess, that I was okay, my grandson asked how I can bake a cake. "The stove is gas, just like the furnace and the water heater. Your grandfather never had great faith in SoCal Edison. And, as you can see right now, that lack of faith was warranted." He nodded.

"Grams, are we still playing miniature golf today?"

"It's your birthday. I'm baking your cake. If the golf course hasn't blown away, we'll play miniature golf. I did promise."

Out came the cell phone. The miniature golf park didn't experience a wind storm at all and our reservation is confirmed. He said he'll make sure his pals know the wind didn't change our plans. He ran out the door. Then he turned and I could see he was trying to make the doorbell ring. "Your power is still out, Grams. See you later."

As I slid the cake pans into the oven, my daughter took out her cell phone. "I'm calling the police, Mom. Or should it be the FBI?" I didn't know. There had been so many authorities here fifteen years ago. Who ended up with the case? FBI? She decided to start with the local police.

No one on the force, who she spoke with, had been here fifteen years ago. And, apparently, the case wasn't interesting enough to still be on anyone's mind. She called the FBI. They were interested. Very interested. First they'd try to trace the call and then tomorrow an agent assigned to the matter would be out. The case is still open. Could I tell them the time the call came. I have an electric clock in the kitchen. It had stopped at 11:17am. The call was maybe ten minutes after that. Lee explained the wind storm and power outage. The agent actually made an appointment. Eleven tomorrow morning. Either the FBI has learned manners in fifteen years or Wesley John Palmer is no longer a matter of extreme urgency or importance. Fifteen years ago there seemed to be an agent underfoot most of the time.

CHAPTER TWO

The cake smells as good as it looks. I finished decorating and changed clothes. When I got to my daughter's home, Wil, the birthday boy, his two best friends, his brother and sister were standing on the front lawn near the downed trees. The kids all told me that someone is coming tomorrow to take care of them. The seven of us fit in my old station wagon. Here we come, Bullwinkle's Miniature Golf. There are downed trees, uprooted hedges, and tangled plants for about a mile. The destruction stopped abruptly and the rest of the trip is the usual well groomed Southern California landscape.

The four boys played ahead of my daughter, granddaughter and me. We deliberately lagged behind. The laughter was a joy to me though my granddaughter, Laurie, is not impressed. She's twelve - someday she'll appreciate her brothers. But right now they're pains in the neck. She had more on her mind - her mother was ahead of her in scoring. She lined up a shot hoping to get through a windmill. Lee looked at me and grinned. Laurie's concentration is incredible. She made the shot.

We met up with the boys at the last hole. Everyone was comparing their scores. The birthday boy won by a single point. We turned in the clubs and balls and headed for the car.

I had offered Wil dinner anywhere local he wanted, except the Derby which is out of my price range. Lee was sure he would want to head to his favorite hamburger joint but he had other ideas. A few years ago, on my birthday, we went to an Italian restaurant that the family used to patronize regularly. Lee's husband, Larry, was home on leave and he insisted we have dinner there. For old times' sake, I believe he said. Evidently, Luigi's impressed Wil and that was his choice.

When I called to make reservations, I was surprised they still remembered me. It's been four years, at least, since that birthday dinner. We used to spend many a Saturday evening there before – well, fifteen years ago.

Luigi's hasn't changed in the thirty plus years I've eaten there. Quiet, understated elegance, wonderful food, and reasonable prices still prevail. Wil's friends, Steve and Donny, were impressed. As a matter of course, with a birthday, a scoop of spumoni is given to everyone at the table. That plus the impeccable service has the two friends in awe. I heard them whispering that this must be costing Wil's Grams a small fortune.

The restaurant was getting busy as we left at 7:30 to go to my house for cake and presents.

Somehow I am not surprised that the power is still off. Declaring that sixteen candles aren't enough light, I brought out several tapers so I could see to cut the cake and Wil could open his gifts. Usually it is lighter at this hour. The wind storm changed the sky somehow. About nine, I took everyone back to my daughter's. She'll get the two friends home. I truly believe it has been a fine birthday for Wil. He happily accepted the leftover cake. A bonus gift, I think he called it. And, it didn't cost a fortune.

Once home, and alone, my thoughts returned to that aborted telephone call. I know it happened. But I don't know how. I hope the FBI agent in the morning will have some information as to where it came from, or how it came at all. The power was off. Maybe I should get a cell phone. But, of course, then Wes wouldn't have the number. But I would have contact with people during times like this. I admit that I resisted moving from this large house primarily so that perhaps, one day, Wes would come home. I don't want a cell phone for the same reason. I have always been convinced that Wes did not disappear alone; someone or something had to have taken him. I am sure. And if he was ever able, he'd call me.

Now he's called and I know no more than I did fifteen years ago. Well, that's not truth. I know now that he is alive. I've wondered often about that.

CHAPTER THREE

The power came on early the next morning. I was up and ready to take a shower in the dark. I was grateful - I wanted a cup of coffee. Mixing a cake by hand is no big deal, but brewing coffee without electricity - I don't think so. I started the coffee before heading to the shower. When dressed, I took a mug of coffee out to the deck to assess the damage from yesterday's wind storm. Most of the potted plants on the deck are fine. One broken pot, a few plants need resetting. The umbrella had been closed or there may have been a lot of damage. It's heavy, and large when open. It could have sailed through the family room doors. The chairs were blown into a corner of the deck railing but none appear damaged. The railing took a beating; I will have to repaint it later. Several cushions are missing but I'm sure they're somewhere in the yard; or maybe even the pool. Lots of loose debris laying around – leaves, branches, papers.

The telephone rang and I ran to answer it. It was Lee. Did I want her to come over when the FBI agent was here? Yes, I did. "I'll come a bit early, Mom. I couldn't sleep last night thinking that Dad is alive somewhere." I told her I knew the feeling. I had a restless night myself.

I put my coffee mug on the counter and went back out. The pool is a disaster. And yes, there are two cushions, at least, that I can see laying in the shallow end. I decided that cleaning the pool is not a priority. The chairs aren't broken but had merely folded when they hit the pool deck. The wind slammed them pretty hard; I feel lucky. They're wood and could have shattered. It took only a few minutes to get them back where they belonged. I walked to the back of the yard. Two cushions were wedged in the holly bush. A book I had been reading on the deck was just laying on top of the privet hedge. No damage to it at all. Mentally I made notes of what needs to be done. Maybe

Wil and Mike can help their grandmother. If not, Laurie will. They often volunteer for odd jobs. Depending on the job, sometimes I pay them. This would definitely be a paid job.

Back inside, I poured more coffee into the mug; then made breakfast. The television usually is not on this early but I hoped to see some local news about the wind storm. There may have been something last night, but TV does take power and I had none. I put my breakfast on the coffee table and began to click my way around the channels. I'm pretty sure there's a local news like program at 8 or 9am. Found a channel with lots of photos. The wind has been classified as a small tornado. There was a swath through town about five blocks wide and over a mile long. Looking at the map they had, I realize I got off easy. The camera showed my daughter's house with her two big trees down and the neighbor across her street lost the roof off his garage. Awnings and canopies in that swath were down and often ruined. Other trees and hedges uprooted. Other swimming pools filled with debris. Yes, I got off easy. I turned off the television and put my dishes in the dishwasher.

I called Lee. Would she ask the kids if they'd care to come restore order to my deck, yard and pool? She said she was sure they would. Laurie was at the school - she's on the track team. School isn't in session but the track coach is. "Just tell them to come when they can. It's bad but not a total disaster. Gloves, they should bring work gloves."

Things I can control are under control. I don't know what to expect from the FBI. Not that they sounded vague; they just said they'd be here. They did say something about trying to trace the call. I don't know how that works. What would it tell me? Where Wes is? What would it tell them? What do they actually know about this whole situation? Fifteen years is a long time to try and remember what an agency knew about Wes; what happened, how, why. It seems that they didn't know anymore than I did at the time. Or, they weren't sharing with me what they knew.

Wes was manager of a large grocery warehouse in Los Angeles. He started with them as a clerk when he was fresh out of college; we had just married. He was twenty-two. Over the years he received promotion after promotion until he was in charge of the whole ball of wax. He was thirty-three then. The warehouse grew quite a bit in those eleven years. Super markets were becoming a big thing. His warehouse serviced some smaller grocers but mainly his customers were two large chains. They had their own brand name warehouses but Wes' warehouse specialized. Two or three times, after he became manager, I have been in a grocery store and actually heard someone say, "If our warehouse doesn't have it, call Wes Palmer." I always told him when I got home and he always said, "Oh, yeah, we had what they wanted." Or something like that. I don't understand grocery distribution at all.

We celebrated Wes' forty-fifth birthday just two weeks before the "incident". I don't know what else to call it. Wil, our oldest grandson who has just turned sixteen, had been born the year before. Wes' birthday dinner was Lee, Larry and the baby, our son Ed and his girlfriend Jane, and us. We went to Luigi's, of course. Back then, we celebrated everything at Luigi's. Our son Ed was two years younger than Lee. Yes, was. That's another story.

Wes decided he was now middle-age and should buy a little red sports car. Larry and Eddy urged him on at dinner that evening. We all laughed until tears rolled down our faces as Wes explained his middle-age driving philosophy. The owner of Luigi's is a long-time friend and suggested perhaps a celebratory bottle of his personal red wine would be in order. He sang Happy Birthday in Italian as he poured the wine. It went well with dinner. Of course, it would. Larry told us that he was joining the Marine Corps. He has a 'specialty' education and the Corps is delighted to have him. He would be leaving for Camp Pendleton in Oceanside in four weeks and then to a place called Camp LeJune. At least, that's what he believes. Maybe it was the other way around. Or I may have misunderstood him completely. But he was leaving for the Marines in a month.

That created the need for a second bottle of wine. Dinner was a marvelous time. I drove home.

The next week was a bit odd. Not for me; Wes said that some union organizer had been on premises and seemed upset that the warehouse was already unionized. Wes talked to most of the employees that week - one on one. They all had the same story. This guy said he was union. They told him they already had a union. Wes said he finally confronted the guy and asked just what his problem was. The answer was not satisfactory. In fact, Wes said it didn't even make sense. He told the guy to leave the property.

That seemed to end the situation. No employee reported seeing the guy after that. And everything appeared back on course. I bring this up only because the FBI tried to make it an issue. I told them that Wes felt the guy was really after something else though he didn't know what. He was convinced the union story was a cover for something. The FBI agreed that was possible but didn't have any explanation either.

Much later I decided the phony union guy was trying to get a lay of the land, so to speak. How things operated and who was in charge of what. The

FBI didn't scoff but they didn't seem to take me seriously either. To this day, I still think that phony unionizer was in on, or aware of, Wes' disappearance.

The next week things were running as usual at the warehouse and at home. Thursday just after noon, Wes called me. He said he was concerned about something and wanted to talk so thought maybe we could go out to eat. He called early so I wouldn't have begun to prepare dinner. I was working part-time then. Wes was very thoughtful that way. I asked what was up and he said, "I don't want to talk about it here, now. I'll call Luigi's and make reservations for six. The restaurant shouldn't be too busy then." I said that was fine with me but we could talk at home. Yeah, but he would like to have dinner out. I said I would be ready to leave when he got home. "I love you, Maddy. See you in a couple hours."

But, he didn't.

He's usually home no later than 5:30. I checked the afternoon news programs. No accidents reported on his usual route. By 6, I was panicky. I called Luigi's thinking I had misunderstood that he was coming home. He always does, to change. Maybe I was supposed to meet him there. They had the reservation, but Mr. Palmer was not there. I told them that he was late getting home then. "Let's cancel the reservation and we'll take our chances when he does get home." They appreciated the consideration and reminded me it was Thursday so there may not be much of a wait.

At 6:30 I called his warehouse. No answer on his direct line so I tried the guard house. The guard, who has been with the company almost as long as Wes, said that he hadn't seen Wes since about 1 o'clock. He said that wasn't all that unusual; but he hadn't seen Wes for several hours. About fifteen minutes later, the guard called back.

"Mrs. Palmer, Wes' car is still in the employee parking lot. I went up to his office. He's not there either. Thursdays the warehouse is closed over night - the deep cleaning crew comes in about midnight. There's no one here - but me. Do you want to call the police, or should I?"

Call the police? I hadn't even thought of that. Of course, I'd been thinking accident on the 110 or something. In the end, we both called the police. And by 6am, the FBI had been called. By whom? I don't know; probably LAPD.

That's pretty much the only clean, clear recollection of Wes' disappearance that I have. Once the FBI was in, I was out. Oh, yes, a bunch of personal questions - any trouble in the marriage and BS like that. But they seemed to sweep me under the rug exhuming me only when they had a string of foolish questions. What will it be like today?

I'm grateful Lee will be here.

Back to my son Edmund. Past tense. Three weeks after his father disappeared, Eddy was run over by a hit and run driver and killed. In broad daylight. Larry, Lee, and I have often believed that Eddy's death had something to do with his father's disappearance. But no one else could see a connection. Hell, I couldn't see a connection either but I know Eddy was in the same spot every day of the week. Someone could have deliberately killed him. He was standing on a street corner waiting to wave elementary school kids across the street. He was a crossing guard every morning - then he went to his accounting job at 10. He was wearing an orange crossing guard vest. He had a large crossing guard sign in his hand. How do you not see that? It was 7:50am.

The FBI was still actively asking questions and searching stuff regarding Wes at the time of Eddy's death. But they saw no connection. The AIC said it was just a very sad coincidence.

CHAPTER FOUR

A glance at the kitchen clock - egads, I haven't reset it yet from yesterday's storm. That took a few minutes as I had to get on a chair to reach the clock. Somewhere I have a small step ladder but it'll take less time to pull up a chair. After the clock was right, I poured another mug of coffee and went out to the deck. A number of plants merely had to be patted back into their pots. I went to the garage to see if I had another 8 inch pot to replace the broken one. Lee pulled into the driveway as I came out of the garage side door. The garage is not attached to the house - there's a four foot breezeway that leads to the back yard. The kids don't have to run through the house when they come to play in the pool. Well, there were many reasons we did that. But they're beside the point.

"Only one broken pot, Mom? Good for you. The neighbors next door lost five or six. She's really upset." Lee followed me back to the deck. The watering can had been blown to the same corner as the chairs. She filled it and watered the plants I had already tamped back into place. "What time is the agent supposed to be here?"

"Eleven." I know she knows. Lee must be nervous to ask. I know I'm pretty antsy myself. I finished repotting the plant. It appears undamaged. I didn't lose one to the storm.

"Well, let's go in and wash our hands. It's 10:30. He might come early. Do you think he expects us to have a file or something?"

"I doubt that. He'll probably have a briefcase with papers in it. He shouldn't expect us to produce anything now. It's been fifteen years and they weren't too excited by what we produced then." I nodded. I remember those stupid interrogations.

Lee rinsed the coffee pot and started a new pot brewing. I must have drank a lot this morning. I went to the bathroom to wash my hands and decided to use the facilities, as Wes used to say. Otherwise, I might have to interrupt the agent just to go. "This is getting pretty pathetic. Good god, Lyn. Get yourself together." I believe I did not say that out loud. I hope I didn't.

The FBI agent turned out to be two guys. And they were precisely on time. We went into the living room. They both had a brief case. They introduced themselves as Agent Harrelson and Agent Tucker. Neither had been here fifteen years ago. Neither looked old enough to have been an agent fifteen years ago. Oh, good grief, how much are we going to have to relive?

Agent Tucker appears to be the AIC. I don't know why I felt that even before he said anything.

"Thank you for notifying us of the telephone call you received yesterday. Fortunately for us, you live in an area of town where the telephone system hasn't been completely updated digitally." He opened his brief case and took out a thin file. Too thin to be the original. "Mrs. Palmer, have you ever seen in Massachusetts?"

"What?" I couldn't have heard him correctly? Massachusetts?

"I asked if you have been to Massachusetts?"

"No. I have never been to Massachusetts. Why do you ask?"

"Have you ever heard of Lowell, Massachusetts?"

"I don't think so. I presume that's a town?"

"Yes, and apparently, the call you received yesterday originated from a bank of telephones outside the Main Library in Lowell, Massachusetts."

Lee and I were both surprised. "You can actually tell what phone?" Lee asked. I doubt she expected an answer. The FBI has never been very forth coming.

Tucker got an odd smile on his face; more like a mouth twist actually. "Well, there are apparently four phones in that bank. We don't know which phone but we can tell it was one of the four. We have agents now in Lowell taking fingerprints from all four phones."

I am sure my mouth dropped open. "You can tell if Wes made the call? You can tell which phone? God lord! That is wonderful as well as amazing."

Harrelson had a smug look. "If you lived, say where your daughter lives, we might not have been so lucky. The telephone company here moves at a snail's pace with upgrades."

They know where Lee lives? She didn't live there fifteen years ago. Creepy.

"So you may be able to confirm that I really did hear Wes' voice yesterday? I'm not crazy. The call was real."

"Yes, we should be able to do that. It's doubtful that the library cleans the pay phones very often. The telephone company seldom does. Do you realize how few pay phones are still in service?"

"Is that a rhetorical question, Agent Harrelson?"

Should have kept my mouth shut. They both, almost immediately, went into standard FBI mode. "Proving that is necessary. Now. We need to establish other times you have heard from your husband in the last fifteen years. Why weren't they reported?"

"There have been no other times, Agent Tucker. I have hoped and prayed for fifteen years to know my husband wasn't dead. Do you think I would not alert you if I had heard something before yesterday? That is an insult. I reported the first and only contact I've had with Wes since the day he disappeared thinking perhaps, just perhaps, the FBI in all its legendary glory could find him for me and bring him home. I had hoped you would be able to tell me not only where he is but why, and how he came to be there."

The two agents exchanged glances. Maybe we weren't supposed to be smart enough to see. I had the feeling they knew a lot more than they were telling us. Lee moved to the edge of her chair - she feels it too. I can tell.

"Once the main hullabaloo was over, after Dad disappeared, we never heard from the FBI again. We had expected some sort of periodic update on what was happening. It never came." Lee took a deep breath before she continued. "Today you insult my Mother. Are you going to give us a fifteen year review now? You know more than you've ever told us. Why haven't we been privy to what's happened?"

Again, the two agents glanced at each other. Tucker looked cornered. Harrelson looked as if he was glad he wasn't the Agent in Charge.

CHAPTER FIVE

Agent Tucker was seated on the couch. He had taken a thin file from his briefcase earlier but now he put the briefcase on the coffee table and started pulling out other various skinny files. He turned and asked Harrelson something. His voice was so low neither Lee nor I could hear him. Harrelson merely nodded. Tucker put his empty briefcase on the floor next to the coffee table. When he looked at us, I couldn't read his emotion. But he was definitely emotional. It scared me. Lee and I were in the club chairs across from the couch. He looked us square in the eye, cleared his throat, and said, "This has been one of the world's greatest screw-ups. I know you should always start at the beginning. But, damn if I know where the beginning really began."

That scared me even more. What in the world could he be referencing? I half expected him to say, "Once upon a time..." But he didn't.

"About a year before your husband's disappearance, he was approached by two men he didn't trust. He didn't like their appearance or their attitude. And he certainly didn't like their proposal. He told them he'd need a day or two to consider if he'd be able to help them. For some reason, they agreed to contact him at the end of that particular week.

"He had some sort of out-of-state meeting with the Independent Grocers Association in Denver that week. He explained that to the two men. That may be the reason they were agreeable to meet later. Do you remember that trip, Mrs. Palmer?"

The incident immediately came to mind. "I didn't go on that trip. Normally I would have but I had had some dental work done and it didn't seem to be healing as I thought it should. I didn't think it would be a good idea to get too far from my dentist. I was surprised that Les agreed with me so readily. I felt it was because I was so miserable and he thought it was wise for me to stay home. Are you saying that wasn't his reasoning?"

Tucker seemed surprised I answered his question as I did - with a question. He chewed on his bottom lip for a second.

"No, I am sure that was the reason. But it did make things easier for him. While in Denver, he contacted the FBI office there. He explained to the desk agent that he had been contacted by two men, Salvadorians he thought. They had a proposition for him involving his warehouse. He didn't want to accept but was afraid to refuse. They had made a few veiled threats. Or what Mr. Palmer construed as threats. Was there some way the Bureau could assure him that they could apprehend this gang, as he called it, if he agreed to their proposition?

"The agent made several calls before Mr. Palmer left Denver. Another agent just happened to run into him and they had lunch for old times' sake - at least that was the story Mr. Palmer gave his associates. This friend just happened to be in Denver and they just happened to run into each other. The agent, of course, had a code name and he said that he would use it as Mr. Palmer's old friend from college if he called. Mr. Palmer was to return the call from a pay phone or other phone not traceable to him.

"When the men with the proposition returned to Mr. Palmer's office, he asked for greater details and agreed to "buy in". We are quite sure no money was exchanged but that was the terminology used. These men would have monthly shipments that required safe storage. All they wanted was a safe, locked place to store small shipments that they could access unquestioned. Mr. Palmer's reputation and his control of the warehouse met their requirements. Nothing else would be required of Mr. Palmer; nothing else.

"When Mr. Palmer next spoke with his college friend, he was able to fill in many details. He said, according to the agent's written report, that at that particular period in time, money had not been discussed. If it had, he missed it. He was afraid that it would be a matter of life or death. The men said a rental fee would be discussed only when he had proven he could protect their shipments."

Lee and I looked at each other - more than slightly amazed. How could Wes have been in on such a deal and manage not to say a word to me? I suppose it was protection for me. Neither Lee nor Edmond lived at home then. But to make a deal with foreigners and the FBI and not say anything? He was a stronger man than I thought.

"Agent Tucker, these shipments - what were they comprised of - what made them so valuable?"

He shuffled some papers. "Opioids."

That shocked me. Wes was death on drugs. Did he agree thinking the FBI could or would somehow shut down this group and keep him out of it?

"Being a warehouse, a truck coming and going would not be suspect. But how could Wes possibly think he could keep the shipments under wraps so to speak? Did the FBI give him guidelines? I just don't understand."

Frankly, I expected him to tell me they couldn't tell me anything. That wasn't the case.

"This pipeline was eventually totally shut down. I don't have the details of the original arrangements other than something about one night a week the warehouse is empty except for the gate guard and a cleaning service that comes in around midnight. Apparently it was agreed that the Salvadorians could enter directly behind them, as if part of the cleaning service. The guard would not question them the first time and would "know" them afterwards. The drugs would be brought in and stored in a locked cage. Not even Mr. Palmer had a key. Pick up of the shipment evidently was handled in the same way. But on pickup, the FBI would follow the shipment out of the city. Before it was distributed, at least half the time, their whereabouts were known and raided. Long enough and far enough from the warehouse, there was never any connection."

By this time, I am trembling badly. The agent's explanation was not totally clear to me All I was sure of was that Wes was involved in drugs. He had US government backing but nonetheless, he had been involved in drugs. That seems so against his principles. What could have possessed him to even consider it? Why did he consider it? Did he think of the FBI when he got to Denver? Or had he thought of it before and that's why he was so relieved I wasn't going with him? There are too many questions. I hope these two guys have many answers.

Lee asked, "Would anyone like coffee? I really need a cup. Well, I think I need a drink but I'm settling for coffee."

Usually the agents would say no, they're on duty. Or some such bullshit. They both said, "Yes, thanks. Black please."

I got up and went to the bathroom. Washing my face helped a little but I am still shocky. This is all almost too much. And it still doesn't tell me where Wes is or why. I came back as Lee sat four mugs of fresh, hot coffee on the coffee table. I murmured thanks and picked up a mug.

The fresh coffee revived me enough to ask "How long did this arrangement go on? And why did it end?"

Harrelson picked up a file folder. "It went on for about a year, we think. Why did it end? Mr. Palmer got spooked about something. He called his college friend and told him some stranger had been poking around saying he was a unionizer. That didn't fit as the warehouse has been unionized for decades. The guy was pushy. And Palmer told him to leave and not come back. That was on Thursday morning. The college friend told him they had enough to close down more than half of the pipeline. Les was concerned because there was a shipment in the warehouse then. It would be picked up that night, he believed. His college friend assured him he'd be okay. The FBI would take care of him. Hold tight. It might be a rough ride." He was reading from one of those thin files from his briefcase.

Lee was unaware that her father had called me that day. She's sitting there nodding, thinking the FBI let him down. I could see that in her face. She has a small storm brewing in her mind. Then I realized the FBI may not know he called me. "Are you aware that Wes called me that Thursday just after lunch. He said he had some stuff he wanted to talk to me about. He made reservations at our favorite restaurant and said he'd be home by 5:30 to change so we could make the 6 o'clock reservations. He never came. Until yesterday, I haven't heard his voice since that telephone call."

The agents were surprised. They didn't know he called me. Both made some sort of note on a couple sheets of paper in the thinnest file. Then Tucker cleared his throat again. "Mrs. Palmer, we were unaware of the call. We were also unaware that the U S Marshals had been notified and about three o'clock they stopped by Mr. Palmer's office. They convinced him who they were and that they had reason to believe his life was in danger. He left with them. They didn't bother to notify the FBI so they may have been unaware we were Palmer's backup. I am sure he convinced them of that at some reasonable point in time. But they have never shared his location. The phone call yesterday is the first clue as to your husband's whereabouts. Once a person is relocated in FWP, the Marshals keep an eye on them as long as the party may be required for federal testimony. We suspect that they have finally told Mr. Palmer that the danger to him is past. And, his first reaction was to call you. This is all supposition.

"However, they also probably have not told him of the collateral damage that did occur."

Lee and I looked at him, puzzled. "Collateral damage?" Lee leaned forward.

Harrelson looked at another file. "Yes, your son Edmond Palmer. When you tried to connect his death fifteen years ago, you were told it was a sad coincident. We discovered some time later; his death was no coincidence."

All I remember is sitting my mug on the table. I woke up on the couch. How can this be?

CHAPTER SIX

The two agents sat on the very edges of the club chairs; Lee had brought another chair for herself. I occupied the entire couch. After a few seconds of utter disbelief and some dizziness, I sat up and put both feet firmly on the floor. I needed a solid connection. My world was in total disarray. Fifteen years ago it fell apart and I've been gradually gathering it together. It is shattered again. Lee handed me my coffee. I took two long swallows. Killing time or collecting thoughts? I truly do not know. I put the cup back on the coffee table.

Firmly, hopefully without rancor, I asked, "Why weren't we told this before? How can Eddy's death possibly be connected? Your own agency assured me I was on the wrong track. It was a sad coincidence." I enunciated slowly and carefully.

If either had been standing, Tucker or Harrelson would be shuffling their feet. I'm sure of it. That look of shame that little boys develop when they've been caught out in a lie is so evident at this moment. Finally Tucker answered. He seemed to take a deep breath before he spoke.

"Before coming here this morning, we had a long discussion with the Director in DC. He said that the case was so perverted, somewhat bungled, and not our fault, we should tell you everything we know. That includes how we presume much of the mess happened. Because we were unaware the U S Marshal was involved, we made several presumptions at the time. Some were spot on; some were not. Even so, things slipped under the radar, so to speak, because there was another entity involved. I am sure things would have been handled differently had we known."

He stopped abruptly. He reminded me of a child's toy. That abrupt stop when the windup spring has come to an end. I wanted to lean over and find his wind up key so I could turn it and keep him talking. I wanted answers.

Finally, it appeared he began to breathe again. It was so odd. Is it that hard to retell?

"A year or so after your son's death, we came across some things that caused us to wonder why they had been written off in the manner they had been dismissed. We interviewed his girlfriend, Jane Stapleton. Well, the two of us didn't, the Bureau interviewed her. She told a most incredible story. She also told us that no one would listen to her before." He picked up yet another skinny file and began to read.

After listening to a sentence or two, I realize this must be a transcript of the interview with Jane.

"Eddy had a friend who worked with the crew that cleaned the warehouse every week. Eddy wanted to solidify a couple details with his friend about a weekend we were planning and drove to the warehouse around midnight. Eddy knew the guard well and never had a problem entering the warehouse. Eddy followed the cleaning crew in. A second group of men followed him in. He asked his friend who they were. His friend didn't know but told him that on several Thursdays they were there. He told Eddy they apparently had permission to be there as they always went to one area, unlocked a cage, and either removed property or left property. They'd lock up and leave - usually in less than half an hour. None of his crew ever approached them as they seemed to belong.

"This intrigued Eddy and he began going out to the warehouse on Thursdays more often. He managed to get close enough to overhear the strangers several times. He told me that there was something fishy going on and he was going to talk to his father to see if he was aware. His father was never on-site when the group was there but Eddy was sure that they had permission to be there. He heard things that truly upset him. Eddy was sure that their inventory was drugs. From what he overheard, they felt that they needed to find a new storage area as lately they had been intercepted too often. It didn't seem they thought the warehouse was responsible in any way for the interception. Even so, Eddy felt his Dad was in danger. The guys didn't sound friendly even talking among themselves.

"I suggested that he go talk to my oldest brother, Richard. Richard is a U S Marshal and I have the impression that the Marshals have intercepted various drug shipments over the years. My brother heard him out and thanked

Eddy. He did say that as far as he knew, there had never been anything that tied the warehouse to drugs. But he would check on what Eddy had told him."

Tucker looked at me and I felt he had quit reading now but was summarizing. What he had just read was definitely a statement from Jane. Jane and Eddy had been an item for quite a while and she would be privy to what he knew or felt. The agent continued reading her statement.

"Two weeks later, there was a shipment in storage. Eddy was sure that it was going to be the last. The Bureau asked why he cared. If the Marshals were on it, what was his concern? But at that time, I am not sure that Eddy was sure that my brother had made any plans to check out what he had told my brother. Eddy was pretty sure that his Dad was going to be eliminated. That was the term he used when he talked to me. That Thursday morning, Eddy called his Dad at the warehouse. He asked if his Dad would meet him for coffee before Eddy went to work at his job at 10. His Dad said yes. I don't know what Eddy and his Dad discussed at that meeting. The next time I spoke to Eddy, his Dad had disappeared. And Eddy wasn't talking."

The agent laid down the folder. "That was what we got from Jane Stapleton. As far as I can tell, the Bureau did nothing about it until after Eddy was killed."

My head is reeling again. I thought I was dizzy before but this is emotional, not physical. A few hours after Wes had coffee with Eddy, Wes called me. What had happened in those few hours between talking to Eddy and calling me? Something definitely had.

"What do you think Eddy and Wes discussed? Do you have a supposition? We were told that the FBI didn't know the Marshals were involved. Why did you think that? Because they didn't inform you?"

Agent Harrelson fidgeted a bit and look at a different file.

"We believe Eddy didn't know the FBI was involved before that morning. We are presuming your husband told him about the arrangement. But maybe Eddy didn't have time to contact the Marshals' office before Wes disappeared. Or, they didn't have time to act or didn't believe it was crucial. We don't know if the Marshals ever contacted Wes prior to spiriting him away. But we were sure then that it was the U S Marshal who took your husband." Agent Harrelson definitely isn't cut out for this time of thing. He looks pretty pale now - as though this statement totally wrung him out.

Wes used to get frustrated watching the evening news quite often. "Why the hell can't the Government work together?" Too often the news indicated that the right hand never knew what the left hand was doing. And now, it appears that may be the why Wes is in Massachusetts.

Lee had been listening quietly. "Agent Tucker, why was my brother killed? Who could possibly know he was even aware. The drugs that were in the locker that night...what happened to them?"

"By the time the cleaning crew was due in, the place was swarming with local police. You know, a lot of cars with flashing red lights going all the while. Your Dad had seemingly disappeared into thin air. His car was in the parking lot. His wallet was in the glove box along with the company cell phone he always carried. The guard said that the group of men that often follow the cleaning crew had come within three hundred yards of the guard shack. The cleaning crew passed through as usual but were detained from entering the warehouse once they reached the it. The guard hadn't been told to restrain entry to anyone so he let them pass. But the second group must have seen the police and decided they'd leave. Their storage area wasn't touched that night. There was no reason for them not to come in as usual - none of the local police were interested in anything but Mr. Palmer's disappearance and had been there since about 7 o'clock."

Lee didn't look satisfied. "How long after that night before the locked cage was investigated?"

Tucker swallowed hard. I could see it. "The day before your brother was run down. We presume that the gang had two weeks to put things together. They made no attempt to get the drugs though I am sure they could have without interference. Surely, this is assumption, they had seen Eddy often at the warehouse. When they knew who he was, again presumption, they decided he was a threat."

Tears spilled down Lee's face. She looked totally defeated. She came to the couch and knelt down. "Why did it take fifteen years for us to hear this? There was never any news about finding a cache of drugs in the warehouse. Was that deliberate? Did you think that it'd save Eddy? Or were you even thinking that far ahead?" She put her head in my lap and sobbed.

Agent Tucker leaned over and patted her shoulder. "I believe nothing was ever said in an effort to save your father's reputation. We didn't know where he was but we were sure he was played. Besmirching a man unable to defend himself is not the way the FBI works. Especially when we had put him in that position."

Showing more bravado that I have, I reached for my coffee. "The question now, Agent Tucker, Agent Harrelson, how do we find my husband?"

CHAPTER SEVEN

"Well, I am not sure. We believe he called you yesterday from the Main Library in Lowell. If his fingerprints prove that, well, I'm not sure what comes next."

"After all this time, and apparent resolution of the case, do you believe the Marshals will divulge his new name? Or where he lives?"

Agent Tucker shook his head. "I don't know. From past experience, I would say no. But maybe, under the circumstances, they'll soften up. I truly have no idea. But we will be in contact with you regarding the finger prints as soon as we hear." He reached into an inside jacket pocket. "This is where you can reach me direct. If your husband calls again, or something else happens that seems pertinent, call me immediately. I don't care what time it is. Call." He handed me a business card – after he had written his direct cell number on the back.

At that moment, I got the feeling he cares. Sincerely cares.

He started putting his skinny little files back into the briefcase. I believe he had referred to each of them while he talked to us. But what more do I know than before they arrived? Only the news about Eddy. Jane married four years ago. She had trouble getting her life back on track as much as we did. She wanted to return the engagement ring and I told her that he'd given it to her - it was hers. I think she wore it until she met Jack Wilson - the man she married. It took her eleven years to begin to live again. I so want to call her. But, I won't. Lee and I have a lot to discuss and digest as soon as the FBI is out of the house.

Both agents stood, shook our hands, and thanked us for our courtesy. They looked as wrung out as I felt. Imagine, I feel sorry for a FBI agent. I walked them to the door and watched as they went down the walk to their car. A nondescript, little, black economy car. I felt sorry for them. I really did. Agent Harrelson turned and waved. That was unexpected. I returned the wave.

As they pulled from the curb, I closed the door. The tears came quickly, hot and stinging. Lee and I huddled in an awkward embrace. While we know what happened to Eddy, we don't know much more about Wes. He was in Lowell, Massachusetts yesterday, we think. Does he live there? Has he been there for fifteen years? I hope someone can tell us something soon.

Lee and I went to the kitchen. At first, I was interested in more coffee. Then I realized it was almost two o'clock. "Want a sandwich, Sweetie?" Lee nodded. She's still processing. She's always been like this. In an hour or less, or more, she'll 'snap on' and be full of thoughts, questions, what nows? I made lunch and took it to the deck. It was still in disarray from yesterday but it was clean enough to sit at the table and eat. I needed the fresh air. I needed a lot more than fresh air but that's what I have. We didn't talk much while we ate. I guess we're both processing.

We ate slowly. Perhaps forty-five minutes later, Lee looked at her watch. "Gotta run, Mom. If Larry can get a tie-line, he'll be calling soon. Okay if I tell him what we know now?"

"Yes, definitely. See if he has any ideas of what we should be doing. He'll be disturbed when he learns about Eddy...even this late. Maybe, not being so close to this mess, he'll have some clear thoughts on what's next. Give him my love."

My daughter hugged me tightly. "We'll find Dad. I know we will."

Her enthusiasm was refreshing yet frightening. She can get so far up on a project that she gets hurt when it fails. I want to believe that we'll find Wes. I truly do. But what if he didn't realize the line went dead - that I didn't hang up on him. He may think I no longer love him; no longer care; no longer wonder about him. Somehow, I have to prevent that from happening.

Early the next morning, the door bell chimed. Wil and Mike and the two friends from the birthday party were at the door. "We've come to see if we can undo whatever the wind did to your yard." We went out onto the deck and I pointed out the major things that should be done. Wil and Mike know where the tools are and, after a few questions, the four of them were untangling the yard. I decided best payment today would be a few dollars and peanut butter cookies. I love baking peanut butter cookies - it goes fast and smells wonderful. And, I can do it without thinking.

The four boys worked steadily for a couple hours. Steve seems to know a lot about swimming pools as he cleaned the filter, cleaned the pool and then cleaned the filter again. The wind had really made a mess of the pool but when he finished, it was immaculate. Donny and Mike worked on the hedges while Wil cleaned the deck and furniture. When finished, they started through the breezeway instead of coming into the house. I went out the kitchen door and met them halfway. "Come in and have some milk and cookies before you go, Guys." They looked at each other and grinned. I do think they had just planned to sneak away but wouldn't argue the point of cookies. We sat at the kitchen table and talked for half an hour. As they left, I gave them each five dollars. "I know this isn't enough but hope it'll do for now." They were pleased and all took a few more cookies to eat as they walked home.

I was cleaning the kitchen when the phone rang. I caught my breath. Then ran to the phone. It was Lee. Larry had called. He was surprised at the FBI and how much they told us. He was surprised that was all they knew but Lee thinks they'd been honest about everything. Larry said he doubted that but if we were happy, okay. His leave for next month has been approved. Of course, my daughter is thrilled with that. This deployment has been a long one.

It was another two days before Agent Tucker called. The agent in Lowell found Wes' fingerprints on two of the phones. Perhaps he realized the line had gone dead and thought it was the telephone. It would make sense then for him to try another phone. Wes was definitely in Lowell four days ago. Tucker said, "I don't want to rain on your parade, Mrs. Palmer. Maybe he doesn't live there. Maybe he was just passing through and decided to call you, maybe based on something he'd been told and he thought it was okay. In a strange town, where would you look for a pay phone? The library seems a likely choice to me." I started to protest. "Then again, out of habit, he may have gone to a pay phone rather than call from his home. And the library seemed a logical choice."

That made better sense to me and I told Tucker so. "Yes, ma'am. I know. I am just trying not to get too worked up here, you know."

"Agent Tucker, I do know. And I appreciate your courtesy and your kindness. This may have all happened fifteen years ago but there are days it seems like yesterday."

"Yes, ma'am. Call me if you need something or if you learn anything we haven't already covered."

"I will. I definitely will. Thank you again." I made sure the card he gave me was on my desk in plain view. Sometimes just knowing I have an option keeps me from using it.

Tears again. I'm not much of a crier. Frustration causes tears. It's a useless emotion and affects me so badly. I decided to go on the computer and see what I can learn about Lowell, Massachusetts. I believe I have heard the name once before now. In a movie, I think. Someone was from there in a movie but I don't know who or what movie. Or maybe not. God, I'm grasping at paper straws.

The website for Lowell is well done. Lots and lots of photographs; though many of them are untitled. Some are obvious -- churches, government, restaurant type buildings, clear signage. Some have no clue but they are pretty. I learned that Lowell is the fifth largest city in the state. Of course, Massachusetts is a small state so what does that really mean? Some of the building photos that look governmental may not be anymore. Lowell was the county seat until 1999 and then the state dissolved county governments. The thing that interested me the most is that the Boston Red Sox have a short season Class A affiliate, the Lowell Spinners, located in Lowell. Like the California Coast League here on the West Coast.

Wes loves baseball. He played basketball and baseball in college but I believe baseball was his true love. If Wes is in Lowell, --- oh, for Pete's sake Lyn, this is stupid. Give it up. It's a given that if Wes is in Lowell, he goes to the ball games.

I went out to the deck to clear my head. Steve laid three cushions on a deck chair. I had seen two at the bottom of the pool. It would be a good idea to see how wet they are - should I throw them in the dryer?

All three were quite wet and I could see he had tried compressing water out of them. Amazing when kids do things you'd hope for but then you are amazed that they do them. It made sense not to wring them but I squeezed hard before turning them over to dry some more. A quick tour of the yard proved comforting. The trees and hedges were clear of debris. The loose branches and sodden leaves were in the yard debris bin in the breezeway. The wet cushions were the only evidence of the wind storm.

It took years to get back in the groove of living. Now everything is unraveling again. I feel at loose ends with no plan just as I had fifteen years ago. It just is not fair that life should be so damned hard sometimes. It just isn't fair.

CHAPTER EIGHT

It was obvious I was headed for a pity party. And that is unacceptable. I've attended too many in the last fifteen years. I took the phone from the family room and plugged it into the jack on the deck. And here I am; a mug of coffee again and a silent phone. It could be a very long afternoon.

No, I can't do this. I went into the house and got my laptop, a pad of paper and a pen. There's no plan in this but it won't appear that I am lounging with no purpose. Though why I should care, or anyone else should care, can't make any difference. After a few minutes, I decided to visit the Lowell website again. Why? I have no idea. But somehow it makes me feel closer to Wes. Yeah, really dumb.

Having exhausted everything the website could offer, I started a timeline on my pad of paper. Timeline of my life with Wes, I guess.

Graduation from high school was 1978. I was one of three people who received a "full ride" scholarship from USC that year at my school. I had applied to half a dozen universities - my grades were great. I was accepted by two and, just as I was about to accept one, I received notice that (if I was still interested in attending USC) they wanted to offer me a scholarship. My application to them had been conditional. I wanted to attend but would need financial assistance. I wasn't afraid or ashamed to ask up front. And that's how I got a "full ride" - books as well as tuition. No housing required as I lived in Los Angeles County. My course of interest was a degree in Library Science.

Beginning the summer of 1979, I began a part-time job at the Los Angeles Main Library. Sometime that fall the person who had been the notary public at the library announced he would be retiring at the beginning of the year. He approached me and asked if I'd be interested in being the notary. The library would pay my fees and bond. As he normally worked evenings and weekends,

I said sure. The schedule for notary work wouldn't have to change much. I could still do my regular job - Notary work wasn't that frequent. I went to a notary public seminar at the Pasadena Hilton Several hours of schooling, a break, and then the Notary Public exam - all in the same day.

And that's where I met Wes.

Wes was in his second year of college - but at UCLA. He was studying Economics and Marketing. I forget why he wanted to be a Notary Public. But he did. Have I ever known? I'm not sure. Well, it's not important.

The class was ready to start when he came in. A few minutes late but the class had not started so he was admitted. There was one chair left - next to me. The ballroom of the Hilton had been filled with long tables with an aisle down the middle. There were pitchers of ice water and paper cups spaced every few feet on the tables.

Twenty minutes into the class, Wes offered to pour a cup of water for me. I shook my head. I was afraid that I'd drink too much water and then agonize for a break. I'm sure I didn't tell him that. The first break was 90 minutes in. Then I accepted his offer of water before running off to the ladies' room. There were a few minutes of the break left when I returned and he struck up a conversation.

Wes was a handsome man even at twenty. Not movie star handsome, but he had one of those pleasant faces that puts everyone at ease. Very good looking. Honestly, I always thought tall, dark and handsome was a catch phrase until I met Wes. The second break was termed "lunch". He asked if I was staying in the hotel to eat. Frankly, I felt I couldn't afford to eat in the hotel and said that I - I had brought my lunch. At that time, there was a 'sort of' snack bar in the lobby. He got a sandwich and he sat with me in the courtyard to eat.

Wes could really talk. Not dumb shit stuff but interesting stuff. I didn't wear a watch in those days and he kept track of time so we'd get back to the seminar in a timely fashion. His car wouldn't start that morning and he bused it to the hotel. That's why he was almost late. The second half of the seminar was the actual notary exam. Took two hours but I felt quite confident about it. Results would be mailed to us within the next two weeks.

Meanwhile, though we attended different schools, we found that we lived within two miles of each other in the San Gabriel Valley. As we left the Hilton, Wes asked for my phone number - that is, if I wouldn't mind that he perhaps would call. I liked him and gave him my number. I told my Mom and she said don't feel bad if he doesn't call. I told her I wouldn't but it'd be nice if he did.

We were married in July 1980.

1980 was an odd year. Wes decided he must be in the wrong field of endeavor but was afraid it was too late to change. Nolan Ryan had just been awarded the largest baseball salary contract ever. One million dollars a year for four years with Houston. We laughed about it - cute joke. We both enjoy baseball though. And then The Blues Brothers - as ridiculous as they could be, had one really great song. "Everybody needs somebody to Love." It really caught on. Maybe we both were studying in the wrong field of endeavor

I didn't have a car and had been busing to USC. Took over an hour and a half and two transfers. Wes had a car and suddenly decided that a husband had a responsibility to get his wife to school. We had a small one-bedroom apartment in Pasadena. I insisted USC was out of his way but he said that was a small matter. I did bus home as he couldn't schedule to match my classes. And often, I went straight to work. Our first Christmas tree was about 20 inches tall, in a pot. We celebrated the new year with friends and family. While different, it was a very good year.

We both graduated in 1981 but I went back to school for another two years. My Dad was disappointed I had not chosen Geology as my major. He is a rather noted geologist. He would pay the tuition if I did two years in geology. I found geology quite interesting. I kept my part-time job at the library. Then my hometown library offered me full time in 1983. I took some time off to give birth to our daughter, Aralee Ilene. Two years later we had a son, Edmond Kendall. I learned to drive in 1983 and Wes bought me a little, clean, used car. I was determined not to put my career on hold and worked part-time. The nice things about libraries - they change but are still the same.

In 1982 Wes took a temporary job with a grocery warehouse. Well, he thought it was temporary. It was full-time, paid well, and he loved the work. It's the only job he ever had -- it wasn't temporary.

Off and on between 1985 and now, Dad has needed a geology research assistant. I was back to working part time and I could juggle my hours when he called on me. My Mother delighted in being a baby-sitter for three or four weeks at a time. Wes laughed and said that had been Dad's idea all along. Get enough certification so I could work with him. Whatever; I enjoy working with Dad. I enjoy geology.

In 1990 we bought this house. And it's been home ever since.

I reread what I have written and can't go any further. Grief overwhelmed me like a flash flood. I put my head on my arms and bawled.

CHAPTER NINE

The sun had set by the time I got myself together. I went to bed. It's not quite nine. I don't care. I am worn out. I am tired. I've had it. Tomorrow has to be a better day.

The telephone woke me. The sun was barely streaking the sky. "Hello?"

"Mrs. Palmer, forgive the hour. I just got a fax from the U S Marshal's office."

I looked at the clock. It was 6:15. AM presumably.

"Agent Tucker, what are you doing working at this hour?"

"Had a project going most of the night. Hadn't really intended to pull an all nighter but I am glad I did. Evidently, the U S Marshal forgets there are three time zones between him and us."

"This involves Wes?" Why else would he call, Lyn? What a dumb question.

"Yes, ma'am, it does. I can read it to you or bring it out to you."

"Bring it out and have breakfast with me. Can you do that? Is it permitted? After all you have worked all night."

"Mrs. Palmer, at this point in time, I don't care if it's permitted or not. It'll take me about half an hour to get to you. Breakfast sounds great."

Half an hour; skip the shower. I washed up and dressed quickly. For a brief moment I wondered why in the world I had made this offer? But it flitted through my mind in a flash. I started the coffee. I set the table for two; if Agent Harrelson comes, it'll take just a minute to add a setting. If he's been up all night, pancakes, bacon, I think there's half a cantaloupe. I nuked the bacon and put juice in a carafe. Eggs are quick no matter how you prepare them. Half batch of pancake batter should be enough even if there are three of us. The stove griddle will warm as I mix the batter. Bacon onto a serving dish and cover with a towel. I am on robopilot. I'm afraid if I stop to think I'll fall apart.

The door bell chimed. Agent Tucker was alone. He had a single file folder in his hands. It has to be good news or I am sure he wouldn't go to this length. Probably breaking regulations; but he looked enthused though tired.

"As I am really hungry, may I show this to you after I've eaten?" I laughed. He's afraid I'll fall apart and he won't get to eat at all. Over thinking, as usual? Maybe not.

Half a batch of pancake batter makes ten medium pancakes. Six fit on the griddle at once. Do you like poached eggs. He nodded. "My favorite but they're a hassle." I cracked four eggs into my microwave cooker, set the timer, and put the last pancakes on the griddle. Agent Tucker looks exhausted but he looks excited. Butter, syrup, jelly. He was standing at the end of the kitchen counter drinking a cup of coffee and watching.

"I mean this as a compliment, Mrs. Palmer. Watching you reminds me of a restaurant chef in the kitchen, precision and purpose."

What an odd compliment. At least he didn't relate me to his mother. "Thank you."

He helped himself to the food. I was starving myself but was afraid to eat too much. The fax he has must be good or he wouldn't be here. Tucker made small talk - how was the storm cleanup coming? Stuff like that. He was surprised when I told him the grandsons and two friends were here yesterday. "You'd never know there was a storm."

Tucker nodded and took two more pancakes. "These aren't from a mix, are they?"

"No, it's a simple recipe. My granddaughter calls it a recipe of one. One cup milk, one cup flour, one egg, one teaspoon vanilla, one tablespoon sugar, and 1/2 teaspoon baking powder."

"That's simple enough. And it makes how many?"

"Ten, this size."

I could see the wheels turning. Maybe he'll make himself some pancakes one fine morning. I took the last piece of bacon, then poured myself more coffee. I nodded toward his cup and he picked it up so I could fill it. He was down to the last few bites on his plate. There was nothing left on the serving dishes. He had been hungry. If he had pulled an all-nighter, did he even have dinner?

He finished and wiped his mouth with his napkin. "Now, for the fax. Forgive me for eating first but -"

"I know. You aren't sure how I'll take this and you were hungry. My Dad says it's better to eat and run than not eat at all." His laugh is wonderful.

He opened the folder. There was a single sheet of paper in it. Almost with a flourish, he picked it out and handed it to me.

All the legal mumbo-jumbo of an agency fax - time, date, etc., etc. "Pursuant to your request to reveal the name of the party previously discussed. He says that he attempted to call his wife this past week but the call was terminated. If she did not terminate the call and would like to speak with him, give her this number. Revealing his name will be his decision. Calls should be placed after 4pm Eastern time as he is gainfully employed." There was a 351 area code and 7 digit number.

I looked up at him. "So it's not up to them? Is that what they're saying? How do I explain the disconnect? Should you call first? I don't know what to do, Agent Tucker."

"For starters, call me Hal. If you want, I can fax back and explain the disconnect saying that it was Mother Nature and the incident was extremely upsetting to you. It is because of the disconnection that the FBI is involved again. Would you like me to do that, Mrs. Palmer?"

It took me a minute to process. Yes, it would be easier if I didn't have to explain anything to Wes when I call. "Hal, I would very much appreciate that. Call me Lyn. We've shared a meal; we need to be friends."

He put both his hands over mine. "Lyn, what is your real name? You said your husband called you something else."

"My name is Madlyn. Not Madelyn, but Madlyn. Why? I don't know. My parents are very educated people and Dad says no one will ever pronounce the E; why bother with it? Wes has always called me Maddy. Everyone else calls me Lyn."

He squeezed my hands gently. For a moment, I was afraid he was going to cry. Then I decided he was just over tired. He stood up. "This is a copy of the original fax and I'll leave it with you. I'll request the Marshal to contact your husband now so that you can call him today. Call me after you've talked to your husband. Will you?"

As I stood, I put my hand on his shoulder. "Hal, you have renewed my faith in the FBI. I wish you could have been the agent I dealt with fifteen years ago. I have hated the Bureau ever since. Thank you for everything. Go get some sleep. I will call you after I've called Massachusetts."

I watched him go out to his car. It wasn't his official car. It wasn't exactly a sports car but it wasn't a Granny sedan either. I smiled as he drove off. If there is a god, then this is an angel.

It was eight o'clock. I called Lee. She cried. "When you talk to Daddy ask him if it's okay if I call him? Oh, Mom."

"Lee, I don't know what to say to him. Do I get flippant and act like it's fifteen years ago? No, I can't do that. I don't know what to say; or how to say it. He'll ask about you, Larry and the baby; he'll ask about Eddy. What do I say? Oh, Lee, I am a bundle of nerves."

"Mom, you know he's not going to call you until you call him. Go take a swim, lay in the sun a while. Think. You have a great imagination - go through a dozen scenarios. Then call me. You have to be calm, cool and collected when you call Daddy."

After cleaning up the kitchen, I decided she was right. I have to imagine every possible scenario. The pool is clean; yes, I am going to swim twenty laps and burn off some of this energy. I usually don't swim alone but today I need to. Then I'll think what to say to the man I have missed so desperately for fifteen years.

CHAPTER TEN

Sudden realization - 4 pm Eastern time is 1 pm here. I called Lee. "Sweetie, why didn't you remind me that Eastern time is three hours ahead of us. I can call in just over an hour."

"Honest to god, Mom. I didn't think of it. Did you take a swim?"

"Yes, and no matter what I think I could say, nothing sounds right."

"Mom. It can't be too heavy. That would destroy both of you. Mom. Just be yourself. You will think of something when he answers the phone. I know you will. Don't sweat the small stuff."

"I know; you're right, Lee. I don't want to make him wish I hadn't called. I have waited for this moment for fifteen years; you'd think I'd be better prepared."

"Oh, Mom, breathe deep, exhale slowly. Repeat. And call me as soon as you hang up with Dad."

I took a shower. I can't bear the smell of pool chlorine. And, believe it or not, I found myself putting on my nicer clothes, even a brief spray of perfume. What am I thinking? This is a telephone call, Lyn. A telephone call. But it's been waiting to happen fifteen years. I should dress up. This is Wesley Palmer. Well, no, I guess it isn't anymore. I had better leave a pen and paper by the phone so I can write down his name. Will he want me to call him something other than Wes? How do I ask that? I can't call Lee back now. She already thinks I've tipped over the edge.

At one o'clock I decided not to pick up the phone. He may want a minute to come in, shower, change, go to the bathroom. The fax didn't say he got home at four; it said call after as he is gainfully employed. Does he get off at three? How far is work from home? Is he expecting my call? The fax didn't say any of those things.

I put a pen and paper by the phone and went to the bathroom. Stalling, that's all I'm doing. Stalling on making a call I've wanted to make for a very long time. Make up your mind, Lyn. Do it or don't. Finally, I did. Good thing rotary phones are out; I'm shaking so much I could never dial eleven numbers in a row correctly.

I could hear the call chase across the country. Sometimes you can really. A little det det det det as it hit different spots on the system. Then, one ring. "Hello?"

"Is this the party to whom I am speaking?" When in the hell did Lily Tomlin join my team?

"Yes, ma'am, it is. Jim Nolan at your service."

"That is a very pleasant name, Mr. Nolan." I wrote it down on my pad.

He chuckled. I could see the little twisty grin that always accompanied that chuckle. "I was hoping you would like it. I have often thought how well Madlyn would go with Nolan." I could hear the tears in his voice. "Are you okay, Maddy?"

"I am now."

There was a long silence. Then he said, "Sure glad the telephone company doesn't charge by the minute anymore."

"Me, too. Tell me all about yourself, Jim. What do you do for a living?"

He actually laughed this time. "You won't believe it. I work for the US Post Office?"

"You're a letter carrier?"

"Oh, no, much loftier than that. I am a mail handler. You know the guy who sorts and separates the mail so it goes to the place it's addressed. I work in a large mail transfer center just outside of Boston"

"How far is that from where you live?"

"About thirty minutes, give or take. It's mostly freeway."

"And exactly where do you live?"

Believe it or not he gave me a street address. I wrote it down. "That's in Lowell, Massachusetts. Lowell is a lot like Monrovia, believe it or not. Size, friendly, community minded. I belong to a bowling league with guys from work and a baseball team sponsored by the city. I have a library card, am registered to vote, and my neighbors all seem to like me."

Tears are slowly sliding down my face and dripping off my chin. He's part of the community. He doesn't need me at all. He's still talking. "My one big problem is the girl I left behind. I am hoping she'll want to come East and visit. And maybe be my main squeeze again."

"Well, you did stand her up your last date. I am sure she's pretty much over that. But you know women."

"Maddy, will you come visit? I'll take time off and show you around. Will you?"

"I'll check airline schedules and stuff and let you know when I can."

"Great. Now how is Lee and Larry? The baby must be sixteen now, right?"

"Larry is still in the Marines. He'll be home on leave in a few weeks. Yes, that baby turned sixteen last week. And he has a brother, Michael, who is fourteen and a sister Laurie who is twelve."

"And Eddy - did he get his promotion?"

I knew this would come up. But I am still not prepared for it. In fact, I had forgotten Eddy had expected a promotion at the accounting firm where he worked.

"Wes, er Jim, sit down." I have watched him on the phone for years. He always starts out standing. If the conversation goes past a few minutes he may sit. We haven't talked that long yet. I heard a chair or something scrape. "Eddy was a victim of a hit and run driver a few weeks after you left. He's dead." I caught my breath hoping to get through this in a sane manner. "He was at the school crossing as usual; not quite 8 o'clock. It was ten minutes from the end of his shift. A car turned across the street, over corrected and ran over Eddy."

If only that explanation will be enough. At least, for now. We can discuss other stuff later, I hope.

"Oh, god, Maddy. I am so sorry I wasn't there to comfort you."

I wanted to say 'if you were here, it wouldn't have happened.' I kept my mouth shut.

"I was still grieving over the loss of my dear husband. It was a terrible time. Janie was here daily. It took her a long, long time to let him go. She married just a few years ago."

There was silence again - only this time I could hear his tears as well as I could feel mine. I am sure he had laid down the phone. He blew his nose. Then, "Maddy, do you still love me?"

"I do love Wes Palmer. I am sure I will love Jim Nolan once I get to know him."

"We have a lot to talk about. I don't know how much you know but I want to tell you everything I know. I was told earlier that when I tried to call you last week, you were in the middle of a wind storm."

"In fact, it was classed a small tornado. The power had gone off. When the phone rang, I was surprised. I answered but the call disconnected almost immediately. That was Wil's sixteenth birthday. The power came on the next morning. But, get this, because the phone company hasn't completely updated to digital, they were able to trace the call. Otherwise, this call we're on right now may never have happened. I don't believe you tried another day." He didn't respond.

"Much damage?"

"No, Lee lost two large trees but other than that everything here ended up in the pool, no real damage. A flower pot - that sort of thing. Wil and Mike and two friends came and cleaned up everything."

"Maddy, I'd love to talk to you forever now but need some time to regroup. I hadn't expected bad news. But I'll call you before I head to bed - if that's okay with you."

"Lee wants to call you. Okay if I give her the number and tell her she can call tomorrow?"

No hesitation. "Absolutely. I'll look forward to her call tomorrow." More silence. "Maddy, I love you. I always have and always will. Please consider coming soon."

"I love you too. I'll check airline schedules and stuff and we'll work something out."

"Goodbye, Sweetheart. I'll call in a few hours."

"Love you." I hung up. Lee was right. It wasn't the end of the world. The conversation went fairly well, I thought. Maybe I should have hedged about Eddy. No, that wouldn't have been right either. The sooner he knows, the sooner he can handle it. I just hope that the reason Eddy was run down doesn't do him in. I know that Wes would think it was his fault. Will Jim Nolan?

CHAPTER ELEVEN

Lee thought the Tomlin quote worked quite well. I got a name without asking. She is kind of doubtful about James Nolan. I asked her what she meant. Well, she didn't honestly know. It just wasn't a name she'd ever associate with Wesley Palmer. I told her I thought that was the whole idea. She laughed, "Of course, Mom. What was I thinking?"

She understood her Dad's need for a couple hours down time. I told her that he accepted Eddy's death but didn't take it well. She, like me, wonders how he'll feel when he learns what the FBI thinks. I told her that I hoped we wouldn't find out for quite a while. Lee is excited that her Dad wants me to come back to Lowell. Then she said, "Wait. Is he going to expect you to stay there?"

"We haven't discussed much other than my going back. And not even that very much. Sweetie, it's been fifteen years. We may not even like each other anymore."

I could see her shaking her head. She can't believe that. "Lee, I haven't even checked airlines or fares yet. I have to go before the summer is over. I have only two months off. Get photos together. He was surprised, though I don't know why, that he has two more grandchildren. By the way, when does Larry get home?"

"His leave starts the first. He has five weeks. Isn't that wonderful?"

I had to agree it was. And it is. He's been gone a year and a half this time.

"Well, I'll call Dad tomorrow just after four. Does he sound the same?"

"He does. There's no change at all. At least, none that I noticed. Let me know how the call goes."

"I will, Mom. Talk to you tomorrow."

As I hung up I hesitated a moment. She doesn't think Jim Nolan sounds like her Dad. My assurances make sense. But there was something about him that didn't ring true. Maybe my imagination. Although I told Lee there was no change, no difference, there was. I can't put my finger on it but there was something. Fifteen years allow a lot of memories that aren't always one hundred percent true, Lyn. Be sensible. He's feeling around too. Love is patient and kind but it's not always faithful He became someone new. Did he allow his old self, his old ties to maintain him? What am I trying to say? I hope he hasn't been screwing around the last fifteen years. Yes, that's it. Oh, my god, what a ridiculous thing to worry about. I'm the one that's been married all this time; not him.

The rest of the day was spent with a calendar, the computer and the telephone. I made no reservations but have a solid of idea of the cost and when of flights. Wes said he'd call tonight before he heads for bed. I want to have all these ducks in a row. Is he off weekends? How many days off can he get? When does he prefer I come in? Is Logan, Boston okay? I hope so. When you start with commuter flights it gets costly. I presume this is on my nickel though nothing has been said one way or the other. I doubt he's even thought about the expense. Wes wouldn't have.

I find myself doing things that make no sense. I have waited fifteen years to find my husband. And here I am, setting the television to record Jeopardy and Wheel. He's going to call just before he goes to bed. That could possibly be around seven o'clock with the time difference. Surely he'll want to talk more than five minutes so perhaps he'll call an hour before he's usually abed. Which used to be eleven. Are these two game shows overriding my passion? Has finding Wes been a bit of a letdown? No, seriously. I've dreamed of this day for so long. How can I be so methodical and nonchalant about it? I'm not shivering with excitement or even too nervous for dinner. What has happened to me? Lyn, wake up. This is what you've waited for so long. Get happy.

Get happy. Get happy. It kept ringing through my mind. I vacuumed the living room and dining room. I dusted. I had changed into jeans and a tee sometime in the afternoon. Not sure when, but here I am, dressed like always. I feel rather foolish when I think that I actually dressed up to make a phone call. My mind may be working but not too well, I'm afraid. I turned on the six o'clock news before I made a sandwich. I do that a lot these days so this is nothing new. Some days I don't feel it's worth cooking for one. I poured a glass of watermelon lemonade and looked for an opened bag of chips in the pantry. There's almost always one.

Not much news tonight; well, not much that interested me. There was some follow-up on the wind storm and they showed a tree company cutting up the two large trees at my daughter's home. I could see a work crew across the street. That neighbor did lose his garage roof or a large part of it. The newscaster mentioned that there was approximately fifteen million dollars in damage from that storm. The storm path was on the north edge of town, around Foothill, and several small businesses lost windows, awnings and some merchandise. From the map shown, I was on the northern most edge of the storm path. No wonder I lucked out.

The sports news was just coming on when the phone rang. Ten of seven. I turned off the television and answered the phone.

"Hello?"

"Maddy?"

"Yep, it's me."

"Maddy, I have been thinking all evening and damn if I know what I want to say to you. I've hoped the opportunity would come one day and now that it's here, I'm speechless."

"That makes two of us. I don't even know where to begin. The why and how you left should be left for a face-to-face. At least, I think so. So much has happened; so much has been said by so many people. I'd like to be able to sit with you quietly somewhere and discuss that. But for fifteen years I have thought of talking to you about things and now, what do I say?"

His response wasn't really a chuckle. But it was in that neighborhood.

"Well, let's begin with when are you coming to Massachusetts?"

"I am off for another five weeks. It has to be within that time. But I know nothing about your schedule, your work hours, shift, nothing that would allow me to make a rationale decision. So, Jim Nolan, when am I coming to Massachusetts?"

For the next fifteen minutes we discussed logistics mostly. It would be most logical if I arrived on a Saturday. He could begin vacation the following Monday. He works five days a week; Monday through Friday. A seniority benefit he said. I had copious notes on flights, times, and costs.

"There are a garden variety of flights. My god, it takes hours to get to Boston. You did intend I fly into Logan, didn't you?"

"Well, it's probably easier and shorter in the long run to come to Boston."

"Okay. I can leave Ontario on a Saturday morning and be in Boston at 4 in the afternoon. Or I can leave Ontario on Friday night and be in Boston on Saturday morning. They both take over seven hours and those are the short flights. Fare doesn't bump much - the red eye saves a hundred and fifty but I honestly believe I am too old for that if I want to be alive on Saturday."

"What kind of fares?"

"Right now for round trip - $450 give or take a few bucks depending on the carrier. Delta or United were the two with the shortest time in travel. The direct flights are outrageously expensive so I've crossed them all off."

"What web site did you use?"

"Travelocity, as always." We've taken several flights to vacation destinations and this site always served us well.

"Are you particular about leaving time? I've just pulled up Travelocity and am looking at the flights now. There's one at 6am and another at 8am. Both have one stopover but both arrive about the same time. I see what you mean about travel time - here's one for less than three hundred but it takes eighteen hours. How desperate could you be to book it? I can book on line and you pick up the ticket and the boarding pass at the airport. Would that be okay? Is your computer handy? We can browse together. I want to decide this first. I don't want to give you a chance to change your mind."

So, for the next several minutes, we are both looking at the same website and making decisions. He wants me to stay two weeks. He found a carrier that you could make changes to your return flight if done within forty-eight hours, at no charge. Although I hadn't really said I don't want to commit to two weeks, I think he sensed the hesitation. Maybe he still knows me fairly well. Maybe.

No backing out now, the decision is made - I leave next Saturday morning for Boston. Perhaps I should have known he'd pay the fare. Perhaps. I don't know Jim that well yet.

He asked what I was doing now. I told him I was still a librarian. No change there. How did I get two months off in the summer? Just lucky, I guess. Actually, I haven't taken a lot of vacation and they wouldn't allow me to roll it over much longer. Jim laughed. Best way to get a longer vacation while looking like the dedicated employee. I protested I was a dedicated employee. We laughed together - as we used to. But the remark slightly rankled.

Then he asked if I ever heard from the warehouse. I told him that Mr. Kellison has kept in touch with me all these years. "The man was devastated when you were gone. Jim, I'll explain a lot of stuff face-to-face. Just know that your reputation is still intact; you were considered a sterling employee. In fact, when I turned fifty-five, four years ago you know, I got a check from the warehouse for $738. I called Mr. Kellison, rather than the accountant, and asked what it was; why did I get it. He said that my husband had been fully vested in the retirement plan when he disappeared. A widow's portion is 50% and even though you hadn't been declared dead, he felt I was about as widowed as a widow could be. But he couldn't issue it before I turned fifty-five. The plan was written that way. He apologized that it took so long to get it rolling. I get a check every month marked retirement benefits."

Long silence. Finally Jim said, "The first few months I barely knew what was going on. And when the dust settled I was still in shock. You're right. That needs to be face-to-face; it's too incredible to discuss on the phone. When I finally was turned loose here, more or less loose, and began working I started worrying about you and money. All I could think was we had been saving for a trip to Peru. Would we ever make it? And then I decided that wasn't important; you might need to hit that nest egg."

"I didn't. It's intact and earning interest. I add a hundred dollars a year to keep the account active. But the interesting thing, and probably the one that saved my neck. Do you remember that million dollar life insurance policy you took out when you turned twenty-five?"

"You don't mean they paid it?"

"Oh, lord no, I refused to declare you dead. You paid the premium annually. If it had been a monthly or quarterly auto deduct, I may have forgotten it. Four or five months after your departure, the annual premium notice for that policy arrived. You had just turned forty-five before you left and the premium had increased. It was more than I had in the bank. I wrote to the company and half-assedly explained what had happened. Some director of finance called and made an appointment to come out to the house. I had all the written records in a file. I told him that I didn't think you were dead and refused to declare it. But I could not afford to make the annual premium which was soon due. He waived that premium and said that I should contact him the next year and we'd see what should/could be done."

"You're kidding! That big company sent out someone who had authority?"

"Oh, yeah. Well, the next year the premium notice arrived and I contacted the man. His name was Shelton, I think. Yes, Thomas Shelton. He asked if he could come to the house the next week and I said of course. I think that over the year he had made some inquiries with authorities. That was the impression he gave me. So he came out. And Wes, he gave me a check for thirty thousand dollars."

"You are joking."

"He said they couldn't pay a claim because I hadn't declared you dead and there was no evidence you were dead. But they would refund the premiums you had paid over those twenty years. He apologized he couldn't get interest for me but hoped the return of premiums would help."

I am not sure, but I think Wes is crying. Thinking back on the day that insurance man came, I remember that I cried. And I cried a lot. We had a thirty year mortgage with ten years left to pay.

Jim/Wes came back on the line. "What goes around comes around, Maddy. You've always been open, honest and trustworthy."

"Well, I went back full-time at the Library. With means to pay the mortgage and utilities, I did fine. Financially, I did fine. Emotionally, I was and am still a wreck. Eddy had insurance. I didn't know that. Did you? I think it was through his employer. It was enough to take care of his end of life expenses including paying off the engagement ring he had just given Janie. Do you remember how excited he was when he told us he was going to ask her to marry him? The ring was so beautiful. I think I told you - she wore it until she met someone she wanted to marry a couple years ago. So, financially, gradually, I made it. But the first couple of years were ramen noodle years."

I don't know why I mentioned Eddy. Because he had insurance? I don't know. Just the thought of my dear son brings tears and they were slowly edging down my face now. Wes was still talking and I tried to bring my mind back to the conversation.

"I am thankful for other people's kindnesses. I was so worried and they kept telling me I had to put you and everyone else out of my mind. I worked in a grocery store for a couple months but management was bad and I left. I even pumped gas for a while but the pay was impossible. Then one of the Marshals told me about a civil service exam that was being given for mail handlers in the Boston area. I took it and I've been USPS ever since - about eleven/twelve years now."

This was the first direct reference to the US Marshal. It probably won't be the last.

We recapped the reservations he had made for me. I made sure I wrote down everything. I agreed to schedule two weeks but also said I didn't know if I could handle two weeks. I'll try. It surprised me, but he seems to know what I mean; where I coming from. Now that he thinks I didn't struggle much after he left, his attitude is a bit easier. Maybe he's been plagued with guilt for fifteen years. Well, it would serve him right. He should have talked to me early on, when things were happening and not wait until the last minute. I need to know what happened that Thursday fifteen years ago.

CHAPTER TWELVE

Jeopardy and Wheel weren't viewed until the next morning. Lee said she'd call me after she talked with her Dad so I didn't call her after my second phone call with him. This was Thursday. I leave a week from Saturday. I am anxious to go. I don't want to go. I don't know what I want. I called the airline to verify whether I could pick up the ticket and boarding pass the same day as the flight or if I had do that earlier. Jim seems sure I can do it all that same day when I check in my luggage. I don't intend to check luggage.

    Luggage. I went out to the garage to see if my luggage was reachable - for me. I have one bag that fits in the overhead nicely and, if I pack carefully, one bag will do. I can surely do laundry in Lowell. Jim washes his clothes somewhere. He plans to call tonight again. Does he live in a house, an apartment, what? Does he have personal laundry facilities or share in a complex or go to the laundromat? I have to ask. I don't want to check a bag. I can see the bag but will have to wait for someone to get it down for me. It's in a sealed plastic bag poised almost directly over my car in the rafters. When did I put it there? Maybe after our vacation in Durango the year before he left. I don't recall going anywhere that required luggage in the last fifteen years.

    The mailman put the mail in the box by the door and rang the doorbell. He's been doing that since I've been getting that retirement check in the mail. For some reason the warehouse isn't set up for automatic deposit. The mailman is a worrier. I believed I shared with him the second check and he said he'd ring the doorbell so I'd know there was something valuable in the mail. A package or something like the check. Some days I see him come and go but don't get to the mailbox for a couple hours. If he rings the doorbell, I go right then. He said before Social Security did everything by direct deposit he used that same system for all of his SSA recipients. "You just can't trust anybody anymore." I echoed his sentiment.

Yesterday I mentioned to Lee that she should gather photos for me to take with me. I'm sure she has some I don't have. I'm going to sort through and scan them to a computer disk to take with me. When she calls this afternoon, I'll ask her to expedite her photo search so they can go on the same disk. I took my camera and walked around the yard; the hibiscus that Wes planted twenty years ago - he won't believe them. The roses along the east wall. A shot of the house from the street. the sun gazer lilies lining the front porch. The pool, the back deck that I refinished two years ago, the privet hedges everyone said would never grow here - hahaha, the summer holly, the hedge of arborvitae, a long view of the yard from the deck.

This took me longer than I had thought. Missed lunch. I had just transferred this morning's photos to a disc when Lee called.

Lee was always Daddy's girl. I had almost forgotten how close they were. She was bubbling and excited as she replayed her call with her Dad.

"Dad says you're going to go see him. Next Saturday? Do you want me to take you to the airport? It'd be nuts to pay parking, even in a long term lot, for two weeks. Dad said you have the details and it's up to you if I play taxi. What cha say Mom? Do you want me to take you to the airport?"

"It's up to you. But it's the day before Larry comes home. Do you want to make that trip twice in two days?"

"Mom! Ontario is not on the other side of the earth, for pete's sake."

"Let's talk about it later. Have you found photos for me to scan to take with me? Baby pictures, birthday parties, first day of school, Larry in uniform. Remember, he joined after your Dad was gone. Pictures of your house. You know, stuff Dads like to see."

"No, but I'll do that tonight. Want to come over for bar-b-q Saturday? Wil is doing chicken and ribs."

"Sure. What should I bring?"

"A salad, I guess. Anyhow, you're right. Dad sounds the same as ever. He told me he works for the post office and has for a while. He bowled a perfect game last year The guys on his team were surprised and they won the tournament. He's catcher on his baseball team. He said there's a Class A short season team in town and he goes to most of the games. And Mom, he said he misses us a whole lot."

When I talked to him last night, neither of us could think of much to say. Old married folk stuff - money and insurance. My 37-year old daughter talks to him and they both have a lot to say. I smiled to myself. At least that relationship doesn't seem to have changed.

I made sure the television was going to record Jeopardy and Wheel. Then the thought, call for a pizza. I haven't had a pizza delivered in a long time. In fact, I haven't had pizza in a long time. I checked for tip money as I got out my credit card. Medium pepperoni with extra cheese and a bottle of Pepsi. The six o'clock news came on just as the pizza was delivered. How long has it been since I've had a pizza and watched the news? A very long time.

The next day I made a potato salad in the morning. Otherwise, I may forget. The last couple weeks have been mind boggling. Some days I feel eighty and other days I feel eight. I finished cleaning the house. Stuff I used to do in one day I have now dragged out over three or four. This is ridiculous. About three I walked down to Lee's, salad and computer disc in hand. Maybe we could scan her photos onto the disc at her house.

And we could. The kids made little tag lines and headlines and sayings for many of the pictures we scanned. It was a fun time. Took hours but everyone enjoyed reliving the photos. We made a section for each of the kids, a section of all the kids, family events, school events. And a couple before Wes was gone. Lee had titled that section "Do you remember?" This may or may not be appropriate but it is what we, as a family, decided we wanted to do. We want this Jim Nolan to know who we are and how we survived without him. Somehow I felt it was necessary to let him know that "life does go on without you".

That sentiment was never voiced aloud. And I may be the only one who feels it. After hearing Lee recount her conversation with her Dad I got the feeling that he was telling her that. Life went on - without you. Of course, she didn't hear it that way.

At ten of seven, I asked Lee if we could call her Dad. "He usually calls me at this time. Last night I forgot to mention I wouldn't be home. It turned into a good gabfest. Each of the grand kids spoke with him. I don't know what was said on his end but they each tried to be cordial and a little personal with a man two of them had never met - and the third didn't remember. Lee chatted for a few minutes before handing the phone to me.

"Wow, Maddy, we have grand kids. They sound like truly wonderful kids. Guess I've missed a hell of a lot. Thank you for holding our family together without me. Thank you for not making me out to be the bad guy for leaving you all. I can tell that only good things have been said about me. I can tell. Thank you."

That threw me off stride for a second. Doesn't he understand that I held this family together because there was no one else to do it? I wasn't going to allow my family to go down the drain because their Dad/granddad bailed out on us. I held my temper in check. I was 'in public'. Quite frankly, I can't justify it either Why am I so angry now? It's over. Fifteen years, it's over.

Or is it?

After we all said goodbye, the photo project seemed to be more important. It was dark by the time I was ready to go home. The kids insisted that they walk with me; it's dark outside Grams. Don't want the bogey man to get you. It was a pleasant walk. They asked questions about their grandfather. Kid questions. What color were his eyes? How tall was he? Did he have dark hair like they did or was it lighter like yours? I assured them that he was tall, dark and handsome with sparkling brown eyes like Mike's. How tall? About six feet two, but that was fifteen years ago. Laurie said, "Grams, I'm sure he didn't grow any taller." I said, "No, but sometimes you shrink when you get older." Well, that was news to them. By this time, we were at my front door. Hugs and kisses and good nights.

The week literally flew by. On Thursday I decided I had better get packing. I laid out outfits that I could interchange tops/bottoms. I want to wear a dress to get there. Wes always preferred me in dresses. The last fifteen years, I've worn mostly pants. I packed two pairs of jeans and six tee shirts. A party dress, dress slacks/shirts, undies and two nightgowns. Dress shoes and sneakers. That was all I could pack into the suitcase. I always carry my ditty bag in my personal carry-on bag. I have a large bag that holds a lot, including my purse, camera, computer disc, phone. I would recheck this Friday evening but I believe I have everything I need for two weeks.

Lee insists she take me to the airport on Saturday morning. The plane leaves at 8am. We left my house at 6:15. The freeway is fairly clear all the way out. She chattered all the way out. When she dropped me off in front of the airline, she said, "Call me when you get there. Remind me later when you're coming home." She's beginning to think I may not make two weeks. I said I would do both.

As I waited in line to board, I realized I hadn't called Hal. He specifically asked me to call after I had talked to Wes. Two weeks and I didn't think once to call and report. Well, too late now.

My reserved seat was on the aisle about two-thirds back. My favorite place to sit. I hadn't realized that I could reserve a seat on this flight but Wes did. It's a long flight with a stopover in Salt Lake City of about an hour. Though

I had a cup of coffee on the plane, I ate breakfast during the layover. Airport prices used to be so much higher than the outside world, but they weren't as bad as I remember. The food was good, hot, and served with a smile.

My seat mates going to Boston were an old couple from Boston. Chatty as all hell. Finally I said that I was going to visit an old friend whom I hadn't seen for several years. Does she live in Boston? I said no, Lowell. Oh, Lowell is such a lovely little town. I was glad to hear that. There was beverage service and snacks. The couple was quieter after that. I leaned back and closed my eyes. I am still not sure about this trip. I'll wake up in a little while and find it has all been a dream.

CHAPTER THIRTEEN

I woke up to an announcement. "We will land in Boston in about ten minutes. Seats and trays upright please." The elderly lady in the middle seat asked if I had had a pleasant nap. I told her if I didn't talk in my sleep, it was. She assured me I hadn't uttered a word.

Leaving a flight is always such a rush, rush situation. Today I took my time. I thanked the flight crew. The pilot suggested I have a great time in Boston. I thanked him. There was a ladies' room just a few hundred feet from the gate. I stopped there, not just to use the facilities but to freshen up a bit. I washed my face, combed my hair, and took a deep breath. Back on the concourse I decided I needed to make a telephone call before I went any further. There were many empty seats at the next gate so I sat down and pulled out my phone. Yes, I finally have a cell phone. It's a flip phone and the kids laugh at it, but I can make and receive calls on it. I looked at the clock over the gate. Not only is it Saturday but early afternoon in California. The phone rang three times. I was ready to hang up when it was answered. "Hello?"

"Hal, this is Lyn Palmer. I should have called you before and I apologize for calling on your day off. I want you to know that I just landed at Logan. I'm still on the concourse but felt I should call you before going any further. I apologize for not calling last week. I hope it's not too late to ask if you have any words of advice?"

Not sounding the least upset, the FBI agent said, "Lyn, take it slow and easy. Don't go with any knee jerk reactions. Have a good time. Call me when you get home."

"Thank you. I just felt you should know where I am."

"While not necessary, it is appreciated. Lyn, feel your way. Don't let old memories kick you in the ass. Pardon the language. While you've known this man a very long time, you really don't know this man. That's not a warning per se; I don't want you to be hurt."

"I appreciate your insight. Hal, I'm scared half to death."

"Of course you are. You're literally on a blind date. Remind yourself of that and don't go overboard to be what you think he remembers. Okay?"

"Okay. Thanks. I'm supposed to stay two weeks but am not going to force myself. Hal, I am sorry I didn't call earlier. This has been a whirlwind and I'm fortunate to have remembered my own name. Thank you for the advice. I promise I will call when I get home."

"Good girl. You're forgiven. I would have just given you the same advice last week. Have a good time."

I put the phone back in my big bag and got on one of those moving walkways. It ends just before the exit of the secured area. Big breath, smooth the hair and the skirt, then walk. Before I exited the hallway to the main concourse, I saw him. He's still tall, dark and handsome. He had a bouquet in one arm and stood still - looking at every person as they passed through that last doorway. Hopefully reflecting a calm I didn't possess, I walked toward him.

The smile on his face was bright enough to light up the entire area. He took one step toward me; I kept walking. And then he ran to me, grabbed me in a big hug, and said, "You haven't changed a bit." The flowers were a bit battered from the hug but I took them, smelled them and smiled. "You remembered my favorite."

"Is this your only bag?"

I nodded. He took the handle of my suitcase. "The car is a million miles away in one of Logan's 'convenient' parking garages." I sort of chuckled.

We walked at a moderate pace; we didn't speak at all until we got to another moving walkway. "This one leads right to the garage we want." That's when I realized there were three moving walkways heading in various directions. Logan is a big airport.

He must have prepaid the parking as he had a ticket that fit into a machine that caused the barrier arm to raise. In ten minutes we were on the streets of downtown Boston.

"Hungry?"

"Peckish."

"We can eat here in town or go on into Lowell. Your choice."

"I don't know anything about either place, Jim. Your choice."

"Let's go to Lowell. We can eat in Boston tomorrow, or whenever. We can stop at the house if you want to freshen up or use the facilities. Or if peckish still means pretty much hungry, we can have some dinner first."

For a moment, I hesitated. "Let's eat first. Peckish does still mean pretty much hungry." I haven't eaten since breakfast. I didn't tell him that but realize I am hungry.

As we drove to Lowell, he pointed out various landmarks. Fenway Park isn't nearly as impressive looking at the outside as it is on television looking on the inside. "There's a lot of history in Boston. We can come down and spend a couple days if you would like. I presume you're still a history nut."

"Yes, I am. And I would like to spend a couple days exploring. Thank you for thinking of it."

"Plain ole American or bar-b-q and brew?"

"Plain ole American sounds good. Too much brew and I'd probably doze off."

"There's a place on Central that I've been to a couple times. Pretty nice called The Keep. We can hit Mill City Bar-b-q and Brew another time. The bowling team goes there once in a while."

There was nothing I could think of to say. Both places must be okay.

"You look quite smashing, Lyn. That is a great color for you."

Wow! A compliment. It is my favorite dress; a plain orange. It's a couple years old but he's never seen it. I bought it for an open house at the Library when we opened a new section two years ago. Afternoon affair so a simple dress.

"Thank you. I rather like it."

Conversation stalled. But, as we were driving, that didn't bother me in the least. I believe in keeping my eye on the road. I should have called Lee before we left the airport. No, I'm sure she didn't expect that but I will call her tonight sometime.

The Keep wasn't extremely busy though. As it is Saturday, I think it might get busy a bit later. It's about six, I think. "May I put my big bag in the trunk? It's a bit conspicuous." I took my purse and phone out and handed the big bag to him. We were greeted warmly. "Reservations?" Jim said, "No, usually before six we've never needed any." A big smile. "Window or corner?" Now if this is some sort of code or sign language, I wonder what it means. If this is everyday conversation, it's pretty weird. Yes, it is usual Q&A for a hostess but it sounds slanted – or something.

"Window, please. We like to people watch." Another big smile. He made it sound to me as though he's only been here a couple times. But this exchange at home in California would say that isn't so. The table is beautifully laid out. Flowers and candles and in front of a window...not real close to the window but I could see the people passing by. A waiter came immediately and handed us each a menu before he poured water. I hadn't opened the menu yet and wondered if we were paying for this kind of service with high menu prices.

The menu was varied and mostly American. The prices would indicate this service was just that - good service. There didn't seem to be any inflated pricing. Good. I'd feel bad if he had chosen a restaurant for its pricey service rather than good food with good service. Oh, my god, I'm mentally rambling. I have got to get myself together.

"Any suggestions, Jim?" I looked at him over the menu.

"I haven't eaten here often enough to form a favorite but the chicken parm is really good."

Back to the menu - there were several different chicken dishes. All reasonably priced. And I do like chicken Parmesan. "Does it come with an angel hair side?"

If you ask for it. Otherwise, it's spaghetti."

"That is what I would like. And a glass of Afftentaler Riesling."

He smiled at me. "Still love your whites, eh?"

I just folded the menu without responding. I always drink white with chicken. He used to also.

CHAPTER FOURTEEN

Dinner was relaxed and not hurried. Never got the impression we were keeping a table too long. The chicken Parmesan was extremely good. Best sauce I've had in ages and this isn't even an Italian restaurant. We small talked. Very small.

We were waiting for dessert - some chocolate creation the waiter declared to be uncommonly delicious. Jim reached across the table and covered my hands with his. "I didn't ask earlier; wasn't thinking. Would you prefer to stay at a hotel? We have a couple in Lowell. I only have one bed at my house. If you'd be more comfortable, I can get you a room."

My god. I hadn't thought of where I would stay when I got here. I am so used to a large house with three bedrooms. I hope that the shock I felt didn't show on my face. He rubbed my hands. "You're still wearing your wedding ring."

I looked down at his hands. "So are you. How are you explaining that, Jim?"

"So far, I haven't had to. I was advised to take it off but couldn't bring myself to that. People aren't real nosy here. But I think they do a lot of speculating. I live alone, I don't chase women. My feeling is that they think I've lost a dear wife and can't accept it. No one has asked. No one has said anything. But that's what I believe they believe."

"It was suggested I divorce you. There's some sort of provision in California law that an absent spouse can be divorced. Publication of intent in the area of last known residence acts as service. But I couldn't see wasting the hundred and eighty-six dollars filing fee."

He began to laugh. I moved my hands from under his. I realized what a stupid statement that was and wanted to cover my mouth. But it wasn't stupid; it was frugality. I lived a lot of that the past fifteen years.

The waiter came just then with the dessert. "I believe you will enjoy this immensely."

Jim was still laughing so I felt it necessary to respond. "It looks incredible, I'm sure we will. Thank you."

I leaned forward to whisper to Jim. "Don't waste the money on a hotel. But remember, I don't fool around on a first date."

Well, that set him off in another round of laughter.

"Yes, ma'am, I do remember."

The chocolate concoction was delicious. It was a hazelnut chocolate cheesecake with whipped cream and chocolate shavings. It tasted as good as it looked. I made a mental note of how it was put together so I can try and recreate it when I get home.

After dinner, we walked around the town for a few blocks. Jim showed me the bowling alley and the movie theater; a small bar he sometimes frequents... you know, the highlights of a small town. The town isn't that small - in reality it's as big as my home town.

Jim's house is more of a bungalow. One bedroom, one bath, nice-sized kitchen, dining room, living room and attached garage. He took my big bag and my suitcase into the bedroom. It is at the back of the house and overlooks a small yard. It's too dark to see the yard but he assured me there is one. I did note that the colors in the bedroom are the same as what were in our bedroom when he left. Not the typical landlord white. I excused myself and went to the bathroom.   I closed the door and turned on the light. It looks exactly like my main guest bathroom. An open cupboard with towels; towels in varying shades of blue and green. Just like my bathroom. One sink with counter on both sides. He had put all of his things on the left side; there was nothing on the right but a box of facial tissue. Plenty of room for my stuff. The walk-in shower had a small bench in the corner. I have one at home just like it as I love a shower but feel I never get my feet clean enough standing on them. It is obvious the bench has been there a while. He didn't run out and buy it just for me. Even the same toothbrush holder. The color of the walls, the tiles. All the same. I didn't open the medicine chest but did check the cupboard below the sink. Good god, cleaning supplies on the left, personal supplies on the right.

Just like my house. I've always thought I set those things up myself, years ago. Was it a joint effort? Did he have that much input? I don't think so. Is this how he has kept close to 'home' even when he's someone else and thousands of miles away? Oh, dear god. Or was it totally unintentional and maybe he doesn't realize it?? More likely.

Then I remembered I came to use the facilities. It was a struggle to blink back the tears. Maybe he has been homesick. I can see that the towel cupboard was added sometime after the house was built. Maybe he missed the house, the conveniences. Then too, maybe it is just easier to fall back on the familiar.

When I returned to the living room, I asked. "Do you own or rent here?"

"I rent with option to buy. Why?"

"The bathroom appears to have had some work on it and I wondered. You mentioned you've been here awhile."

"Yeah, that was the only thing in the house that I didn't care for. I asked the landlord if I could do a bit of painting and stuff. Stiff New Englander. 'Just remember; anything you add is a leasehold improvement and stays when you go.' I said oh yes sir. Then a couple years ago he asked if I'd be willing to sign a lease. I had already been here about five years. Sure, why not? Then he said, 'It could be a lease with option to buy.' And the advantage of that, Sir? 'Well, if you decide you'd like to buy the house, the rent you've paid after signing the lease would be counted toward the down payment.' I don't know if he really likes me or if he's just interested in getting rid of the house. I checked. His property taxes aren't that bad. So I signed the lease."

Now I really want to see that back yard. I doubt hibiscus would grow here but my backyard is an eclectic collection of plants. Wes likes flowers and plants and was always finding something he wanted to try to grow. And everything always grew.

Jim turned the television on to a station that played just music. "Would you like something to drink? I have a good whiskey, some gin, and some sodas."

"What are you making for yourself?" I wanted something but soda on top of that cheesecake would have been too much sweet. But I wanted to talk to him so wasn't sure about alcohol.

"A martini sounds good to me. I don't have any olives but do have ice and sweet vermouth."

"Olives are superfluous. A dry martini sounds great."

Wes never drank without crackers or something. Said crackers kept him from drinking too much. Sure enough, he had a box of cheese crackers tucked under his arm when he brought the martinis. I don't know how, but he had a small dish stuffed inside the box and after sitting down the two drinks, he shook crackers into the dish. He put it between the martinis.

He sat down before he handed me the martini. "Made the way you like it; three drops of vermouth."

I took a small sip. It was even my favorite gin.

"Here's to a new friendship. Jim and Maddy." We touched glasses. There was a small ping.

After a few minutes he leaned back and said, "We need to talk. Do you want to go first?"

"No. I don't. I have no idea what happened fifteen years ago. Why you stood me up for dinner at Luigi's. You go first. Your story will be longer, I'm sure. Please, go first."

CHAPTER FIFTEEN

Wes took another sip of his martini. He turned on the couch and sort of leaned on the arm so he was facing me. Another small sip before he put the glass on the coffee table.

"It starts long before that Thursday. That's how I think of it - that Thursday. In February, early in February, two men in suits came to the warehouse office and asked to speak to me. They asked for me by name - Wesley Palmer. Anna was my secretary. They gave her a business card. Do you remember Anna? She always appeared slightly intimidated just by living but she was not naive. She asked if they had an appointment. She knew they didn't. They said no they didn't know they'd be in this area of town but need to speak to Mr. Palmer. She asked them to take a seat and she'd see if she could locate me. I was in the warehouse talking to a new Kroger driver. She dialed the desk in the loading area and asked if I was in the vicinity. I came to the phone.

"Instead of saying two men are here to see you from Acme Supply, she said, "Is Mr. Palmer in the vicinity? There are two gentlemen here to see him." I knew she knew it was me on the line. I had identified myself when I picked up the phone. "When is he due back? He didn't tell me he was going to be out of the warehouse."

I spoke quietly. "What's up, Anna? Don't you like the look of these guys or something?"

"Yes, that's right. No, they didn't have an appointment. You know Mr. Palmer never misses appointments."

Again, I barely whispered, "Tell them whoever you're talking to sees him coming in. Can they wait five minutes?"

"Oh, great, just a minute." I heard her quiz them. And apparently, they could wait. "When he comes in please ask him to come up to his office asap. Thanks."

"Before I went up, I asked Dave Wilkerson to see if he saw any strange cars near the front door. He did. A big, classy, shiny, Caddy. He said it almost looked like a pimp car. You know Dave. Anything bigger than a Gremlin is a pimp car. But I figured Anna's sixth sense had kicked in. The guys couldn't be anything good.

"And, of course, they weren't.

"They actually had business cards for Acme Supply. You know I am a Wile E Coyote fan but kept my mouth shut. Maybe they thought they were being clever. Anyhow I came in close to ten minutes later with my hand out and an apology for keeping them waiting.

"They explained that they sometimes dealt in fairly expensive goods and were looking for a warehouse with space they could rent. They had particulars on the space. So happens we had a cage that could be locked. Remember when IGA was running a special on some sort of electronic thing and they wanted it separate from their own warehouse as it wouldn't be secure enough there? Well, that's the cage. Seldom been used since then.

"I told them it'd be $125 a month rental; first month in advance. Then they were curious about access. They preferred to come when the warehouse wasn't extremely busy. That's how we arrived at Thursday night. I took them downstairs and showed them the cage and which door was closest access, etc. etc., I am not sure how they knew when the cleaning crew came but the guards said they followed the cleaning crew in. Any Thursday that Acme came they followed the cleaning crew. We went back upstairs and I asked Anna for a monthly rental contract. They signed it, paid the first month in cash and that was that. I thought.

"I agreed with Anna. There was something really off about these two guys."

I sipped at my martini for a couple minutes. "This was in February?"

"Right."

"Something must have gone sour. What?"

"Anna sent them a payment request in mid-March. Mr. Slocum, one of the suits, stopped by the office. They had decided they weren't going to pay. I protested. How long does it take the fire department to get up to Greystone on an average day? I asked what they were talking about. It seems they wanted the cage rent free. The fact that he said Greystone scared me. We lived on

Greystone. Was he making a threat? He sneered. I think it was supposed to be a smile. Well, I could take it as I wanted. Then he said, "I would advise you think twice before calling the cops. You have two kids. You don't want anything happening to them, do you?"

"It didn't sound good to me. I had no idea what was in those shipments and if they were so damned valuable why doesn't he just pay the rent? He got up to leave and said we could just call the police ourselves and tell them what you've got locked up in that cage downstairs."

They were blackmailing you? But why? A small rental fee and there'd be absolutely no interference from anyone."

Wes ate a handful of crackers. "That's what made no sense to me. But that threat made me sure it was something illegal in that cage. I told him that I'd get back to him by the end of next week. I had to think about his proposition. Surprisingly, he said okay. We were going to that IGA meeting in Denver that week. Remember? But you didn't go because your dental work was killing you. While I was in Denver, I contacted the FBI. I told them I was working with a pair of idiots and told them the whole story. I told them I had rented the space without question but now it seems they wanted to involve me in it somehow. Rather than paying rent and coming and going, they wanted me to be a fall guy or something. A co-conspirator or something. But why?

"The FBI showed me a series of photos and I was able to pick out both guys. The FBI was quite concerned that these guys would try to involve and intimidate me. They had been on FBI radar for two years but every time they thought they had them, someone else ended up arrested. But I had a rental agreement with them. I figured it'd be pretty hard for them to blame me. I'm just a guy renting out a warehouse cage. The FBI said this was the first time they'd ever signed an agreement. I argued it's only $125 a month. I just don't get it.

"The FBI laid out a plan which pretty much excluded me. The new part time night guard I hired that month was a Fibbie. I figured everything was under control. The bad guys would lay the blame on me but this time it wouldn't work."

He drained his martini. "Want another?" I handed him my glass. His story is, after all, the weak end of this tale. It's validating what the agents told Lee and me a few weeks ago. When he came back with two fresh drinks, he continued.

"Then one day maybe a month before that Thursday, Eddy came into the office. Anna had already left for the day. He said that he needed to talk to me. He had a bad feeling about the rental cage. He told me that he's been coming in more often with the cleaning crew and the people who rent the cage were usually right behind him. Sometimes they picked up, sometimes they left product. He had managed to get close enough to the cage to hear them talking and he was absolutely positive that the next shipment, or maybe the next after that one, would be the last. They had been intercepted a number of times though they were sure the warehouse location wasn't known. It was coincidntal but it was time to move on and eliminate any witnesses.

"He was sure they were talking about me. So he and Jane went to Jane's brother who is a U S Marshal and told him what they thought was going on. Including the idea that they planned to get rid of me so I couldn't identify them. Apparently they didn't consider Anna a credible threat.

"That Thursday morning, Eddy called me and asked if I could meet him for coffee before he went to work. I said sure. I thought he'd heard something about the promotion he was hoping to get. But instead, he told me that the US Marshal had been monitoring this gang and they agreed with Eddy; the gang wanted to get rid of me. He said that the Marshal wanted to put me in FWP as soon as possible. That blew my mind. I had a meeting with Safeway at 11 and when it was over, I called you. At three, two US Marshals came in, plain clothes, and told me they were putting me under federal protection. They made it sound like it'd be a week or so until this gang was rounded up. I told them I had talked with the FBI and they were in place to do something as well. Shouldn't they talk to the FBI first? No. They walked me out to my car. I thought it was a courtesy and I could go home. No. Put my wallet and any other ID, including my phone, into the glove box. I said the phone was company property. Put it in the glove box.

"I did that. I took our wedding photo out of my wallet and slipped it into my pocket. They put me in a plain unmarked car and that was the end of Wesley Palmer - effectively."

CHAPTER SIXTEEN

It took me more than a minute to respond. Try as I may, I just don't get it. "Explain this to me in simple English, Wes. How could renting a space in your warehouse make you a target for the Feds? I don't get it."

He didn't look irritated or exasperated. "It took me a while. In fact, a long while. This particular group of people were high interest smugglers of high grade opiates. Every time the Feds thought they had them, they didn't. All they had was a warehouse that had agreed to rent to them. They never signed paperwork so there was never a trail to them. The warehouse guy became the fall guy. A lot of them were aware and took a chance. Until they made threats, I had no idea what they were really into. I suspected they were not legal but didn't know. I have been told that the product was something new and really lethal. It wasn't wide spread but they were making an inroad. Because I paid attention, made them sign a lease, got an address, etc. etc. they decided that intimidation would be the only way to continue using the warehouse. Actually, all they had to do was pay the damn monthly rent. You have to admit the warehouse is well located near the railroad, airports and freeways. The usual mode of operation was to use a location until there was the possibility of discovery. How they could tell that, I don't know. Then they would pull out 80% of what they had stored and anonymously tip off the Feds. They lost a little of their profit, got a little guy convicted and they'd go on. The Feds had no one to prosecute but the warehouse guy. This time though, because the product was new, different, worth more, they thought they'd have to eliminate me. They may not have remembered I had a rental agreement. A signed rental agreement. Though it wasn't worth the paper it was written on. Except there was a genuine mailing address. Thank god they forgot Anna could identify them too."

The martini was still cold. I sipped at it while I wanted to gulp it down and ask for another. This still makes no sense to me. What kind of drug could possibly be so valuable that they'd kill people for it?

"Okay. The Marshals stuff you into their car. Then what?"

"They drove to the Federal Building downtown and we went into an office. Someone took my photo and an hour later, I had a California driver's license with a new name."

"That's when you became James Nolan?"

"No. I needed a license because I needed identification. We then went to LAX. I think I wasn't supposed to know where we were going but I'm not blind. I know that KSTL is the airport designation for St. Louis Lambert Airport. And I saw the arch before we landed."

"But if you were flying with the Feds were you on a commercial airliner?"

"No, but they have rules for non-commercial flights as well. However, I don't remember ever having to show that license. Maybe I did. I was in a bit of a daze by this time. I don't even remember the name on it."

"Wes, this is getting deeper and deeper. Should I have brought my boots?"

"Maddy, how do you think I felt? In St. Louis at their headquarters, they literally produced James Allan Nolan. In three days I had a passport, a Missouri driver's license, a birth certificate, and had been fingerprinted. They gave me a resume that reflected my abilities; phony companies with telephone numbers that would verify my work history; my education."

"Fingerprinted?"

"Yeah, supposedly they'd go into the National Registry in case I applied for a job at a place that requires fingerprints, or in case I wanted to be a Notary Public again. Wes Palmer was eliminated."

"But that can't be. The FBI proved you had called me from a pay phone at the Library here in Lowell. They took your fingerprints off two phones. If they had put them through the National Registry, Wesley John Palmer would not have been identified."

Wes looked stunned. "They took my fingerprints from the phone? That's how you found me? How can that be?"

For more than a minute I just sat there trying to figure out if Wes was lying to me and was covering up more than I knew or if there had been a fluke. I got up and went to the bedroom to get my phone. He followed me. "What are you doing?"

"I'm going to get an answer to this fingerprint thing - tonight."

"How?"

I called Hal Tucker. The phone rang only twice. Evidently he checked caller ID before he answered. I would too - though it was only about 8pm on the West Coast. It was still Saturday. "Lyn, are you okay?"

"No, Agent Tucker, I'm not." I relayed the whole conversation to him. The whole conversation. He listened and asked a question or two when I didn't explain something well. "The thing I want to know, is how could the FBI have traced Wes' fingerprints through the National Registry?"

Silence. Then, "I don't know but let me make a call. I'll call you back within the hour. Lyn, are you okay?"

"Yes. And thank you." I disconnected.

"What the hell? You have the FBI on speed dial?"

"This Agent is the only person in the entire Federal Bureau of Investigation that has given me any help. He's found out things for me that I never knew and never would have known without his help. A lot of things."

"Like what?"

"Like who ran over Eddy and why."

"What?"

"You know that Eddy went to the US Marshal on your behalf. You've told me that. What you didn't tell me, because you probably didn't know, is that the person who rented the warehouse had seen Eddy around the warehouse several nights. He found out who Eddy was. The night of that Thursday this man, or men, had planned on coming in and taking part of their stash before getting rid of you. You'd be dead and there would be drugs in the warehouse. Eddy had overheard that the week before and alerted the Marshals. He wasn't sure how it'd happen but maybe a car accident on the way to work in the morning. That's why the Marshals moved so fast. They saved your life. There were police swarming the warehouse because you had disappeared. The bad guys didn't go into the warehouse. They could have as the police weren't interested in anything but you. No one would have paid any attention to a crew with a key removing their property. Three weeks later, Eddy was run over. It was deliberate. There were five school kids and a parent who witnessed it. They described the car and two helped a sketch artist draw the driver. You were gone but Eddy might still be a threat. Their stash was never picked up. The FBI removed it much later - when no attempt was made to recover it. The FBI, well Agent Tucker, told Lee and me that it was a hundred million dollars of something called Fentanyl, or something like that. There wasn't much news about the drug until the last few years but it sat in your warehouse for months. I think it was one of the drugs that Michael Jackson overdosed on."

Wes sat there, head cradled in his hands. I an sure he was crying. I went out to the kitchen and made two more martinis. I can't have a worse headache in the morning than I have right now. I came back and sat his drink on the table in front of him. Several minutes later he sat up - his face was wet with tears.

"So, he saved my life and lost his own. That is just wrong. Why did he wait so long to tell me? I could have told the FBI the whole story as apparently they don't talk with the US Marshal. Oh, dear god, Maddy, I am responsible for my son's death. Oh dear god." He sobbed but the tears had stopped.

He picked up the martini. "I should have bought another bottle. One's not going to do it."

I reached over and took the drink out of his hand. "I finally find you and you plan to drink yourself to death?" I put the drink on the table. He grabbed me and hugged me so tightly I could scarcely breathe.

My phone rang. I checked the caller ID. I hadn't called Lee yet. But it was Tucker. "This is Lyn."

Hal said, "Are you sure you're okay?"

"Yes, I am."

"I found the technician who ran the fingerprints. He didn't go through the National Registry as he thought the US Marshal would have made changes fifteen years ago. He went through the State Fingerprint Registry. Remember, Wes was a Notary Public for a whole lot of years. Every six years he renewed his bond which required new fingerprints. You're a Notary. You know that."

"Yes, I know that. But since the fingerprints were taken here in Lowell...."

"The technician here had requested they be faxed to him. He was way ahead of us. He figured there'd be no Wesley Palmer in the National Registry. And, he was right. Does that answer your question?"

"Yes, Hal, it does. Thank you for taking my call."

"Take care, Lyn. I'm here if you have any other questions."

"Thanks." I disconnected.

"Hal? You call the agent by his first name?"

"Yes, I learned it the day he came to the house with the information from the US Marshal that they couldn't tell me your name but they'd pass the question on to you. If you wanted me to know, you would tell me."

"They said that? They wouldn't tell you who I was or where?"

"Nope. They wouldn't and Agent Tucker finally beat them down to saying they'd let you decide. He figured that was an absolute win - a true victory for him. The US Marshal is an efficient and valuable unit but they don't play well with others."

We sat together on the couch sipping our martinis. I was getting very tired. I had started the morning on California time, lost three hours coming East and have now had three excellent martinis. I stood up and announced. "I'm going to shower and go to bed."

And I did.

CHAPTER SEVENTEEN

I woke once during the night to a call from Nature. It took me a few seconds to put myself where I was. Wes was curled behind me, as he was wont to do fifteen years ago. That was the first puzzle to my sleeping mind. Then I had to remember where the bathroom was. Thankfully, Wes has a nightlight in the bathroom as I do at home. His little clock in the bathroom told me it was 3:15. When I returned to bed, he had rolled over. I was glad as I couldn't remember how I used to get back into bed without waking him.

When I woke the second time, the other side of the bed was empty. I didn't have a headache after all. I was sure I would. Martinis haven't been on my daily routine - heck not even a weekly routine. Coffee, I could smell coffee. A bedside clock announced 8am. I seldom sleep that late. Wait, it's only five at home. Oh well. I put on my slippers and went to the bathroom to wash my hands and face before I padded out to the kitchen. Wes was at the table reading the newspaper. The coffee pot was on the counter and an empty cup sat by it. I filled the cup and went to the table.

"May I have whatever section you're done with?"

Without a word he handed me the sports section. That was always the first part of the paper he read. He was in his 'bedtime Bermudas', barefoot and bare chested, like always. He likes pajamas but not long ones. There is actually a short pajama bottom sold separately so he must not be the only guy who prefers them. The Red Sox are in Chicago for the weekend - they lost Friday, won yesterday. The paper covered both leagues fairly; but emphasis was on the home team, of course.

He handed me another section of the paper. "Should you call Lee?"

"Not for another hour. She's picking Larry up at the airport at 11, but it's just after five now."

Wes laid down the paper. "Now I understand why you wanted this discussion face-to-face. It definitely could not happen by telephone. Maddy, I don't know what you are thinking of me right now. Whatever it is, I'm sure I've earned it. I did not know anything that happened at home after that Thursday. And, though you refrained from saying it, I should have known renting space to those two hoodlums was idiotic to begin with. As things played out, they would have used the space through intimidation as I am sure they'd done to other warehouses. They were very menacing but I was sure with the FBI on my side, things would work out. Maybe they would, maybe they wouldn't. As I have bitched for forty years - why can't the U S Government agencies work with each other? They're all worse than a ball team who sulks when they lose. We've lost fifteen years due to the hubris of the US Marshal."

While I wasn't sure I agreed totally with that or not, there was nothing I could say to appease him. I'm not sure he was looking for appeasement, or forgiveness, or anything else. Maybe he just wanted to be validated as a loving husband and father who took a wrong turn. I don't know. So I said nothing. I just drank my coffee and went back to the newspaper. The first section has a great banner. The Lowell Sun. Out of habit I checked the pub box on the bottom of page 2. Why should I care who the editor is or how to contact the opinion desk? I don't. When I was a kid, I worked for our local paper. The editor said the best way to tell anything about a newspaper is how much information they give the public about accessing the people running the paper. The Lowell Sun is a good public paper. They tell you how to access nearly everyone but the janitor.

The front page news must be pretty much the same everywhere. An article of import to the area; an article regarding national news; and a feel good story continued on page 5.

I read the first section pretty quickly as it was national news mostly after page one. And I've been following those news on television. Then he handed me the Life section or whatever they call it. The comics, puzzles, the doctor column, the advice column - all the good stuff. I resisted asking for a pen to do the puzzles. It's not my paper.

Wes got up and poured himself another cup of coffee. "What would you like to do today? There's a matinee ball game at 1:30. I usually have coffee at home; go out for brunch; and then hit the ball park if there's a game."

"The Red Sox are in Chicago."

"True, but their farm team is right here in Lowell and they are a really good team this year. I expect four or five of them will be called up to Fenway next season."

"That's right. Lee said you mentioned a short season Class A team. I'm still a baseball fan."

So it was decided. Coffee/newspaper, brunch, ball game. I finished reading the comics and the columns. There was a recipe for a pumpkin pecan bread attached to a story on the first page of the section about a local couple who have opened their own bakery. Reads really well. I was going to ask if I could cut out the recipe but decided I can go on line when I get home to retrieve it. Wes has always made jokes about my cutting out recipes. Of course, he has always eaten well from those recipes but that's beside the point. I poured a second cup of coffee and checked the time. Lee is probably up now. She's anxious to pick up Larry.

The phone rang three times before Laurie answered. "Grams, you didn't call last night. Is everything all right?"

"Sure is Dear Heart. Your grandpa picked me up at the airport in Boston and fought the Saturday traffic out of town. Lowell is really a nice town. We had a great dinner - chicken Parmesan with angel hair. We walked around town so I could see stuff. Nice movie theater - looks great, playing the new Star Wars. Your grandpa's house is kind of little but very nice. I am going to check out the back yard when I get off the phone. We talked awhile and I went to bed. I should've called but kept forgetting there's a 3-hour time difference. Are you all going to the airport?"

"Oh, yeah. Mom doesn't get Dad alone right away. He's going to be home for a whole month. I'll tell him you're in Boston, or wherever it is you are, but look forward to seeing him. Okay?"

"Absolutely. That's exactly what I am doing. Tell your Mom that we're going to a ballgame this afternoon. Hold on a minute." I turned to Wes. "What's the name of the team?" "Spinners, we going to see the Spinners."

"Did you want to talk to Mom?"

"She's probably making your breakfast right now. No, I don't need to talk to her. Just tell her I arrived safely and have been talking your Grandpa's ears off."

"Okay, Grams. Have a good vacation. Mom says call tomorrow so she can talk to you. Okay?"

"I certainly will. Hug your Dad for me. Bye."

Wes sat at the table. "I am having a hard time reconciling three grandchildren."

"Get your laptop. I brought a disc." Can you believe it? I had almost forgotten the disc of photos in all the mess of last night.

"I am going shower and dress first, Maddy. Last night I just fell into bed when I finally got off the couch."

While he was in the shower, I realized he had partially opened a dresser drawer. I am sure it was open last night. I just didn't see it. The drawer was empty. I transferred stuff from my suitcase to the drawer. And there were empty hangers at one end of the closet. I hung my dress and good slacks and shirt. I zipped my suitcase closed and stood it on end in the closet under my stuff. Then I got dressed. Going to a ball game? Jeans, tee, and an over shirt and sneakers. I was sitting on the couch with the disc in my hand by the time he was dressed.

"So what is this?" He fit the disc into the tray of his laptop.

"We thought maybe you'd like to see the people and places you left behind. We gathered up our favorite photos and scanned them to the disc. Well, the first twenty or so, I took this past week."

The first photo was the house taken from the street. It looks really great. Wes sat there for several minutes before clicking to the next picture. He exclaimed over all of those photos. His flowers, plants, hedges. The deck. "Wow, that looks like new." "I refinished it a couple years ago." The pool and yard. He leaned back and looked at his hibiscus. "And everyone said it wouldn't grow."

Then we got into the photos the kids had titled. Birthdays, school, family events. He was amazed. More than once he said, "Mike looks just like I did at that age. Is he the only one with brown eyes?" It's funny as I never saw the similarity before he mentioned it. But, damn if Mike doesn't look like a young Wes. And yes, he's the only one with brown eyes.

Every once in a while, a picture brought tears to his eyes. Mostly he was just excited at seeing the kids grow. We had a few good shots of Eddy and Jane; some just of Eddy. He came back to the beginning of the disc. The house and yard.

"I have thought of this so often. I missed the house, the neighborhood, everything about our daily life. But in a one-bedroom house you can't really replicate what I had. Come see my back yard."

That admission causes me to believe that the color schemes, the bathroom cupboards, the shower stool were, in fact, an early attempt to hold on to what he had left behind.

He tried but never succeeded with a hibiscus here. But he has roses and arborvitae and lilies. He created a small fountain in one corner that is surrounded by low growing peonies. There are two small benches in that little corner. Nothing like this at my house, but it certainly is attractive.

All of a sudden he said, "Good lord, look at the time. Do you mind eating at the ballpark?"

"Do they have something other than hot dogs?"

"Oh, yeah, they're as sophisticated as Fenway. You can get a nice salad and sandwich. Matinee games are usually kind of crowded so if we leave now, we have time to eat some lunch at the cafe before settling in for the game."

We went into the house and I got my purse, phone and camera. He laughed at me. "I should have known you wouldn't use your phone as a camera, Maddy." I wasn't sure how to take that. And honestly, I don't know how. I should have just shown him it was a flip phone without camera abilities. Didn't think of it at the time.

Once inside the ball park, while Wes ordered lunch, I bought myself a Spinners' ball cap. This isn't a fancy park and is pretty much open. Without a cap, the glare might keep me from really getting into the game. It was a good game. And I enjoyed it. I picked out three players and asked if they were on his list to be called up. They were. Sharp, alert players.

We drove around and he pointed out different places of interest. Much of the town looks like an old colonial town, which I guess it is. One place there is a plaque that said "Incorporated in 1826 to serve as a mill town, Lowell was named after <u>Francis Cabot Lowell</u>, a local figure in <u>the Industrial Revolution</u>. The city became known as the cradle of the American Industrial Revolution." As Wes said, "There's a lot of history here on the East Coast. A whole lot." I am fascinated. And as an educational Librarian I am thinking of a new exhibit for my library. I didn't mention it though. But I will say something to Lee to see if she thinks it's a good idea.

During the day, Wes was recognized often. I heard "Hey, Jim," quite a few times. Only one man asked who I was. He didn't come out and say it bluntly. I waited to hear what Wes would say. "Someone from a former life. We grew up in the same town. Here for a visit." His friend offered his hand, "Stan Rogerts." I shook it and said "Lyn Palmer."

Couldn't disagree with any of that explanation. We grew up in the same town all right. We grew up together in the same house. We were both very early 20s when we married. We sure did grow up together.

Dinner was at the Mill Grill & Brew or whatever. The place he had mentioned last night. It's more like a pub but there is a good-sized dining room. The food was very good. It was after nine before we were back at the house.

Weekdays Wes has a different routine. Up and take the paper to a small cafe around the corner from his house. We drank coffee and read the paper there. Usually he says he doesn't read the paper as he has to get to work. But he takes it with him to read at lunch. He never has liked reading a morning paper at night. I always figured the news doesn't change that much from morning to night and the comics don't change at all. Instead of going to work, we visited some of the museums in Lowell. Had lunch at a food cart in a park.

"I still know how to cook, Wes. We could buy a few groceries at least to make breakfast or something."

"Pancakes?"

"Sure. Now which of these ingredients do you have at home?"

Turns out he didn't have the basics at all. So I bought what I'd need for pancakes, eggs, and bacon. The maple syrup was the real stuff. What a joy to find it. Some syrups are so insipid. He didn't want me to go to the hassle of making dinner while I was there. He said, "It's not much of a vacation if you do everything you do at home." While I agreed, eating out so often doesn't sound so great to me. But he does it all the time. And has for fifteen years. When he was home, years ago, we went out a couple times a month. That was enjoyable.

The next morning, after breakfast at home, Wes said, "Would you like to go down to Boston maybe Thursday or Friday and spend the weekend? Lots of history in Boston; we could take in a Red Sox game. You've never been to Fenway. I know you want to see the Green Monster for yourself, close up and personal like.

"I've stayed at three different hotels that are practically in the outfield of Fenway. The Commonwealth isn't a luxury hotel but has everything. The Verb is the closest and I liked it. But the one I think I liked best was The Boston Hotel Buckminster. These three are within walking distance of the park. I mean really close. Like next door."

"Prices?"

"They're about the same. You can get a 4-day weekend for under five hundred bucks."

For someone who has had to watch their money closely until they turned fifty-five, that sounds like a lot of money. But looking at it realistically, compared to hotel prices at home, all three would be considered inexpensive. "The Boston Hotel Buckminster sounds more impressive. Do you think you can get reservations this late? It is still summer."

"Don't know but why don't I call and find out." He went on line, to get the phone number, I think. He could have made reservations on line but he has always insisted that you can get a better rate if you talk to 'somebody'. In half an hour we had reservations for Friday through Monday. "Getting two weekdays with the weekend gives you a better rate." Damned if I knew anything about that. I wonder how often he's gone to Boston? He works down there. Is this how he spends his time off? I'm not sure I want to ask. No, I don't. This is one thing I don't need to know.

"There's just one thing, Maddy. You have got to start calling me Jim. Someone is going to overhear and what do I tell them?"

I didn't admit it to him but I have been deliberately calling him Wes. I tried out Jim at the very beginning and, well, he seemed too comfortable. I'm sorry but this trip was a mistake. I find myself resenting him, not what he has, but how easy life seems to have been for him; and still is. I suffered for fifteen years - badly for eleven. His suffering, his discomfort, appears to have lasted a few months; maybe a year with occasional pangs.

CHAPTER EIGHTEEN

"Are you still a history nut, Maddy."

"Does one ever recover from that kind of mania? Of course, I am."

"Want to run over to Lexington? Lots of history in this state. I have been all over it and if you like we can turn this into a history vacation. We talked about doing this once or twice as I recall."

And so, for a week we visited history. There was so much to see in Boston. Freedom Trail, Minute Man National Historic Park, Bunker Hill memorial. The Boston Hotel Buckminster is the perfect location for history nuts and/or baseball nuts. We arrived there early afternoon on Friday. We could see Fenway from the hotel but we didn't go to the Friday night game. It sounded quite enthusiastic though. Dinner in a quiet restaurant recommended by the concierge. Drinks later in the hotel bar. This was one of three vacations on our bucket list. Places we intended to go after Wes retired. Now I wonder why we hadn't just taken a vacation? Why were we waiting for retirement? We were both working and it would have been affordable when we were in our early forties.

The hotel has cooked-to-order breakfasts every morning. There is a charge - this isn't your usual complimentary breakfast. The charge is less than at an outside restaurant but it isn't cheap either. There is a chef in a white coat and tall cap who prepares whatever you want from a fairly extensive menu. Fairly extensive menu for this sort of venue, anyhow.

A very short walk took us to the light rail station. Armed with maps and brochures from the hotel, we saw a lot of history without parking fees or traffic jams. We didn't light rail every time but certainly had a wonderful time when we did. There were a couple days I was tired when we got back to the hotel.

The concierge gave us a list of nearby restaurants that he thought we'd like. While all were nice, none had over the moon prices.

Saturday evening we went to Fenway Park. I was surprised that decent seats were available. The Toronto Blue Jays were in Boston. It was a really good, close game. The Red Sox got a one run lead in the seventh inning and held on to it to win.

Sunday we took the Cityview 'hop on hop off 'trolley tour. The Old North Church is a highlight of the trip. It is amazing how well preserved it is. And the area around it reflects the past quite well. It is maintained wonderfully. I could be happy and go back to Lowell then but we had another day in Boston. Don't get me wrong. I loved every minute of it. And, I called him Jim.

On Tuesday, we left Boston after a nice breakfast at the hotel and drove back to Lowell.

On the way back, Jim showed me the mail center where he works. My god, it is huge. He says they sort mail for most of the eastern seaboard there. For some reason, I have always thought he wouldn't like being an employee. He's always been a boss man. But, evidently, he really likes this job.

Once we were in Lowell, I asked to stop at the grocery store. Bread, juice and a melon. I love pancakes but don't want to eat them every morning. A couple mornings we ate breakfast out on our way to somewhere. I love a variety at breakfast - it may be my favorite meal of the day. We ate in Wednesday and Thursday.

Friday arrived and Jim asked if I brought a dressy dress. I told him indeed I had. He had made reservations at one of the hotels for dinner and dancing. It was my last night. We stopped at a couple clubs in Boston and danced a bit but not an evening of dancing. Just a tune or two while we had a drink. Dinner and dancing used to be a really big deal. I find that it still is.

Dancing can be very intimate; I had forgotten that. This entire two weeks we have held hands, hugged a couple times. At night I woke often to find him curled next to me. We've kissed but that has been it. Deliberately. So dancing for a couple hours was almost a new sensation. I went to the ladies' room at one point and realized I was rather flushed. I had a stern talk with myself before I returned to the table. This has been a first date, a blind date, just like Hal suggested. And I don't monkey around on first dates. Strangely enough, I wasn't that interested in monkeying around. Wes could always turn me on. Jim - not so much. He's still tall, dark, and handsome but over these two weeks I've seen him differently than ever before. I realize this is petty. He doesn't seem to have taken the last fifteen years as hard as I have. I'm going to have to realign my thinking, I guess. But there are subtle changes that I'm not sure I like about him.

It was close to last dance when Jim asked me to marry him. I looked him square in the eye and said, "Slight problem, Jim. I'm still married to Wesley Palmer."

For some reason, he thought the marriage was automatically over when he became someone else. I told him, legally I am still married. He said, "Will you consider going home and getting a divorce?" I thought about that for a minute. There is not a single benefit being married to Wes. His retirement from the warehouse will continue anyway. Mr. Kellison told me that even if I remarried I was entitled to it. The warehouse isn't set up like Social Security.

Perhaps I hesitated too long. "Well, would you?"

"Jim, this is the first time I've really thought about getting a divorce. It's not a decision you make without thinking about it."

"You mean in fifteen years you never thought about it?"

"Never."

"Well, will you think about it?"

"Yes, I will. I will even discuss it with my daughter. Would that be okay?" I don't know why I was feeling snide all of a sudden. But that's what it was - pure snide. He didn't pick up on it. That's a not so subtle difference. Wes would have jumped on that bit of snide like a canary on seeds.

"Good idea. I'll mention it to her sometime after I know you've talked to her. Lee is level-headed; I'm surprised she never suggested it to you before."

"Really? Jim, my daughter has always believed she'll get her father back. Divorce just never entered the picture."

He seemed pleased with that response. We danced one more dance and called it a night. Even though it was late, we sat in his back yard and talked. He still wants to go to Peru. He was glad that savings account was still intact. "You cannot know how hard it was for me to make sure I never touched it. Some day you'd be home and we'd do all sorts of grand things."

I couldn't fall asleep and found myself wondering if he had been saving anything in all these years toward that trip to Peru. Yes, more snide. But if it is as important to him as he sounds it is, wouldn't it have been logical to save toward it and hope to merge monies if we were ever reunited?

We left for the airport at noon. Traffic was surprisingly light so we had time for lunch at a small cafe we'd discovered earlier in the week. He hugged me tight and whispered that he loved me. I teared up as I believe that was the only time in two weeks he said it and sounded like he meant it.

"I love you too." Trouble is, though I didn't tell him, I love Wes Palmer. I'm not sure yet about James Nolan.

CHAPTER NINETEEN

Though I gained three hours heading home, the trip lasted too long; even longer than going. I had one stopover, in Denver. It was supposed to be an hour and six minutes but there was some nature of delay and it was nearly three hours before we boarded to continue. No reason for the delay. It's not a holiday; wasn't the weather; the other plane just wasn't at the gate when it was supposed to be. I called Lee and suggested she check on line for a new arrival time. As always with Lee, it was no problem. She did say that they planned dinner at Luigi's at seven. Larry thought it would be a great way to celebrate your homecoming and Dad's location. She'll alert Luigi's if we're going to be late.

From Boston to Denver, I tried to sleep. The alternative to sleeping was thinking and I am not ready to think this through yet. I went through the photos on my camera. Some of Wes' house and yard, Fenway Park, historical sites up the wazoo, the Spinners game, and several of Lowell itself. I know the grand kids want to see what kind of town it is. I told them during one phone call that it was a lot like our own town. Not overly big, friendly people, nice shops, good streets. All Lowell has that we don't have, I told them, is a whole lot of history and a Red Sox farm team. So I took photos to prove all that.

And there are several photos of Wes. Some of the two of us. People are so friendly. They see a couple, one holding a camera, and immediately offer to take your photo in front of whatever landmark you happen to be in front of. No fooling. I think there are five or six photos of the two of us at some historical place. Photos taken by absolute strangers. Of course, we are all smiley and happy in the photos. Though come to think of it, there wasn't a single day that we had a major disagreement about anything. I'm not even sure we had any minor disagreements. It was a pleasant vacation. One to cross off the list of things to do after we retired.

The subject of divorce won't be brought up at dinner tonight. The kids are probably old enough to understand the legal ramifications of this situation, but it might put a damper on the evening. I'm not willing to take that chance. But I thought a lot about it all the way from Boston to Denver. Wes wants me to legally divorce him so that I can legally marry him. As Jim, of course. There were times during the past two weeks that he mentioned marriage - wouldn't this be a great place to get married. Doesn't take long to get a license, etc. around here. When he finally actually brought it up he was surprised that I was still legally married to Wes Palmer. Even after we discussed it, I believe he was having a hard time with the idea.

While I am willing to divorce Wes, I am not sure I want to marry Jim. I can't say that he's changed. Because I believe he hasn't, not that much. But I have. I didn't realize how much my thinking had to change when I was suddenly on my own with a mortgage, taxes, and a part-time job. Yes, I suffered through those things and I am a better person for it. Therein lies the crux of the matter. Listening to his litany of woes for his first few months on his own, I had difficulty equating them with the problems I had on my own. And mine lasted eleven years, until his retirement pension kicked in.

Dealing with the authorities, juggling money, death of a son, all seem much larger than his list of worries. He had backing; he couldn't fail. He may have missed me and the house and all the good things we had but he had replacements. He had a house, he got a job, he bought a car, he could not fail. The Feds needed him as a witness. And they would make sure no harm came to him before then. Well, or after testifying either, if it came to that. I missed him. But I worried that I couldn't save the house. I sold his truck. I lucked out on his insurance. And years down the road I got his retirement. But it's difficult for one person to juggle that many balls in the air without dropping even one. I did it, but it wasn't easy. He's been living the high life for fifteen years. I only got close to my original level four years ago when the warehouse started paying his retirement. For ten years I did not buy a new pair of shoes. For ten years I did not go to a movie or out to eat unless it was with family and they paid their share. It's difficult for a grandmother to not be able to take a grandchild somewhere special for their birthday. Until I turned fifty-five, I felt like a pauper. Wes went to Boston for long weekends, ballgames, movies, bowling, and eating out all the time. And he complains how much he suffered. His lame apology was just that - lame. He should have known, he thought, blah, blah, blah.

Good grief - my biggest problem now is that I resent him. I resent that he threw away our good life and sabotaged mine for a decade. No wonder I can't love James Nolan. He's the enemy.

I don't know how the airline did it, but we landed only forty-five minutes late. The pilot said something about a tail wind, for a change, out of Denver. As I left the secured area of the Ontario Airport, three grand kids came running for a hug. Wil took my wheelie bag; Mike took my big carry-on and Laurie took my arm.

Chatter, chatter. Dad's been home two weeks and boy are we glad. We went hiking up the canyon to the waterfall. Dad backpacked a picnic lunch. Mom stepped on a snake but it was a little garden snake but she screamed pretty loud anyhow. Yada, yada, yada. Did you take pictures? Did you know we're going to Luigi's for dinner? Will you tell us all about Grandpa?

It was that question that made me glad I had come to terms with myself before we landed. Now that I realize I resent Jim Nolan, I can tell them about their grandpa. Larry and Lee were waiting for us. Larry hugged me closely. "I hope this meeting was as wonderful as we all wish." I just smiled.

Lee hugged me tightly. "Is Dad okay?"

"Honey, he's better than okay. He has it made. He's happy where he is."

At dinner, my camera was passed around several times. Laurie asked, "What did Grandpa think of the pictures we sent?"

"He was amazed. He was absolutely stunned at how handsome his grandchildren are. But poor Mike, Grandpa thinks you look just like him when he was fourteen."

The camera had to go around again to the photos of Wes and Wes and me. His siblings decided Mike doesn't look like Grandpa at all. But his Mom and Dad can see a very strong resemblance. It was a joyous meal. Of course, we couldn't tell anyone why it was so joyous. The reason if asked? I had been on a history junket for two weeks and had a marvelous time but am delighted to be home.

They dropped me off at home. I told Lee that I needed to speak to her, and Larry too, about something totally serious. Maybe in a day or two they could come for a cookout and the kids could spend some time in the pool. Could that be arranged in their schedule. Definitely.

"Is it something to do with you and Dad?"

"It does." I shouldn't have said anything. She's going to be thinking possible reconciliation. And it's just the opposite.

CHAPTER TWENTY

Sunday morning life looked a bit better than it had on Saturday morning. I laid in bed for quite a while after I woke, just to reflect on the past two weeks. I reflect better lying down. The two weeks were well spent. I saw American history; history I had studied and often wondered what the area was like where this history took place. History books frequently gloss over details about an area. Or it paints it so darkly, you wonder why anyone would fight over it. I had never been to Massachusetts and found it to be a wonderful place. The image I had in my mind, and from textbook photos, of the Boston Tea Party, for instance, was so far wrong. No wonder I never really understood the import, or the impact, of the dumping of tea in the harbor. We happened to be there during a reenactment. Very interesting. There may have been extra drama but it was history.

Now I want to visit Pennsylvania just to get the landscape in mind for so many battles; for Gettysburg, Valley Forge, and other places. I am sure now my mental image doesn't even come close to the real thing.

So for history's sake, and my enlightenment, the past two weeks were absolutely wonderful. But I hadn't gone for history's sake. My enlightenment in things other than history is what I am reflecting on. I wish I hadn't gone. Perhaps this is what Agent Tucker was trying to tell me. I am sure that is why he asked each time I spoke with him if I was all right. He may not know me personally, but he knows human nature. And sometimes, human nature comes through at its worse when a person feels cheated, or deprived, or put upon. It certainly did this time. I wonder if Agent Tucker thought it might turn out like this? Didn't he once say something about memories not being 100% perfect? The fantasy I had created was a farce. Couldn't have been further from actuality. That devastated me. It should have made feel better - that both of us hadn't suffered so cruelly. But, I don't work that way. Before this, I always felt I was a fair and open person.   Someone who could be happy for someone else's better fortune. I have let myself down. I'm not that way at all. When Milly Simms won a hundred thousand dollars in the lottery a couple years ago, I was happy for her. And it didn't bother me in the least that I hadn't won. For a lot of reasons, one - I seldom buy lottery tickets; two - it was chance. She had no effect on the outcome other than she had bought a ticket. I was genuinely pleased she had won.

The situation with Wes/Jim doesn't fit that mold. There was no chance about it. He had made a mistake, well really several, and it affected the whole family. He, however, came out smelling like a rose. No, I can't be happy for him without being sad for myself.

I am delighted that he has suggested I file for divorce. I can do that easier than I could declare him dead. We're not talking money here - we're talking conscience. I don't want him dead. I no longer wish to be married to him. I don't want to be married to his new image either. Resentment will overcome love every time. It would take me twenty years to shed the resentment I am feeling. I'm smart enough to know that. Living alone is not that difficult. I've done it for fifteen years under good circumstances and bad. I prefer to live alone rather than live in resentment. He won't understand or believe that. But that's okay. He doesn't have to.

I got up and took a long warm shower and washed my hair. Airplanes always make my hair feel dirty. There wasn't much in the kitchen to eat so I dressed and went out for breakfast before going to the market. I've asked the kids to come over for a cook out or something. I bought a lot of groceries. I'll make three or four salads and that fancy chocolate dessert we had in Lowell. It is a straight forward dessert - it's just put together fancy. Chicken and burgers sound good to me.

Once I was home I called Lee and she thought that tomorrow would be an excellent day to come. She asked if I would consider staying with the kids so she and Larry could take off for a few days. Of course, let's discuss it tomorrow. We decided on two o'clock but not eat until later. Give us time to visit, review my photos, kids can swim a lot, and the three of us could talk. She asked what she should bring. Whatever you want to drink; I just came from the market and didn't buy a single thing to drink except milk. She laughed. She would bring drinks.

I went through and dusted the house. Wil and Mike mowed the lawn while I was gone. I had the mailman hold my mail so will get that in the morning. I prepared the salads for tomorrow and tonight will do the cheesecake. Eating out is great and often fun. But after two weeks of it, I don't have to eat out again for a long while. Breakfast this morning is my last meal out for a while.

Monday I decided to call Agent Tucker. I should let him know I've returned home in one piece. And I believe he expects a report. He wasn't sure I should go.

He answered on the second ring. "Lyn, how are you? How was your visit?"

I told him about where I'd gone and what I did and what I'd seen. He asked about Jim. I told him that Jim had asked me to come home and divorce Wes. Tucker didn't sound surprised.

"When did he realize you were still married to Palmer?"

"Not until I pointed it out to him. I believe he hoped to get married while I was there. I told him it wouldn't work. I was still married to Wesley Palmer. He didn't quite understand the legality of that and I told him that he had not been declared dead so I have been, in fact, married to him all this time - and still am. He said go home and get a divorce."

"And are you going to?"

"Oh, yes."

"So you can marry Jim Nolan?"

"No."

Long silence. "I thought you would want to marry him. It took you so long to find him."

"You're right, Hal. I really wanted to find him. I didn't know a lot of things before I went to Lowell. I found him. He's in good health, has a job, is leasing a house with option to buy, people around town know him and seemingly respect him. He's the perfect example of the 'man you would want to take home to Mother.' But I don't want to marry him. Not now, not ever."

Hal cleared his throat. "I believe I suggested you might not want to go visit him."

"You did. And if I had known then what I know now, I wouldn't have gone. But I had to find out from the horse's mouth, so to speak. just why we were in the position we are in. I felt I had to go."

"Well, filing for divorce won't be that difficult. I can walk you through it."

"Are you super busy this afternoon?"

"Why do you ask?"

"My daughter and son-in-law are coming over for a cook out this afternoon. I plan to tell them I am divorcing her father. She's going to be all jazzed thinking of reconciliation. You can explain the legality of the divorce and why it's a good move. You do think it's a good move, don't you?"

"Yes, I do. You should have done it long ago. But when she learns you aren't planning to marry her father, then what?"

"Well, maybe you can back me up when I tell her I resent him so badly it would be a bad thing to do."

"Now you know why I thought you shouldn't go. I don't know you well, Lyn. But I've felt a sense of justice in you from Day One. When you found that he's not had more than a month or two of "bad" days, I knew your dander would rise. And rightfully so. Perhaps if he could have explained circumstances to you differently, things could be okay. But I have a feeling the unvarnished truth didn't cut it as well as he expected. You are an unvarnished truth sort of person, you know. And it rankled you that you're the one who suffered for what he'd done."

"Not just me, Hal. My only son was killed because of his father. Wes felt sincere remorse over that, but it doesn't bring Eddy back. From what he told me, there were several times he could have done things differently. Do you know if the people who rented his warehouse were ever brought to justice?"

"Yes, they were. Eddy's death was a key part of that conviction. They seemed to believe that by not retrieving that last shipment they'd be okay. But between Eddy and that last shipment, that pipeline was shut down for nearly a decade. I think it's up and running again as it seems a lot of these designer drugs are coming back but that particular group are all in jail. That's why the Marshals finally told Wes they weren't monitoring him any longer."

"Am I a bad person for not wanting to remarry Wes...er, Jim."

"Nope. You should have divorced him a long time ago and found someone who could love you as you deserve."

His answer surprised me. "Can you stop by later this afternoon? There will be plenty of food around four or five but I'd like backup when I talk to my daughter. I think her husband will understand but I'm not so sure about Lee."

"I can't make it until about three. Soon enough?"

"Thank you, Hal. I am glad I didn't listen to you. I could have pined myself to death if I hadn't."

"Well, we certainly don't want that happening, Lyn. See you around three."

CHAPTER TWENTY-ONE

We all gathered around the deck table looking at my big monitor. Seeing photos on the camera was great but is much better when viewed so much bigger. I put all the photos from my camera on a disc this morning. Don't want to chance losing any. The kids are really enthused. Seeing their grandfather for, literally, the first time. They loved the history shots but came back to the pictures of Wes and I several times. Larry chuckled when I explained how we happened to have so many good pictures of the two of us. Not a single selfie in the bunch.

Lee et al had been here nearly an hour when the doorbell rang. Wil got up to answer it. It wasn't until he was nearly to the door when I realized it was probably Hal Tucker. It was. I heard him introduce himself and ask Wil if his Grandmother was in. Wil said, "Sure, we're on the deck looking at her vacation pics. Come on back." Wil had a slight look of awe on his face as he came onto the deck. "Grams, Agent Tucker from the FBI is here to see you."

I stood as did Larry. Larry reached across the table to shake Hal's hand. I invited him to have a chair. He motioned to the monitor. "Vacation pics, huh?" Wil flipped back to the beginning of the disc.

"Gram's a history nut. She got some neat pictures of the Boston Tea Party." He made it sound as though I had been there in December 1773. Hal sat down and watched with seeming interest as Wil narrated most of my vacation. When he got to a picture of Wes and I, he said, "These are my grandparents. Though I suppose you know that."

Hal said, "I have never met your grandfather but I do know your Grams."

The kids are all in swim suits and decided this is a good time to go swimming. "Call us when supper's ready." That's Mike, always hungry.

When they were out of earshot, Hal became all FBI. "Lee, nice to see you again. How much leave do you have left, Larry?"

"Three weeks, Sir."

Hal smiled. "I no longer wear the uniform, Larry. The name is Hal."

"You were a Marine, Sir?"

"For twenty years, and I decided I just didn't need that crap any more. Where was your basic?"

The two talked military for a couple minutes. I hadn't known Hal had been a Marine but I could see what he was doing now. Larry will automatically side with him. It's the training.

They shook hands again and Hal said, "Lyn asked me to stop by this afternoon to help clarify a decision that she and her husband have made while she was in Massachusetts."

Lee looked at me with question marks fairly shooting at me.

"The former Wesley John Palmer is now James Allan Nolan. He wants to marry your mother. She explained to him that she was still married to Wesley Palmer. Jim didn't understand how that could be. I am sure, as you're not as close to the situation as he is, that you both do understand. Lyn did not have Wesley Palmer declared dead. As a result, she is still legally married to him. She called me this morning to ask how to go about this type of divorce as it is not common and why should she have to wait six months for a divorce to be finalized. I told her she didn't if I walked her petition through the courts. It is a fairly standard petition of absentee spouse dissolution of marriage except - if I can ex parte the petition to the family law judge, it could be immediate."

"Explain ex parte, Hal." Larry is not up on court terms.

"Nearly every day in the court's calendar there is a blank spot. The court being each individual judge. This blank spot is for people who have some nature of case that belongs in that judge's court but want advice before court is in session, or have a question of some other nature. Ex parte means an action for one party, no opposition. No notice of the action is given. You knock on his door and request to see him ex parte, out of the court. I believe if the petition itself is in order, the judge would look at it, ask a few questions, sign it and it never goes to public court. I could be sure that a divorce petition for your mother-in-law is in order. I, as an agent of the FBI, would have the answers for his questions. I can see no reason why he wouldn't sign the order. One of the good things about this is that such a petition would not be on the court calendar and wouldn't be listed in the newspaper under "dissolutions". I am sure the judge would have compassion to play down this seemingly last detail of this case. And the other thing, if the Judge accepts the petition as an ex parte action, which I'm sure he will under the circumstances, you do not have to run a public notice in the local paper notifying Wesley Palmer that you're seeking a divorce. That not only is costly but, in this instance, a farce as there no longer is a Wesley Palmer."

Lee and Larry both nodded. So far they're with it.

"And that would mean that my mother could marry again, legally?"

"Exactly, Lee, she'd be like any other divorcee - free as a bird, to marry or not."

"So, my mother could then marry James Nolan?"

"If she was so inclined. But she wouldn't have to marry anyone. Or, she could marry anyone."

I could see that Lee might be getting a hint that I didn't intend to marry her Dad. She leaned over to Larry and talked so quietly I couldn't hear her. Hal looked at me and kind of raised his eyebrows. I shrugged. I have no clue what she might be saying to her husband.

"So Mom asked you to come today to explain this to us?"

"She did."

"Mom, why didn't you explain it to us yourself?"

"Quite frankly, I didn't know all that. That's why I got an expert. I couldn't explain it to your father very well. He was really upset with the idea that all this time I have been married and he has not. He finally just said to go home and get a divorce."

She shook her head. Okay, that sank in. Then, and I expected it, "When are you going to marry Dad, or Jim Nolan?"

"Lee, I don't believe I will marry your Dad - no matter what name he has. I learned so much about him these past weeks. I don't think I can marry him."

The look on her face was amazement and shock. "What?"

"Honey, your father is a different man. Or perhaps it is me that's different. I believe I would not be happy with him. I'm fifty-nine, Lee. I have had a hard fifteen years. I don't think we fit anymore."

Well, I didn't expect tears but they sure came. Larry patted her hand then put his arm across her shoulders. "Sweetie, that's how Mom feels right now. That could change. Don't cry on her parade. She has a right to think this through. Don't push."

She sat very still for a moment before smiling weakly. "You're right. Some things take more processing than others."

Larry turned to Hal. "Hal, do you have to go back to headquarters immediately? Can you stay and swim awhile, maybe have some supper?"

Hal looked surprised. "Let me call in and see what's rolling." He took out his phone and stepped into the family room. He was on the phone perhaps two minutes.

"I didn't think to bring a swim suit, Larry. Do you have a spare in your pocket?"

Larry jumped up. "Better than that, Sir. Wait until you see the dressing room. Cubbies to put your street clothes in, a wide selection of swim trunks. a shower and towels. Even a good shampoo. Of course, Lyn expects everyone to rinse their suits and hang them on a rack. You won't believe this dressing room. Lyn built it herself."

Hal put his phone inside his briefcase, took it into the family room and returned. "Lead the way, Master Sergeant."

I never heard them discuss rank. How did he know that Larry had been field promoted to master sergeant recently? The dressing room is at the far end of the deck. We could hear the murmur of their voices. Lee looked at me. "Mom, are you positive you aren't going to marry Dad?"

"Positive is a very strong word, Lee. At this moment, I am positive. Maybe it's not your Dad who has changed; maybe it is me."

CHAPTER TWENTY-TWO

My son-in-law is forty. And I had guessed that Agent Tucker was also. But he told Larry that he had spent twenty years in the Corps. And he's been with the FBI at least a dozen. How old is he? When the two came out of the dressing room, they were laughing and enjoying each other's company. Two young men in swim trunks running down the steps and headed for the pool - they look the same age. Tucker is in excellent shape; perhaps even better than Larry and Larry is active duty. Two cannonballs into the pool. "Oohrah." The kids were delighted as the men proceeded to show them an old Marine Corps pool game. Now I couldn't testify that it was an Old Marine Corps pool game but they convinced the kids it was. It looked like a lot of good exercise and a lot of fun. Zigzag laps without running into each other and some other antics. At zig you swim right; at zag you swim left.

Lee sat smiling. I know how it feels to watch a man you love have fun. And when your children are with him, also having fun, it's only better.

The five in the pool played hard for half an hour and then, another old Marine Corps game, how long can you float and lap the pool only using your feet? Or something like that. It calmed the pool down and everyone was having fun floating.

It wasn't long before Laurie, the only girl in the pool, came running to the edge of the deck. "Dad wants to know how long to chow?"

Lee and I looked at each other. "Twenty minutes but you don't have to dress." She went running back to the pool and yelled, "Hey, Dad, watch this." She was at the deep end and did an aerial somersault into the pool. It was quite an athletic move - full somersault from a dead stand.

Hal clapped his hands. "That was beautiful, Laurie. But don't ever do it if you're here alone." I could see his reasoning - if she had failed she could have landed hard on the pool deck.

"Oh, don't worry, I won't. I nearly killed myself once." She lapped the pool and came up behind her Dad and hugged him. "Grams say twenty minutes - you don't have to dress."

Lee had decided late yesterday I should hold off on chicken on the grill. I forget her reasoning - something about chicken three days in a row or something. So we were just grilling burgers. I had turned on the grill when the guys got in the pool. We brought out the salads. Yes, I got carried away but I am so tired of restaurant food. Potato salad, macaroni salad, coleslaw, and tomatoes/onions/cucumber in Italian dressing. Lee got down a large bowl and put chips into it. I already had the condiments in the carry basket. Paper plates and silverware were ready. Lee had an ice chest full of beer and soda. The famous red cups were last to go on the side table.

I put a dozen burgers on the grill. Laurie came up and went into the dressing room. I know she used the facilities but she has a short robe hanging there. But she said, "I have to wash my hands. I want to smell the meat not the pool."

Lee told me. "She just wants a head start on her brothers. But as there's company maybe she'll be more ladylike than usual."

I laughed. It would be hard for that child, even at twelve, to not be ladylike.

The boys came running up. Facilities in the dressing room and washing their hands. People have always marveled at that but we raised them to always wash their hands before eating, especially hamburgers. I flipped the burgers just about when Larry and Hal came across the yard. They too washed their hands. I agree with Laurie - chlorine is not the best dinner companion.

The kids all got a plate and a bun and lined up for a burger. I asked Hal how he liked his cooked. "Medium or well, Lyn, whatever you've got." In a short time we were around the table passing salads and condiments and enjoying an early supper. I put the extra burgers on buns and sat them in the middle of the table. The kids were telling Lee all about the old Marine Corps games with such enthusiasm that even if it's something the guys made up, it was worthwhile. I could see that it was a definite exercise workout program. We're not going to have any fat kids around here.

Larry and Hal were comparing notes. They'd both been at LeJune; Hal was at Twenty-Nine Palms for a short while. Both had gone to Oceanside and

Camp Butler on Okinawa. There were actually a couple of career men they both know. The kids are listening but soon lost interest. Mike wanted to know if there was dessert or should he toss his plate. I told him there was dessert but it was special and I'd put it on a clean plate. "Keep your fork."

I leaned back eating slowly and enjoying a cold beer. It had been so long since I've heard this kind of talk between men. It was obvious Hal had been a commissioned office - rather than come up through the ranks. Finally, Larry asked the question I was interested in. "At what rank did you retire, Hal?" They were sitting on the opposite side of the table, next to each other. I strained to hear.

Rather nonchalantly he reached for the potato salad, "Lieutenant Colonel." Larry said, "Honest to god?" "Yep. That's okay, isn't it?" "Absolutely. No wonder I keep wanting to call you Sir." I saw a little smile on Lee's face. I saw one on Hal's.

"Larry, I left the Corps nearly fifteen years ago. I buffeted around a year or so trying out jobs with structure but not bullied structure. How I landed with the Bureau I don't know. It's structure but not a damn soul calls me Sir. I was lucky and landed in OTS immediately out of basic. My Dad knew someone who knew someone. I thought I'd be a Marine forever. And, I guess I am, just not in uniform."

"Good god, man, you look my age. You can't be." Larry was flummoxed but good. So was I.

"No, I've got several years on you, Larry. I hope you don't mind."

I went in to get the dessert. How interesting, He's over fifty and I pegged him for a kid like Larry. Lee followed me in. "Need any help, Mom?"

"No, Hon, I'm just getting dessert out of the fridge. Oh, bring the cake server, will you? I forgot to get it out of the drawer."

When the kids saw the cheesecake with the chocolate shavings on top, they all came running back to the table. "What is that, Grams." Wil wiggled his nose. "It smells like chocolate."

"Well, dear boy, that's because it is. With hazelnuts. I had this at dinner in Lowell the first night I was there and it was so good I thought I'd make one for you. This is my own recipe, I forgot to ask for one at the restaurant, but I'm pretty sure it's good enough to eat."

Lee handled me the cake server and the kids lined up with the plates in hand. The four of us still had food on our plates. About three minutes later all three kids said, "Grams, it's really good. Your recipe is perfect. Will there be seconds?" Both boys had a second burger but I guess they really did have a workout in the pool.

"If there's any left after your Dad and Mr. Tucker have some, yes there will be seconds."

It was about six when Hal's phone rang. He stepped inside the family room to take the call. He came out a few minutes later and said, "Wow, they missed me. I told them I'd be in the office in an hour or so." He finished eating and said, "Miz Palmer, may I have a slice of that delicious dessert? I don't want to leave too much for the boys to worry about." Larry and Lee both laughed. I gave him a slice on a clean plate. As he was eating he said, to no one in particular, "I have thoroughly enjoyed this afternoon." He ate the cheesecake and said, "The kids are right. Grams, it's really good. Your recipe is perfect."

"Guess I'd better shower and get going. It was a slow day at the office. Now, do I have this right, I have to rinse my trunks and hang them on the rack?" Everyone laughed and he went to the dressing room. When he came out he was all FBI again.

"Thanks, Larry, for getting my foot in the door for supper. I appreciate it. Thanks, Lyn, for having me over. I hope that everyone understands what we discussed."

Lee and Larry both nodded. I walked him to his car. Not to the front door but to his car. "Thank you for being such an excellent guest. My son-in-law is in awe and the kids think you're gold. I do believe Lee understands the situation now. She'll harp on me as she loves her Dad but now she understands the logistics."

"Lyn, thanks for allowing me to be a part of your family for a few hours. This is my best day in the FBI."

He got in his little car and zipped off. I don't know how long I stood on the curb.

CHAPTER TWENTY-THREE

When I retook my seat at the table, Larry said, "He's one hell of a nice guy. How did you meet him?"

"He drew the short straw when I caught that call from Wes, in the middle of the wind storm."

"Well, I'm glad he did. Hell of a nice guy."

I cut myself a piece of cheesecake and motioned to Lee - yes, she would like some. I saw that she had already served Larry. We sat and ate cheesecake while the kids all went to see if they could improve their float time in the pool.

"Hal is going to talk to their legal department tomorrow to see when they can complete an absent spouse petition. He believes it should have been done at least twelve years ago but no one followed through. I think it was mentioned then and when I said no thanks I never heard from the FBI again. They just kind of shut the book on the Palmers."

"Mom, you could've told us what Hal did. He didn't really need to come."

"He did. I didn't know about ex parte or any of that stuff. I knew there was a special petition but didn't know if I had to have a private attorney or go to the Bureau or what. He did have to come."

She shook her head but I believe she finally agrees with me. Was she upset that he had come and wowed her husband and children? Usually she's more flexible and friendly. I'm not saying she wasn't friendly but I don't recall that she was either. Doesn't she trust him? He seems forthright to me. What can he possibly gain by being helpful?

"Lyn, Lee says you will watch the kids for us for a few days."

"Absolutely. They can stay here and we'll swim every day while you're gone. Have you decided where you're going?"

"Morro Bay. I am going on line tonight to make reservations. I hope I can - summer and all. But I need to know what days are best for you, and how many."

"Check and see what's available and book it and let me know. I am available starting Wednesday, as in day after tomorrow, until your leave ends."

He kissed my cheek. "Thanks, Lyn, a lot. I'll call you later tonight and let you know what we've been able to book."

Then he offered help to clean the table and return stuff to the kitchen. I told him Lee and I had it. So he cleaned the grill and then jumped in the pool with his children. They were just goofing off and swimming now - no Marine Corps games. But I am sure they'll play them the next time they're in the pool.

The sun was low on the horizon when they packed up their ice chest and headed home. The kids were enthused. I sent 3 slices of cheesecake home with them. Surprisingly, for as much food as there had been, there was very little left. Lunch tomorrow will wipe out all leftovers.

I poured a glass of tea intending to watch television for a while. I almost forgot I had asked the television to record Jeopardy and Wheel and decided to watch both programs now. The telephone rang. It was Jim - an hour later than usual.

He asked about the trip home. Oh, yeah, I didn't call him Saturday when I got home. I told him that Lee and Larry had planned dinner and it was late when I got home. "I thought you'd call Sunday and when you didn't I figured you were out."

"I went in for the Sox game. They won't be home for a couple weekends. Even with the time difference, I figured it was too late to call. The Spinners have won their last four games. How is Larry?" I must be tired; his conversation seems almost disjointed.

"Well, he got a field promotion to Master Sergeant last month. He has three weeks leave left. They're going up to Morro Bay for a couple days. The kids are going to stay with me. So if you call in the evening, you'll be able to talk with them. You should get to know them. They loved my vacation photos. Mike thinks he does resemble you; his siblings don't agree but he doesn't care."

"Thanks for copying your photos onto a disc for me. I'm going to take it to work and show some of the guys the lady I met while I was on vacation."

"Oh, Jim, do you really think you should?" "Why not. You're getting divorced soon, aren't you?"

"Well, if you're going to show off photos, perhaps you should take off your wedding ring. Your friends might think you're serious then."

"Good idea. I will do that. And you are filing for divorce?"

"As a matter of fact, I spoke with a FBI agent today about that. He thinks they can run it by a judge ex parte and get it settled immediately. I guess I'll have to wait and see." I doubt that he knows what ex parte means but he didn't ask. Maybe once I said I spoke to someone about it today, he quit listening. I don't know. "How was work today?"

"Took me a while to get in the groove. Two weeks off at once is a new experience. But by lunch I was with it again. How were things at the house when you got back?"

"Wil and Mike had mowed the yard. Everything looked good."

We chitchatted for a few more minutes. He admitted that he made his own breakfast this morning. He said it was kind of nice. In half an hour he signed off and I turned on Jeopardy. It was nearly 9.

Somehow he sounded 'off' tonight. Probably my imagination. Should I have told him how resentful I am? Would he understand it? Watching Lee and her family today makes me wish that I felt differently. I remember too well sitting on that deck years ago with friends watching our kids play in the pool. The Dads always waited until the kids had been in a while before they joined them. The Moms and I never swam at neighborhood cook outs. I wonder why. We did swim other times but usually not when the guys were around. Was it some kind of archaic behavior that floated around in the 90s? I vaguely remember a few times that I thought we were all Stepford Wives. I was just a teenager when the original came out. But the image stuck with me a long time.

A long time. I am slowly coming to the realization that my married life was kind of patterned on that movie. Wives had certain duties and I vowed to complete them properly. I was going to be the best wife anyone could ever have. The house was always clean; I threw good parties; I raised polite children. When the remake came out, I didn't go see it. I think it was just before Wes vanished. Maybe I should have. Maybe the second time around I would have realized it was all BS and when Wes vanished, I would have just packed up and let go of the life I had so carefully constructed. Maybe I wouldn't be so resentful now - I lived the perfect life without the perfect husband, with no husband at all. I didn't have to do it. It's not his fault I wanted to keep everything I considered necessary to live.

Lee had put a couple bottles of beer in the fridge before she went home. I went to the kitchen and got one before settling down to Jeopardy.

Damn, life is just too complicated. Do I want to pick up where I left off fifteen years ago? I don't think so. It was a comfortable life. Would it be now? Massachusetts is a wonderful state and full of history but I believe I don't want to add any of my history to it. I've put my heart and soul into this house. Do I want to leave it? I have a job that I love. Do I want to leave it?

Even if I wasn't resentful...even. I don't want to leave what I have, not even for Wes. My days as a Stepford Wife are over. I'd rather be alone than leave what I've built here. It's comfortable. It's what I know.

CHAPTER TWENTY-FOUR

It is after ten and I'm foraging in the fridge. There is a slice of cheesecake but that would be overkill. I just want something crunchy. Is there any celery left? Should be. Before I could open the crisper drawer, the telephone rang.

It was Larry. He was laughing. They'd scored big in Morro Bay. He'd been on line and found the "perfect" hotel. But seven days cost nearly a thousand dollars. So he thought he'd check what six days cost. But he hit eight instead of six in error. But, it was barely eight hundred for eight days. How could that be? He and Lee decided to call the hotel direct instead of trying to figure out what was wrong with the website. Well, nothing is wrong with the website; they're trying a new kind of pricing which will eliminate a couple days of laundry, yada, yada. So $792 for eight days was correct. Larry said that sounded really good providing they could get the eight days they'd entered on the website as he was home on leave. Oh, military? Yes. What eight days? This Wednesday through the following Wednesday. $792 less a ten percent military discount. They were staying at the Embarcadero Hotel for $712 for eight days. It's reputed to be the best in Morro Bay. I could hear his elation. What a deal.

It's been a while since I've been to Morro Bay. But I remember that hotel. "Larry, it's right on the Center. Right at the port. Cross the street and fall in the ocean. Their big drawback is no in-house restaurant. There's a small restaurant directly on the edge of the dock across from it. When we were there the restaurant was overpriced and not that great. But the hotel is a marvelous stay."

He was very excited. There are plenty of restaurants in the area. Besides they want Morro Bay as a base camp so they can visit Los Osos and Cayucos and San Luis Obispo. I remember all those little towns. Well, San Luis Obispo isn't that small anymore but the others still are. Larry will bring the kids and their gear over Wednesday morning. How early was too early?

"Six is too early; seven would be fine. I can feed them breakfast."

So it was decided that I will have three visitors beginning Wednesday. He'll bring them to me then go back to the house to finish loading their stuff and secure the premises. Would the kids and I stop by daily for the mail? And check on things?

Of course we would. I can imagine that the kids are already making plans.

Tuesday I went to the grocery store to stock up food to begin the grand kid week. I checked to be sure that the bedrooms were visitor ready. Eddy's bedroom has bunk beds and Lee's a double bed. Vacuum and dust; double check the Jack/Jill bathroom for supplies; open the windows to air out the rooms. When I went to bed Tuesday night, I was ready for a grandchild invasion. It's been a while since I've had all three at one time. Two years? Maybe three?

It doesn't take long to get into a routine. With meals, swimming, walking to their house for the mail, we seemed busy most of the time. Their grandfather called every night. There are three extensions in the house and frequently they were all on the line at one time. I am sure Wes appreciated that as he didn't have to repeat stuff three times. They would chat about twenty minutes or so than pass the phone to me. I seldom had much to say. He talked about his job or the Spinners but seldom anything personal. I felt that perhaps he had decided that remarrying me was not in his best interests or he was tired of trying to persuade me to reconsider. Either way, the calls were more pleasant. I felt no pressure from him to do something I wasn't ready to do.

Larry and Lee called every evening about nine. They talked to all three at once usually. Then I gave them a quick update of the day. The kids went to bed about ten.

Other than cooking three meals a day on a regular schedule, my days weren't altered much at all.

On the sixth day, Monday, Hal called. The legal department had finished the petition for dissolution and would like me to review it. If it's what I want and/or expect, he'd like to try for an ex parte with Judge Johannson of the Family Court Division on Thursday. Did I have to go with him? He didn't think so; but he would double check. I hoped not as Larry and Lee won't be back until late afternoon on Thursday. I didn't mention that to him, however. Hal asked if he could he stop over this afternoon? If something's not quite what I expect, there would be time to correct it. I said, "I am here all day, come when convenient for you."

I didn't mention it to the kids. No particular reason; I just didn't think of it. And I didn't mention the kids to him. So, surprise for everybody maybe.

I checked to be sure I had lemonade and soda. I want to offer him a cool drink but he will be "on the clock". We, the kids and I, had baked cookies on Sunday evening. So there'll be a snack to offer as well. Chocolate chip and peanut butter. Double batches of both. When the kids are around I always make double batches of cookies.

When I am at home during the summer, I wear knee length shorts, a tee shirt and sneakers. I have gotten so comfortable with Hal, I didn't think to change. Around 12:30 or so, we made sandwiches and took them with chips and drinks to the deck table. We had finished eating but were discussing if we should walk over and check for mail before swimming or after. We haven't created a time schedule to pick up the mail. Wil says someone might realize it and so it's better to go at different times. As far as I know, they haven't had any thefts or vandalism in their neighborhood. Perhaps this is just preventive things they've picked up from television. There's a lot of theft and vandalism on TV. Of maybe from their Dad. He's very security conscience, even installed an alarm system in their house.

It's been my habit to leave my front door open when I am at home. There's a nice sturdy screen door with a latch and, if I'm home, that should be sufficient. Laurie was in the kitchen looking for another bag of chips in the pantry when the doorbell rang. She yelled, "I'll get it." So the boys and I stayed put. I heard her giggling. That's odd. She came through the family room door literally dragging Hal by the hand. "Look who I found at the door, Grams. Agent Tucker!" She was delighted to see him. The boys jumped up and ran around the table to shake his hand.

Mike said, "Oops, briefcase. You must be working. Any chance you can stay and swim a while? We've been working on floating." Wil laughed, "And we getting better at zig and zag, too."

I sat there and watched the FBI agent being mobbed by three kids and didn't do a thing about it. Finally, Hal said, "I've got official business with your Grams. When that's done I'll call and see how desperate they are for good help at the office."

Laurie asked if he would like some lemonade, tea, or a soda. She could offer him three kinds of soda. "Lemonade would be great, Laurie. I am parched."

She ran off and the boys sat down. To my great surprise, he came and kissed me on the cheek. "How are you today, Grams?" He didn't blush or flush or stammer. I believe he doesn't realize what he had done. It seemed like second nature; habit.

"Perhaps I should ask how you are. Being mugged by three teens must be hard to take." He laughed. I never realized what a happy laugh he has.

"Wait, one is a pre-teen mugger. Frankly, that's the greatest reception I've ever had as an FBI agent." The boys were beaming. Laurie brought out the tallest glass in my cupboard half-filled with ice and with lemonade to the top. It was quite pretty - for a glass of lemonade. She sat it on the table in front of the empty chair next to me. Good grief, I hadn't even invited him to sit yet. But he took her gesture as indicating his place. He sat down and took a long drink of lemonade. "Excellent, Laurie, just the right amount of ice. Thank you. Now if you three don't mind, I really do have FBI business that needs to be handled this afternoon."

The boys headed for the dressing room. They're going to try and guilt him into staying a while. Laurie said, "We have cookies too, Agent Tucker. I'll bring you some." And she left for the kitchen.

He looked at me positively beaming. She brought a small plate she put together just for him. Cookies laying in a circle - three chocolate chip, three peanut butter. The boys were out of the dressing room and she went in and changed. I could feel a full charge coming up soon. Looking at this man, I realized - he doesn't have and never has had children. I wonder if he's married or has ever married. I don't see a ring but sometimes FBI agents don't wear rings. I heard someone say that fifteen years ago, though I don't remember the context.

"Larry and Lee on vacation?"

"How did you guess?" Big smile.

He ate two cookies, had some more lemonade and then opened the briefcase. "This is really straight forward. I believe I have all the assets properly listed. If I missed any, let me know; if there are some falsely listed, let me know. While this is an absent partner petition, all the information on a regular petition for dissolution has to be listed. Later if the absent partner shows up, he has no claim on any of the joint assets of the marriage. This has never happened that I know of but you know the law always errs on the side of caution."

Surprisingly, the petition was fairly long. At the beginning is the reason for this type petition. The FBI had stated that it is believed the respondent was entered into the Federal Witness Protection by the US Marshal fifteen years ago. Exact date unknown but presumed to be... The US Marshal will neither confirm or deny this supposition. However, it is also possible the respondent is deceased. The petitioner, being a loyal and loving partner, did not want to declare the respondent as deceased. The Agent in Charge of the original case involving the disappearance of the respondent should have suggested, at that time, that Petitioner file for divorce before he closed the case. However, that was not done. The Federal Bureau recently reviewed the case and interviewed Petitioner and made the suggestion to divorce Respondent. Petitioner has agreed and offers this petition.

There is a listing of all the known assets that Wes and I had at the time of his disappearance. I didn't realize then that such a list had been made. But it appeared to be an old list as the line item that was Wes' truck was lined through and marked sold. The million dollar life insurance policy was lined through and marked return of premiums under circumstances. And the retirement fund that the warehouse began to pay me four years ago had been added.

There was also a listing of all debts owed. At the time of the list, there was a mortgage and a few other debts. Eddy's funeral expenses were listed. It was a couple months before we learned he had insurance. They were also lined out. Try as I may, I cannot remember ever giving any of this information to the FBI in the weeks following Wes' disappearance. I must have; it's too accurate to be a guesstimate.

The petition continued with the facts of family - very short.

Then came the section that began - Petitioner prays the court will grant a dissolution of this union. There were other 'Petitioner prays the court' statements that Hal says it is formal language saying that I, the petitioner, would like the court to sign this damn piece of paper and declare the marriage dissolved.

I laughed. "Are you serious?"

"Honest to god, Lyn, when a petitioner prays to the court they're just summarizing the basic items in the petition for the benefit of the court. A couple Agents have seen a judge read the first page or two of a petition and then flip to the "Prayer" section without reading fourteen pages of whatever."

"Wow! That's incredible."

"It is. Our head legal beagle says you don't have to go with me for an ex parte meeting with the judge. As a Federal Agent, believe it or not, I am credible enough alone. Judge Johannson has ex parte time at 12:45 Thursday.

He's the only family court judge I know personally. I'm going to be outside his door at noon. It's first come, first served on ex parte. I want to be first. Ex parte is often to clarify something an attorney wants to bring up later in the courtroom. Sometimes it's for a matter so trivial it will save the court time. I explained that the other day. Sometimes it for stuff like this; we'd rather no one knows the FBI didn't follow through on something. First come, first serve, until the court's allotted ex parte time is over. And it's usually not much more than half an hour."

I shook my head. It made sense to me to do it this way. Hal showed me where to sign the petition - in two places. And then he notarized both signatures. He had me sign his notary record and my part was done.

"By this time Thursday, I believe your divorce will be final." He leaned back in the chair and ate cookies and drank his lemonade. The kids had been watching and they ran across the lawn to see if he would call his office and maybe stay a while.

There was too much going on at his office but he promised he would be back tomorrow and he would stay and swim for a while. Laurie, great little hostess, said, "We could wait lunch for you, Mr. Tucker."

He glanced up at me. "Laurie, if your Grams doesn't mind, I would appreciate it. It may be 1:30. I'm going to be sitting on a chair in a hallway at the courthouse tomorrow at lunch time. After lunch, we'll spend some time in the pool. I will notify the office before I head to the courthouse that I am out the rest of the day."

I smiled. He knew I would agree. He was missing lunch on my behalf.

CHAPTER TWENTY-FIVE

The kids spent an hour in the pool before we walked to their house to collect the mail. Their street was very quiet; Laurie says it always is. The boys wanted to check something in the back yard before we left. They were gone quite a while. When they came around the house, Mike looked as though he had been crying.

"What's up?"

Wil said, "Someone killed Mrs. Lagger's cat. It's in our back yard."

"Wasn't that cat ancient? Maybe he died of old age."

Mike blew his nose. "I don't think so, Grams. Who do we call about a murder?"

I called Animal Control and the local police. Of course, it led to numerous questions requiring answers and it was nearly four o'clock before we got back to my house. The officer who responded said there's been a few other cases of this type of thing lately. Animal Control took the cat away and one officer went to tell Mrs. Lagger - two doors down. The second officer suggested we check the inside of the house.

The kids went in and were gone five or six minutes. Everything looked fine. Wil reset the alarm and I thanked the officer for responding so quickly.

The walk home was a bit somber. The boys had never seen anything like that. I'm glad Laurie hadn't gone with them around the house outside. I heard Mike tell Wil that he was going to mention it to Agent Tucker to see if the FBI ever gets involved in cat murder.

Everyone wanted macaroni and cheese for dinner. It is my personal go-to comfort food but I was unaware they had the same idea. Of course, their Mom was a mac 'n cheese kid. I should expect no less. At dinner, we discussed what we could have for lunch tomorrow to impress Agent Tucker. I asked why we were trying to impress him?

Almost in unison, "So he'll want to come back sometimes."

He really has made an impression with my grandchildren.

Four or five ideas were floated around the table. Then Mike said, "Why don't we make our Crazy Cook salad?" "Yeah, yeah." The other two agreed.

Crazy Cook salad? Oh, yes. A few years ago, the four of us had gone to the movies. Afterwards we stopped at a nice restaurant for dinner. I ordered a Chef's salad. They thought it looked interesting. One weekend when Lee had a seminar to attend for work, the kids were with me and decided they'd like one of those Cook salads I had. After distilling it, I realized they were talking Chef's salad. I didn't have all the traditional ingredients but enough to call it a chef's salad. We added a couple ingredients not usually included and, of necessity, skipped a couple that usually are. Over time, we've pretty well developed our own recipe and call it a Crazy Cook's salad. Even their Dad likes it.

After the dishes were in the dishwasher and the pans were put away, we did an inventory. Did we have enough ingredients to make it? We did.

The next morning at breakfast I asked whose turn it was to do dressing room laundry. Wil said he was pretty sure it was his turn. He got the used towel basket and picked up all the suits on the rack. "I sure like your new washer, Grams. I have forty-eight minutes before I put stuff in the drier."

Last year I had to replace my old washer and dryer. First improvements to the place in fifteen years. The old washer didn't tell you anything. You had to listen carefully to see if it was still running. Wil kept an eye on the clock and got the laundry into the dryer.

Everyone has an assigned role in preparing this salad and so the next day, around eleven, we started the chopping and dicing. Wil makes the bacon in the microwave. He's gotten very good at getting it nice and crisp and then crumbling it perfectly. He also juliennes the beets. Mike is in charge of the boiled eggs, bleu cheese crumbles, and he also makes carrot curls. Laurie's main job is dicing the tomatoes. She has it down to a science. She also slices the radishes. The ham and chicken were diced and each in their own covered container and I was preparing the lettuce base. I add thinly sliced celery and green onions to the lettuce. Everything has its own covered dish.

I had just put the cover on the lettuce dish when the door bell chimed. It was not yet noon. As everyone else was occupied, I went to the door. It was Hal.

"Was there a problem? It's not noon yet?"

"No, not at all. May I come in and tell you what happened?"

"Of course, I'm just surprised to see you so early."

The kids were delighted to see him but dismayed as lunch wasn't ready. He said that a major miracle had happened and he hadn't expected lunch at noon anyhow. They kept working at preparing the salad ingredients. Hal and I went to the living room.

"Major miracle?"

He put his briefcase on the coffee table. He was on the couch exactly where he had been sitting the morning he and Agent Harrelson sat that first day we met. He opened the briefcase and handed me two copies of the petition. I looked at him, "What?" It had the purple filed stamp on it.

"Ordinarily, we would give one copy to the US Marshal to serve on their witness. But, as we know who and where he is, do you want to mail it to him yourself? If not, I'll get it over to the Federal Building tomorrow."

"But, it's so early. I thought you wouldn't see the judge until 12:45."

"That's where the miracle comes in. Public parking was jammed, so was jury parking. When I told the office yesterday I was going to the courthouse today, several agents asked if I would file something for them while I was there. I figured if I went in quite early, I could do that and still be outside the judge's office by noon. So, I said sure why not. Here I was 9:30 and no parking. The FBI vehicles are known by the courthouse guards so I figured I'd parking in the judicial parking lot. Lots of space. I had locked the car and I spotted Judge Johannson coming through the parking lot gate. I headed him off.

"Sir, is there a problem? 'Oh, Good morning Agent Tucker. Well, sort of. Miriam has fallen and the doctor would like to speak to me in the Emergency Room.' I made noises about I hope nothing was broken but sounded doubtful if the doctor wants to talk to you. He agreed. I said Damn, I was hoping to see you ex parte this afternoon. 'Something urgent, Tucker?' Not really, Sir, but in reviewing files for storage I found an oversight that should have been handled fifteen years ago. 'Really? For the FBI that's unusual.' So I told him what it was and he asked if I had the petition with me.' I told him I was going to the clerks' office to file some other stuff so yes, I did have it. He said 'Let me see it.' I put the briefcase on the hood of his car and got out your petition. He looked at the Petitioner's name and said 'This is one of the saddest cases in this County. Madlyn never asked for a divorce?' I told him that you were probably in shock at the time and no one followed up. 'Why now, Tucker? Has she met someone?' No sir, I don't think so. But she's not yet sixty and should be allowed to live a normal live. Being married to a ghost isn't normal. He reached into his inside pocket, pulled out a pen, and signed the petition - right there on the hood of the car. I shook his hand and thanked him a zillion times. And he said, "It must be right. Otherwise why would we meet like this in a parking lot where you shouldn't even be parked?" He laughed and laughed and laughed then got into his car and drove away."

I literally fell back into the chair I was perched on. "It's final? It's done?"

"It's even filed and here are your copies. I just filed it with everyone else's stuff. The clerk had no idea I had nearly shanghaied the judge in the parking lot."

Like an idiot, I started crying. For the first time in a long time, things feel right. I never thought I would someday divorce the love of my life. I never thought the love of my life would leave me either. Hal's comment to the judge "married to a ghost" was so right on. Hal moved from the couch and came to my chair. "Lyn, it's over. You don't need to waste any more tears on Wesley Palmer." He helped me stand and he hugged me.

Then he asked, "Do you need to supervise your kitchen crew?"

"Probably not, they've gotten really great at this dish. It's one they created."

"Really? Can I come watch?"

We went into the kitchen. The kids were still at the island but it looked like they were pretty well finished. Mike looked up. "Grams, do I steam the asparagus for one minute or two? I have forgotten."

"Two, on half power."

Hal looked back and forth between us. "The kids have devised a salad called Crazy Cook salad. It's a Chef's Salad that's not traditional. We deleted stuff and added stuff but we finally have it down to a science. The first time we made it, there was half a bunch of asparagus in the fridge. It's not super great raw. The next time we micro-steamed it for two minutes on half power. Absolutely perfect."

All Hal could really see was a series of small plastic storage dishes and half a bunch of asparagus. Laurie said, "We can eat anytime, Agent Tucker. If you're ready, we are."

I took a clear glass pitcher from the cupboard, The bleu cheese dressing has been blending overnight and should be perfect. I spooned the dressing into the pitcher. "Now we're ready. Let's set the table."

Laurie handed a handful of silverware to Hal. "I have to get the biscuit bites into the oven. They take nine minutes." I had forgotten the biscuits altogether even though I had mixed the dough an hour ago. They are cheese biscuits but dropped by teaspoon so they're two or 3 bites each. A regular recipe of biscuits, with cheese added, makes about five dozen bite sized biscuits.

By the time Laurie had the biscuit bites into a bread basket, the guys have set the table. They have integrated Hal into the process and he is folding napkins to put by the forks. They popped the lids and put all the small storage dishes on the lazy susan. I put lettuce into each of five flat bowls and Laurie put them at each place. We decided that if it's a Crazy Cook salad, everyone makes their own - in case someone doesn't like something. I believe everyone eats everything though. The dishes were arranged according to Laurie's idea of how each ingredient is added. She showed Hal how to make his salad - he is sitting to her left.

The susan had almost made a complete turn before Hal asked, "What is this, Laurie?"

"Oh, bleu cheese crumbles. Sprinkle them all over the salad, lay the asparagus across, four sections of hard-boiled egg in a circle and then the dressing." I must admit, her salad looks absolutely beautiful. Hal did as instructed; the boys and I were one or two ingredients behind as we waited for the lazy susan. When everyone had a completed salad in front of them, the kids said, in unison, "Here's to all the crazy cooks in the world. Long may they cook."

In an aside, Laurie said to Hal, "There's enough of everything. If you want more, just spin for it."

We ate and talked, and talked and ate. The boys asked if the FBI handled cat murders. No, usually not, though there may be extenuating circumstances. The boys told him what they had found at their house yesterday. And then they made sure he had the rest of the day off. Did he know any other Marine Corps pool games? Yes, of course he did. But they're better played with two people who know them. Yada, yada, yada.

Lunch had gone on more than an hour when the doorbell rang, followed almost immediately by a "Yoohoo, anybody home?" Lee and Larry were back earlier than expected. The kids all made a dash for the front door. They literally dragged their parents back to the dining room. Were they hungry? There is enough left for two more crazy cook salads. I got up to get salad bowls and forks while Larry shook hands with Hal. Lee went to the bathroom.

When Lee came in to the dining room she asked Larry what he wanted to drink. He looked around the table and saw lemonade, then spied a pitcher partially full. "Just bring me a glass with some ice, there is lemonade." She brought two glasses and put a chair between the boys. I was surprised either of them remembered the ritual of building your own crazy cook salad. The lettuce was in the middle with the dressing and the lemonade. Hal watched as they created a dish he'd never heard of two hours ago. I wondered what he was thinking.

Once they had food in front of them, Larry asked, "Is it customary for the FBI to come to lunch?"

Hal blushed.

Wil said, "Agent Tucker had to file something for Grams at the courthouse. We told him he had to come for lunch and a swim."

Mike said, "And it was a big miracle that everything got done. And the bigger miracle is that Agent Tucker told his office yesterday he wouldn't be in today after he left the courthouse."

Laurie said, "And he's our friend, Dad. He's not here now as the FBI. As soon as he gave Grams the papers, he was just Mr. Tucker again."

Lee looked across Mike at me. "He got the divorce petition filed?"

I nodded. "He did indeed. And later I'm sure you can convince him to tell you why it was a miracle it happened today."

Hal blushed again. I think that is so neat that a man over fifty still knows how to blush, and when.

CHAPTER TWENTY-SIX

The kids were ready to change to swim when Wil remembered his laundry in the dryer. All three kids went to the laundry room and folded towels and folded and sorted swim suits so they could put them back in the dressing room. Once that was done, the boys told Laurie they had first dibs on changing. She didn't seem to mind. Her Dad and Hal were sitting on the top step of the deck and she sat down next to Hal and laid her head on his arm. He looked surprised but put his arm around her. Larry seemed a bit surprised. So did I. I went back to the kitchen to clean up.

Lee and I were loading the dishwasher when Larry came to the kitchen. "Lyn, we stopped at the house. What's the crime scene tape all about in the back yard?"

"Yesterday we found your neighbor's cat murdered in the back yard. Police and Animal Control came. We checked inside the house. Nothing was disturbed."

"Scared the bejeebers out of me. We probably wouldn't have come over immediately otherwise."

"Well, I'm glad you did. I think the kids have nearly overwhelmed Hal. He seems to be handling it pretty well though. He told them he knows more Marine Corps pool games. After being asked, of course."

"Oh, I am sure he does. I'm sure you realize they aren't games but regulation water training."

"Figured that out the first day. The two of you chanting in perfect cadence. No doubt it wasn't a game. But the kids love it. They've gotten really good at floating using only their toes to guide them. I was sure then it was special training of some sort."

"Thanks for watching them. We had a marvelous vacation; absolutely spectacular in fact." No worries about the crime scene tape so he went out to the dressing room. I wondered how long it would take him.

He and Hal sat on the top step of the deck watching the kids in the pool. Both were in swim trunks. Probably deciding what piece of training to fool the kids with next.

Lee filled the lemonade pitcher with more ice and lemonade before we went out to sit on the deck. She had so many great stories about their eight days away. She said, "It was marvelous to spend all day free as birds and then come home at night and call our little 'peeps'. It anchored us enough so we could thoroughly enjoy the freedom the next day. I know, that sounds drippy. But it's nice to be able to just 'do' and then realize why you do at the end of the day. You'd never know I majored in language would you? I can't really say anything as beautifully as I think it."

"I understood what you meant. And it was beautiful."

She asked if I had a blank disc; she'd like to transfer her vacation pictures now so the kids could see them on a monitor later. She spent a while doing that. And I found myself wondering if I had enough cash to take everyone to dinner. I didn't feel like cooking and it would be appropriate to end a vacation with a special meal. I called Luigi's and asked for a 6:30 reservation for a party of seven. I'm going to presume Hal will be available. He told the kids he had taken off the rest of the day. Presumption is not a good thing but he's been very human lately. Not at all the tough FBI agent who was here for the first time so recently. I wonder if his partner is aware he's spending time here? Probably not. I wonder if it's against regulation? So far, he's had a legitimate excuse for every visit.

I hadn't checked the mail today. As everyone seemed busy doing something, I thought I should while I'm still thinking of it. Credit card statement and bank statement. Oh, I could take us to dinner. I hadn't even thought of the card; zero balance right now. There was a postcard - not a picture post card like you send on vacation, just a postcard like you buy at the post office. The address was badly written but legible. But it didn't have a first name, just Palmer. On the reverse it said, "All things are not as they seem at all times." No signature. I couldn't make out the postmark. While the statement is an obvious statement of fact, who felt it necessary to remind me of that? And why? I'm going to turn it over to the FBI, just as soon as he's out of the pool.

Lee was on the deck looking at her vacation pictures on my big monitor screen. I went out and she asked if I knew where this was? I did. Cayucos pier. And this? The nature point at Los Osos. "How long has it been since you've been there, Mom?"

"Seventeen years. We spent five days at Morro Bay and used it as a base just as you did. But we were there over the New Year. They had a couple barges off shore loaded with fireworks. We stood on a little platform and leaned against the railing - half freezing our tokas off. Then, after the fireworks at midnight, we followed the noise and ended up at a party. Never found out who the host was, but it was a great party. I think it was around three am when we got back to the hotel."

"Mom, are you romantically interested in Agent Tucker?"

I am sure my face looked shocked as I truly was. "No, Lyn, whatever gave you that idea?"

"Laurie thinks he hugged you this afternoon."

"He did. But I don't think it was a romantic gesture. He'd just given me the final and filed copies of the divorce. I got emotional and cried. He hugged me and then suggested we check on the kitchen crew. The kids were putting together the ingredients for their salad."

She looked as though she wanted to believe me, but didn't. Thank goodness the kids hadn't seen him kiss me on the cheek yesterday. I wouldn't have had an answer for that. Still don't. It had to be some reflex but damned if I know to what.

We went through her photos and I asked questions or made comments. I love the coast and Morro Bay is so nicely located to be convenient to other smaller places of interest. The men got out of the pool and headed to the deck. They sat on the top step and asked what we were doing. Lee moved the monitor screen down to the deck floor and clicked through. Hal asked a couple of questions about different landmarks, etc. Perhaps he hasn't been up the California coast.

I could see the clock in the family room. "By the way, we have reservations at Luigi's for 6:30. Maybe we should call in the troops and start getting ready."

Hal got up. "I'll shower first and get out of your way."

"Aren't you going with us?"

He stopped short and turned around. "I didn't know I was invited."

Larry laughed. "Hal, you'll have to learn that around here if we're eating, playing, or whatever - if you're here, you're included. Have you been to Luigi's?"

"No. I know where it is but haven't indulged."

"Well, let's get dressed then call in the kids. 6:30, Lyn?"

"Yes, I could have said seven but didn't realize how many photos there were."

The guys were showered and dressed in fifteen minutes. Larry called in the kids. "We are going out for an after vacation dinner. Want to shower and get dressed?"

Laurie said, "I want to change clothes so I'll shower in my own bathroom. Okay? I promise, I'll bring the towel and suit back out."

Larry told Hal, "We go to Luigi's a lot. Usually as a small celebration for something. Today it would have been just the end of our vacation. But I understand you got the divorce petition filed."

"I did. When the Judge asked why the FBI was concerned after all this time, I told him it should have been handled years ago. It is not normal to be married to a ghost. He agreed and signed the petition."

Wil tapped Hal on the shoulder. "You should tell Dad where you were when you met the Judge." He was kind of teen-age smirky. "The Judge called Hal out." Larry looked at Hal. "Sounds intriguing. Didn't you go ex parte?"

Hal reddened just a little and told the whole story. Larry was whooping by the end. Then he soberly said, "You didn't mention we know where Wes is and he wants to marry Lyn?"

"Oh, lord no, Larry. The judge remembered the original case. Said it was the saddest thing ever to happen in this county. He wondered if Madlyn had found someone. That's when I said it wasn't normal to be married to a ghost."

Larry turned to me. "Why would Judge Johannson call you by your first name, Lyn?"

"Larry, I've know the judge for years. He's on the Library Board of Directors. I never realized he was a family court judge."

By this time, Laurie is dressed and ready to go. Her Dad has a nice big SUV and said he'd drive.

Luigi's was just getting busy. Everyone was delighted to see us again so soon. Hal looked around as if he was drinking in the atmosphere. The aroma is delightful; the staff is attentive; the food is great. They had saved us a round table in the front corner. We could watch the people on the street through the starched lace curtains.

Unfortunately, at that moment in time, it reminded me of Lowell, Massachusetts. Where Jim and I had a window table and I ordered chicken Parmesan. I checked the menu; I was going to order something else - anything else.

CHAPTER TWENTY-SEVEN

Dinner was a happy time. Lee and Larry told about their vacation. Larry said, "And Lyn, you are right. Two people, one holding a camera, standing in front of something scenic - some stranger will ask if you'd like them to take your picture. Happened nearly every day. On the Cayucos Pier an older gentleman saw us pause at the end of the pier. We were looking actually at how the mobile home park on the bay had grown but he thought we were in awe at the ocean. It was so clear, so calm, with just an occasional white cap. It was definitely picture perfect. I think that was our first stranger aided photo. It wasn't the last, though."

They were taking turns with cute stories. Or awesome seascapes, you know, vacation exhilaration. They had visited Questa College. Lee had considered attending there as a friend of hers had. But it didn't offer something in particular she wanted. The campus is so beautiful. I remember visiting it.

Hal asked, "Is Jill Stearns still president? Her brother and I were roommates in college. I still hear from him occasionally. He's certainly proud of her. I don't recall what field her PhD is in but Norm says she is brilliant."

That took the conversation toward education and Hal asked Wil if he had decided what school he'd like to attend. "You should really be looking now. Those last two years just run away from you if you're not careful."

Wil said he'd been making some inquiries but hasn't settled on any school in particular. Laurie popped up, "I'm going to keep my grades up and see if I can get into USC on scholarship like Grams did." Her Dad almost choked. Larry had gone to UCLA. He and I have had a minor rivalry going for years.

Hal said, "Forget I said anything. I was not aware of a family rivalry."

We all laughed and went back to talking about the vacation. Thankfully, it was a Thursday and, while the restaurant was busy, it wasn't hectic. We never had the feeling we should be hurrying. Larry asked Hal a few personal questions that fell into the general vein. He graduated from Pepperdine and then went back east to go to law school. Which school? Columbia. That's in New York, isn't it?

Wil asked, "What was your LSAT score?"

Hal looked a bit embarrassed. "180."

"Wow! Why didn't you become a lawyer? With a score like that you sure have the smarts."

None of the rest of us knew anything about LSAT scores. Must be close to perfect for Wil to be so impressed. I'm going to Google it when I get home. (It's 180.)

"Actually, Wil, I was a lawyer. I passed the State Bar in New York but there's no reciprocity between New York and California. After living in New York to go to school, I decided I didn't want to live in New York. My folk told me to come home and take the California bar. So that's what I did. And passed. I joined the Marines and spent several years with JAG. Then I was moved from the Navy Yard to the Pentagon. I traveled a lot after that. At twenty years I left the Corps and shortly after joined the FBI."

Wil wasn't the only one impressed. Larry and Lee looked astonished. As for me, I knew he was smart but had no idea just how smart. If he maintains any kind of relationship with Hal, I am sure Wil will make good choices for his education.

The waiter asked if we were interested in dessert. I mentioned there was none at home so if You want dessert, now is the time. The grand kids all wanted tiramisu. I believed they've never had it. Hal and I both chose the Mascarpone and Dark Chocolate Cream in White Chocolate Cups.

He said with a name that long it has to be good. Larry ordered cannoli and Lee the chocolate amaretto cake.

The waiter smiled. "It is marvelous when a family can disagree on dessert and they all order the very best." That seemed so convoluted and yet made so much sense. The kids were impressed with their choice. Hal asked if they'd ever had tiramisu before. Nope. But they've heard about it. We all laughed.

The check came and was given to me. I made the request when we were seated. Both guys reached for it and I reminded them that I was the one celebrating the most. The total was quite reasonable.

Larry dropped Hal and me at my house. "Your briefcase is in the living room. And, I got something in the mail today that I think you should see."

Once inside, he got his briefcase and sat it on the coffee table. "What did you get in the mail?"

The postcard was on top of the stack of mail I had opened earlier. "This."

I reached for it but Hal said, "Wait. It probably has a dozen set of fingerprints on it already but let's keep it that way. Do you have tweezers or something so you can flip it over?"

"Look at the address first. I couldn't see anything but a last name this afternoon. But under this light it looks like it says Mrs. or Ms. Palmer. But the interesting thing is the message." I gripped two paperclips together and turned the postcard over.

Hal read it over several times. "All things are not as they seem at all times. That is really strange, Lyn. Can you slip it into an envelope for me? I think out lab should look at it. Maybe they can bring up a postmark."

I have envelopes in a drawer and pulled one out. Using the two paperclips again, I picked up the postcard and put it in the envelope. "It makes no sense. I hope your lab guys can come up with something. I have a gut feeling it has something to do with Jim Nolan."

"I feel the same way. I don't know why but I feel he has something to do with this. No, I don't think he sent it, but I think he's involved somehow."

Hal put it in a pocket in his briefcase. "I'll keep you posted."

"Hal – wait. Maybe it would be a good idea for the FBI to send the divorce petition to the US Marshal. Make sure they know it's been done. It makes no difference to me if they pass it on to him or not. But maybe they should handle it. I believe I should send him anything right now." He nodded. The mail was on top of the two copies of the filed petition. I handed him one of them.

He reopened his brief case and dropped it on top of the Bureau's file copy. "And Lyn - thank you for a wonderful dinner. The conversation was as good as the food. That seldom is the case. And the day was perfection - all the way through. Your Grandchildren really take the cake though. Thank you. I'll call you in a day or two."

He picked up his briefcase and was out the door. I stood in the doorway and watched him. He waved as he got into the car. I kind of laughed to myself. Agent Harrelson waved to me the first time I met the them. I'm pretty sure they don't teach the 'wave' in FBI School. Or do they? The message waiting light was blinking on the telephone. It was Jim. "Guess you're out. I'll call tomorrow."

CHAPTER TWENTY-EIGHT

I slept longer than usual that Friday. The house was so quiet and there was nothing I had to get up and do. The kids never seemed noisy while they were here but they must have been. It is so quiet now. I put the coffee on to perk and decided to call to see how Miriam Johannson is doing. Hal had mentioned that the Judge was on his way to the ER when he met him in the parking lot.

The housekeeper answered the phone - which is fairly usual. I asked how Mrs. J was doing today. I think the housekeeper's name is Kathy or something with a K. I told her a friend had run into the judge leaving the courthouse yesterday. She laughed. "Aren't small towns wonderful? A few others have also called this morning. Mrs. J suffered a fractured hip. She'll be in the hospital a few days. She's at Methodist, Room 2312."

"Thank you for the information. I certainly didn't want to disturb the Judge."

"May I tell him who called?"

"Of course, this is Madlyn Palmer. I'm the librarian."

"Oh, I know the name, Mrs. Palmer. I hear it often after Library Board meetings. The Judge is impressed with you, you know."

"No, I didn't know. I guess that's a good thing."

"That didn't come out as I had planned. He's thrilled he was retained on the Board again this year. Is it custom to change board members often or is he just happy with the position?"

Somehow that seemed like an odd question to me. "There's a Library Board election every six years. It is seldom that anyone is voted off. We've had a few retire though and then the hunt is on to replace them. But seldom is anyone voted off."

"Oh, good. He's a very nice man, you know."

"Yes, I do know. He's effective on the board and always open to new ideas. You needn't tell him I said that though."

She laughed, "Thank you for calling. I'll be sure the Judge is aware."

After that exchange, I figured I should go visit Miriam. I know her well enough I believe. She's not that much older than I and we've met on several occasions. I'll pick up a good magazine and go visiting. I called Methodist Hospital. It's been ages since I've visited anyone there. What are the hours for visiting? Noon to 8pm. At one, I was sitting by her bedside listening to how she fell.

She was grateful for the magazine as she's not a television addict and was bored. "It's a clean break, but an odd break. I'll be here about a week, I've been told. Thank goodness replacement is not necessary."

We chatted about town news and library stuff. There is a good size clock on the wall in her room. That could be depressing but it was convenient and I didn't overstay. She thanked me again for the magazine as I left.

So here I am, out and about, and hungry. There are so many little restaurants on my way home. I decided to eat wherever I found a good parking space. Turned out to be a small Mexican eatery. I haven't been here in ages. There are several patrons even though it is nearly two in the afternoon. And I know many of them. A group of three women wave me down as I am being seated. "Come sit with us, Madlyn. It's been ages." I looked at the waiter seating me - he smiled and handed me a menu.

The three all work for a local escrow office. There have been a very few times when their Notary Public was out of the office when they needed a Notary. They called the library and I came to their rescue. "How can be you out of the library this time of day?"

"It's not a prison, you know." Laughs all round. "Actually, I haven't taken any vacation for some time and the Board insisted I take some of it now. I protested. There are so many programs going on during the summer. Too bad; take it or lose it. Well, you know, I still have that I earned it I deserve it attitude and said okay. I go back to work in ten days." More laughs.

Lots of chit-chat and family news that I have missed in the past few months. When it came to family news, I told them my son-in-law is home on leave. He's been promoted to Master Sergeant recently and felt he had enough stripes to ask for leave. I told them I had just gotten home from a two-week history vacation in the Boston area and have some great ideas for a new exhibit for the library.

So I was able to hold my place in the gossip area. Perhaps I should do stuff like this more often. Felt so invigorated when I got home. The kids had done the dressing room laundry yesterday so there wasn't enough to do again today. I changed the sheets on all the beds so did do laundry. For the rest of the day, I was a homemaker. When working I do things when I have time - so not everything is done at once. What a feeling of accomplishment to get the laundry done and beds remade in the same day.

Even though the television is recording my two game shows, I turned them on to watch 'live'. Between the two, Jim called. "Called last night, you must have been out."

"Either that or I just didn't answer the phone."

"That doesn't sound like something you'd do, Maddy. What's up?"

"Well, it seems you presume you know what I'd do or not do. You haven't been home in fifteen years. Just how would you know?" Why was I feeling so challenged?

"Oh, come on, you haven't changed that much. While you were here, I could pretty well predict what you'd say or do. You just haven't changed much."

"That's kind of an insult, Jim. I believe I have changed a lot, a whole lot, in fifteen years."

"Well, maybe in some things, but I can still read you like a book."

That wasn't just a slap in the face - it was a big red flag. This is not something Wes would have said or done. Maybe I am wrong. Maybe it is him who has changed and not me. No. I know that is not true. I am not the same person I was fifteen years ago.

"I'm sorry you believe that, Jim. You might get a hell of a shock someday."

"What's biting you, Maddy? You sound just a little distressed. Totally unlike you. You don't stress easily."

"Maybe it's just little things. A friend of mine fell and broke her hip. I saw her today. And it's the first day the kids haven't been here. Maybe I am stressed without really thinking so. But I doubt it."

"See? There are things bugging you. Why don't you just sell the house and pack up and move to Lowell? Things are not very stressful here. I'm sure you saw that."

"Why, after fighting to keep everything I have for so long, would I want to sell it and move thousands of miles away?"

"You would be with me. Doesn't that count for anything?"

"I always thought so. Now, I'm not so sure."

"Maddy, this is me you're talking to. You know you still love me. I could tell when you were here. I could tell that you wished I had ignored your silly "I don't monkey around on first dates" thing."

"Sorry, Jim. But that is not true. I was married to another man when I saw you in Lowell. I could not, would not, break my vows."

"You said you talked to someone about filing for divorce. Have you filed?"

"I filed but you know, under the circumstances, the US Marshal has to serve you. It'll be messy, maybe."

"I don't care. The Marshal knows who and where I am. The court doesn't care who serves the papers. And you know it."

It was obvious that he has forgotten the conversation we had that service could be done by publication in the instance of a missing spouse. I'm not reminding him. Hal didn't know if, or when, the Marshal would serve him with the final divorce paper. "Jim, you're thinking of the common, ordinary, run-of-the-mill dissolution. You and I don't fit that category."

"Come on, Babe, you know you still love me."

"Do you still love me? You know I don't like to be called Babe."

"Maddy, you know I love you. If this house is too small, we'll have the proceeds from that house and we can buy something bigger; something more your style."

"Careful, Jim. It almost sounds like you're wanting to marry me for my money."

He laughed. "That's my girl. I have always loved your sense of humor."

"Well, don't get used to it. I am hanging up now."

"Maddy, Maddy, Maddy, I love you, Girl." And he hung up.

I was shaking. This doesn't sound like Wes at all. And if this is how Jim is, I'm definitely not interested. My solace is that the divorce is final. He has no right to anything. I found the taped episode of Wheel for the night and turned it on. Some of those contestants are so dense. They miss the obvious puzzles. I was shaking from my call with Jim and shaking my head at the apparent idiocy of these contestants. I shouldn't have bothered watching. The telephone rang just as the program ended. I checked caller ID. It was Lee. "Larry just got a call. He has to report Sunday. Good thing we got our time in when we did. He's losing a week but he got most of his leave."

"From what little I overheard, he didn't have a swimming pool where he's been. If you all want to come over tomorrow to swim and stay for supper, just say so."

"He's not sure he'll be going back to the same place. But, it's doubtful there's an available pool anywhere in the general area that he can use. I'll ask and call you in the morning. Do you have a direct number for Hal? Larry wants to call him. Hal planned to give it to him last evening but I think we all ate too much to remember something like that."

"Wait. The first day he was here he gave me a direct number. Let me find it." It was on my desk; I've used it to call him a couple times. "Here it is. Ready?" She was and I gave her the number.

I know we all thought that a month leave was extraordinary. Larry got three and a half weeks. He won't complain, much, about reporting early. But his children will. Those last few days were theirs.

CHAPTER TWENTY-NINE

And so, we were all together again on Saturday. Larry and Hal spent a lot of time talking. I can't imagine about what but it seemed serious. They played for an hour in the pool with the kids and then lined them up on the pool chairs and talked to them. It seemed serious. It appears to me that Larry knows more about where he's going than he's letting on. Maybe Hal will be talkative - if it's not high security or something. I won't ask tonight. I won't ask tomorrow. I won't ask at all unless I think it's necessary I know what they discussed.

Larry brought chicken and ribs to grill. I made a couple salads and a dessert. Lee made sure there were drinks. We ate late afternoon so Larry could go home and pack. He wants to be sure all of is uniforms are ready-to-wear.

The kids left with promises to come swim in a couple days. I said that would be good as I haven't been in the pool much this year and miss it. And I haven't. I swim when Lee and the kids, or just the kids, are here. The pool has been really busy this summer. The kids gave me hugs and ran to the car. Larry hugged me and thanked me for being here. He and Hal shook hands and agreed to keep in contact. Lee was almost in tears and just gave me a peck on the cheek as she got in the car. They drove off leaving Hal and I standing on the curb. I think this is the first time I've entertained Hal as Hal and not as Agent Tucker. Of course, I hadn't invited him; Larry had. But still, it's a first.

We walked back to the house and I began picking up and straightening things. Finished loading the dishwasher. Hal cleaned the grill. It's so unlike Larry to not do that. He's worried about something. Hal did a credible job with the grill though I have the feeling it's not something he has done or does do on a regular basis. I thanked him and told him he really didn't need to do it.

Yeah, he knows. He seems so somber. Where can Larry be going? It's serious.

It was too early to ask if he'd heard anything about the postcard, so I didn't. However, he said that the lab had managed to raise the postmark. It was 2054-. "Dash?"

"Evidently, there are many agencies, buildings in the 20540 zip code packet and this is how it's printed if mail is picked up in the building and that particular sending agency doesn't have their own mail room."

"Where is it located?"

"Washington, DC."

"Someone in Washington DC is sending me mystery postcards?"

"Evidently. But remember, a lot of big office buildings have an outgoing mail slot in their lobby. So it could just be someone passing by. Hey, I'm surprised the lab contacted me with this tidbit. They must not be too busy. Though I told them it possibly related to an open file. By the way, does your ex still call every night?"

I liked the sound of that 'ex'. "No, not every night. He did while the kids were here."

"What's he talk about when he does call?"

"He used to tell me how much he has missed me over the years. Done little things that made no sense since I wasn't there. What he's been doing; where he goes. Thanked me for the great history tour that had been under his nose all these years. Reminisce about things - old and new. But lately it's I should sell the house and move back to Lowell and marry him. If the house he's in is too small we'd have enough money to buy something I like better. I told him last time he called that it sounds more like he wants to marry me for my money. He said he's always loved my sense of humor. But, really, Hal. I doubt his sincerity."

"Wonder if he's ever been to DC?"

"Never thought to ask him. I am amazed at how often it seems he goes to Boston. Wonder what he does in off-season, baseball season?"

"You could ask him, Lyn."

"I don't want him to think I'm that interested in what he does."

"Ah, yes, there is that."

Just then the phone rang. ID showed it was Jim. I said to Hal, "pick up the kitchen phone as I pick up. You don't know him but you may spot something in his voice."

So, he did.

"Hey, Babe, what 'cha doing?"

"How many times have we discussed you calling me Babe?"

"I forget. You're still a damn good looking woman. I was half afraid that I wouldn't recognize you at Logan when I picked you up -- weight gain or gray hair or something."

"Well, thanks a lot. How encouraging that if I wasn't the old me - what did you plan to do? Just walk away?"

"Don't be silly, Maddy. I'm just giving you a bad time. So what were you doing just now?"

"Cleaning the grill. Larry et al were here for a cookout. The balance of his leave has been canceled."

"Didn't he just get a promotion? Shouldn't that count for something?"

"The way promotions usually go they do count for something; more responsibility. He's not kicking. He got three and a half weeks. He had planned to take the kids to Disneyland Monday but I believe he hadn't told them so no big deal there."

"Why don't you take them to Disneyland? It's been a while since you've been there, hasn't it?"

"Jim, do you have any idea what it costs to get into Disneyland these days? I don't have that kind of money."

"Well, sell the house, take them to Disneyland and move here."

"Yeah, right. By the way, curiosity. Have you visited DC since you've been back there?"

"As in Washington DC? Hell, no. Why would I?"

"That was always part of the history trip. I just figured since you're so much closer maybe you have gone."

"Maddy, darling, it's four hundred and fifty miles to DC from here. No, I haven't been there and don't plan on going."

"Okay. Just wondering. Well, Jim, I need to get back to my grill."

"Love you girl. I'm waiting for you to get divorced so you can marry me."

"Right."

"Good night, Maddy. Sleep well."

And he hung up.

Making sure I had hung up, Hal hung up the kitchen phone. "Is this how he is all the time?"

"No, just the last couple weeks. Before it was all sweetness and light. Babe is new – he called me that a couple times and we had words about it. That was twenty years ago. But he seems to deliberately work it in now."

"If I was trying to woo someone I loved to give up her world and move thousands of miles to join me, I wouldn't be spending her money and being so off-handed. To say that he was afraid he wouldn't recognize you - that makes no sense. Were you ever overweight in your life?"

"No. That stung. I hadn't even imagined he'd look any different than when I had seen him fifteen years ago as he left for work. I didn't gain weight at all; wore the same clothes actually for ten years. He's rude and crass. He's never been either. It's almost like he's telling me what he thinks I want to hear but is trying to discourage my coming back. Or, am I deluding myself?"

"That is exactly how it sounds. Lyn, did you hear a little hum on the line? Very faint but a hum?"

"I thought I did a few nights ago. But sometimes I get a buzz of tinnitus so I dismissed it. Yes, it seemed there tonight. It doesn't interrupt the conversation and doesn't seem to be constant but lately he's been so 'off' that I haven't paid attention. Did you hear a hum?"

"I did. Either his phone is tapped or the call was being recorded there, at his home. I think recorded. We had a case a couple years ago where the man kept saying there was a hum on his line but he attributed it to his telephone company and even complained to them. We found a recorder in the next room and it was connected to his phone. This wasn't a wire tap but plain old recording machine. The bad guy rented a room from him and it wasn't a good thing. The hum I hear reminds me of that. But why would Jim be recording his calls to you? And why would his general demeanor change at the same time? Something isn't right. The next time he calls, if you hear the hum, I want you to say to him, "Jim, is someone recording this call? I hear a weird hum that reminds me of that time Eddy was going to blackmail Lee."

I looked at him in shock, or horror. "How do you know about that? He was twelve and she was fourteen? I'd forgotten it until you mentioned it."

"Oh my god, you mean it really did happen? I made that up because I figure he'd try to find something to say because he didn't remember but he didn't want whomever to know he didn't remember."

Laugh - all I could do was laugh. "You made it up? Are you sure don't have teenagers? It's almost a given that a younger brother is going to try and extort something from his older sister at some time. And if he thinks she's talking to friends and telling secrets, well, he records the phone calls."

Hal shook his head. "No, I don't have teenagers. And being an only child, I guess I missed out. Well, maybe he won't remember. Maybe he will. But his response would tell us something, I think. But you're never sure when he'll call. Maybe we could 'borrow' some recording equipment that doesn't hum from my office. We connect it to the phone and when caller ID indicates it's the party you want to record, you hit the little red button before you answer the phone. Shall we do it? Lyn, something is going on in Lowell and if we can prove it, I'll reopen the file and contact our offices in Boston."

My mind is whirling. Is Wes in trouble again? Is Hal reading in something not there? Why is Wes/Jim behaving as he has been lately? I've known him for nearly forty years. Can people's manner of speaking change overnight? He's never been crass or crude, even when he's had too much to drink. Maybe he has a brain tumor. Oh, good god, now what? I realize that Hal is waiting for an answer.

"Rather than 'borrow' the equipment, why not report this and reopen the file. If it's nothing, we have egg on our face. If it's something, we get the Cupie Doll."

Hal stood still for a moment. "How would I look with egg on my face?"

"More importantly, how cute will you look holding a Cupie Doll?"

CHAPTER THIRTY

Hal was reluctant to ask for the equipment and I understand that. Even though he had suggested it. I understand impulse remarks. I also told him that maybe Jim/Wes is trying reverse psychology. He has done that before. If he thought I really wanted to do something and he, for some reason, believed it was not a good idea. Sometimes even after he had mentioned it himself. Hal couldn't quite see that. "That doesn't make sense, Lyn."

"Come on, Hal. Hasn't someone ever tried to convince you that you want to do something, something you don't want to do. So you play along and get it so messy, they back down and say forget it?"

He seemed to think for a moment. "Not me, but I have seen my Dad unconvince my Mother of things by agreeing so disagreeably she changed her mind."

"Bingo. That almost sounds like what Jim is doing. Do you suppose that after I left he met someone and is feeling kind of sappy over her and suddenly realizes that he's practically got me packing to come back and marry him? So now it's reversed psychology time. He's done it before."

"That could be it. Maybe he's recording the calls to see if he's making any headway - or which way the wind is blowing. I know sometimes when I'm on a call, I hear everything but don't have time to really analyze it."

"Maybe I should tell him the divorce is final. The US Marshal has the paperwork and is supposed to notify him."

"And then see what he says?"

"Exactly. If it sounds like panic, I'll tell him that I'm right back at the beginning. I do not want to leave California and the family, friends and home I have here. I've thought about it and I'm not coming."

"He may call your bluff."

"Hal, I'm not bluffing."

"You're not?"

"At the very beginning, I was so overwhelmed and so excited I could have walked to Massachusetts. It had been a very long hard fifteen years. There was still ten years mortgage on the house. No one wanted to refinance and give me lower payments because, well, mainly because I was a woman. I had a job and a good one but... I sold his truck and convinced the bank to allow me to make a large payment and refinance the balance. We'd been customers for years and the new manager saw the sense in it. Property taxes can be a killer. I paid them in two payments and ate mac 'n cheese for three months. A house this size takes a lot of maintenance. And the dressing room was unfinished - the plumbing was in. Nothing else; no framing, no floor. I got very adept with a hammer and paint brush. The project stalled often for lack of funds. And if you look closely you'll see some imperfections. I'm a librarian not a carpenter. Property taxes come every year. I lucked out the second year and had a decent tax refund as I was back to work full-time. I saved it for property taxes. Utilities are brutal. I lived in two rooms to conserve electricity and gas. We had two savings accounts. One is for a trip to Peru. I never touched it but added a hundred a year to keep the account active. I couldn't let the state get it for going dormant. I could have paid property taxes from that account but that was the only thing I had that said there is a future; he'll be back. The other savings account I used sparingly for things that had to be paid. Then I talked to his life insurance company, they talked to the FBI, and returned premiums paid and canceled the policy. I couldn't afford to pay the premiums anyhow. That was a good sized chuck of money and things righted around. It still was very close but I could add a salad to the mac 'n cheese. Then when I turned fifty-five, his employer at the time he disappeared began paying me Wes' retirement. He was fully vested when he disappeared. But the fund was written that even widow's mite couldn't be paid until she was fifty-five. Finally, I could breathe. One of the first things I did was buy a new pair of shoes.

"Then I went to Massachusetts. He lives in a small one bedroom house with a backyard where he's planted stuff. A lot of pretty and expensive stuff. He goes into Boston regularly for a weekend to watch the sports teams. He has a job that pays well, benefits, the whole works. He has a nice car. He goes out to eat every single meal. He's well known and liked in his town. Other than missing what he had, he has never suffered a single day. He has done very well without me.

"I am not bluffing. I resent him so much that the love I once had has soured. We talked a lot when I was there. He said the first couple of months were agony. That's all, Hal. A couple of months. He admitted he knew better when he made the deal that took him away. But, it was just a bad deal after all. He missed me on special days but it sounded that he didn't miss me every day and every night. And he admitted he fell into being James Nolan rather easily. No big obstacles to overcome. His life never really changed. Just it's location.

"I will ask him point blank if there is any reason I should not come. Any reason he has - right now. If anyone had told me twenty-five years ago, or even fifteen years ago, that I could fall out of love with Wes, I wouldn't have believed it. But the trip proved to me one thing - while for fifteen years he was my reason for fighting on, I wasn't his. He fell out of love as soon as he changed his name. He was free to start over. He said that's what they told him to do and he believes he has done it pretty well."

"Lyn, did you ever think that maybe there isn't someone else? Maybe he likes being free of the responsibility of loving someone other than himself."

That thought had never occurred to me. But it makes perfect sense. Perfect sense.

Hal asked, "Do you think you'll ever trust anyone to love again?"

I laughed. "Hal, the only person I have to trust to love again is myself. What kind of person could be so resentful that they'd throw away twenty-four years of marriage? I have to learn to trust me. I can't take the chance of hurting someone else."

Hal was still in the kitchen by the phone. "Lyn, is there any beer in the fridge?"

"Beer?"

"Yes, I feel the need for a beer."

"I don't think there is any. I have some gin, good gin. Would a martini do? Shaken, not stirred."

"Yes, that would be fine." He missed the 007 reference entirely.

Somehow I never thought of Hal as a martini man; heck, I didn't associate alcohol with him at all. He's a bit stiff - which I attribute to his job. I put two glasses into the freezer and got out the gin and vermouth. The glasses had just frosted when I took them out. "I hope you like dry martinis. They're the only drink I know how to make." Ice in the shaker, gin in the ice. Three drops of vermouth in each glass, swirl it around and dump it out. Shake the gin and pour into the glasses.

He had been watching. It only takes a few minutes. I handed him a glass and held mine up in a half salute. He touched the rim of his glass to mine. Ping. A slow sip and 'ahhh.' Good lord, Hal could be a bonafide martini drinker.

We sat on the stools at the kitchen island and sipped our martinis. Not a word was spoken for at least ten minutes.

"Lyn, where did you learn to make a martini?"

"One summer I worked in a law office. The principle drank martinis. I was a file clerk. One afternoon he wanted a martini and no one else was available. I told him I wasn't old enough to drink and didn't know how to make a martini. "Let me show you, my dear." He did. After that, every afternoon just before I left the office, he would say "Madlyn, my dear, please make a martini for me on your way out." I didn't learn much that I didn't already know at that job, but I can make a very dry martini perfectly."

Hal was laughing. "Let me guess. Elmo Gustafson."

"Yes, how did you know?"

"I interviewed with him for a job when I came home from New York. It was a late in the day interview. He asked if I would care for a martini as he enjoyed one every afternoon. I said no thank you. I didn't get the job. I've often wondered if I would have if I'd accepted a martini."

"Well, I'm glad you didn't."

"What?"

"Your whole life would have been different. No USMC, no FBI, and I would never have met you."

He sat there for another few minutes before asking, "Do you suppose I might have a second?"

I put a clean glass in the freezer, rinsed out the shaker, and made another martini.

"Absolutely wonderful."

Again a pleasant long silence. I have few friends that I can sit with, say nothing and yet be totally connected to them. That's how I am feeling now, totally connected.

He excused himself and went to the bathroom. When he came out he said, "Okay. So our plan is the next time Jim calls you're going to give him the boot. To hell with his reverse psychology or whatever it is he's doing. Correct?" I nodded.

Hal didn't look drunk, didn't act drunk. He went to the couch and laid down and promptly fell asleep. I covered him with an afghan and put his shoes under the coffee table. It was about ten, so I turned on 'Dateline' in the family room. I'll have to remember he's a one martini man.

CHAPTER THIRTY-ONE

Sunday broke bright and clear. A typical August day. I looked out my bedroom window – Hal's car was still at the curb. I dressed, washed up, brushed my teeth and went to the kitchen to start a pot of coffee. He was still on the couch - it appeared he hadn't moved at all during the night. I set the table for two. Hopefully he will wake without a headache.

I went out to bring in the newspaper. For some reason, Randy never hits the porch with the Sunday paper. I went halfway down the walkway to retrieve it. As I came in, Hal sat up. He shook his head, probably wondering where he was. I waited for him to say something. He looked at me. I was in a skirt and sleeveless blouse this morning. "Well, I would guess it isn't Saturday anymore."

"And you believe that because?"

"You're wearing something different than I remember."

"Would you care for a cup of coffee before or after you shower?"

He seemed to process that for a minute before answering. "Probably after."

"Second door on the right. If you would like a change of clothes, there may or may not be something suitable in the top dresser drawer. There are shorts and jeans in the closet as well as shirts that don't say anything. I think you're the right size. Since Wil and Mike were in this bedroom this past week, there's probably shaving cream. Top drawer of the vanity in the bathroom has new toothbrushes, disposable razors and stuff. If you need something, just shout."

"Do you have people fall asleep on your couch often, Lyn?"

"No, you may be the first. You don't have to change after you shower, but it does look as though you slept in your clothes."

"You seem rather prepared for visitors, is what I mean."

"When you raise teenagers, you never know if you'll feed two or twenty or sleep one or five. Even though mine are gone, the grand kids often forget stuff. They don't wear Uncle Eddy's clothes; neither have the stature yet. But you look his size. If nothing fits, well, you're stuck with wrinkles."

He walked down the hall. God, I should have handled that differently. What is wrong with me these days? I went back to the table, poured my coffee and opened the newspaper. About twenty minutes later Hal emerged from the bedroom. He was dressed in Bermuda length shorts and a colorful shirt. His own shoes are casuals and he will look just fine. He turned around and said, "Well, am I suitable now?"

"Hal, you were suitable before. I thought you'd be more comfortable in clean clothes. Now, do you want pancakes, eggs, and bacon or toast, bacon, and eggs?"

He looked slightly stunned. "You're going to feed me too?"

"Well, it's impolite to eat in front of guests, and I plan to have breakfast."

"Pancakes sound good."

"How do you like your eggs?"

"Well, I like them poached but I know that's a hassle. Over easy would be fine."

"Here's the paper. Here's your coffee. Breakfast shortly."

I cook bacon and poach eggs in the microwave. I mixed the pancake batter. There was some melon in the fridge. I poured juice in a pitcher and put it on the table. He looked up at me but said nothing. There were juice glasses at both place settings. He poured himself some juice and went back to the paper. Syrup. I hadn't put syrup on the table. Thanks to the microwave, breakfast was on the table in a short while. I poached two eggs and put them in a small dish and sat it on his plate.

"Please serve yourself, Hal. I have no idea how much of anything you want."

Damn, I embarrassed him again. But he did fix his plate and begin to eat. "Okay. Exactly what happened last night? I'm not sure."

"We discussed Wes/Jim and why he's doing whatever it is that he's doing. We decided that the next time he calls I will kick him to the curb. We discussed this over a martini. And you had a second one. You went to the bathroom and came back, recited what I was to do next call from Jim, then you laid down. You were asleep before I could even say good night."

"Really? That simple?"

"Yes, that simple. Do you usually cause a scene or something?"

"No, I usually don't drink unless it's wine at dinner or I'm at home."

"Well, with your limited capacity, I certainly understand the wisdom of that."

His face reddened again. I put my hand on top of his. "Hal, you were a perfect gentleman. We discussed a problem and you were not impaired while doing so. We made a determination. And, you had intelligent input. You laid down when you felt you couldn't function."

"I do remember our discussion. I don't remember anything after excusing myself to go to the bathroom. This has never happened to me before."

"Have you ever had two very dry martinis in an hour before?"

He sat quietly. "No, no, I haven't. Do you suppose that explains it all?"

I laughed at him. "Of course. What else could it be? Gin is very insidious."

We spent more than an hour at the breakfast table. We talked, read the paper, discussed the news, and ate. It was a typical Sunday morning. Or used to be years ago. Though I think it was a new experience for Hal. "Well, what do you have planned for the day, Hal?"

He looked blank. "I don't think I planned anything. It's Sunday. Do you have something planned?"

His phone rang. It was not quite ten. "Thanks for calling. Good luck. I'll do my best. Keep in touch." That type of conversation was what I heard. He came back to the table but, before he could say anything, the house phone rang. It was Larry. He wanted to say goodbye. They were leaving for the airport. He mentioned he had talked to Hal this morning. I didn't tell him I knew. He said he had asked Hal to help me keep an eye on his family. He thinks this is going to be another long deployment. I told him I thought that was a brilliant idea as the kids like Hal a lot.

"Yeah, they do. I am surprised." I suggested that perhaps they could see his good qualities in Hal.

"Lyn, I couldn't hope for much more." He promised to keep in touch.

When I returned to the table, Hal said, "Larry Baxter is one fine man. It is amazing how you meet people sometimes."

"Yes, it is truly a wonder. Makes you almost believe there is a life force controlling the planet."

He nodded. "Now, do you have something planned for the day?"

"I thought of going to the Arboretum. There's a new orchid house I would like to check out."

Again, he nodded. "Am I dressed properly to go to the Arboretum?"

"As a matter of fact, you are. Should we pack a lunch or worry about eating afterward?" Hal is a very bright man. But these kind of simple questions just seem to blow his mind. He looked confused. "Oh, I am sorry, Hal. I shouldn't have assumed you wanted to spend the day looking at orchid houses. I'm feeling much too comfortable with you."

"I'm not FBI every minute of every day, Lyn. Usually, unless there's something really big happening, I have every weekend off - just like normal people."

Now I was embarrassed. I started to say something wise ass about normal people. But he held up his hand. "I know what you mean. But it just verifies that we meet people who can affect our lives in very strange ways."

We put the dishes in the dishwasher and cleaned up the kitchen. While we talked I learned that he had not been to the Arboretum since he was in grade school. Then his primary interest was the 'Tarzan' area. He was totally unaware of the gardens and green houses or the other 'history' there.

We spent several hours in the Arboretum. Hal was fascinated with the entire place – and believe me, we saw the entire place. Late afternoon he said, "Early dinner or really late lunch?"

"What's the difference?"

"Where we eat."

"Oh. Well, you choose. It seems I've made most of the decisions lately."

At first, I thought he was going to protest that. Then, maybe he realized I was right. At any rate, he decided we would have an early dinner. "I have a few things I want to do before I get to work tomorrow. Hope you don't mind an early dinner."

Expecting a call from Jim that evening, I went over what I would say to him. But he didn't call. So much for that. Knowing Hal was home working I decided not to call him. I am sure he has more important cases than this one. In fact, is this even an open case anymore? When he brought me home, he gathered up his dirty clothes and promised to return the ones he had on - washed and ready to go back into the emergency dressing drawer. Saturday was the first time he had visited my home without a briefcase in hand. I found myself hoping it wasn't the last. Larry Baxter is correct. Hal is a fine man.

CHAPTER THIRTY-TWO

Jim didn't called Monday or Tuesday either. This is the longest stretch since I returned from Massachusetts. Maybe Hal is right. Jim likes his current status. He may have been like me – excited to be reunited. Fifteen years can cause a lot of good, perhaps false, memories. My visit may have made him realize he's happy alone.

Wednesday was a busy day. I went back to work. Evidently I wasn't expected back so soon but I was tired of being at home. So much happened while I was on vacation at home and at the Library. Things were not as neat and tidy as I like them but I kept my mouth shut. My vacation came as a surprise to us all. I didn't go charging in with these grand ideas I've developed while on vacation though. I know better than that. Don't get me wrong, everyone seemed genuinely pleased I was back. They had been rotating, or maybe just juggling, my duties for several weeks. My office was untouched except for a pile of things in my in-box. Stuff they didn't know how to handle or didn't want to handle for me. Fine with me.

I picked up some dinner on the way home. It was almost seven when I arrived at my own front door. A long day. I kicked off my shoes and sat my dinner package on the island in the kitchen.

The telephone rang. It was Jim.

He started by apologizing for calling earlier than usual. I reminded him that he had no duty to call at all. It was his choice. Yeah, good, he supposed I was right. The line sounded a bit different than usual. I took the phone to the family room and sat in my favorite chair. He chatted about a couple things. Finally I asked him if he was calling from home. Why did I ask?

"Lately there's been a slight hum on the line but tonight it's almost an echo."

"Hum?"

"Do you remember when Eddy was going to blackmail Aralee and tried to record her phone calls?"

Slight pause. "My god, that was a very long time ago. But, yeah, I remember,"

"When we finally found out what was going on and listened to his recordings, there was a very slight hum. And the last few times I've talked with you, there was a slight hum. Were you recording our calls for some reason, Jim?"

Dead silence. Finally, "It may have been the microwave tower near the house, Maddy."

"I didn't see it so never thought of a microwave tower. I suppose that could account for a hum. Are you calling from home now? There's no hum."

"Damnit, Maddy, what is this? An inquisition? No, I'm not calling from home. I'm still at work. Sometimes I get the swing shift."

"Calm down. I was just asking."

"Did Larry get off okay?"

"He left Sunday morning. The kids are devastated. They may be over Saturday. I don't know. School starts in two weeks. Lee and I haven't talked much this week. Sounds like Larry is expecting another long deployment."

"Too bad. A guy should be home helping raise his children."

"Agreed. But he is career Marine."

"Well, I have to get back to work. Just wanted to check in." And with that, he hung up. What a wacky phone call. No opportunity to tell him I wasn't moving to Lowell. But the reaction to the hum was something. Do I call Hal? It's not important; I'll just make a note of it in case he asks later if I've heard from Jim. I retrieved my dinner and a glass of tea and settled down in front of the television. How odd? Microwave tower? I got up and got my photo disc and laptop. I took several pictures of his house and yard and surrounding area. Microwave tower? I don't think so. An hour later I am sure he's lying. I haven't been gone long enough to erect a microwave tower and there is none visible in any of my pictures. Not even one of those 'cleverly' disguised towers.

My dinner was cold, but it was still tasty. It was late enough now that I went to the taped versions of the shows I watch. Guess I'll continue taping them. Seems I never watch them in real time anymore.

Saturday in the mail was another pencil written postcard; just like the first. This message said, "A man is known by the silence he keeps." The message was much more legible than the first card but the postmark was still blurred. I put it into an envelope, wrote the date on the envelope and left a message for Hal on his office phone.

Monday morning he called me at the Library. "Lyn, what's this weird message you left for me? You could have called my direct line."

"It isn't vital. At least, I don't think so. I didn't want you to think I was going to ruin another weekend for you."

"Well, that's something you've never done. What's the postmark on the card? Is it legible?"

"No, it's blurred again. I can make out a 2. That's it. I presume it's DC though I don't know that."

"What time do you leave the Library? I'd like to pick up the postcard and have it examined."

"Usually I'm out of here by 5:30. Things have smoothed out and I'm pretty much back on my regular schedule."

"I'll try to be at your house by 6. The comment is well-known. I wonder if its author is a clue or it's was just a convenient saying? Anyhow, I'll see you around 6."

"Hal, Oliver Herford is the author of this. Another similar quote was by Aesop, "A man is known by the company he keeps." Herford was a writer and illustrator in the late 1800s in England. His father was a minister who moved his family from England to Chicago and later to Boston. I can't see where he relates to anything."

"Interesting. Maybe it's just the quote not the author then. See you this evening."

My day was busy. I laid out my idea for a history exhibit - industrial revolution theme. Lowell was/is the center of a lot of milling and manufacturing and the way the City exhibits that information is clever. It would be an exhibit for next year but it may take more work than I imagine. Our little area of the world has had enough industrial revolution to make a good Exhibit. Everyone likes the idea. I had a few photos to show them that I carefully culled from my vacation disc. One of the interns asked if I was writing off my vacation on my tax return. I hope the glare I gave him was enough. He's new and has not made a good impression on me yet. He was hired as a temp in July. Thank god for that. However, I need to get rid of him by the end of September or he will be a regular employee. I marked my calendar - I don't want to forget to show him the door before his 90 day anniversary. I don't like his attitude.

On the way home, I realized that I haven't heard from Jim since Wednesday After the last phone call, that is even more interesting. Guess I'd better mention the call to Hal. He may get more out of it than I did.

By the time I reached the house I remembered where the first quote came from. It's not an exact version of the quote but very close. Plato 370BC - Phaedrus. Though, as Hal suggested, it more likely is the quote that should concern us rather than its author.

Hal's car was at the curb. Where was Hal? I heard voices and walked through the breezeway to the back yard. Wil's friend Steve was standing with the vacuum wand in his hand by the pool. I'm sure that Steve doesn't know Hal. "What's up, guys?"

"Hi, Mrs. P., I'm being questioned by the FBI."

"Hal?"

"Just wondered who he was. When I first saw him he was just kneeling by the pool and I didn't see a uniform or a service truck."

"Hal, this is Steve. He's a friend of Wil's. He helped clean up the mess after the windstorm and he comes by ever so often to check on the cleanliness of the pool. Steve, this is Agent Tucker of the FBI. He's come by hopefully with some news of Wil's grandpa."

They shook hands. Hal apologized to Steve and Steve said, "Oh, no apology, Sir. We all have a responsibility for each other and especially for Wil's Grams. If it's okay, I 'd like to clean the pool this evening. Meant to come last week but I knew Wil's Dad was still home and they might be here."

I hugged the boy. "Thank you so much, Steve. Stop at the house before you leave." Out of earshot, Hal said, "I feel like an idiot. You never mentioned having a pool service." "I don't. Since the wind storm Steve has come by on a half way regular basis. I give him twenty bucks for cleaning the pool. He does a more thorough job than I do. He tried to refuse the money at first and I told him he would hurt my feelings if he didn't take it."

We went back through the breezeway as the deck doors are locked from the inside.

"Let's see the new postcard." I went to my desk and got the envelope. He pulled on a blue glove and took it out. "There is something we're missing. Can you think of anything that binds the two quotations together?"

"It seems so secretive. Things aren't what they seem always and a man and silence. Do you suppose it's a reference somehow to Jim? Is he what he seems? Is he keeping something silent? I don't know - but it's weird."

We couldn't make any connection of any sort between the authors and anything we were aware of. Then I remembered the telephone call.

"Jim called Wednesday, earlier than usual. The line had a different sound and I asked him if he was calling from home. No, he was working swing shift, he was at work. Why would I ask and I told him I'd heard a hum the last couple times I spoke with him. Sort of like the time Eddy was trying to blackmail his sister. The silence was so long I thought he'd hung up. Then he said that he remembered the incident - my god how long ago was that. But he laid the hum to a microwave tower near his house. Hal, there is no microwave tower near his house; not even one in disguise. There's nothing taller than forty-five or fifty feet for blocks. He says I evidently just didn't see it. What the hell was this - the Inquisition? Then he asked if Larry got off okay. I said yes. And he hung up."

"What did you say he does for a living?"

"He's a mail handler at the Boston Sorting Center, USPS."

"I'm going to ask the lab to check this postcard for fingerprints, as usual. But to start with a known set - Jim Nolan. If he works at a sorting center, he might be able to put an unpostmarked item in a packet to DC. If caught, DC would postmark it."

"Aren't we stretching now?"

"Maybe, but maybe Jim is trying to tell us something. And it involves someone or something else - ergo his home phone is recorded or tapped."

"That's really stretching, Hal. Really."

Steve knocked at the family room doors. I took my wallet from my purse and went to let him in. "I hope my coming without calling doesn't give you problems, Mrs. P. I didn't know you were back to work already."

"No problem, Steve. None at all. Agent Tucker wanted to run some ideas past me. Who knows what may come of it. I appreciate your diligence with the pool." I handed him a twenty. "Is that enough taking harassment into consideration?"

He laughed and hugged me. "I'll let you know when the price goes up. I'm just glad you know people who look out for you." He skipped down the deck stairs and out the breezeway. I relocked the doors and put my wallet back in my purse. Hal is watching me. "Is there anyone that isn't charmed by your grandmotherly ways, Mrs. P?"

"Well, there is one FBI agent who is still wary of me. Other than that, nope, no one at all."

For the longest minute, Hal stood looking at me. "Maybe the FBI knows what a femme fatale you really are, Mrs. P."

What a comeback. Maybe I've underestimated this man. "What a marvelous thing for you to say, Agent Tucker."

"Let me add another marvelous statement. I'm starving. May I buy you dinner?"

CHAPTER THIRTY- THREE

Hal said he'd rather stay in town for dinner. I said fine with me. There are a lot of great places to eat here. How about Mexican? Sounds good. Surprisingly, or maybe not, he went to my family's favorite Mexican restaurant. Well, I'm sure it's the favorite of many families. There are always specials offered for dinner. I read the board before we sat down and knew exactly what I wanted. The waiter brought chips and salsa; did we want a drink before dinner.

Hal looked at me. "I'd like a beer with dinner but nothing before." Hal thought that sounded like a grand idea. We were ready to order. The waiter seemed glad. The place was a bit busy even at seven. We ordered the same special. A very cold beer arrived about two minutes ahead of a very hot plate. I didn't want to discuss anything of import and Hal apparently didn't either. We are in a public place in a town that believes my husband has been missing for more than a decade.

Hal started talking about the Arboretum. He was amazed at how extensive it has become. I said it is surprising that things grow a bit in forty years. He looked at me and said, "Probably forty-five. I wonder why we never visited it again? Have there always been so many peacocks?"

I nodded. "They roam the streets and people complain. Their shriek at sunrise is the worse alarm clock in the world. My family used to live south of where I live now - on Foothill. There was a pomegranate tree in the back yard. At sundown it was filled with roosting peacocks."

The intern kid from the Library came in with a couple of adults. Looked like his parents possibly. I leaned close to Hal. "The kid in the yellow striped shirt that just came in -"

"Yeah, what about him?'

"They hired him as a temp intern at the Library. Rude little bastard. He makes remarks that are not appropriate in every meeting he's been in since I've been back. I have to fire him by the end of September or I'm stuck with him."

"Ow! I can see that would be a problem for you. Do you have to tell him why you're dismissing him? Is that policy at the Library?"

"Since he's an intern, I think I can just say it was a summer position and he's no longer needed. At least, I hope so. We won't be replacing him. I'm going to check with our legal beagle tomorrow. I hate to say this but look at the man he's with. Doesn't he look familiar?"

I was afraid I'd get caught staring. But I looked again. They were standing in the foyer waiting to be seated. "Oh, my god, I think that's Congressman Mason. This is his second year in congress and hasn't been a stellar representative. Personal opinion, of course. The kid probably feels he's privileged and can say offhand remarks at will. Should I have a talk with him tomorrow? Not about his lineage but his language?".

Hal signaled for another beer. Did I want another? No, I was good.

"That might be a good idea. Phrase it in such a way that he's making himself look like an ass. If he protests or disagrees, remind him he's temporary. You just hope he'll clean up his act for the rest of his time with the Library. If he doesn't, get rid of him sooner than later. You don't need a verbal and a written warning for temporary help -- if it's before their ninety days."

I had forgotten that Hal is an attorney. Evidently, he keeps up with the law.

Hal's second beer arrived and I asked for a few more chips. I believe I eat as many chips as entree when I eat here. We talked about a lot of things. He apologized that he hadn't returned the borrowed clothes yet. I reminded him that they were there only because I couldn't bear to throw them away. It's not like they were in constant demand.

That got him started on Eddy. How old was he when he died? He'd just turned twenty-one. Hal said he was a good sized kid then? "I never thought of his size. He was about one fifty and six foot something. Why do you ask?"

"When I tried on the clothes, they fit as if they were my own. I was amazed. I am six foot three and one sixty-two. Was he an athlete?"

"No, he was an accountant. He did play a lot of baseball and basketball with his friends but he wasn't really an athlete. Are you an athlete? You've never mentioned sports. Well, I suppose in your line of work, sports isn't a common topic."

"I work out, mainly because I am so sedentary. I go to the Y to swim regularly. Except this summer, I've been swimming at the Palmer pool. I was just curious about him. I've been thinking a lot about him lately and how he must have felt when -- well, you know. He did what he thought was right and his Dad was gone anyhow. Twenty-one. What a shame. He sure collected a lot of crazy tee-shirts. I'd forgotten most of those sayings."

"His Dad used to say, 'good god Eddy, does every shirt you wear have to reflect your beliefs? And Eddy would say, 'not every shirt Dad, some reflect my religion'. He got this terrific job in Pasadena. He figured he'd save gas money if he lived closer in. Though he didn't pay rent at home. He and two buddies rented a small house. When it got too loud there – I guess there were frequent loud weekends - Eddy would come home for a few days. That's why there are so few clothes in that bedroom. He didn't live at home."

The waiter asked if we saved room for dessert. I told him that I had cleaned my plate and there was no room left. Hal said, "Got so tied up in the burrito, I forgot there could be dessert." In a few minutes, a check was on the table. Hal said, "Thank you for coming to dinner with me. It was most enjoyable."

We navigated through the restaurant and ended up walking past Congressman Mason's table. I don't know what possessed me. "Good evening, Thad. See you tomorrow." I just kept walking. I heard his mother say, "Who was that, Thaddeus?" We were out of hearing range but I wish I knew how he responded to her.

In the car, Hal said, "Oh, Lyn, that was cruel and grand at the same time. Wonder if he remembers who you are?"

"Guess I'll find out tomorrow, won't I?"

The drive was short and quiet. I haven't thought how Eddy must have felt when his Dad disappeared after he'd made an effort to save him. I think of Eddy often but only how I feel, never how he must have felt about things. I have no idea what Hal was thinking. Maybe it was just usual end of the work day thoughts. I don't know.

Hal walked me to the door. I invited him in. He said he was going back to the office for a few hours. If I need him, just call. I watched him drive away - feeling things I haven't felt in a long time. Motherly love for my son; and a warm feeling for the man I just had dinner with.

CHAPTER THIRTY-FOUR

The Library opens daily at nine am. But on Tuesday all staff reports by eight. I hold a weekly State of the Library meeting. This is a rather large library with many and varied departments. Each week we review attendance in each area to our best guesstimate, any problems, needs, etc. Today is no different, even though I've been gone all summer. From going through my in-box I found that this meeting wasn't held every Tuesday of my absence. That bugs me as, to me, this is one of the most importance functions of my position. However, it's too late for any action now other than to emphasis the need to know what is happening in the complex.

At eight, every employee (including custodial) is in place but one. Yep, our summer intern. He came strolling into the meeting about ten minutes late. This was no time to chew on him as we have less than an hour to complete the meeting. Everything seems in pretty good order until we get to the front reading room. This was created when there was an addition to the library two years ago. There's a central reading room, has always been, in the middle of the building —standard newspapers and magazines and comfy chairs. The front reading room is behind the main desk – to one side and is adjacent to one of the many pairs of public restrooms we have. It has couches, comfy chairs, newspapers, magazines, free coffee and a shelf with a sign that says "I'm reading this." This reading room, like the other, is open to everyone and anyone. As it is located close to the front door, the users have primarily been homeless or poverty level readers. Nearly all of them possess a library card but many homeless will not check out a book. They read in the front reading room, put a bookmark with their name on it in place and put it on the "I'm reading this." shelf. We do not re-shelf those books. When they finish a book, they return it to the Front desk. There are several older people who aren't homeless but you can tell money is tight. Many of them don't dress well and won't go to the Central Reading Room. The coffee is free and a system has been worked out to be sure there's always coffee. There is no coffee in the CRR.

However, today there is a complaint. And apparently, it's happened two or three times recently. The person responsible for coffee hasn't been responsible. No one knows this unless one of the readers comments to the front desk. So it may have happened more than we know. Many of them are hesitant to do so as they are afraid the free coffee may disappear entirely. There is bowl that says 'donate if you can' but the coffee is free.

Having not been here for nearly seven weeks, I don't know who is scheduled to do what. Well, I do have this week's schedule but not the past weeks. I asked for comment. Who could explain this? No one spoke. Who is responsible? Yep, our summer intern. I asked him for an explanation. Why has there been a complaint of no coffee. The system is fool proof if you use it. He began an excuse by ranting about coddling the homeless. He was quite verbal. I said, "Thaddeus, stop right there. Evidently you are unaware this library is a public building. Regardless of community standing, everyone has the right to use this building. As soon as you have completed your 'first of the day chore' report to my office."

He grumbled and mumbled under his breath. We finished the list of departments. I had a schedule of duties for the week in my hand. Thaddeus is responsible for front reading room coffee. He didn't show up in half an hour at my office. All he had to do was roll out a cart that should have been prepared the evening before and plug it in. I went to the reading room. No one, no coffee either. I went to the kitchen and he's there measuring coffee into the top of the 32-cup coffee pot.

"When you were hired, Thad, were you aware this would be one of your duties here?"

"Hell, no. Making coffee isn't working in a library."

"Well, it is here. Who trained you for this task?"

"Jeanine."

"Jeanine has been here for several years. I am sure she trained you the proper way. Why have you deviated from your training?"

"I tried to tell you in the meeting and you shut me down. Homeless people are low life's." He had finished measuring the coffee; I checked that there was water in the pot. "Take this to the front reading room and get it perking." He grumbled and I followed him.

He looked at the little donation bowl. "Look at this. Eighty-five cents."

"That was supposed to be picked up last night. Did you move the coffee pot to the kitchen last night? You were supposed to set up this morning's coffee last night; I'm sure Jeanine told you that."

"Yeh, but that's a pain in the ass. I get out of here late then."

Just then one of the front desk librarians came in. She had been eavesdropping, I'm sure. "Excuse me, Mrs. Palmer. I wanted to get some coffee."

"By any chance, Helen, have you heard any of my conversation with Thad?"

She flushed. "I'm sorry, Mrs. Palmer, I didn't mean..."

"That's okay, Helen. I need a witness anyhow. Thaddeus Mason, your summer internship is canceled. You are not timely; you refuse to follow orders; and you are insolent, foul mouthed and a disgrace to the library staff. If you have any personal possessions in your locker, you have five minutes to clear out. And, I will be talking to the Board about revoking your library privileges."

While I expected Helen to be shocked, or upset, she almost looked relieved. I followed Thad to the employee area and watched him take a few things out of his locker. He stood upright - like he was facing a bear and wanted to look larger. "Do you have any idea who my father is?"

"Well, of course I do, Thad. I saw you with your parents at dinner last night. I didn't think you knew who I was. But I'm not firing your father. I'm firing you. He can come talk with me if he thinks it'll change my mind, but it won't."

He stomped out and I followed him to the front door. Helen was back at the desk by this time. "I am so glad he's gone."

That sounds like another situation I need to check out. I went back to my office before I realized that I am shaking like an aspen - from top to bottom.

CHAPTER THIRTY-FIVE

The rest of the day went well. Several of the staff, when they learned I had booted Thaddeus Mason out the door, stopped by my office. And every one of them had the same opinion of him. He was bad news from the first day. I pulled his application - a member of the board had recommended him for a summer internship. Frank Cartwright. I don't know Frank all that well. He's been on the board for two years. Perhaps I should call him. He's the owner of a small machine shop that has been around for decades.

Frank himself answered the phone. I introduced myself and told him I had called to talk to him about Thaddeus Mason. "Ah, yes, how is he working out?" I told him he wasn't; that I canceled his internship this morning. At first, he was very huffy. Then he calmed and asked why. I told him.

"Damn right he should be ousted. How did he last so long?"

I explained that I had been out for a few weeks. The board had hired Thaddeus while I was gone. Apparently my people didn't have the authority to speak to anyone. Or thought they didn't. They could have called me but no one thought of that.

I told him about the usual Tuesday meeting and I went into detail about it as it happened Today. "Mr. Cartwright, as you recommended him, I believe I have the obligation to let you know he didn't work out."

He kind of made hmm noises and finally said, "Well, I've never liked the lad myself but his father is an old and dear friend. He was hoping we could fit the boy in somewhere that would straighten him out a bit."

"So Thad's father is aware of his behavior? He thought what could possibly happen at a library? Is that it?"

"Well, when you put it that way, it does sound a bit ridiculous. I'll let Congressman Mason know it was a failure."

"The boy used his father as a threat. I told him to bring him on. I was firing him, not his father. He was not too happy I didn't kneel and bow."

"Mrs. Palmer, you did what was right. Not just what you thought is right but what is right. The lad thinks too highly of himself and, as you discovered, believes his father is omnipotent."

"My staff is too relieved that he is gone. I am hoping there's nothing more that I learn about him."

"I appreciate your calling me. That's more than most people would do. I'll have to stop by the Library some day and get reacquainted with you. Thank you again for the call."

I had the staff schedule and determined who would be able to handle the front reading room coffee for the rest of the week. No one else on the staff minds doing it. Most feel honored that they're able to contribute a bit of comfort to someone. There are many elderly readers who truly appreciate the free coffee. It's not just the homeless.

That taken care of, I got back to work.

About two thirty, Hal called. "I hate to bother you at work but a case Harrelson and I have been chasing for a year is finally on the move. We'll be out of town for a few days. I'll have my phone with me if you need to call."

"It'd have to be rather over-the-top for me to call you when you're out on assignment. I can save up everything and you can call when you're back in town."

"One of the things I like about you, Lyn. You're sensible. By the way, did the kid you spoke to last night know who you were?"

"No. Do you have two minutes for the whole story?"

"Absolutely."

I gave him a quick version including that I had called his sponsor. "Right thing to do all the way. If I can, I'll call you this week. Can't promise a thing. But maybe."

"You're not obligated to call, Hal. But it would be pleasant."

"Yes, yes, it would. Take care of yourself."

Such a bright spot in the day. I actually found myself humming all afternoon. A new sensation. But it can't be FBI protocol. My case isn't even open, is it? I smiled to myself. But maybe to someone, Lyn, it is important.

I did spot interviews with the staff. Apparently Thaddeus Mason had verged on harassment but not enough to do anything legal about it. I would have though. There are a few I haven't talked with but covered about seventy-five percent of my staff. I told them all he is not allowed in the Library.

That will probably backfire on me but I don't want him in my library bothering my people. On the way home, I stopped and got a pastrami sandwich. I had somehow missed lunch and was getting hungry. The phone was ringing as I walked through the door. It was Congressman Mason wanting to explode about my treatment of his son. "Congressman, the Library opens at nine in the morning. I'll be happy to speak to you there, in my office."

He didn't like that idea and I told him I don't bring business home with me. I asked if he recalled where the Library was located. "I've lived in this town for twenty years, young lady. Of course, I know where the Library is located."

"Congressman, I was born in this town. Longevity is not your strong suit tonight. Goodbye."

That probably wasn't the best idea but I was hungry, tired, and sick of the name Mason. But I did make sure my doors were locked and pulled the kitchen curtains before I sat down to eat. Again, early, Jim called. I wasn't quite finished eating.

"Maddy, I am sorry that I'm calling early, again. Still on swing shift. First time in a long time. Now tell me again what you were trying to say about my phone at home. You think someone is recording my calls?"

"Jim, you called several times before I heard a noise on your line. And while I was there, I never heard it. Are you in trouble? Why would someone be bugging your phone?"

"In trouble? What do you mean?"

"I don't know but in the movies the bad guys always bug the good guy's phone to try and catch him saying something about them that they don't like. Have you made any enemies since you've been there? Is there somebody new in town that you've accidentally crossed?"

He was really quiet. I could hear shouting behind him that sounded like guys trying to talk over equipment noise or something. Like I imagine a mail sorting facility might sound like. "I may have pulled a real dumb thing a couple weeks ago but I don't think it'd come to bugging my phone."

"You're not known for doing dumb things. Who did you cross? Is this why you call me from work?"

"One of the Marshals has been bugging me to help him out a little. He's not been with the Marshals a long time. I never heard of him until the week after you left."

"Have you mentioned it to any of the other Marshals? Are you sure he is an U S Marshal? What kind of help is he looking for that makes you hesitate? You used to be a real helpful, Nelly."

"I almost ran an errand for him when I went to the last Red Sox game. But he said something that put me off and I ended up staying home and watching the game on TV."

"What did he say?"

"He said I'd been with the Marshals for a long time and things aren't always what they seem. I've been 'sanitized' and no one would think of looking at me."

"Jim, isn't there one Marshal that you had more contact with? One that you could meet somewhere? One you trust? This guy sounds no good. If you've been sanitized by the Marshals does he mean that you're above reproach?"

"That's what I wondered. I developed a hell of a cold the morning I was supposed to go to Boston and called him and coughed and hacked and said I wasn't going. Perhaps another time."

"A real cold?"

"No, but two days later when I called you, you asked about the hum on the line. I'm finally free, no monitoring Maddy, and now I'm scared."

"You have to make contact with someone you trust. Maybe they're testing you. Maybe he's a rotten apple. Be careful.

"I've got to get back to work. The guys tease me about calling the beautiful dame I met on vacation especially since I took off my wedding ring. I can take that kind of ribbing. I still love you, Maddy." He hung up.

I went to my computer and wrote down everything I could remember from the conversation. When I got to the point where the guy said things aren't always what they seem, I got the shivers. I won't call Hal but I will keep this conversation for him to read when he gets back. The first postcard said "All things are not as they seem at all times." Is this strange Marshal sending me clues to help hang Jim for something? And why would he do that? Does he think I'm coming back and he can involve me somehow, in something? Or is he warning me away from Jim? Or is Jim trying to hit my sympathy button to get me back there? Should I call the US Marshal? No. Not until I talk to Hal. Something really weird is going on in Lowell, Massachusetts. Really weird. None of it makes sense.

CHAPTER THIRTY-SIX

Congressman Mason came to the Library around eleven on Wednesday morning. I was in my office catching up on some correspondence. Alice, my secretary and right hand person, pushed the intercom and said, almost in a whisper, "Congressman Mason is here to see you Mrs. Palmer."

"Ask him to wait just a moment. I'll be right with him."

"I could have said send him in but I read once that when dealing with an arrogant bully, make 'em wait a few minutes. From the phone call last night, I believe he falls into that category. I tidied my desk, counted to fifty and hit the intercom. "Alice, please show in the Congressman."

As he came through the door, I stood behind my desk and put out my right hand. "It is a pleasure to meet you personally, Sir. I must say you look much younger than your campaign ads."

He almost preened. I could see the wind had begun leaving his sails of anger.

"Mrs. Palmer. How long have you worked for the Library?"

"In what capacity, Congressman?"

"Haven't you always been director?"

"Oh heavens, no. I worked my way up. It took me fifteen years to achieve this position."

"And you've been director for how long?"

"Is there an end to this question, Sir? What difference does it make if I've been director two or twenty years. You've come to bitch about my treatment of your son. You've heard his side. Are you at all interested in mine? Or that of my staff?"

The wind was completely gone from his sails. He plopped down in the chair in front of my desk.

"Damnit, Madlyn, he's my only son."

"And I, Sir, am Mrs. Palmer."

"Mrs. Palmer, do you have any idea what it is like to have a son, raise him up and find out that he's lazy, arrogant, inconsiderate and lies?"

"No, I don't. I had a son, raised him up, sent him to college, saw him get a fine job and then get run over and killed by a hit-and-run driver. I can't imagine a son such as you've described."

Oh, I admit that was dirty pool. Now even his arrogant look vanished.

"All right. Tell me what happened yesterday."

"Do you want me to start with the staff meeting he arrived at ten minutes late or the discussion wherein I fired him?

"Oh, hell, begin at the beginning."

And I did, even using the words that Thad had used. The disrespect of others and of me. I told him that I was going to petition the Board to revoke his Library privileges. He terrified some of my staff, verging on harassment. He mocked others for their behavior. "And what angered me most was when he stood up, thrust out his scrawny chest and said, "Do you know who my father is?

"That, Sir, tipped me right over the edge. I spoke to him as a friend when I left Rudy's Monday evening and he didn't even know who I was. Did he? His mother asked. I didn't hear his answer but I will lay you odds it was not 'my boss', the director at the library, or Mrs. Palmer. Was it?"

Mason isn't that old a man - probably seventy. But at this very moment, he looks ninety-going on two hundred. "I apologize."

"Congressman, you know very well you cannot apologize for someone else, for their attitude or their behavior. I'd accept an apology from Thaddeus, but he will not be allowed back in this library ever again if I have anything to do with it."

"I don't know what to do."

"Send him to military school. Even one year will teach him to take orders.

"He looked at me as though I was suddenly surrounded by a heavenly glow."

"That may be what I have to do. His grades aren't bad but he'll never get into college. He can't complete an entry essay. His command of the language, as you have heard, is vulgar."

"Don't try for West Point. He'd need references and I'm not sure you'll find any."

"Well, our neighbor Frank Cartwright, he's on the library board, recommended Thad for this summer internship. Maybe…"

"I spoke to Mr. Cartwright yesterday. I felt an obligation to let him know that Thad didn't work out. I believe he won't write another reference."

He looked defeated. He took a check out of his pocket. "I was going to use this as bribe money to get him back in your good graces. I can see that you're out of good graces. So put it into the building fund or whatever the hell fund you've got going now."

He threw a check on the desk and walked out.

"Ten thousand dollars?" I chased after him. "Mr. Mason, are you serious?"

"Damn right. I haven't ponied up any money to the library in years." He walked out.

"Alice, did you hear that? The Library has just been given ten thousand dollars because we stood up to the Congressman."

"Do we tell the Board or the newspapers?"

I laughed. "The Board. But don't tell them why."

Believe me, the rest of the day was one of my very best as Director of the Library. Alice told the staff at breaks, and whenever she ran into them, that Congressman Mason donated ten thousand dollars to the library. At first, everyone thought Thad would be coming back. The girl eavesdrops and said, "No, just the opposite because Mrs. Palmer won't take him back."

I laughed all the way home. It was about six. I hadn't heard from Lee for a couple days so gave her a call. She had just heard from Larry for the first time since he left. He was fine and already missing us all. I said, "Why don't we gather the kiddos and go out for dinner? I've had a glorious day and need to tell someone I love.

"The idea struck her as a good one. She and the kids pulled into my driveway half an hour later. Where could we go to supper? How about Chinese? Anyone like Chinese? We all do and there's a small place we used to go that's still in business. Lee said, "Mom, we haven't been there since Dad left. Maybe it's changed.

"Maybe it has. Maybe for the better."

We were warmly welcomed. The old owners are still there. We had been seated for some time when Mae, the wife, came to the table and asked if I remembered her. I told her I certainly did and apologized for taking fifteen years to come back. Lee introduced her kids. "Wil, Mike, Laurie, this is Mae Wong. I know you've heard me talk about the good old days and how many diners it took to get free egg rolls here." They poured on the charm.

It was exciting to them to go someplace and meet people that knew their grandfather. Someone who knew their mother when she was their age.

Mrs. Wong expressed her condolences for Eddy. "He was my favorite boy." She didn't mention Wes but it's awkward - what do you say when someone just disappears? Her husband Bill would be back in a few minutes and will be so surprised and excited to see us.

Was I glad or sad we had come? I know the tears were very close to dropping. Lee was so delighted. I never knew how much she had enjoyed eating here. And we had from the time she was about seven until after she married Larry. She spun tales for her children and I could verify nearly every one. There were a few things I had not known - they were teenage secrets at the time.

Lee directed the menu for the kids; she was sure she knew what they would like best. I ordered a half order of orange chicken. Mae also brought me a small platter of rumaki - on the house. Wes and I always ordered the rumaki. I did cry a little then. I can't help it. Too much is happening now.

We spent nearly two hours eating and visiting with old friends. Lee had lost touch with their son and was delighted to hear he was a doctor in Simi Valley now. "I always knew he could do it. We had great dreams when he started med school."

She didn't add "And then Dad disappeared and we all put life on hold for a while." But she could have. That was why she lost track of her friend. I wonder now how many other friends were casualties of Wes' disappearance. I know I lost some.

A lot of chatter in the back seat going home; a deep silence in the front. It's amazing how you can put away happy things when something tragic happens. I have to start living again. We were almost all the way home when Lee asked what great thing had happened that I wanted to go to dinner? We laughed. I told her that I'll call her tomorrow. I don't want to spoil the Feeling tonight.

She shook her head. "Oh, Mom."

CHAPTER THIRTY-SEVEN

Jim called every night that week. I told him Larry had finally called Lee and he's okay. So we went out to dinner. To the Moon Palace and saw Bill and Mae. They are still making the best rumaki in the state. He was surprised it was the first time I'd been there in fifteen years. He just doesn't get it yet. Obviously, we grieved more than he. Of course, we had also lost Eddy.

"You don't understand at all, do you? I damn near quit living after you were gone and Eddy was killed. If I didn't have the job at the library, I could have curled up and died. Of course, going back full-time just when I did was providential. They made me Head Librarian and later changed the title to Director. The college education finally paid off. Of course, it's a City job and still doesn't pay really well."

"I didn't know you ran the place now, Maddy. You never mentioned that."

"I guess there were too many important things to talk about. How long are you going to work swing shift?"

"Three months is the longest unless you petition to stay on swing. It's okay but I tend to get up too late to really do anything. I get off at eleven, and it's often after one before I hit the hay. I'm getting old, Maddy. I don't wake up as easy as I used to do. But I agreed to trade shifts while Clancy's wife is undergoing some kind of chemotherapy. That'll be three months for sure. Maybe more. Clancy is permanent swing."

There wasn't much to say. He called every night. We talked about ten minutes. He complained about a lot of stuff but didn't mention the mystery Marshal again. That concerns me. Wes used to be able to smell a rat - he was suspicious of a lot of people. Now all of a sudden he is but he isn't.

I have to quit worrying about him. I still care but I still resent him. I lost fifteen years. A week of these calls and I realize I haven't kicked him to the curb as Hal and I had discussed. I'm not even sure any more exactly what I was going to say or how. It sounds to me that he's gotten into something more than nefarious. I keep urging him to contact someone in the Marshal's office he's sure of, someone he knows. This guy could be playing him for a sucker. He wants him to move stuff - and it sounds like he wants him to move it through the mail sorting center where he works. I asked him if he wouldn't have more problems then. I believe I have very little influence with him anymore but I have planted the seed that USPS gets pretty pissy when people use the mail for all the wrong reasons.

"Wes, please. Go to the last handler you had. The guy you mentioned to me the first day I was in Lowell. He sounds like a square shooter; an upright citizen. Don't do it for me. Do it for your grandchildren. They are so elated that maybe someday they can come visit you, meet you, get to know you. Do it for them. Contact a Marshal you know you can trust. You're not being monitored any more. This guy sounds awfully bad - and you feel it too."

"Yeah. He hasn't come out and said he wants to move contraband, but the less he says, the more I wonder about him. Maybe if he'd just say, Hey Jim, I want to send a couple kilos to my bro, it'd be easier. But I don't know what to make of him. He's a real quiet guy. But persistent as hell. I think maybe he has tapped my phone to be sure I'm not calling the authorities."

"Doesn't he know you have a cell phone?"

"I don't think so. I keep it on silent when I'm out and I am sure I've never mentioned it. And I wasn't allowed one for quite a while. So, no, I think he's unaware I have a cell."

"Take care of yourself. I don't know what else to advise other than find someone you know really is a Marshal. You've sort of been in this position before. And you know how that turned out"

As with most of the conversations, I made a note of this one in my computer. I'm ready to call the US Marshal myself but don't know where to start. What a mess.

Hal and Harrelson are evidently still chasing their case. He hasn't called. He warned me so I'm not worried. But since I first met him ten weeks ago, this is the longest period of time that I haven't heard from him. And, I miss him. I don't know if I find amazing or amusing.

Jim's calls stopped abruptly after I practically begged him to go to an U S Marshal he knew well; one he trusted. Four nights without a call. I don't miss his calls so much as worry why he isn't calling. He was really distressed that last call. I am sure it's a real crisis of some nature as I believe he's beyond trying to convince me to come back to Lowell. Something is definitely happening in his life. I'm not sure that even he has a clue what. I hope he goes for help.

The library is running along smoothly. The Board of Directors wonder how I ever convinced Tightwad Mason to contribute to the new growth fund. I told them we just see eye-to-eye on several issues, non-political issues, and he felt generous. There was a nice article in the paper and Congressman Mason called me to say thank you for your understanding. "By the way, Thaddeus is at a school in Utah designed for boys with behavioral problems. It's not a military school but they say they can change his attitudes toward life and living. Of course, this is not for publication, the organization suggested that his mother and I get some counseling so we don't undo everything when he returns home. Evidently, Edith and I are permissive parents to the point of kowtowing. Can you believe that?"

Of course, I couldn't. Of course, I do but would never tell the Congressman. Perhaps there's hope for the whole family.

Labor Day passed without notice, practically. Usually Lee and kids would have been here swimming and grilling. But everyone seemed so tied up in other things. Laurie thought her Dad might call. She's pretty sure they don't celebrate Labor Day wherever he is. I didn't push. They spent a lot of time here this summer. Kids are back in school and seem happy with their new classes.

Even Wil. He's a junior this year and has the usual blah reaction to things. He isn't interested in sports at all, except swimming. He's applied for the swim team but, as he hasn't ever been involved in sports at all, he's not sure he'll get in. There are tryouts to get on the team. I told him with all the swimming he's done over this summer alone, he should be a shoo in.

"That would be nice, Grams. Dad and Hal put a lot of effort into us this summer in the pool. I'd like to show them it paid off. I think I'd be a good addition to the team. This is the first year I've been interested in sports. Why should that be a handicap?"

"Wil, there are a lot of people, coaches especially, who believe to be really good in a sport you have to have invested in it your whole childhood. You have been a swimmer your whole childhood; just not competitive.

"I compete with my sister and brother every time we're in the pool. I don't win every time though."

"When are the tryouts for the swim team?.

"This Saturday morning."

"Do you know any of the current team members?"

"A couple, vaguely. None of my buds are swimmers, except Steve and Donnie, and they aren't interested in competition. We swim for fun. You know that."

Actually, I wasn't aware that kids swam for anything but fun. But I agreed. "Just remember all the tips you got from your Dad and Hal."

This was Thursday afternoon. He and Mike came to mow the lawn after school. Mid- September already. The summer has flown by. Laurie is in the eighth grade and hating it. She complains that the girls all act like babies. I wish I had the wisdom to explain to her that while she is only twelve, she's experienced so much more than her peers. With a Dad in the military, she has had to look at things differently than most girls. Instead, I told her that she was wise beyond her years because she was so damn smart. That made her laugh. She will be thirteen in a couple months.

Saturday morning Wil called at eight. "Think good thoughts, Grams. Tryouts start in a few minutes. Because I'm the new guy, I go first."

I wondered what kind of tryouts they have where the applicants go one at a time. "Call me when it's over. You'll ace it, Wil."

The house was cleaned by ten. No word from Wil. I baked cookies. No word from Wil. At 11:30 he called. "Grams, you will not believe it. I did everything I was told to do first go round and did it at my best. Dives, underwater, floats, baby stuff. Then a while later, I had to do stuff with three other guys. It wasn't as hard as zig and zag so I aced that test, whatever it was. Then, there was a six-man race; ten laps. Aced it. Came in first by 9 seconds. Then some sort of float test. Compared to the wiggle your toes float - this baby was so easy I was surprised it was considered a test. Aced it too. They had room for three new swimmers. Some sort of state law on number you have on a team in competition - like baseball. Coach announced two seniors and a junior - yeah, I made it. The coach asked me who I had been training with, you don't get that good alone. I told him my Dad was home for a month and he and a friend of his worked with me and my sibs."

"Coach said, "Let your Dad and his friend know that they should be teaching high school swimming. You are the product of excellent training." Can you imagine, Grams? Dad might be able to call tonight. Sure hope he'll be pleased. Tell Hal when you talk to him. Okay?"

"Hal's off on assignment but I'll definitely pass on the news that he's a good coach and you're on the school team."

"Thanks, Grams. Gotta run. Mom's here to pick me up." I settled down on the deck with a new book. I couldn't help but compare Wil to Thad. Thad is just a year older than Wil. They're like night and day. And the difference was in the parenting; I'm absolutely positive. Wil sounded so pleased; not with himself exactly but that he had done well because of his Dad.

That night Jim called. I had been right sort of. The guy had said he'd not been with the Marshals for long. Jim misunderstood him. He had not been with them for long as he had been dismissed a couple years ago. He had the understanding Jim was some sort of drug lord being hidden. He got it all mixed up thinking Jim had been more or less protected because of who he was, not what he knew. Jim went to the last guy he had contact with. "You suggested it and I finally realized I had to do something. One of the guys I work with had an idea I was trouble. He said he wrote to you twice to try and convince you to steer clear of me. He didn't say how he got the address but he had seen your picture and figured you were too nice a lady to get involved with me. He has no idea who I used to be or that I used to be someone else. Or who you really are. Why didn't you mention that he wrote you?"

"I don't know what he's talking about. To my knowledge, I have received no mail from someone you work with. Maybe he had a wrong address."

"No, he said he sent it to Ms Palmer because he couldn't remember your first name. He knew you were a librarian. But he said he sent you two postcards with warnings."

"Are you joking? Those postcards were warnings? I took them as warnings but couldn't figure out what the hell they were warning me about. He sent two old quotes. How was I supposed to know they were warnings regarding you? They weren't signed; no return address. How could I have deciphered what they meant? Good lord, I turned them over to the FBI.

Jim was quiet a long time. "Well, that's that. Guess I'll tell him you got them and decided maybe I was a bad choice. And then, you weren't sure they were about me or some other guy so you tossed them. Next time he should be more explicit."

"He may get a knock on his door from the FBI. The postcards were postmarked in Washington DC and being so mysterious, they're being tested for fingerprints. Do you want to tell him that? Because of the postmark, the FBI thought someone in a mail sorting center elsewhere could have routed them to DC for mailing. I hope that doesn't happen, but it could. Be prepared. They thought you had something to do with the postcards. You fit the profile. "What happened to your mystery Marshal?" I am chuckling. It's actually funny.

"I don't really know. But a team came out and debugged my house. I haven't seen him since."

"So the guy you went to knew who he was?"

"Yeah, I guess so. Thanks for the good advice, Maddy. You probably saved my bacon."

I gave him the news that Wil made the school swim team and then said good night. I typed everything into my computer. I don't know how much of it to believe. It sounds pretty farfetched.

CHAPTER THIRTY-EIGHT

Wil spent extra time at the pool He wanted to hone his diving skills. Hal taught him a lot about diving but we don't have a board. The coach said he'd be able to spend some extra time at school. No problem. The first meet went well. Wil's team won. Wil didn't compete in any diving. Says he's not good enough. But the fact he won or placed in every event he did enter was more than sufficient. The coach admitted to Lee that the school hadn't won a swim meet at all last year so he was excited.

Larry was thrilled with the news. Wil told him what the coach had said about him teaching swimming. Larry reminded Wil that you need a teaching certificate to teach in high school in California. Wil said, "Then get one, Dad. The Marines will put you through school." Larry laughed over that. He told Lee he was pleased Wil thought he could do anything. "How the hell do I live up to that, Sweets?" Lee didn't know. A few minutes later their tie line ended. Hopefully Larry can call next week.

Jim didn't call for a few days. In a way, I was relieved. It's hard work for me to stay upbeat while talking to him. He's changed a lot. He used to be the go getter, the leader of the pack. He's sounded timid and unsure of nearly everything the last few calls. I hate to admit it, but I've been going to the store more in the early evening instead of on the way home. Hoping I'll miss his call? Yep, that's the whole idea. But I never missed a call; he wasn't calling. While he didn't say goodbye last time, maybe he intended to. That's okay.

Wil is becoming BMOC much to his sister's chagrin. I told her that she wasn't in high school yet. How does she know these things and why does it bother her? All of her silly friends in the eighth grade have older sisters who are gaga over Wil. Can you imagine, Grams? Will!! I laughed at her.

She's probably thinks I was laughing with her.

It's almost the end of September. I floated the idea of a monthly schedule at the Library. We've worked on a weekly ever since I can remember. No one has ever complained but I think it'd allow for more personal planning if you knew a month ahead when you're working. I have a schedule sketched out and think it is fair and better than the weekly way. I have spent hours on it and think it's good.

Everyone gets a 3-day off stretch in the month and more weekend days off. Not necessarily Saturday and Sunday together. But for a long time I realized some employees seldom got a weekend day off. No one has ever complained but as I grow older, I am beginning to treasure weekend days. Hopefully working four ten hour days will not be a killer when you getting three days off that week.

I reviewed it twice more and was just ready to send it to my computer at the Library when the phone rang. It was after nine. Hope it's not an emergency.

It was Hal. "Lyn, Harrelson and I are at an airport in Tennessee. We are finally coming back to the land of milk and honey."

"Tennessee? That's mid-America if I ever heard. Case closed?"

"Indeed. Sure as hell took long enough but we did it."

"What time is it in Tennessee?"

"Probably around midnight or half past. Our plane boards in ten minutes. I just wanted to hear your voice, make sure you remember me, and to let you know I'll be available for dinner tomorrow. Or today, as the case may be."

"Tomorrow here. Wonderful. Dinner is at seven. Come early if you want to swim, or talk, or peel potatoes."

"I have missed your sense of humor, Lyn. See you tomorrow. Did I just invite myself to dinner?"

"You did and I accepted." We both laughed and he hung up.

For some reason I had pretty well convinced myself that the case he was chasing couldn't take this long and he was weaning himself from me - or weaning me from him. We have seen a lot of each other this summer. But he will be here tomorrow for dinner. The market closes at midnight. I put on my shoes and went shopping. This has to be a special dinner. Who knows where or what he's been eating?

It was after midnight when I went to bed. A pot roast is ready to go in the crock pot in the morning. I made a cheesecake tonight and it will be ready to be topped with peaches and whipped cream tomorrow when I get home.

I remember the chocolate cheesecake with hazelnuts I made one of the first times he was here. It looked spectacular. This cheesecake will be much better.

Alice and I reviewed the October schedule I have drawn up. I wasn't sure it would work as everything has been week to week for at least fourteen years. Maybe longer than that. She went over it employee by employee. "Mrs. P., you seem to have remembered birthdays. No one is scheduled on their birthday."

"Is that bad?" There are three birthdays in October; three different weeks.

"No, but we've always have cake on birthdays."

"Look at the footnotes." I had scheduled one afternoon to celebrate birthdays of the month. "A cake comes in at noon and everyone can or cannot gather then. But the cake is available the rest of the afternoon. We don't do presents so I thought this would work. You think it won't?"

"We could just skip the monthly cake and have an hour of cake the first day after the birthday."

She mulled it over. I could see she was seriously concerned about missing a cake on your birthday versus having your birthday off... "It'll work. And I think it's a good idea. You can get two pieces of cake if you want. When we only have an hour, it's kind of hard and sometimes the cake is good enough for a second slice."

Well, I admit, I had not taken a second slice of cake into the calculation. Alice is in her early thirties but there are days I swear she's fourteen.

I told her where I had saved the thirty-eight schedules on the server. "So you think we can post and distribute this today?"

"Absolutely."

"Add a large note at the bottom - maybe 24 point type. "This is a trial schedule. If you see anything you believe won't work, please see Mrs. P".

"Believe it or not, in an environment as small as a public library, a massive schedule change is a massive change. Or can be. There are thirty-eight people involved, most full-time. But I had found on the weekly schedule part-timers were sometimes working eight or nine four hour shifts in a row. That's not right.

The rule was no one worked more than five shifts in a week. If a part-timer worked Tuesday through Saturday one week, 5 shifts, but was assigned Sunday through Wednesday the next, 4 shifts. Rule satisfied. However, it was 9 shifts in a row. I just hope I haven't stirred up a hornet's nest.

We had an older employee who made up the schedule until he retired in August. He was a carryover from the last head Librarian, a long time carryover. When I got back from vacation, I assumed his job and decided weekly schedules don't work. Fairly.

After one o'clock the day dragged by - barely pushing the seconds past to make a minute. I toured the Library. I do that on occasion to check what's happening. Today I did it because I could not sit still. I keep thinking about dinner. What I have left to do. But, it was apparent that nearly everyone had already seen their new schedule. And they thought I was doing my job to check reactions. I was overwhelmed with the comments. Thank yous and Wow I have my birthday off and three days in a row off, what did I do to deserve that? When that person found everyone had a 3-day stretch off in the month, he hugged me as I passed through his area. Working four ten hour shifts was not an issue. It made sense. He'd still get his forty hours. Yea. Just goes to show-what's happened before and done for years isn't always the best. Too bad Jacob didn't retire sooner. I had never really paid attention to the work schedule. It took me days to do this one month, but I have a formula now.

I went home, took a shower, changed my clothes and went to work on what hopefully would be the nicest and best meal I've ever made. The doorbell chimed at 6:40. I looked at the clock, surprised. From a day that crawled to one that raced, well this was it. I was pretty much ready. The table looks great and the aroma from the resting pot roast was delicious. I opened the door to a man who looked extremely happy to be where he was. He had a beautiful small bouquet of flowers in one hand and a package in the other.

"Did you ring the bell with your nose?" He laughed and handed me the flowers. Then hugged me as though he was afraid I'd get away.

"My god how I've missed you. I believe I have never been so lonely in my entire life. This was the longest month of the year."

To be honest, I was surprised. I've never seen him so up. That's the only word for it – UP. And I didn't expect such a declaration. "It really has been long. More like forty-nine days than twenty-nine."

He was all smiles. "You counted the days?"

How could I tell him it was because so much has happened. I admit though, I missed him a lot. I got a short vase and put water in it. The flowers looked perfect on the kitchen table. "You have a good eye for flowers. They look as though you chose them just for that spot."

"I chose them because they were the most colorful flowers in the shop. I'm celebrating being home and having closed the nastiest case of the decade. I chose them because I wanted to give them to you. They are almost as beautiful as you are. Almost."

Wow. I am bowled over. What do you say in a situation like this?

"Agent Tucker, you've been gone a long time and are delirious. Be careful. You may say something you regret or I take seriously.".

"That is a consideration, Lyn. I am really happy to be home - er, back in California. You never realize how good it is until it isn't.".

"Go wash your hands. Supper in ten minutes." He trotted down the hall to the guest bathroom. I had to smile. He's really a good looking man, especially when he's happy.

Dinner went exceptionally well. I promised dessert and coffee shortly.

"Dessert?" "Yes, dessert. Fresh peach cheesecake. You do like peaches, don't you?"

He laughed. "You're the cream in my coffee; you're the peach in my pie. Lyn, I love peaches."

That he should sing that line tickled me. It is one of my father's favorite tunes. "I am pretty sure those aren't the real lyrics, Hal."

"I know the real lyrics, I don't want to say something I might take seriously later."

"Oh, Hal, you are such a wonderful man." He blushed.

"Speaking of such, you haven't opened my gift yet." He went to the counter where he had set it when he came in. "We really weren't in a boutique area of the world most of the time we were working, but one afternoon Tom and I were in downtown Murfreesboro. There was a small jewelry store next to the building we were using as decoy cover. I spied something in the window and told Tom to rap on the window if we needed to move. I made a purchase and was back outside before he said, 'now.' I risked my cover for this because it reminds me of you." He said it matter-of-factly but I think it was a real issue. Wonder if Tom Harrelson made comment? Or what comment?

With that story, I opened the small box with great caution. Inside was a jeweler's box, blue velvet. Inside that was a pendant on a gold chain. Two books together suspended on a gold loop from the chain. They were enameled with their fore edges in gold. The clasp was a lobster claw. I took the necklace out gently. The enamel is bright red with blue lines. I was shaking a bit; what a surprise; so beautiful. The clasp was so easy to open. I put it on.

"How does it look?" I turned to Hal. I know I was flushed; I could feel the warmth in my face. "Oh, Hal, this is too expensive a gift for me to accept. It's too beautiful to refuse. You are so mean."

He looked like the cat that swallowed the canary. Pleased with himself. "Then you like it?"

"Oh, yes. Thank you for risking cover. I realize that's a serious matter."

He kissed me very gently. "I think I've risked my cover again. It's difficult being Agent Tucker when I'm with you. Like the song really goes, you're the cream in my coffee, you're the salt in my stew, you will always be my necessity, I'd be lost without you." He didn't sing it this time. He kissed me again.

I cried.

We sat together not saying anything for several minutes. I don't know what he was thinking but I realized I had never felt so at peace. I felt safe. And loved. Not wanting to break the spell, I knew I had to do it. "Ready for dessert? Coffee with it?"

"Absolutely."

Together we cleared the table and loaded the dishwasher. I took the cheese cake from the fridge. It looked as I planned...perfect. We sat at the table to eat. He said, "Okay, you've heard all you can hear about my month, how was yours?"

"Well, the best news first. Wil tried out for the school swim team. He's a junior and has never tried out for sports before. He was sure he'd not make the team because of that. The coach asked who he'd been training with and he said my Dad and a friend of his. Coach Snider thinks you should be teaching swimming. He told Wil that his technique was so perfect in so many areas that Wil's Dad and friend had to be professional swimmers. Guess Wil said. No, Sir, they're both Marines.

The school didn't win a single meet last year. They've participated in two and won both so far this year. "Laurie says her brother is becoming BMOC. He's working on his board diving. The coach says that's his only weak point and it's not that weak."

I could see the pride wash over Hal's face. "Does Larry know?"

"Yes, he has called home twice. And Wil got to break the news the second time. Larry is so pleased. No remarks about the summer, just good boy. Show 'em the Baxter way to win."

"What else?"

"Remember I told you about getting rid of Thaddeus Mason? Did I tell you his father donated ten thousand dollars to the Library? Mainly because I stood up to him!"

"My god, Lyn. What a triumph! And the Library actually benefited."

"Well, just getting Thaddeus out of there was a benefit. He was a real burr under the saddle for most of the staff. Mason has sent him off to Utah to a behavioral school."

"Anything else?"

I told him about the dinner Lee, the kids and I shared at the Moon Palace. The kids were excited as their mom has actually told them a few stories about the place. And to think you could be gone for so long and people still know you and remember things about you. "It was a trip down memory lane, Hal. But a very cleansing one."

"Wow. Anything else?"

"I've talked with Jim and he's told me a wild story. I've recapped the conversations on my laptop so you could read through them. I'm not at all sure any or all of it is fairy tale or truth. Do you want to read them? If he's truthful, you can stop the postcard fingerprinting exercise."

"Let's see what you've got.".

I refilled our coffee cups and opened the laptop. I had tried to be concise so there wouldn't be too many questions. Must have succeeded as he read for about twenty minutes, making notes in a small notebook he had in his pocket. He reread the last conversation at least twice.

"May I have another slice of cheesecake, Lyn?"

That surprised me. I took the cheesecake from the fridge and cut another slice. I refilled the coffee cups again.

"Believe him. We came back to rumors of trouble in the US Marshal office. And it sounds exactly like the story Jim told you. A bad apple with incorrect data, ousted from the service, trying to blackmail certain FWP participants into working for him. There were three. Two went along with him; the third reached out for help. Must have been Jim. I'll be damned; we thought it was one of those stories that circulate that are only half truths. The office will be interested to learn that the Marshals actually did screw up. But it still doesn't explain the postcards to me. Nothing in the rumor about that. But, if the guy was a good friend of Jim's he may have thought he was saving you from a bad deal."

"But unsigned old quotes?"

"My dear, you are a Librarian. Librarians know every old quote in the world and they can just feel when someone is doing wrong. Don't you know anything? I feel if we really study the quotes, we can figure out what he was trying to tell you. Of course, it would've been smart for him to let you know who they related to. Misguided but faithful. At least, he did tell Jim or we'd still be wondering. The lab found your fingerprints, your mailman's and several partial sets they couldn't identify."

He sat quietly eating his peach cheesecake. "You know, Lyn. This is the best peach cheesecake I have ever eaten."

"Have you eaten many peach cheesecakes, Hal?"

"Nope. But this is definitely the best."

CHAPTER THIRTY-NINE

We sat together quietly for a long while. Next to each other, his arm around my waist. "You know, Lyn, I think we should get to know each other. Listening to your litany of things that happened while I was gone made me realize that, while I truly believe I love you, I don't know anything about you? Does that make sense?"

I leaned my head on his shoulder. I know I know little about him so figured I'd ask questions first. "Yes, it does. Are you from Southern California? I have the impression you are."

"Born and bred. Altadena was home for a long time. My folks moved to Apalachicola, Florida seven years ago. I call them once a week unless I'm working. They're both in their eighties and love to fish. So, it was a logical choice, they say. I don't get down too often so they're always glad to see me when I do make it. I think you pretty well know my professional time line. When I was in high school, six three was still really tall. Nowadays, it's kind of standard. I played basketball at John Muir and baseball, second base usually. I wasn't exceptionally great at either but could stand my ground against the competition. I've never married. Have had a couple of lady friends but I was too reserved or old-fashioned or not spontaneous enough, or something. I'm not really sure what my deficiency is but I just never measured up. My mother says they were just the wrong women. I figured they were pretty nice but maybe nice wasn't what they wanted me to feel. I don't know. I quit looking. I am pretty sure it's no crime to be single. Then all of a sudden I realize I'll be fifty-seven November 19th."

"November 19th? Guess whose birthday that is? Oh my god, she'll be in seventh heaven."

"Laurie?"

"She'll be thirteen. We have tried to figure out why that child has glommed on to you as she has. She's no shrinking violet but she's never immediately become attached to someone, especially an older male, as she has to you. Maybe it's just the birthday....birds of a feather, you know."

"Oh, shoot, I thought it was my charm and good looks."

"They may have played a part. She thinks you are really special. I am sure you have noticed. Cookies specially arranged on a plate. The tallest glass for lemonade. Personal instructions on how to construct a Crazy Cook salad. Pulling you in from the front door by your hand."

We chuckled. "When her birthday comes up - and it will soon - you can act surprised and say 'that's my birthday too'. We might be surprised at her reaction."

"Now you know everything about me, Lyn. How about you?"

"I was born and raised less than a mile from where we are sitting. I wasn't expected for a few weeks and when Mom went into labor, Dad freaked. I was delivered by two firemen on Flag Day, June 14th. My Dad was thrilled; his favorite sister's birthday was the 14th. Her name was Madelyn. But my Dad said skip the E - he knew from experience no one ever pronounced it anyhow. My brother Edmond was killed on the USS Stark in 1987. My Dad is a geologist, Mom passed in 2001. Dad travels the world and sends picture postcards once in a while. I think he's in Australia now. I married in 1980 and I think you know the rest."

"Now we have statistics."

"But we don't know each other. Right?" I could see that he hadn't really thought beyond data.

"Right. I guess we have to spend some time together to get to know one another. And actually, we have done that this summer. I've gotten to know a lot about you. Stuff you probably don't realize. It's obvious family means a great deal to you. You are kind, and gracious, and caring. Oh, and forgiving. I am sure most women would be put out with my passing out on the couch. You didn't laugh at me and you didn't criticize. You pointed the way to the shower, clean clothes and then cooked breakfast for me. You invited me to spend the afternoon checking something you were interested in but you didn't make it an issue. You entrusted me to find your missing husband. You cried in all the right places. I think you are the genuine article. I've watched you with your children and grandchildren and gone home at night jealous."

How can I possibly respond to this? I am overwhelmed, totally. Unable to say a word, I turned and kissed him with all the passion that has been building in me. He returned the kiss, Oh, so gently.

"I've watched you too, Agent Tucker. My granddaughter isn't the only grandchild who admires you. And you treat them with the respect most people reserve only for adults, or superiors. My son-in-law bonded with you immediately. It's not because you're both Marines. He's a very discerning man. He sees something in you that he likes and trusts. He normally would not ask someone he'd known so short a time to look out for his family. You work together well - whether it's at the grill or grilling the kids in the pool. My daughter has been wary of you because of all the love she feels flowing toward you from her family. How can she trust someone who so easily has enchanted her entire family? I think she's warming up to you though."

"Do you like movies? Maybe once in a while we could find a movie we'd both like. Then stop for ice cream afterwards. And if we can't find a movie we both like, we could find some old film on Netflix or something and still have ice cream."

"Hal, we could just have ice cream on the deck and watch the stars."

"You do swim, don't you?"

"Yes, I do. I taught the grand kids. Their Dad is in the Marines and Lee has worked some odd hours. I swim when they're here. I saw a program about swimming alone after fifty-five so I don't. But I do swim. I don't zig; I don't zag; but I can float."

He laughed. How I love his laugh. "It sounds to me that we could be a perfect pair. Want to give it a chance? Madlyn Palmer, will you go steady with me? It's a serious commitment, Lyn. I don't have a class ring to give you but maybe the pendant can be my promise to you to be a good boyfriend, a steady beau."

I fingered the pendant. It pretty much sums up my life. The fact that it is two books and not one makes me wonder if he had this in mind all along. And, I feel that he would believe that a promise ring at this point would be overreach. He is such a mystery.

"Is that such a difficult question, Lyn? Should I not be asking it now?"

"No, it's not difficult at all. I am just a bit overwhelmed. Hal, I'm going to be sixty. Are you sure you want to team up with an old broad like me?"

"Okay Librarian, what is one of Jules Renard's most famous quotes about age?"

"Jules Renard. The French author who died in 1910 or so?"

"Yes, that one."

"Are you sure I know it?"

"You're a librarian, of course you know."

I laid my head on his shoulder. Jules Renard. Ah, yes. "It's not how old you are, it's how you are old."

"See? Librarians know all the quotes. Age doesn't mean diddly. And you aren't quite two and a half years older than I. My Mother is four years older than my Dad. Age means nothing."

"Yes."

"Yes, what?" He looked really confused.

"Yes, I'd like to go steady with you, Hal."

Who would expect at fifty-nine to be 'going steady' with someone? I had a couple 'steady' boyfriends in school but no long lived relationships. And Wes? We never went steady, per se, he didn't offer a token of faithfulness until he gave me an engagement ring. Maybe the earlier women in Hal's life were right - maybe he is too reserved or old-fashioned or not spontaneous. But it's not a crime to be any of those things either. I rather like them.

CHAPTER FORTY

October kind of sneaked up on me. When I'm happy, I lose track of time. The new schedule at the Library seemed to change the atmosphere somehow. One of the older custodians knocked on my door after the Tuesday morning staff meeting. I wondered why he hadn't said something in the meeting and, fortunately, I didn't ask him. He knocked on my door. Alice was on break. "Do you have a minute, Mrs. P."

"Of course, Albert, come in and sit a spell." He sat in a chair across the desk from me.

"Mrs. P, do you know long I've worked here at the Library?"

"Well, let me think." I counted on my fingers. "I think thirty-one or thirty-two years, Albert."

"Yes, ma'am. thirty-two years come March."

I waited. I know he didn't come just to remind me how long he'd worked here or even to verify I knew.

"I took my schedule home to show my wife - I always do that of course. She looked at it and asked if we have someone new at the Library and I told her no, Mrs. P. took over the scheduling – Jacob retired. She said that I should come tell you that it is obvious to her that you respect us employees. She pointed out to me how comfortable my schedule is now. Comfortable is the word she used, Mrs. P. Comfortable. She's planning us a little trip out of town on my 3-days off this month. And inviting the Preacher and his wife to dinner on my Sunday off. Mrs. P. I haven't had a Sunday off in twenty years. And a friend is getting married on my Saturday off. I won't miss a day's pay to go. Mrs. P, comfortable isn't a big enough word. I was thinking to retire after my birthday next year. I don't think so now. I'm comfortable."

"Well, I am grateful for your wife's pleasure. And very pleased you won't be retiring next year. You are a very valuable employee, Albert. Very valuable." I got up and went around the desk to hug him and he hugged me back. He left the office with a real jaunty spring in his step.

This is not what I had expected, hoped for, or planned. But it's a good thing. A very good thing. After Albert left my office, I sat there wondering if all changes can be this impactful, this good.

Now that I have agreed to go steady with Hal, there are going to be changes. No doubt.

Will my daughter react as graciously as Albert when she realizes that I will never remarry her father under any name? She's been bristly since the divorce is final. She so desperately wants a reunion. There is no way I can explain to her what I've been able to convey to Hal, and to Jim. Things seemed okay to her, so they were. There were very few times she may have realized how great a struggle it was for me to make ends meet. There's no way she can understand resentment. And even though I'm softening on that, I don't love her Dad. He seems too content where he is - and I could not be. I believe I have changed and he has not. She'll blame Hal. My feelings for her father were set in stone before I had any feelings for Hal. Lee may not believe it but I know it is true. Why does living have to be so difficult some times?

Several employees commented on my books pendant. I told them all it was a gift from a dear friend. It looks so rich and yet so simple. I have worn it every day since he gave it to me. One of the first things Hal did ask, during our get to know you conversation, was if I preferred dinner out on a Friday or a Saturday evening. I asked, "Do you dance?" He gave me an odd look. "Well, I took Cotillion in high school. My father insisted a well-bred man should at least be able to waltz."

"Do you dance? I know you can, but do you?"

"I haven't in a long while.""

Do you enjoy dancing?"

He stammered. "I don't really know. It's not something I do regularly. Why do you ask?"

"I love to dance. I love good music. And there are a few restaurants here in the San Gabriel Valley that offer dancing and dinner. Usually on Saturdays."

"Could we practice first? I'm more than rusty. I'm not sure how much I remember."

"Come over Friday and we'll dance on the deck. I'd never embarrass you in public."

"Want dinner first and then we'll dance the night away; or the will night dance me away?"

"You may bowl yourself over but the night will never harm you."

"I'll pick you up at seven. Over dinner you can tell me what kind of dances you like and I'll tell you if I know anything about them at all. If I fail miserably, will you still love me?"

I laughed and said, "Well, I'll have to think that over."

For a minute I think he didn't realize it was a joke. Then I'm sure he saw me smiling. I know he has a good sense of humor but evidently it hasn't been in use much more than his dancing skills. There are so many little restaurants in this area. Hal seems to know a lot of them. Of course, he doesn't cook much either, probably.

On Friday, he chose a place I'd never been. And I really enjoyed it. The food was great and the people were friendly. He says he's here for breakfast usually. I realized then I don't know where he lives. I'll have to ask later.

It was after 8:30 when we reached my house. I turned on the family room lights and the deck lights. I have a very great record player and some super dance records. Yes, vinyl. We had established at dinner that he was still familiar with the waltz and sort of the fox trot. So that's what we started with. He's better than he knows. We called it a night around 10:30. Hal was quite exhilarated. He didn't step on me once.

"Now tell me again why we're doing this?"

"There are some nice restaurants with good dance floors. One or two dances, a drink, and dinner and it's a special evening. If you find you don't really like dancing, we'll just eat elsewhere. I have missed dancing a whole lot. I realize that's not your fault. Perhaps I'm being selfish but I was brought up to believe dancing was a fine date. The Library holds a fund raising gala every year that includes dancing. I hope you would care to escort me and dance."

"That gala is when?"

"December 10th. I'll add your name to the mailing list if you give me your home address. The invitations go out November 5th, I think.

"He lives in a small, older apartment complex just a few blocks from Lee's. Nice neighborhood.

"I have a library card, Lyn. So I am probably on the list already." Of course, he would be the type man who owns a library card. Well, that's okay. I know now where he lives.

After he left I panicked. I agree to go steady with this man and am now imposing myself and my desires on him. This isn't good. It may change his mind about me. Maybe I'm not the gentle, kind, understanding person he believes me to be. How can I take back this evening? I find someone who loves me and I'm going to blow it. Is dancing that important? Is it?

CHAPTER FORTY-ONE

Lee called early Saturday morning to ask if the kids could come over in the afternoon. She would like to go to a Blue Star meeting and it might last a couple hours. Even though Wil is sixteen she'd rather they were supervised. Of course, when should I expect them? The meeting is at two here in town. So around 1: 30 probably.

When Hal left last night, he asked if I had plans for Saturday. I told him not that I was aware of so I called him. He sounded half asleep.

"Did I wake you? I'm sorry."

"No, no, I wasn't asleep. I was listening to some music. You got me going last night and I realized I have a CD of my Dad's that is some pretty smooth music. What's up?"

"I told you I had no plans for today. Lee just called. She's going to a Blue Star Meeting and wondered if the kids could come over. It's nice enough to swim. Do you want to come swim today? They'll be here early afternoon."

No hesitation. "Hey, that would be great. Haven't seen them for a while. Can we coax Grams into swimming too?"

"It won't take much coaxing. I haven't been in the pool for a couple months I think."

"Terrific. Do you have a yellow bathing suit?"

"By chance, I do. Why?"

"I just think you must look terrific in a yellow suit."

"Well, come see. I didn't mention I might call you so you will be a surprise."

"I love surprises - even when they're me." He was laughing when he hung up.

When the kids arrived, I was in my yellow swim suit and a long shirt. "You're going to swim with us today? Hooray. Do you want to learn to float with your toes?"

"Well, I don't know about that." Peals of laughter. They were changed and in the pool almost immediately. We did laps first. I always do laps first. And then it turned into a four-man race. I noticed that Wil's turns at the end of the pool have gotten really quick. After I came in second twice, I pulled up on the side and declared I was out of shape. I saw Hal come through the breezeway and he put his finger to his lips. He quietly went into the dressing room. The kids were unaware he was here.

In a few minutes he came out and ran across the yard and yelled as he dived into the pool. Not a cannonball, just a clean dive. What a lot of fun. Three kids ganged up on him and laughed and shouted. "You sneaked up on us. Did Grams know you were coming?"

He swam over to the edge where I was sitting.

"Thanks for the yellow suit, Lyn." I slid off the rim and we stood arm in arm for a few minutes. Mike yelled, "Let's lap again." And the five of us swam the length of the pool a couple times.

Hal pulled up to the edge and said, "No wonder you guys swim like fish; your Grams is a mermaid." We just swam around for a few minutes before I got out of the pool. I toweled my hair and sat on one of the pool chairs. The kids wanted to zig-zag. Hal said, "Well, with only one calling it's not as good." That was okay. They wanted to anyhow. I wrapped my towel around me and went to the deck. I need a glass of lemonade.

I watched them play for about an hour. Then I called out, "Anyone want ice cream?" Silly question. By the time they were out of the pool, I had gathered bowls, spoons, scoops, two flavors of ice cream and two flavors of syrup. Everyone made his own sundae. Laurie said, "Grams, my birthday is coming up pretty soon. You told me to think about what I wanted to do for my birthday. I've been thinking." I looked over her head at Hal. He was grinning. I could sense he was getting ready to surprise her.

"You have a birthday soon? How old are you going to be?"

"Thirteen."

"Oh, gracious, another teenager. When will this happen?"

"November 19th."

If I didn't know him, I would swear he had no idea that was her birthday. "Really? November 19th?"

"Yeah. That's it."

"There's some mistake. You can't have that birthday, Laurie. That's my birthday and I've had it longer than you have."

"November 19th is your birthday? No way. You're teasing me."

"No, I'm not. Ask your grandmother."

"Grams?"

"Yes, Laurie, Hal's birthday is November 19th. He's going to be really old though so maybe he'll let you have it alone. Though he's probably used to it and might not."

"Come on, Hal. How old are you going to be?" Now she had to know how old he was. I had the feeling she'd fight for the date until she realized it made no difference.

"Are you ready for this? I'm older than your Dad and almost as old as your Grams."

"No you're not. Grams? How old is Hal going to be?"

"Promise you'll still love him?" Her head bobbed up and down. The boys are standing by – actually interested. "Fifty-seven."

"No he's not."

"Yep, he is." "Wow Hal, for an old guy, you sure are young." Hal and I roared.

He looked at me, "See. It's not how old you are, it's how you are old." We finished our sundaes and the four of them decided to float awhile. I took the dishes and stuff into the house and put the ice cream away.

I was just loading the dishwasher when Lee came in" "You swam today? Kids still in the pool?"

"Yes to both." She went out on the deck.

Then she came back in. "Is that Hal Tucker with them in the pool?" "It is. You know I don't like to leave them unsupervised."

She started to say something then evidently decided not to. She went out on the deck and waved. The kids yelled, "One more lap and we'll be up." Hal came with them and greeted her warmly. She wasn't rude but didn't seem exceptionally cordial either.

"We were discussing Laurie's birthday. Has she mentioned what she would like to do?"

Lee shook her head. "No, I'm surprised she hasn't brought it up before."

"It's three weeks away. Guess she just thought of it."

I didn't mention it was Hal's birthday also. I'll let Laurie or the boys tell her that. Meanwhile, I don't know if Laurie has decided what she wants to do for her birthday. We got so far afield with Hal's surprise. Laurie called an hour later. "Grams, we got side tracked when we were talking about birthdays. Mom is not too happy that it's Hal's birthday too. She thinks I won't get anything special. I told her you promised that anything within reason is your present. Is bowling within reason? We were talking about bowling when we were swimming. Hal says he can't remember ever bowling. Can we go bowling and invite Hal instead of another friend?"

"Laurie, bowling is definitely within reason. As for who you invite - that's up to you. If you'd rather invite Hal instead of a girlfriend, I have no problem with that. Or you can invite Hal and a girlfriend."

"Well, that's what I'd like to do. Invite Hal. But Grams, when we go back to your house for cake, can we have a cake for Hal too? Make it a surprise party for him. The guys think that'd be a neat trick. Hal would sure be surprised. And it would be only right." Hal is sitting within ear shot of me. I doubt that he's listening but then, he's heard his name so he maybe is. "Yes, that would work. I can do that. It is your birthday."

"He's close by, isn't he?"

"Yes, indeed."

"Okay then. It's settled. We go bowling, to Rudy's and to your house for Hal's surprise party. Is that a plan or is that a plan?"

"Laurie, it is an excellent plan. We'll have to start at two o'clock to fit it all in."

"Okay. The guys and I will plan Hal's party, except for the cake. You know, Grams. We sure like him."

"Well, Sweetie, you aren't alone."

She giggled. "Yeah, we know. I hung up and said, "We finally got around to planning Laurie's birthday. Actually, all the input I have is paying and baking a cake."

"So what did she decide?"

"She wants to go bowling." "You're joking."

"Nope, and I understand you will be invited." He got up and walked over to me.

"Lyn, you have one hell of a nice family. I love you all." He hugged me and said, "Are we eating in or out?"

"Either or. Your choice. But in is fine with me." Frankly, I hadn't planned on seeing Hal today. I had bought some fresh crab at the market; going to indulge a little. I have enough to make two crab Louie salads. I have hard boiled eggs, avocado, tomatoes, lettuce. Yes, that will be dinner. Better get the dressing made now so it blends a bit. After the kids and Lee had gone home, we swam for a while. We're both dressed but in our bare feet.

Hal asked, "Do we have time to practice the fox trot before dinner?"

"I need to prepare a dressing but then, yep, we have time. Let's stay in the family room. I don't feel like putting on my shoes." I don't know why he laughed at that, but he did. He brought the record player inside and got things set up while I made my favorite spicy Thousand Island dressing.

CHAPTER FORTY-TWO

My daughter is being a pain in the ass. Two days before Laurie's birthday she learns that Laurie has invited Hal, and only Hal, as her special birthday guest. She hopes he knows where the Crosley Lanes are. Evidently, he's not being invited to ride to the party with everyone else. When Laurie heard that, she said that she would ride with Hal to make sure he knew where the bowling lanes were located. That didn't help at all.

Laurie called me at the Library, absolutely furious. "Laurie, you know what your Mother's problem is with Hal, don't you?. "Yeah, Grams. He's your friend and she thinks that why you don't want to remarry Gramps."

"Laurie, between you and me, Hal and I are good friends but that didn't happen until after I went to Massachusetts. He seems to be the only one that understands that people change a lot in fifteen years. I no longer love your Gramps as more than just a friend. I could talk to Hal about how and why I thought Gramps and I changed and weren't really suited to each other. I could talk to him because he hadn't already formed an opinion about what should happen. I do like Hal a lot. And he will be upset to learn that your Mom is going to penalize all of us because of her ideas. He may decide he shouldn't come. Ask her to call me, or better yet, come up to my house later so we can discuss this."

"Do you think she'll come see you?" "I don't know. But we have to give her a chance to do what is right before she hurts Hal's feelings."

"Love you, Grams. I hope you can pound some sense into my Mother."

"Hadn't planned on any pounding, but I will try very hard. There's more than a single birthday party riding on this."

"Yeah, I figured that."

"Laurie, you know that I love you?"

"Of course, Grams. But you should be able to love anybody you want to - not just family." "Thank you. I knew you understood."

And I certainly hope her mother has the same wisdom as her almost thirteen-year-old. I can only imagine what had to have been said for Laurie to call me at the Library. I've never heard her quite so distressed. She has never called me at work before. On the way home I stopped to pick up bread and milk. When I got home, Lee and the kids were sitting in their car at the curb. She used to walk up, now she's driving? Oh, well. I pulled into the driveway and took my groceries to the door. They waited until I had unlocked the door before anyone got out of the car. The kids were subdued but didn't look exceptionally disturbed.

Their mother however had that righteous indignation look she wears so well. "You're usually home earlier."

Bit of a snap. I heard it well. "Occasionally I feel the need to buy bread and milk."

The kids went out on the deck and sat on the top step. Evidently, they don't expect to stay long. I put my groceries away. "Would you like a cup of coffee?" Lee said nothing but I measured coffee into a filter and started a pot anyhow. I usually do for my own supper. "I don't think coffee quite makes it." "How about a martini? I don't have any beer."

"Be serious, Mother. I came to talk to you about Laurie's birthday party and her choice of guests."

"I think it is so wise of you to allow your children a choice of guests to their parties." Oh, what a glare. But it shut her up for a minute.

"You know very well what I mean, Mother."

"Apparently, I don't, Aralee. Would you like to sit at the table or in the living room for your talk?" She pulled out a chair in the kitchen and sat down. The coffee was done. I poured myself a cup and sat across from her. She looked slightly bewildered but must have realized she'd already declined coffee.

"My daughter wants to invite your friend Hal to her birthday party." The stress on your friend was definite.

"I thought Hal was her friend also. Her friend, her brothers' friend, her father's friend."

"At thirteen, she should be inviting little girl friends to her birthday party."

"It's not really a party, Aralee. It is a chosen function that her grandmother is paying for as a gift for her birthday. I have done this for the boys as well."

"Well, Wil didn't invite Hal to his gift function."

"Aralee, none of us even knew Hal then. We met him the next day. You were here. Remember? You seem extremely upset primarily because it is Hal. Your father used to tell you to not hate anyone until you knew them well enough to hate them really good."

"Funny you should reference something my Father said."

"Why? I was married to him for a very long time. I reference him frequently when appropriate."

"Then why are you so damned determined to not remarry him? Everything is legal now. I think that Hal has influenced you because he's interested in you himself. He should stay out of family business."

"Aralee, perhaps you should stay out of your parents' business. Your Father and I have come to an agreement that we don't 'fit' anymore. We've both lived alone for fifteen years; he loves it. I don't. Because of circumstances, and public opinion, he will never return to Southern California. And I will never move to Massachusetts. We aren't the same people we were fifteen years ago. What about that is so hard for you to understand? I resent that I was married to him all that time and he was single. He had not a care in the world. He couldn't fail. He had backup. I had nothing. I resent that. How can you not see that? He likes his lifestyle. Things are good for him."

"Well, Hal is sure being friendly."

"Aralee, what is wrong with that? I am not married and neither is he. Hal is a good person who has a tough job. Think back on when we first met him. Did he come on strong to either of us? No, of course not. He was kind, considerate, and almost as upset as we were. Over the weeks, circumstances has put him in contact with me and my family many times. And he likes us. And, Aralee Ilene Palmer Baxter, I like him. He's concerned about my well-being He's asked me to see him exclusively. That is so funny as I have seen no one for fifteen years. I lost fifteen years of my life because of your Father. Hal is not trying to make up for those fifteen years. He just wants the next fifteen to be kind to me, good for me. I care very much for him. Your children can see and understand that. They like him too but not because he likes me but because he cares for them. If Laurie wants to invite a caring friend for her birthday, why are you trying to block it? Because you don't like him? You don't know him well enough to not like him as strongly as you think you don't. But keeping him away from the bowling alley is not the way to show your disapproval. He won't come if you are that insistent but he'll be here for cake; he'll be at Rudy's for supper. You can't keep him from either of those places because he will be with me - they're my gift to Laurie. So make up your mind right now. Are you going to give Hal a chance? You might actually like him. Is he invited to the bowling alley or not? It's decision time."

I refilled my coffee cup and sat down again. I can't read her at all. Her face is stone. She's not looking at me either. Without warning she laid her head on her arms and started to cry. Well, it was more like bawling. Loud and messy. I put a tissue in her hand. She blew her nose. The tears were falling but the bawling had ceased. All I could do was drink my coffee and wait. I looked at the clock.

Nearly five minutes later, she raised her head. "Are you going to marry, Hal?"

"He hasn't asked me to marry him. He's just asked me to date him so we can get to know each other. He may decide we're not a good match. I don't know. I may decide we don't fit. He hasn't asked but if he does, I'll probably ask when." I handed her the box of tissues.

She wiped her face and blew her nose again. "I'm a real screw-up, Mom. Hal can come to the party." That's progress. I was afraid to say anything else at the moment. I sipped a bit more coffee and waited. "Forgive me, Mom, for putting my nose into your business. I guess when you have a dream it's hard to let it go. We've found Dad. I should be glad about that. I never thought about what all those years meant to you or how they affected you. You always just soldiered on. I am sorry. I really am sorry for being such a butt head."

All I could do was hug her. I'm sorry too because I can't say 'that's okay.' I'm sure I'll get around to it but right now, I can't. As long as she understands, and she seems to, I'll let it go. "Go wash your face, Lee. The kids will think I've been beating you or something." She went to the bathroom and I went to the deck. "Hey, guys, what if we order a couple pizzas? Nobody feels like cooking dinner."

Laurie said, "Is everything okay? "Well, Hal is coming to the party." All three of them grinned. I think that was their entire concern.

CHAPTER FORTY-THREE

It was agreed that Hal and I would meet the family at the bowling lanes. I had made reservations for one lane for two hours, prepaid. But Laurie said they'd wait for us. She and the boys had come over earlier to "decorate" the deck and family room. "Grams, don't let Hal go near the family room."

So, when he arrived I was ready to leave. He didn't think it was odd that I kept him waiting at the door while I got my purse. Thank goodness. I kind of indicated that I wanted to make sure they didn't have a problem accessing the lane or anything since the last names are different. It was a beautiful Saturday afternoon.

As we drove the five or six miles to the Bowling Alley, he said, "This is the kind of day I like to walk the beach."

"Me too. Which beach do you prefer?" "Just for walking? Laguna." Hal was watching the road but conversing. I'm used to driving and this was new. Riding with someone. "It has been years since I walked Laguna. Sometimes it was too crowded and we would head to Malibu."

"Malibu this time of year is usually perfect walking. Want to go tomorrow?"

"That would be so relaxing. If you're serious, I'm game, Hal."

"Believe me, I'm serious. Why haven't I thought of walking the beach before now. Oh, probably because November and December are chilly and I've been busy. Do those sound like good reasons, Lyn?"

"You are a nut. Those are excellent reasons. Let's talk about this later. There's the drive to the Lanes."

We could see Lee had just pulled in as the kids were just getting out of the car. Hal pulled in next to her car. Laurie came running. "I'm so glad you could come, Hal." Little does he know just how sincerely she means that. The confrontation with my daughter did not go beyond my grandchildren. And they didn't know what happened except their Mom capitulated and he was invited. We signed in, got shoes and balls, instructions on the scoring and was pointed toward our lane.

We decided to have two teams and compete. I had to laugh. We drew straws - Team One, Laurie, Lee, and Hal. Team Two, Wil, Mike and me. The boys were moaning. I said, "Wait a minute. Didn't Hal say he doesn't know anything about bowling?" I know Laurie had said something about that not too long ago. Well, Hal is a fast learner but Team Two prevailed. We had enough time to bowl some more and Laurie suggested we just bowl every man for himself. It was a fun time. She won, Mike came in second, I was third, Wil was fourth, Hal was fifth and Lee had the lowest score. We didn't have time to play a full ten frames but everyone bowled seven.

Hal didn't know you could reserve a lane for a predetermined time period. "How convenient."

A lively dinner at Rudy's. We were headed for home about 6:30 for cake. We pulled up and the kids made a mad dash for the party area. They had one thing left to do. Hal said maybe he was glad he never raised teenagers. He and Lee commiserated together. I was shocked, and pleased. She righted around to a decent human being by the time we had gotten to the third frame in the team game. Probably because Hal talked to her as a teammate. He wasn't pushing himself on her. He wasn't trying to impress her. He just talked to her.

The cakes were on a decorated table in the family room. I handed ice cream and scoops to the kids. The party was all set to begin. They had begged me to keep Hal busy in the kitchen or something so he and I were the last to enter the family room.

There was a banner that said "Happy Birthday, Hal." They had bought number candles for his cake - a red five and a yellow seven. There were a couple small packages by his cake. As he came in, Wil lit the 57 and they sang Happy Birthday. Ever see an FBI agent wipe away tears? We all did. But, as he said later, "I wasn't FBI at that moment." Wil explained the number candles. "First of all, we didn't think we could afford fifty-seven candles, and second, we'd have to alert the fire department."

Everyone laughed, especially Hal. The cakes were different and everyone had a slice of each. Hal looked so pleased. I could tell he was having a hard time processing something. Later I asked him when was his last birthday cake? He said, "My folks were moving to Florida. It was my big 5 O and Mom had the restaurant serve a small cake at dinner. Seven years. It's been seven years."

He was still in awe. The kids gave him a very nice professional looking necktie. Lee gave him a tie tac. I gave him a belt buckle - not too elaborate but with an engraving of Cassiopeia. He had pointed out different stars and mentioned the constellations that dominated the winter skies. I think we were floating in the pool and looking at the stars. So, the double party turned out perfect.

My daughter seems to have come to her senses. Hal was very surprised. It was great. And, he found out he likes to bowl. He's not too bad at it...only one gutter ball the entire time we played. When the ball finally drifted into the gutter Hal said, "Oh, Snickle Fritz." We're going to hear phrase that for a long time. The kids love it. They've already talked to Hal about maybe playing again some Saturday.

After Lee et al were gone, Hal looked at me and declared I could be very clever and crafty. He thinks he likes that in a woman. "Let's get an early start tomorrow, Lyn. There's a little restaurant in Malibu very close to the beach. We could have coffee and a pastry before hitting the sand. Morning really is best. Afternoon can do horrible things to your beautiful complexion."

I nodded. There aren't many men who worry about your complexion. "Bring an extra pair of shoes. There's nothing worse than sand between your toes when you'd like to have a restful lunch."

"Are you speaking from experience, Hal?"

He laughed. "Marine Corps experience at Oceanside. Some things stay with you forever, I believe. On another note - I have never returned the clothes I borrowed. I think I'll wear them tomorrow and return them later. What do you think?"

I wanted to say good idea as you probably don't have any walking shorts but decided that would be crass and cruel. "Sounds good to me. I believe I'll wear walking shorts also."

"Walking shorts to walk the beach. Lyn, you are indeed crafty and clever."

"What time should I expect to see your smiling face. Early to you may not be early to me." "Seven? Is seven too early? It'll take an hour to get to Malibu."

"Seven is perfect." He kissed me good night, picked up his leftover cake (which I insisted he take, Laurie took hers), his birthday gifts, his birthday banner, and whistled his way to his car. I thought to myself... "There goes one very happy man."

There wasn't much clean up left to do. Lee had been quite helpful. I took a slow, warm shower and was in bed in half an hour. I must be getting old. Even good days exhaust me.

CHAPTER FORTY-FOUR

The eastern sky was streamers of red, gold and pink. Not a cloud to be seen. Sunday traffic was fairly light this morning. Even though we're more than half way through November, the temperature at seven was sixty-four degrees. We were both in walking shorts and tennis shoes. I brought a pair of sandals to change to after we left the beach.

Hal was in a great mood this morning. Perhaps he is every morning but today he chatted and replayed last night and talked about dancing and bowling. He enjoyed bowling a lot and wondered why he had never bowled before. "I may have turned fifty-seven yesterdays, Lyn. But I feel younger today then I have in a very long time. The world looks better today somehow. I am sure that's because I am driving along in beautiful weather, headed toward a beautiful beach, with the woman I love beside me. I'm sure that makes a man younger."

There's little you can say to a remark like that. I patted his knee. "Remember it's how you are old. You haven't put on your cardigan and slippers and eased into a rocker yet." He laughed but said nothing.

The little restaurant he had in mind was open and there was parking right in front. There's a flagstone walk to the front steps. It looks as though it's been on this little hillside forever. There were only a few other patrons. A man behind a counter came across the floor carrying a coffee pot and two mugs. "Would you like something with your coffee?" Hal asked if there were any raspberry croissants left? The man laughed, "You've been here before, haven't you? There are three left. Not quite so many early risers this morning."

"I knew it was my lucky day. Lyn, would you care for a raspberry croissant? It's unlike anything you've ever eaten."

"Absolutely. It is why we came." He had said coffee and pastries last night. The man poured coffee, made some little motion and Hal said, "No, black is best. Thanks." The man returned with two large, crusty and flaky, golden brown pastries on plates, and two forks. Hal asked if Mr. Moon still owned the restaurant.

The man said, "Yes, but he seldom comes in much anymore. He is ninety now. You look familiar but I am sure I don't know you."

Hal offered his hand. "I spent a summer down here the year before I went to New York to law school. I happened in one day and Mr. Moon was being rather verbal as his dish washer had quit working. I asked if I could help. He said 'can you fix the dishwasher or do you want to wash them by hand?' I looked at the dishwasher, saw the problem and in twenty minutes it was working again. He gave me a raspberry croissant that looked like this. What else do I owe you, Son. I said nothing, a pastry like this is payment enough. Well, after that I stopped in every morning. But if I got here after 8:15, the croissants were usually sold out. My last morning, I told him I was leaving the next day for law school but I'd try to get down once in a while. It was three years before I came back but he still remembered me. Please tell him that Hal Tucker stopped by for a raspberry croissant."

The man laughed. "He'll remember you. In fact, once in a while he mentions you. Usually when the dishwasher in on the fritz. I thought it was a swear phrase. Where's Hal when I need him?" Hal hasn't always been so reserved as he seems now. What a fascinating little tidbit. We ate our fabulous pastries and the man refilled our coffee. Hal paid the tab and we walked back to the car.

"Mr. Moon is a different sort. Real rough exterior. The morning I told him it was my last; that I was off to school; he gave me a hundred dollars. I tried to refuse it and he said you'll need it. Wait until you see the price of law books. He was right." Hal opened the car door for me and said, "There's a little cove not far from here and we can park close."

We spent a couple hours walking the beach. The little cove was fairly secluded and there were no other people on that section of the beach. There was a drift log that was dry and we sat on it for quite a while just talking. It was almost as if, on his fifty-seventh birthday, a little spring inside him had begun to work again. Crazy tales about his childhood. His Dad worked at JPL for a lot of years; his Mother was an associate professor or something at Cal Tech. He is an only child and spent a lot of time alone as a kid. When he looks back now he says he can't remember who suggested he might want to be an attorney. He didn't think it was him. Of course, he is pretty sure he was the one who decided he wanted to be a Marine. The sun was just about straight overhead when we returned to the parking lot. We both used the facilities there before going to the car.

"Did you bring shoes in that little bundle of yours?"

"No, I brought sandals." He had to think that over.

He laughed. "Do you have sand in your shoes now?"

"No, not much. I poured it out in the restroom. I brought a small towel though so I can clean my feet before I put on clean sandals."

"May I borrow it when you've finished? I didn't think that far ahead." We both wiped our feet and put on clean shoes. In all the years I've come to the beach, no one has ever suggested it before. Clean shoes. Hmm. He's meticulous without being tedious. That's good. I'm a bit of a slob. He pulled onto the highway and headed north. I figured we were headed home. Nope. Not quite two miles later he pulled in the parking area of a seafood house.

"After that crab Louie you made for me, I've been hungry for seafood. They get fresh fish every day here." Lunch lasted quite a while, and we ate quite well. Then we headed for home. "Do you think I can handle one very dry martini?"

"You have a full stomach, you aren't stressed, yes, I'll bet you could."

"I enjoyed both martinis last time. I'd like to prove that I can handle 'em this time."

"You're going to try for two?"

"No. But I believe one would be the finishing touch to this day."

We sat on my deck and sipped our martinis. It had been a day totally unexpected. There is so much to know about Hal Tucker. Not Hal Tucker of the FBI but the Hal Tucker that is sitting next to me enjoying the sunset. He's still jazzed over his surprise party. He sort of reconnected to his much younger self in Malibu. And he has shown me a side of him that I truly enjoy. Neither of us had spoken for quite a while when he said, "By the way, should I rent a tux for the Library's Gala?"

CHAPTER FORTY-FIVE

The Gala. I could lose my job over this year's Gala. The last several years the Board has elected to hold it at the Hilton Hotel in Pasadena. We have nice larger hotels closer to us but the Hilton is old, tried and true. Except, of the monies received, too much goes for expenses. To me that is not a good fundraiser. In March, before the first board meeting after last year's Gala, Albert, Antonio, and I went into the Hilton with a measuring tape. The rent has been five grand. They provide two bars and four bartenders for an open bar. That expense was greater than the rent. Then, they insisted on a sit-down dinner and that was expensive. Even at five hundred dollars a plate, the attendance wasn't enough to add many dollars to the Library. We determined that the lobby of the Library plus the first mezzanine was only forty square feet short of the space in the hotel.

I went to the Board with an entirely new idea for this year's Gala. Several of our young part-timers are computer whizzes and they made bar charts, pie charts and graphs for me. I proposed to send invitations to every person over twenty-one who holds a library card. Not the heavy ivory invitations with RSVP cards and envelopes, but a printed invitation with lots of information. There has been expansion to the Library in the last two years and I was willing to wager 80% of library card holders haven't seen them. Children's area, computer room, new reading room, theater (we show two movies a week plus recitals for local studios), and new meeting rooms available for public use. Instead of five hundred dollars and a free meal (ha), make it one hundred dollars, we'll serve appetizers and have a bar, but bring your checkbook. We have been limiting your decision on how much you'd like to gift the Library by charging five hundred dollars for the evening. Check out the facilities and write a check accordingly.

That was the message I wanted to send to the library members. Several employees had input. We wrote a great flyer. We worked on it diligently so it would say something in addition to we want your money. Catering appetizers is less expensive than a sit-down meal. Library staff would do everything but be the band and tend bar; we'd hire that. Usually there are a hundred and twenty to a hundred and fifty attendees. What if we had seven or eight hundred attendees with big checkbooks? The Board waffled but after seeing the numerous charts decided, "What the hell. Let's take the chance. We can't really lose too much. Hold the Gala at the Library and invite Library card holders instead of just the big shots."

I sent a personal invitation to Congressman Mason thanking him for his donation and inviting him to tour the library during the Gala. Perhaps he'd better understand my love for it. There was a lot of dissension in the ranks. Not my people, the Board. I may lose my job over this but I think the little people who read will back me up.

I told Hal I was going to buy a new long dress but not a fancy dress. I would be hostessing the event, but formal wear was not required. I am sure it says so on the invitation – which admittedly was more of an informational flyer than anything. The invitation was boxed and in the middle of the page. The invitations were mailed on November fifth. Thank goodness for our bulk rate license. I am not sure I got a count of library card holders over age twenty-one but it was several thousand for sure. We put an age on the mailings because there would be alcohol. Also, I didn't want our 'young' members to think they should pony up a hundred dollars to tout the library. Most of them visit often.

To prepare for the Gala on a personal level, Hal said he really needed to hone his dancing skills. I invited him to dinner every Wednesday which included dance lessons at the newly created Palmer Studio in my family room. Most Saturdays we went out for dinner and, surprisingly, he ventured onto the dance floor several times during an evening. I didn't coach or coax. But he watched other couples on the floor and thought he could do that well. He is really a fine dancer. He remembers more of the Cotillion lessons than he thought. And he pays attention when I teach him a new step.

The responses and hundred dollar checks started pouring in on the eighth or ninth of November. At library staff meetings we began assigning positions for each staff member. Whatever area you normally work; you'd be the host or hostess of that area for the evening. Two part- timers would be working with the caterer. And in areas where there are two responsible employees, one would lead a tour and the other host their area. I suggested they trade off during the evening. We scheduled tours every half hour (figured there'd be five) or the public could wander. We want them to see the Library.

Each tour was the same. We based our tours on some many of us have taken in big museums. I worked on dialogue for weeks. We would lock areas that are not public. We made name tags for staff - who they are and what their job is. On December first, the caterer called for a head count. Alice had been tallying and making a check in chart, etc, she told him nine hundred. He didn't hesitate but said, "Great."

Check in would be at the front desk. Bar and Band stations were established on paper. The actual areas would be set up the day of the Gala. One bar downstairs at the far end of the lobby and one on the first floor mezzanine. The band would be just off center to the back of the main lobby almost under the mezzanine. The morning of December tenth, we had a meeting and every department told what they'd be emphasizing to those touring - either to a tour group or individual. The theater was going to have an old cartoon reel on loop and serve mini bags of popcorn. (We have big bags for movie days.) If this turns out to be a flop, so be it.

But I learned this group works well together and to a man has great pride in the Library. I went home at five and changed. Everyone had a scheduled window to change. The group wanted some uniformity and I didn't want tee shirts so it was decided everyone would wear something green. It wouldn't be the same green, but all staff would be in green. I found a simple, long gown at the mall. So simple it was almost elegant.

We closed at six with a large notice that the Library would reopen at eight. Last minute check-ups in every department. The last few to change hurried to get back to their areas. You could think we were expecting the Queen. At eight the line went half way round the block. I had a little speech and gave it hourly during the evening. The band was good and it seemed to me that the part of the lobby set aside for dancing was busy all evening. After the first tour started, Hal arrived. "My god, how many people are here?"

"I don't know but they just keep coming. The front desk staff has been busy all evening. Alice thinks eighty percent of those registered are here already."

"Can you take time to dance? I never imagined it'd be this busy."

"Of course, I can. It may encourage others to dance though it seems the floor is active."

We both circulated through the crowd and whenever we got back to the dance floor, we danced. That was about every twenty or twenty-five minutes. Hal said he looked for possible trouble spots and found none. He figured a minor security detail was a good idea. It was an amazing evening. Amazing. While it was supposed to end at 10:30, it didn't.

Congressman Mason came about nine, took the tour and wrote us another large check. We had a large fishbowl type dish on a pedestal under a spotlight. It was filling up fast. The Congressman handed his check to me personally and I said, "Come with me while I deposit it in the bowl." A lot of people recognized him and he was most gracious saying 'the library has changed my life.' There were a lot of checks in the bowl. A lot.

There was even press coverage. Some of our card holders work for different newspapers. They spotted Hal and I on the dance floor - nice shot. Congressman Mason and I at the fishbowl. Most of the Library Board members were there and immortalized by the Star News and the Valley Tribune. I look forward to their coverage. I hope it's positive. I hadn't notified the press but probably should have. But the coverage of the Library Gala the last couple years has been sorry. We finally cleared the Library and locked the doors.

The staff met in the front reading room. Hal was amazed. We were all in green and he whispered, "Looks like a family photo setting." I laughed and agreed.

I got everyone's attention and announced, "First, Mr. Tucker says that we look like a family waiting for a photographer. We are family and he's going to take our picture. Gather together." Hal grinned at me, got out his phone and took three shots. Then I said, "This isn't usually done but, Alice get a calculator. We're going to see if we succeeded or not." Most of the staff was aware that the entire Board was not on board with my idea. And some of them were concerned for my job.

Everyone found a seat; someone brought in a tray of leftover appetizers. Two calculators appeared. I began reading the amounts on the checks. They went from five dollars to (drum roll) fifteen thousand. A lot were for fifty dollars, several for a hundred, big amounts, little amounts. There over eight hundred checks. Both calculators came to the same amount, $164,615. Everybody was hugging each other, some of the older staff were crying. This was more than twice the gross of last year and our expenses were a quarter of last year.

With a long tape in hand, I asked for quiet and officially announced the total. "The Board will be more than surprised. I am asking Jack, Bill and Rick to make new bar charts, pie charts and flow charts. We have proven a point. When you want something supported, ask those who use it."

"Helen, how many people actually were here tonight?"

She flushed. "I am happy to say we checked in eight hundred ninety-one persons. They all hold a library card but I only knew a couple hundred of them, people who come in often. A few asked if a donation beyond their entry fee was required and I told them no. A hundred bucks was heavy for some of them."

Then I remembered another chunk of money. "The total we just added up does not include the registration fees. I know there were several who registered who didn't attend and we'll get all the data together in the next few days. But I would venture that will be close to ninety thousand dollars more. We aren't waiting for the March Board meeting to let the Board know. I believe the gross is close to a quarter of a million dollars; close, very close."

Wild cheers. "We'll clean up tomorrow. Good night and thank you." Everyone went to their area to secure it and turn off the lights. Albert made sure all the outer doors were locked. He reported to me that the hatches were battened down. Then added, "Thanks, Mrs. P. We all knew you were doing the right thing." Hal walked me to my car. "Guess you're not losing your job, Lyn. I'll follow you home. It's kind of Late."

CHAPTER FORTY-SIX

It was nearly two am but he came in. We had a root beer. Yes, root beer. I was tired and a martini would have put me out. As soon as I was in the door, I asked to see the photos he had taken at the library. "These are really great, Hal. Thank you. Will you transfer them to my computer? I think there's enough money to create a full page thank you with a photo for the newspaper." He thought that would be quite appropriate.

I am still wound up but exhausted. Too much Adrenalin to sleep. We talked. About everything. Starting back when I was a kid and coming up to tonight. He asked questions and I answered without thinking - I'm sure I said what I honestly felt. What did I like best in school? Were my grades good? Did I participate in sports? Did I go to the Senior Prom. I was tired but he was curious. There were a lot of empty spots that the FBI hadn't probed. He went back much further than fifteen years. Does that upset me? No. Not in the least. Should it? Maybe under different circumstances. But he's a fifty-seven year old bachelor. Just doing his job.

Finally I asked him, "Hal, why all the questions?" "Lyn, I have never been so smitten by someone in my life. I believe that I have found the right woman. I called my Mother this morning and she said, "It certainly sounds like you have. Someone who has drawn out all the good parts of you; someone who has reminded you of the fun parts of living. I told you that someday you'd meet the right woman. I believe you have."

I was surprised he called his Mother. But pleased. He's an only child; I shouldn't expect less. He was still talking. "I told her about your grandchildren and the surprise party. She asked how I met you and I told her you were a closed case that was reopened and I caught the call. That bothered her and I told her that it was a very old missing person case that hadn't been closed properly. But it's all settled now and, in the meantime, I met your family, told her your son-in-law and I know a lot of the same people. That he's active Marines. Hell, Lyn, I told her everything not classified and she wants to meet you someday. So does Dad. He says remember he's eighty plus.

"But, doing this has left me in a peculiar position. I know exactly, well kind of exactly, how I feel about you. But I don't know what you feel about me. From what I've seen, I realize you may not be interested in me at all - you are a very caring, compassionate person. And everyone you know probably thinks you really like them, really care for them. Even Congressman Mason. You made his night. But he may have made yours, too. Your staff is respectful to everyone but they defer to you. They all really care about you because they are sure you care about them. "So, my question, or one of them, do you care for me as a matter of course, because I'm a nice guy and that's just how you are? Or do you care for me because I'm me and mean a great deal to you?"

"Hal, I don't know how to say this. I care for you because you are you. You make me smile. I find myself humming when I think of you. I see in you a loving, caring man. My grandchildren have never made a mistake when it comes to choosing people to love. My daughter has decided you're not the big bad wolf. My son-in-law bonded with a handshake. I don't always go along with the family. But this time, I do. You mean a lot to them and you mean a great deal to me. And you're tall, fair and extremely handsome. But most of all, I'd be lost without you." He sat there a long time and I mentally kicked myself. Did I even tell him I think I love him? Love is such a huge word; I'm afraid of it. I keep worrying that this is not real but rebound. Even after fifteen years.

"Lyn, the question is 'Do you love me?" I took both his hands. "More than you can ever know. Hal Tucker, I do love you."

He breathed such a huge sigh of relief, I think he must have been oxygen starved for a while. "Good. Great. One more question. Will you marry me? I don't know much about romance and stuff and probably have given you no reason to believe that I can learn. I think we're a good match; I truly do. You love to cook and I love to eat. We both like walking the beach. We both have love of family. But best of all I love you and you love me.

"Will you marry me?"

"When? Hal?" I told Lee that if he asked, I'd want to know only when.

"Today."

"Doesn't the great state of California require a license to marry?"

"Details. We'll get a license."

That was so funny coming from him that I began to laugh. His face crumpled. I pulled him into a very close hug and whispered, "Does the FBI know how cavalier you can be about laws?"

He looked down at me. "No. So marry me. Then you can't testify against me." Big grin.

"Let's consider three grandchildren who would be devastated if their favorite friend married their grandmother and they weren't there. I'm not putting you off; but we have to consider the others involved. My family and yours. Harold Tucker, you know more about romance than any person I've ever known. You are kind, gentle, caring, and funny.

"I love you most dearly and I accept your proposal of marriage."

He drew me closer. "Thank you. I will make sure you never regret it. I love you; I truly do."

"Hal, I think you are such a romantic and sincerely hope that, when reality ups and kicks you in the fanny in the morning, you won't regret having asked me. You are such a delightful human being. I truly do love you. For a few weeks, I allowed myself to believe my feelings for you were rebound. Silly? Yes, I've been alone for so long but honestly considered myself married. So I thought, this is too good to be true. It's rebound. But any time I thought of being without you, I couldn't stand it. When you were on assignment that long month, I thought maybe you were trying to wean you from me, or me from you. That you felt you had been totally unprofessional and was looking for a way out. That month was one of the saddest I have ever had to endure. Truly. I will try to be the woman your Mother thinks I am. Now go home. I want to go to work tomorrow. It's after four am."

"Is it? Oh, Lyn, I didn't mean to keep you up all night. I'm sorry. No, I'm not. I love you and will see you tomorrow at the Library. You don't have to go in but you will. Just to crow with your staff if no other reason."

Hal kissed her a dozen times and she walked him to the door. "See you later, love you."

Lyn smiled as she reset her alarm to eight. "Grandmother used to say sometimes you have to sleep fast. I never knew what she meant by that. Until now.

"Three hours later the alarm sounded. Lyn was up, relatively awake, dressed, and out the door before nine. She found the employee parking lot jammed. Thank goodness for a designated parking space. Every staff member is here this morning even though not all are scheduled to work. They want to revel in the success of the fundraiser the Board thought would be a flop. They want be sure their areas are clean, shiny, and ready for a new day. But most of all, they want to crow with their Director. It was a night to crow about, after all.

Before leaving the Library last night, Lyn figured that after expenses, they had raised five times the fundraiser gross result of the prior year. A quarter million dollars. There had been close to nine hundred people in the building the night before. The entire staff is still in party mode. The cleanup in each department went quickly and the library opened at ten, its usual Sunday opening time.

Sundays at the library are always slow starting. The staff made sure all evidence of the party the night before was gone. Lyn did a cursory inspection of the fourteen restrooms. She was sure they were spotless but she knew the maintenance crew had huge amounts of trash to carry out plus other cleaning jobs a large crowd creates. The restrooms are sometimes last on the list.

She went to the kitchen and pulled one of the trays of leftovers from the party out of the refrigerator. Break times start about eleven but today is a different day. No one could have had much sleep. And many may not have eaten breakfast either. Lyn went to the front desk and asked Helen to let everyone know there were leftovers in the kitchen. It was after ten when Hal showed up at Lyn's office. Alice, Lyn's assistant, greeted him. She hasn't seen him often in the Library but he came last evening to help Albert and Rick in their 'security' rounds during the party. He said as many people were expected, there could be some sort of problem. The custodial crew acts as security and appreciated the extra help. Two of the usual crew are part time but they were assigned to the caterer for the Gala.

"Mr. Tucker, how did the photos turn out. Were we all smiling and beautiful?"

"They are perfect. Mrs. P says she's going to create a full-page thank you for the newspapers and put the photograph of the staff in the middle.'"

That sounds like a great idea. We should thank all the library card holders who came and gave."

"I believe she's working on that as well."

Lyn heard them talking and opened her office door. "Good morning, Mr. Tucker. Did you get any sleep?

"I didn't set the alarm and slept in." He kissed her - in front of Alice. Alice was surprised. And giggled. Lyn has often said Alice is thirty-one going on fourteen.

"Alice, as you are my personal assistant, I want you to be the first to hear the news." Alice's eyes got very wide. "Mr. Tucker asked me at 3am this morning to marry him. I said yes."

Alice ran around in a tight little circle and then hugged her boss. "You two look so great together. Every time you were on the dance floor last night, we all just stopped and watched. You are so beautiful together." She paused, "I don't see a ring."

Hal Tucker laughed. "Alice, have you ever done anything on the spur of the moment? Something you'd thought about doing but never did? And then, just of the blue, you do it and you don't have a ring to put on the finger?"

"You mean you didn't intend to ask Mrs. P to marry you?"

"Alice, I've thought about it for weeks but never thought I'd get up the nerve. Since she was driving home alone and it was almost two am, I followed to make sure she got home okay. Then she asked me to transfer the photos to her computer. We talked about the evening. She's sure she still has a job. We had a couple root beers. And I was so jazzed about the evening and how I feel about her, I asked before I remembered I didn't have a ring to give her."

Alice was fourteen at the moment. "Oh, Mr. Tucker, that is so romantic. When are you getting married?"

Hal laughed. "I wanted to get married today but Mrs. P reminded me that we have to have a license in the great state of California.".

Alice giggled. "You are so funny, Mr. Tucker."

"We have families to consider, Alice, so we haven't set a date." Lyn put her arm around her assistant. "We have family, Mr. Tucker's job, my staff - lots to consider. But you'll be among the first to know."

"Can I tell anybody?"

Hal and Lyn both laughed. He said, "Alice, you may tell everybody." Alice turned and danced out of the office. Hal pulled Lyn to him. "I hope you don't mind that everyone knows?"

"Not at all." She kissed him softly. "I didn't expect to see you so early."

"Should I leave?"

"Of course not. I was just ready to clipboard my way through the building and check with everyone on how they feel their department was viewed last night. Did the patrons see their department as they see it? Were there complaints or suggestions? How many people did they talk to, etc.? Do they think we have anything special to relate to the Board - besides the totals.

"May I accompany you?"

"Well, Alice will have spread the word by now. Be ready to shake a lot of hands. My staff is kind of old-fashioned."

CHAPTER FORTY-SEVEN

Lyn started with the front desk. She asked if anyone had come who had not registered? "Yes, there were three, Mrs. P. We told them to put their hundred dollar check in the fishbowl." Helen gave her a folder. "I made note of their names. I was sure you'd want to know.".

"I am working on a full page thank you ad for the newspapers. Do you think we should make it a two full pages facing each other - and list every donor by name? Alphabetically, of course." Helen and Janice thought that would be a splendid idea. Both women were quite pleased that the fundraiser had done so well. Helen has been with the Library about twenty years; Janice only twelve.

"Now, my second question. We've never handled a crowd this large at one time before. Is there any way we should change how we register people? We have other events; of course not on this scale. Or, is our current method acceptable?"

"We had the list on the computer. It was really a breeze. And Jack had put a little program in that gave us a total as we went. No, we're good." Lyn was satisfied. Helen would definitely know. "Thank you, both. Excellent job last night. The line was long at eight but there seemed to be no real delay in getting people checked in. Great job."

"Mrs. P, is it true that you are engaged to be married?"

"Yes, it is. You both know Mr. Tucker, don't you? Not everyone does but you're on the front line and may have seen him on occasion." Hal had stood to one side. He wanted to accompany Lyn but not get in her business.

Both women nodded. "Yes, we know him. We watched you dance last evening. Couldn't miss that." Lyn looked at Hal. Yep, he was blushing.

Good report from the central reading room though perhaps a few more waste baskets would be nice. Not just because of the crowd last night, but they have noticed people getting up to walk all the way across the room to a waste container. A larger group made it more obvious. Lyn made note. The two in charge reported that several people were unaware that the Library has daily papers from seven states and four other cities within the state. Many guests had also commented on the excellent selection of magazines. Lyn wrote, "Waste baskets for main reading room. Tell Board of praise for selection of reading material." A couple Board members have questioned what they consider an outrageous yearly subscription expense.

Turned out that the most mentioned item requested by the different departments was waste baskets. The need has always been there; it just wasn't recognized until there were a lot of people in the area at once. The computer room had comments that a second printer might be a good investment. The staff has noted that several times there has been a wait for printing; and at times, confusion by patrons thinking their print was next in queue. There are twenty computers. A few visitors last night had commented on only one printer. Lyn and the staff decided that two additional printers would be sufficient and each computer would have a choice of printers. "I'll take it to the Board when I make our Gala report." She made a note on her clipboard.

The children's area had received hundreds of favorable comments. Lyn was surprised that the play area, the daily reading circle, and educational toys were that important to some people. Mostly grandparents, the staff said. The theater also received kudos and the staff had put out a clipboard asking for movie suggestions. There were seven pages, many duplicate titles, but seven pages of movies they would come to see.

The staff on the third floor asked the most. Several guests had commented how nice it would be to be able to purchase a drink when on the terrace. Could a small coffee bar be added to the terrace? There is always staff on duty on the third floor so no additional staff would be needed. The third floor terrace was a new addition two years ago and has been very popular even during inclement weather. The staff had sketched an idea this morning based on last night's comments. Hal looked at it and said that the plumbing would be the expensive part, depending on where things are already in place. Otherwise, a couple thousand would do the job. The staff nodded; that's what they had thought also. Lyn added their sketch to the clipboard.

It was mid-afternoon when Lyn and Hal completed her rounds. They stopped in the kitchen. The leftover goodie tray was empty. "Hal, is there another tray in the fridge? I think the caterer said he left three. We ate one last night so there should be another." There was indeed. Hal sat the tray on the counter and Lyn put the empty on the top of the fridge. They sat at a small table with coffee, food, and Lyn's clipboard. Hal was impressed. There weren't any frivolous complaints or requests.

There was a lot of feedback. Library patrons were surprised at what they could find at the Library; what events take place weekly; how easy to come and go. Many hadn't seen the Library since the expanded lobby and front reading room were added. Several updated their information with the front desk during the evening. "It's none of my business, but I believe you may have gotten more than just money from this fundraiser."

"You're right on that. Some of this stuff should have been obvious; some not so much. We found little chinks in our offerings. Nothing vital but if I can convince the Board, we should have the perfect Library in no time."

"I was thinking good will. Perhaps a revival in reading."

"That too. I am going to get the boys started on new charts. We're going to wow the Library Board. I am going to ask for a special, short Board meeting before Christmas." Hal shook his head. "Why wait until the end of March? The newspapers will be full of the Gala next week. Get permission to do the things you have on that clipboard before year end."

"That's exactly what I hope to do, Dear Sir."

"Do you have plans for dinner?"

"Hal, leftovers were the first food of the day. I haven't thought as far as dinner."

"Same here. Guess that's why I'm asking. And we do have some talking to do." Lyn nodded. "One big thing. Telling Lee. Wish we had a way to call Larry; he'll get this all second hand. I hope it won't be too slanted."

"I think that once he hears, he'll make an effort to call me. Tie-line time is always up for grabs but isn't always time convenient at both ends. He has to do a lot of planning to be able to call home at a time when Lee and kids are there. I'll ask Lee to ask him to call me whenever. I always have my phone. Then we have to agree on a list to discuss with him."

In actuality, there was nothing that had to be discussed with Larry other than how to handle Lee. She has said she knows her parents will never remarry but she hasn't been tested yet. Lyn doesn't want a meltdown. At three o'clock, Lyn went to the front desk to tell Helen she was going home. Helen said that one by the one, the staff not scheduled to work today had also been leaving. Lyn went to the local pharmacy that has a photo development department.

Could they possibly produce forty 8 x 10 prints before Monday closing? One image? Yes. Of course they could.

By five, Hal and Lyn were at Luigi's. Several of the employees had been at the Gala and commented on what a great time they had. They hadn't realized how much the Library has expanded in the last few years. And, they were impressed with the Gala itself. Hal put his hand on hers. "See? It really was as great as we think."

The rest of the week was busy at the Library. People who hadn't been in for years, who had come to the Gala, started borrowing books again. A number used the computer lab for the first time. Traffic began to increase almost immediately. It was almost as though people had forgotten the Library was there until the Gala. Lyn called the newspapers and was told, yes, to list all the donors, she would need a full page. She developed a very attractive thank you page. One of the photos Hal took that night was the centerpiece. The staff was listed, alphabetically, under the photo. The paper agreed to do that page in color. Hal was right. The picture looked like a large family. The varying shades of green only added to that illusion. There was a large thank you banner at the top and a small paragraph at the bottom which listed the gross income from the Gala and directed the reader to the page to the left for a list of the nine hundred fifteen donors. The caterer and band were referenced by name and thanked and praised. And, total attendance was noted.

The newspaper said the donor list might be in six point type but Lyn said as long as they were all listed. She submitted the alphabetical list from the library computer. "Can you do columns?"

Monday on the way home from work, she picked up the forty photographs. The first order of business at the Tuesday morning meeting was to give every employee a copy of the photo. To her recollection, there has never been a photo of the entire Library Staff. Everyone was surprised and quite pleased. The developing company put a title on the bottom of the photo stating Library Staff and the date it was taken. Lyn had one copy in a frame which will be hung somewhere prominent. Minor detail at this point.

The meeting went smoothly as there was really very little that hadn't already been discussed this week. Lyn invited Lee and the kids to dinner on Saturday. Hal brought flowers for the dining room table - this was not a kitchen affair. He showed up at three to help prepare a special meal. He learned how to set a moderately formal dining table. Lyn had not talked with Lee or kids all week other than to invite them to dinner. She said that happens from time to time and they knew she was overwhelmed with the Gala and its aftermath. And, it was the last week of school before the year-end holidays. Hal was concerned with Lee's reaction. He hoped she was reconciled to the idea her mother was not going to remarry her father. She says she is but he is still worried. He wasn't concerned about the grandchildren's reactions. They consider him their best friend. But their mother? Another story.

CHAPTER FORTY-EIGHT

At six, Lyn took off her apron and excused herself. She took a shower, changed into fresh clothes and fixed her hair. When she came back to the living room, Hal asked if she would like a martini before company arrived. Absolutely. They talked about who should make the announcement and when. They decided to wait until the table was cleared for dessert. And perhaps break the news the same way they had to Alice on Sunday. Rather off-handed, but effective.

The doorbell rang just before seven. Everyone wanted to know how the Gala turned out. Lyn said, "There will be a two-page spread in the paper tomorrow. But come sit and I'll tell you all about it at dinner."

Food was on the table in a very few minutes. Laurie sat to Hal's right. Wil sat next to her, across from his mother, and Mike sat to Hal's left. Seats weren't assigned but Lyn is sure when they found Hal would be at dinner, the kids tossed a coin to see who sat next to him. Or called dibs or however kids determine things these days. "You look pretty happy so I guess you still have a job, Mom."

"I do that. Well, I think so. The Board hasn't met yet but the Gala turned out to be the biggest success in the Library's history. Be sure to read the paper tomorrow. Meanwhile, I'll try to remember it all. It was amazing. We closed the Library at six to get last minute details in place; check with the bars and the band. You know, all the stuff that has to be ready when the doors open. The Gala began at eight. By eight o'clock, when we opened the doors, people were in a line wrapped half way around the building. The streets must have been parked full for blocks."

For the next several minutes, Lyn regaled her daughter and grandchildren with everything she could remember from that evening. The food; how good the band was most of the Library Board came; Congressman Mason came; the newspaper sent a reporter. The newspaper said the photos taken at the Gala would follow her two-page ad. "It'll all be in the newspaper tomorrow." Hal said that he had gone so he could dance with Lyn. The kids laughed but he assured them he can dance. He filled in a few details that Lyn may not have even known. He said he also acted sort of like part of the Library security team. Everyone nodded. That made good sense.

Hal and Lyn cleared the table for dessert. Rather than serving it aside, Lyn put dessert and plates in front of her and served from the table. "The whole thing was supposed to be over at 10:30. It wasn't. We finally got the Library emptied about midnight. I decided to total up the checks that had been given that night. Total, registration and checks, is over a quarter of a million dollars."

Whoops and hoorahs around the table. "The smallest check was five dollars, but remember whoever wrote it had already given us a hundred dollars for registration. The biggest check was for fifteen thousand." Louder whoops and wows.

"I got home at 2am. Hal followed me because it was so late. He took a group photo of the staff when we were getting ready to total the checks. I asked him to put them on my computer. One of those pictures will be in tomorrow's paper. I was tired but couldn't sleep. We decided a drink would knock us both out so Hal got a couple root beers from the fridge and we toasted the Gala."

The whole family was excited. It sounded like a really great evening.

Hal said, "And since your Grams was in such a good mood, I asked her to marry me."

Dead silence.

Lyn said, "And I accepted."

The kids cheered and got up to hug Hal and their grandmother. Such excitement. Hal and Lyn watched Lee. She was processing what she'd just heard. Lyn got a bit worried because Lee didn't say anything for several minutes.

The kids were back in their places and eating dessert before their mother said, "Have you set a date? I hope Larry can be here. He's the only logical man to give the bride away." And then she cried. Softly, but tears ran down her cheeks. She lifted her head and said, "Welcome to the family, Hal. You have no idea what you've gotten yourself into."

CHAPTER FORTY-NINE

The newspaper was incredible. Well, Lyn thought so. The front page of the Living Section had a photo of she and Hal on the dance floor in the middle of the page above the fold. The cut line says Library Director Madlyn Palmer dances with Library Patron Harold Tucker at annual Gala. See inside for more photos. Other usual Sunday articles filled the front page of the section. Page two was the list of donors. The type was small but the entire list was there in columns. It was very impressive. Page three was the Thank You from Your Library Staff just as Lyn had planned it. Page four were photos of several Library Board Members, Congressman Mason, the Mayor and his wife, three of other prominent business people. Page five was filled with small photos taken during the evening of numerous Library Patrons. A photo of the band and a filled dance floor; a photo of the mezzanine bar and, directly in the middle of the page, a slightly larger photo of just Lyn standing by the fishbowl filled with checks. And it was all in color.

Hal called Lyn saying he had the newspaper. Should he buy another? "It's pretty spectacular, Lyn. Pretty spectacular. Should I get two to send to my folk and your Dad?""

Thank you for thinking of that. Buy three. I want an extra." The president of the Library Board called on Monday to see if an hour's meeting on Tuesday afternoon would be agreeable with her. At the Library, of course. He said that he read the newspaper yesterday. Apparently the Gala was everything she had predicted. He'd like to see the numbers and hear the feedback. Two o'clock; he'd have the Board secretary notify everyone. Lyn hung up the phone.

Board secretary? For the last eight years, Alice has been taking meeting minutes. But she isn't considered the Board secretary. She just takes meeting minutes as required by law. Lyn has been at every Board meeting for the last sixteen years and can't recall ever knowing who is the Board secretary. Oh, well. It's his call. Lyn checked the list.

The president of the Library Board had not attended the Gala. The newspaper must have been one hell of a shock to him.

"That turkey."

Lyn called her computer whizzes together. "We have all the detail to do the charts and graphs as we did last year. Is there time? All of a sudden, Mr. Swanson wants a Board Meeting tomorrow afternoon." The three young men laughed. "Mrs. P, they're practically finished already. We need definite expense numbers and the charts are done."

For the next hour, Lyn and her whiz kids worked on creating extremely impressive charts and graphs. Income and expenses for this year alone; compared to the last Gala and then the charts they'd produced to sell this Gala idea. Details were precise - if you couldn't follow the charts you were blind or just totally ignorant. Lyn said she told the guys she didn't like to use that kind of language regarding the Board but she did agree. Even she could follow the bouncing ball. Everyone laughed.

That evening, about seven, Jim called from Massachusetts. He hadn't called in a while. Lyn was surprised. He had been at his local library this afternoon. He saw the Gala in the newspaper. His library, as most others, subscribe to several local and out-of-area papers.

"Just called to congratulate you on your successful gala. That guy in the picture dancing with you - is that my competition?"

"Jim, we've had this discussion. You aren't in the running anymore. Remember?"

"Yeah. Well, he looks like he dances okay. But that's the guy, isn't it?"

"It is, Jim. That's the guy."

"Well, congrats on showing up the Library Board. Looks like it was one helluva party."

"It was. Doesn't the staff look great?"

"Yep. One big happy family. That's your forte, Maddy. I'm proud to know you."

And he hung up.

Lyn sat with the phone in her lap. "Why didn't I tell him I'm going to marry Hal? The opportunity was right there." Abashed that she hadn't said more, she put the phone back on the table.

Tuesday morning, Lyn alerted the staff there would be a board meeting at two. Everyone was surprised. She told them that the President of the Board hadn't been at the Gala. Evidently, he was blown away with the newspaper coverage. He called yesterday to set the day and time. There were several murmurs among the staff. This didn't sound right.

One of the public rooms was set up for the Board Meeting. Water in pitchers, glasses, pad and pen at every seat. Jeanine asked if she wanted coffee for the meeting and Lyn said, "Not this one. I have a feeling it's going to be short and sweet. At least, I hope it'll be sweet." Jeanine repeated the remark to a couple other Staffers. Wonder what she meant? The whole place was on edge by two. Lyn was unaware she had set such a tone although some of the staff had been on edge since she made the announcement of the meeting.

Just before two, Alice took her note pad and three pens to the conference room. She always sits to the left and slightly behind the Board President. Lyn stood at the door and welcomed each board member as they came in. Swanson arrived a few minutes after two. Alice thought, "Late to his own party. wow" She made note at the top of the minutes that the Board Chair was late. The meeting was called to order and Swanson declared there was only one item on the agenda. He hadn't asked Lyn to print an agenda for him, as he does usually. The one item was dismissing the Library Director, Madlyn Palmer.

The shouts from the other directors were loud and long. Judge Johannson asked to be recognized.

"What the hell is your problem, Tom? Why would we dismiss Madlyn? She just pulled off the most successful fund raiser ever held for the library."

"Well, as I see it, she did it without proper authority from the Library Board."

"And how do you figure that?"

"When was she given permission to use the Library for such an activity?"

Three or four others asked to be recognized. Richard Haley, owner of the hardware store, stood. "Last March Mrs. Palmer showed us the error of our ways of raising funds at a formal sit-down dinner. She had charts and graphs showing that barely twenty percent of funds raised were profit. We were impressed with her presentation. Then at the June meeting, Mrs. Palmer offered a plan which she believed would be a better money maker. We asked her to get definite figures and solid estimates. In the September meeting, she did. We took a vote. I think there was only two dissenting. You weren't one of them, I'm pretty sure."

Lyn stood up. "If you wish to wait about three minutes, I will get the official minutes book so those meetings can be reviewed."

Swanson said, "What do you mean official minutes book?"

Bill Walker, a local attorney, stood. "Mr. Swanson, any organization registered in California that has a Board of Directors is required to have minutes taken at every meeting and entered into an official minute book. Alice has been taking our Board minutes long before you even moved to town. Does anyone here doubt what Mr. Haley has just recalled?"

Everyone shook their head. No. They were here and definitely recall that while it seemed a foolish venture, go ahead. We couldn't do much worse than in the past. Four or five people verbalized that at one time. They didn't bother to be recognized by the chair. Alice made note of them by name however in the minutes.

Judge Johannson asked Lyn if she had charts, graphs and data relating to the December 10th Gala. Of course she did. The boys had set up three tripods for her prior to the start of the meeting. Mr. Swanson shouted, "This is not on my agenda."

Judge Johannson replied, "You didn't publish an agenda prior to the meeting. We are adding to it."

Swanson was red-faced and puffing. "You can't do that."

"Roberts' Rules of Order says that I can. And so, I will. Mrs. Palmer, please walk us through the dollar signs."

Lyn had rehearsed a short message using the charts. The Board applauded when she finished.

Judge Johannson stood. Swanson was getting very, very upset. His position was being usurped and he wasn't going to stand for it. The two men had words. Alice took down every word. Then the Judge said, "I propose we change the wording of Mr. Swanson's original agenda item." Everyone looked at one another. "What?"

"The one item that should be on the agenda is the ousting of the Director of the Library Board. Swanson were you even at the Gala?"

Red in face and sputtering, he said, "No. I never got an invitation."

Lyn stood. "One was sent to you. Alice, can you pull up the list of card holders on that tablet?"

"Yes, ma'am." She pushed two buttons and found Mr. Swanson's Library Card information. She read off the date issued and the address listed.

"I moved from that address five years ago. Just how incompetent is this Library?"

Lyn asked, "Did you notify the Library you had moved? We don't have a crystal ball at our disposal here."

Now he was really hot.

Alice was diligently taking notes. Judge Johannson asked for a motion to remove Mr. Swanson from the Library Board. Not just as director, but from the Board. Bill Walker made the motion, Mr. Haley seconded it. The vote was unanimous.

Lyn stood again. "Mr. Swanson, you were in every meeting where this Gala was discussed. You were the Chairman of the Library Board. Why would you believe you had to be personally invited?"

"Swanson had no answer. Mr. Walker asked what he intended to prove by removing Mrs. Palmer from her position? "Well, look at the newspaper. How self-serving can you get? She was prominently photographed several times. It was the Madlyn Palmer Gala, if you ask me."

"She and the staff collected a quarter of a million dollars for the Library. Mrs. Palmer doesn't even get a raise for her brilliant ideas. And it was the Madlyn Palmer Gala. She's the Director of the Library; she is the face of the Library. We've voted you out. Leave. If you want to be notified about Library activities, stop at the front desk and change your address." Judge Johannson sat down. He felt he may have overstepped but apparently no one else thought so.

Swanson gathered his jacket and left the room. He had brought a file folder with him but he left it laying on the table. Later, when the crew cleaned the room they took the folder to Lyn. "This was on the table in the conference room. We don't toss what we don't know."

Swanson had intended to nominate his daughter for the position of Library Director. She was graduating in January with a degree in Library Science. Lyn put the file in her desk. It won't be fair, but if Tammy Swanson ever applies for a job here - she may not get it. The sins of the parent. Lyn felt very sorry for Tammy. She's never met her but it must be hell living with a father like this.

Haley walked Swanson to the front desk and then out. Once Swanson was out of the building, the rest of the Library Board went over the facts and figures with Lyn., again They were suitably impressed. They approved every item she requested including a coffee bar on the third floor terrace. Someone said, "Didn't Mrs. Palmer say once that if you want something supported, go to the people who use it? This definitely indicates she was right. Is it true that she doesn't get a raise for doing a good job?"

Judge Johannson asked Lyn. "When was your last raise, Mrs. Palmer?"

Lyn had to think a moment. "I think it was six years ago. I think."

"When did the staff last receive raises?"

"We've managed a cost of living raise every year since I've been director."

Haley wanted to know why she hadn't received one also. "The Library Board never thought it was necessary. I guess."

Alice is taking notes as she hasn't heard a motion to dismiss yet.

"Well, something should be done to correct that. When is the next scheduled Board meeting?"

"End of March."

Judge Johannson called for a motion to dismiss; and a second. The meeting was over. Lyn and Alice shook hands as everyone left. Then Alice said, "Mrs. P, what just happened here?"

"Lyn laughed, "I was going to ask you. You were the one taking notes."

"I'm going to go transcribe them right now. The meeting starts saying you should be fired and ends saying you should get a raise. Neither thing happened. But the Board Director was tossed out. This is crazy. At least, everyone was happy with the Gala report."

"Alice, I believe if you check, everyone on the Board now was at the Gala. I believe we didn't have to do much explaining. They all experienced it."

The two women walked back to their office. What a wild and wacky meeting. "Alice, as usual, this meeting is confidential."

"Yes, Mrs. P. It'll be hard not to blab, but I won't."

CHAPTER FIFTY

Alice transcribed the minutes as soon as she got back to her computer. She asked me to proof read. Which she usually asks. Wow, what a whirlwind meeting that was. I cannot believe that Mr. Swanson would make such a suggestion right on the heels of a successful fundraising. His daughter can't be so inept that she needs this kind of help. Alice says she'd lay odds the poor girl has no clue.

I am sure there will be an agenda distributed before the March meeting. First thing should be to select a new director for the Library Board. They may decide to fill the vacancy left by Swanson's departure with someone to finish his term. I think they will do that as election for the Library Board isn't due for another year.

My whiz kids came to see how their graphs and charts were accepted. I told them that the Board was absolutely overwhelmed. "You showed them money; how we got it; how we spent it and how much is left. They have approved every single thing we asked for. I am calling the architect in the morning to discuss the third floor coffee bar. And if the three of you can decide what printers we should buy, let me know and I'll issue a purchase order. The fact that we collected opinions seemed to count a great deal. And the fact there were no real negatives comments made them know that this staff is doing everything right. It was quite a meeting."

Helen stopped by Lyn's office on her break. "What's with Mr. Swanson? Was he ill? It looked like he was being escorted out though. He was pretty upset that we didn't have his new address. And when we found out he moved years ago, I made a mistake and called him on it."

"Well, Helen, don't worry about it. One of his major complaints was that he didn't get invited to the Gala personally. I'm sure you realize he was the only Board member who wasn't there. One of the other Board members called him on the old address. For some reason, he was in a bad mood and seemed to want to cause trouble. He's no longer on the Board, however. His conduct was unbecoming an officer of the Library."

"Wow. Other than that, how went the meeting?"

"Splendidly. They approved everything we asked for from wastebaskets, to two printers, and even the terrace coffee bar."

"Money really does talk, doesn't it, Mrs. P?"

"Well, mine sure knows how to say goodbye, Helen."

Helen laughed and waved and went to the kitchen for a cup of coffee.

Alice was putting the transcribed notes into the Minutes book. "You sure glossed that over well, Mrs. P. No wonder you're the Director.".

"Actually, Alice, I think it's something you learn with age. Ready for a cup of coffee? I honestly feel like I need a martini but coffee will have to do."

The two went to the kitchen. There were a few other employees on break. They all wanted to know about the wedding. When, where, all the good stuff. "Are you going to wear white, Mrs. P."

"No. I did when I married Mr. Palmer. Once is enough. Though I've been single a long time, it's almost tempting. I think I'd like a nice pastel. What color would make a good wedding dress for me?"

"Does Mr. Tucker have a favorite color?"

"Good question. Once when he and my grandchildren were swimming, and I was going to join them, he asked if I had a yellow swim suit. But I don't know if that's a favorite color or not. He said he just thought I'd look good in a yellow swim suit. And, somehow, it just doesn't seem like a wedding color.".

"Oh, he's right. With your hair, yellow would be good.".

"Are you going to look for a wedding venue?" One of the girls from the main reading room, Jessica, was married last fall. She was married in her church.

"We haven't even talked venue yet. But I'm not sure I like the idea of getting married in a place that's there just to get married in."

Rachel from the children's area. "Why don't you get married here? At the Library."

They all clamored that would be a good idea. "We know there's room for a good band and the lobby is a great dance floor. You could just have cake and champagne. Or finger food like the Gala. Patrons are still raving over some of the food that night."

Lyn realized that while she had accepted a proposal of marriage, she had absolutely no idea what needed to be done. Maybe they could just elope. The girls were all chattering; sounds like some excellent ideas floating around. She looked at her watch. "I hate to be a spoil sport, but I need to get back to work." She stood up and finished her coffee in two quick swallows.

They all decided maybe they should too. They chattered as they left the kitchen. Alice said, "If you need any ideas, Mrs. P, sounds like we all have at least one."

Walking back to their office, Lyn told Alice, "I'm going to talk to Mr. Tucker and ask if he has preferences. He's never been married and may have some ideas. Sounds like my staff could put together a pretty good wedding and reception though."

Lyn stopped for ice cream on the way home. She couldn't decide and ended buying four flavors; rocky road, strawberry, vanilla and Dutch dark chocolate. She fixed a sandwich around seven and sat down to write to her Dad. He's in Australia, she thinks. He has a postal box with the National Geology Society and they route his mail to wherever he is. She hasn't written in some months and realized the postage is going to kill her now. He doesn't know she found Wes or that she spent two weeks with him and discovered he's not the man he once was. She didn't gloss the situation but did emphasis that, when she realized he'd been able to go on without her, she had wasted fifteen years of not living life to the fullest.

She told him how she met Hal and how falling in love with him was so gradual she was unaware until she woke up one day and decided she cared a whole lot. Lyn's Dad is a romantic. He's told her so many times. A good geologist has to be, he told her. There's so much romance in nature - the way the earth formed and is forming. Lyn was sure he'd understand what she was trying to say.

Lyn asked if he was going to be anywhere near the United States in the next year. She knows he gave her away a long time ago; would he care to do it again? If not, she certainly understands. "But Dad, I want you to meet this man someday. In many ways, he reminds me of you. He is taller; but he's a dark blond with blue eyes; in good physical shape. And he is passionate about things. He loves my grandchildren deeply. There is no doubt. He and Laurie share a birthday. He's fifty-seven, Dad, but looks younger than Lee's husband. He's a trained attorney; a Lieutenant Colonel in the Marine Corps (retired), and now he works for the Federal Bureau of Investigation. And that's how I met him. He found Wes."

Then, she wrote, "In all this mess, I learned why my Eddy was killed. And, Dad, I'm not sure but maybe because Wes was at the root of it, maybe that's why I just cannot remarry him. I filed for divorce earlier this year - after sixteen years." Lyn wants her Dad to know why Wes was in Witness Protection. Maybe he can tell her how to rid herself of the anger when she learned her son was murdered because of his father. Lyn poured her heart out in hopes her Dad could help her rationalize her thinking.

Lyn reread the letter; it was single spaced but still took eight pieces of paper, both sides. She ended it saying, "We have not set a wedding date. If you'll be in the area, let me know when. If you can't get to the States this coming year, it's okay. But, I'd like very much to have you walk me down the aisle one more time."

She addressed the letter, weighed it and put two overseas stamps on it. The post office is on her way to work. She'll mail it tomorrow. The sandwich was gone and she filled a bowl with dark chocolate ice cream.

It was nearly nine when the phone rang. Hal calling to check on her day and wish her a good night. He had just finished a case; he thought he'd be done earlier. Lyn told him that was fine; she wrote a long sixteen-page letter to her father.

"Speaking of parents, mine wonder if we can come visit them in Florida on the next 3-day federal holiday."

"Well, the next is MLK day, third Monday in January and then Washington's Birthday, third Monday in February. Which do you prefer? Or do your folk prefer?"

"Probably January, but that's too short notice for me to get off. Federal holiday or not, I'm on call and I think Florida is out of my call range. But I believe I can wrangle February. How about you?"

"Yes, I can do February, I'm sure."

"How did the Library Board meeting go? Did they approve your various requests?"

"Are you at the office?"

"Yes, why?"

"Because the Board Meeting isn't a two-minute story. Will you be here for dinner tomorrow? It is Wednesday."

"Absolutely. If you're going to be up a while, I'll stop at your house on my way home now. I'd like to hear this Board meeting saga before tomorrow."

"At this moment, I am elbows deep in a dish of dark chocolate ice cream. I'll be up a while."

"Don't eat it all. I'd like to try dark chocolate ice cream. It'll take me half an hour but I'll be there, if you don't mind."

"Thank you. The story will knock your socks off. I can promise you that. I have four flavors of ice cream in the freezer but will save you some of this good stuff."

Quick 'see you soons' and the call ended. Lyn started a pot of coffee.

CHAPTER FIFTY-ONE

Hal and Lyn sat on the family room couch to eat their second bowl of ice cream. Hal had laughed so hard earlier, he had to go wash his face to sober up. He couldn't believe anyone could have made such an error in judgment as Swanson had done. They were still chuckling over some of the remarks that actually got entered into the minutes of the meeting. Rules are that the minute taker stops only when told something was off the record or otherwise was not being admitted or the meeting was adjourned. The dialogue between Swanson and the Judge was in black and white. Swanson is such an idiot.

"Hal, I've done some map looking to see where your parents live. How do you get there? Fly into Tallahassee?"

"That's how I've always done it. There is a small airport at Apalachicola, or so I've heard. I've never seen it. My folk live in a pretty small place so as soon as a date is set I'll call for hotel reservations. I've done it nearly every time when I've gone. I am claustrophobic on their boat. Doesn't hurt their feelings. Last time I went, I got a suite at the Coombs House and they stayed on shore with me. We had a really great time. I'll see if they want to do it again."

"They live on a boat?"

"Yeah, it's pretty good sized but I'm pretty good sized too and I feel really cramped." "Well, whatever you think is best. Just let me know the dates so I can be sure things are covered here. How long have they lived there?"

"Seven years now. Apalachicola is known for its oysters, shrimp and blue crab. They do have clams but oysters and shrimp are their primary crops. They don't fish commercially but do fish daily, I understand."

It seems odd to Lyn that living sea creatures are considered crops. She knows it's true, but still strange.

"Do you want some more ice cream?" Lyn finally decided she'd had enough but she was a bowl ahead of Hal.

"No, I'm good. I've got to get going. Tomorrow's already looking nasty. Have to sit in on a couple depositions. God, how I hate that. Some attorneys will ask the same question three different ways hoping to trip up the witness he's deposing. It's time consuming and usually not very effective. It's supposed to be an interrogation not an inquisition. Every time I get snagged into this kind of duty, I remember why I decided to become a Marine."

They took the ice cream bowls to the kitchen. Hal put both arms around Lyn and just smiled. "You really did say yes, didn't you?"

"I really did.

He nuzzled her neck before kissing her. "I am so glad. What time is dinner tomorrow?"

Lyn laughed. "Maybe the way to a man's heart is through his stomach. Get here when you can. Do you like pork chops?"

"Yes, ma'am, I do. I should be here by seven. The deposition is in Santa Monica but the deposing attorney is a jackass. He'll ask questions right up to five o'clock, I'm pretty sure."

Lyn watched from the door as he got into his car and drove away. She leaned against the door after throwing the latch. "He is so genuine. I am so lucky. I sure hope his parents like me. I'm more nervous at fifty-nine then I was at nineteen meeting Wes' parents. Ridiculous."

The Library was already busy when she got there at 9:15. On the way, Lyn stopped by the caterer's office with the three pans from Gala leftovers. She paid an advance to the caterer and he hasn't sent a final bill yet. It would be good to get it paid before the end of the year. She had estimated the final for her reports. The caterer was delighted to see her and thanked her for the nice recognition in her thank you ad in the newspaper.

"That was the most innovative thank you I've ever seen in the Star News. Did you do it yourself?"

"Sure did. A friend took the photo when we decided to stay and add up the checks. Usually that's done the next day but we were sure - well, if you must know the Library Board thought this was the stupidest idea I've come up with in twenty years. As you read, it wasn't. That night we all wanted to know if we had been right."

"Well, it made an impact. We've had four calls since the paper came out that I doubt we would have gotten before. People think we're too small for big stuff. Your thank you indicated nine hundred attendees or something like that. All of a sudden, we don't look so small. Wait, I've got your final statement on my desk. I was going to write you a note, when I sent it, to thank you. But, as I've done that in person, I'll just give you the bill."

He went into his office and returned with a single sheet of paper. "I have given you credit for two helpers; the kids you assigned to us were terrific. I would have paid fifty dollars if I had hired them myself so gave you the credit."

"But you didn't have to do that. I was so relieved when you got a head count of nine hundred and you said, okay, like it was an everyday affair."

"Well, I did give you the credit anyhow. If it'll make you feel better about it, consider it my donation to the Gala. Thank you for the opportunity. If you have anything else we can help with, let us know. I should tell you that we had expected a head count of maybe three hundred. When you said nine, I sat down fast. But I knew we could do it and we did."

"Definitely. We've gotten rave reviews on the food nearly every day since. Patrons check out a book and say "by the way" and tell us how yummy, delicious, spectacular, something was at the Gala. You are at the top of our catering list. If you need a reference for someone in particular, send them over."

Lyn stopped at the front desk. "Things on an even keel, Helen?"

"Yes, ma'am. You move fast. There are two technicians in the computer room installing two new printers and making sure the computers can choose any one of the three."

"The guys knew what they wanted, what we needed, so we just called yesterday afternoon to see if the store had it in stock. Good, we can get it paid before year end. I hate dragging debt into a new year. By the way, are the signs made for Noon Closing on Christmas Eve and Closed Christmas Day? I haven't seen them and we just days away from the holiday."

"Oh, Tom brought them down about half an hour ago." She reached below the front desk and pulled out the signs. "They'll go up Friday morning."

"Let's put them up Thursday. Tomorrow. Better to give an extra day's notice. Agreed?"

"Absolutely. Thursday."

The rest of the day was busy. Year end reports take a while but go faster if you start on them early. It was nearly noon before Lyn got up to the computer room. The technicians were just finishing up. There were little cards taped to the computers reminding people of a new system for printing. "Did you bring me an invoice?"

"Well, good afternoon to you too, Mrs. P. Of course, we brought you an invoice. What do you think of the new printers?"

"I like the size. Looks like they'll do more than the old one."

"Exactly. We put print instructions on the computers. If you have a print job under ten pages, no duplicates and collating, please use printer #1. That way when Grandma comes in to write a nasty letter to the bank, her print job is done in thirty seconds and the big print jobs aren't inconvenienced."

"Should we have a copier? We don't have a copier just for public use. What if Grandma wants to send a copy with her letter to the bank? Or save a copy for her file. We need a copier. Stop down at my office before you leave. I want to give you a purchase order for a handy-dandy copier. One like PIP has - well, maybe two steps down. Make it a copier like I have at home with scan and fax capabilities. Well, the commercial version of what I have at home. Do you have brochures with you or shall I just go on line? Where's Rick?"

Rick came in the room just then. "Looking for me?".

Lyn told him what else she wanted in the computer room. "I have information on it. Wait." He went to his desk and returned with an illustrated brochure. Lyn took it. "Yes, that's it there. Come down to my office and make sure I make the purchase order out properly. You do agree this is a good idea?".

"Oh, yeah. I just came from your office to use your copier."

They both laughed and Lyn suggested he should have mentioned this before. "I don't get up here often. When something is necessary, let me know and we'll work it out."

"Yes, ma'am Mrs. P. I keep forgetting you're reasonable."

Lyn laughed. "How long have you been here, Rick?" She shook her head and went back to her office. Rick celebrates his tenth year of Library employment in April. He knows his Director is more than reasonable.

CHAPTER FIFTY-TWO

It was nearly seven before Hal arrived for dinner that Wednesday evening. While he couldn't tell her what the case was, he did mention the deposition was explosive. It should have been researched better. The person was definitely an unwilling participant and, more than once, verbally attacked the attorney. The attorney who was supposed to be supporting him from the defendant's attorney didn't do well in support or defense. He was more shocked than the plaintiff's attorney. Numerous times.

"I thought I knew all the swear words in the world from the Marines. Wrong. I learned a whole raft of new ones today. The guy is quite a colorful speaker."

"Saturday is Christmas Eve, Hal. Lee and kiddos come for dinner and our family celebration. Will you be available? I realized this afternoon that I hadn't mentioned it to you before. If you can't make it, okay. But the kids will expect you now. I think your new position in the family makes them believe you're on tap for anything family related."

"When do you want me to be here? I'm learning how to be a second cook and can help."

"Well, I am thinking I should have a tree this year. There hasn't been one for sixteen years. I know the Boy Scout tree lot is open until ten tonight. Do you want to go with me to get a tree?"

"Decorations. Do you have decorations?"

"In the garage rafters there are a lot of decorations - inside, outside and tree. In plastic wrapped boxes."

"Let's get a tree tonight and tomorrow I'll come over as soon as I can to get the decorations down and get the tree party ready. Little late for outside stuff but whatever you want, I am sure I can do it."

After dinner, Hal and Lyn took her car to the Boy Scout lot and found a very handsome five-foot tree. "Is this big enough, Lyn. I'm taller than it is."

"Good, then there won't be any hassle putting the star on top."

True to his word, Hal was at Lyn's by 5:30 Thursday. He brought a change of clothes and once redressed, got into the rafters in the garage. He was concerned how he'd know which boxes were which until he saw they were labeled. "Tree, outside lights, inside decorations." He brought down the two boxes marked tree. Then, on a whim, went back for the boxes that said inside.

Lyn had put chicken and rice in the crock pot before going to the Library that morning. Once the tree decorations were in the family room, she suggested they have dinner and then tackle the tree.

Hal was going through the tree box, laying things out in some sort of order. "Okay, dinner first. Hey, you even saved the tinsel. Wow, this is high grade stuff, not like the stuff they sell nowadays."

"I have always saved tinsel and usually buy one new box a year. I forgot to buy tinsel but it'll be okay. It's a smaller tree."

They discussed their day over dinner. Hal hadn't eaten chicken and rice since he lived at home. "This stuff is so good. I forget how great home cooking is. How did you know this was one of my fa-vor-ite foods?"

"Lucky, I guess. It is one of my fa-vor-ites."

The tree fit into the stand first try. They moved a chair so the tree would be in the corner by the outer doors. Hal put the lights on and she was surprised at how precise he seemed to be in their placement. He insisted they be lighted when he put them on. Wes just wound them around the tree and then spent an hour trying to make them look right. Once the lights were on the tree, the serious business of decorating began. Hal said, "Oh, gotta run to the car. Nearly forgot something."

He had bought an ornament for her. "It's our first year, sort of, and I wanted something special on the tree." Lyn cried a little. How thoughtful of him to be so sentimental. Our first year, sort of. "I bought it but you should hang it." It was a blue and silver bell that reflected the lights around it. The year was engraved on the silver. Lyn placed it at her eye level, a foot from the top. Perfect.

When they were down to tinsel, Lyn asked if he'd care for a drink. "What do you have in mind?"

"All the usual, it's just that we've been at this two hours and I'm thirsty."

They took a break, had a martini, and sat looking at the tree; it was almost completely trimmed. Lyn realized they had not disagreed on a single thing.

She and Wes argued about nearly every placement. And hanging tinsel with Wes was torture - he just threw it on the branches. Well, in a few minutes I guess I'll find out what kind of tinsel person Hal is.

They each had a bundle of recycled tinsel and stood on opposite sides of the tree. If he was a thrower, she didn't want to know. He wasn't. They finished their tinsel at about the same time and when looking at the tree, you couldn't tell who had done which side. Big smile.

"I knew you were a keeper."

Hal had no idea what that meant but he liked the sound of it.

"If you decide you want some inside stuff, I put those boxes on the work bench and you can do whatever tomorrow. If you decide you don't want to delve into them, I'll put them back in the rafters when I come over Saturday." Lyn was already thinking of maybe putting a few things up. Wreath on the door maybe? She'd think about it at work Friday.

It was after ten when Hal gathered his work clothes and headed home. Lyn had done most of her shopping on line this year, as usual, and would spend tomorrow evening wrapping. That is, if she stopped at Thrifty and bought some tape and paper. "This year has been all out of sorts - in every facet of my life. I am glad there is a tree this year. The kids will be surprised as I've never had a tree in their lifetime...except the first year but Wil was too young to enjoy or remember it."

Hal had put the tree light switch in a very accessible spot. Lyn turned off the tree lights and went to bed. This was like starting life all over. She had been so pleased to see the familiar ornaments and regretted not having a tree for so long. Sleep came quickly.

The huge tree at the library had been decorated for more than a week. Seeing it after decorating her own, she realized that her staff had put up the tree and decorated it. All she had done was order it. Has she participated in tree decoration at work at all? "I don't think so. Somehow I just didn't really do Christmas after Wes was gone. How could I have done that? And why didn't her family say anything? Come to Grandma's for Christmas but no decorations there. It hadn't been a holly, jolly Christmas at the Palmer house for a long time.

Damn Wes.

As soon as the bank opened that Friday morning, Lyn was there. She had convinced the Board a couple years ago that Christmas bonuses were necessary and they should be cash. Lyn had sent the bank a list of cash she wanted; how many of what bills. Addressed envelopes were already in her desk. She left the bank with a lot of cash and hurried back to the Library. For the next hour she stuffed money into envelopes and sealed them with a holiday sticker. Bonus was determined on longevity. Lyn added a personal note on many of the cards. It took all morning.

Lyn had argued to get the bonus and succeeded. She had argued to distribute it the week before Christmas and lost. She never got reasoning for the Board's decision but decided a bonus is good no matter when you get it. Especially if it is cash.

Friday went by quickly. Lyn stopped for tape and gift wrap on the way home. Then decided she didn't feel like making dinner and stopped for takeout. A bit of decorating - boughs, balls and bows on the fireplace mantel and a wreath on the front door. Wrap ten packages and it's done. Hal called about seven to check in. Another day of depositions but no more until after the new year. How was your day, etc.? Sleep well. I love you. She felt really Christmasy as she wrapped packages. "Hal always brightens my day."

The telephone rang at ten. It was Jim. "I figured you were decorating the tree or wrapping packages and would still be up."

"Merry Christmas, Jim."

"Merry Christmas, Maddy. It's snowing here. Going to be a white Christmas for sure. I was going to wait and call tomorrow but figure the kids and Lee will be there and I didn't want to interrupt."

"Thank you for that. They'll be here for dinner and to open presents. But how would you know that?"

"I just guessed since there aren't kids at home that's what you'd do. So Lee's kids could be home for Santa presents Sunday morning."

"Well, you're right. Have a nice holiday, Jim."

"Thanks, Maddy. I'll try but there's no real incentive."

"Merry Christmas, Jim."

"Same to you, Maddy. Bye."

"Goodbye, Jim."

For a brief moment, Lyn was sad. Then she thought, "He's survived for sixteen years without us. He surely has a routine by now for holidays. I am not going to feel sorry for him. I'm not."

She arranged her packages under the tree. How nice that looked. The family room was festive. First time in a long time. A smile came as she turned off the lights and went to bed. Tomorrow was Christmas Eve.

CHAPTER FIFTY-THREE

Saturday morning Lyn went to the Library. It is custom that every employee stops by the Library on Christmas Eve, scheduled or not, to receive a Christmas bonus. Lyn would prefer to have a small celebration at noon, as the Library closes at noon on Christmas Eve, but she took a poll a couple years ago telling the staff what the Board had decided about bonus distribution; when would be the best time? This was the unanimous vote. She was sad; it seems so impersonal.

She left for home with a bag full of gifts. Her staff always thinks of her. They were appalled to learn she doesn't get a Christmas bonus. But, she received gifts from her staff before she got the bonus approved, so there you are. The bonus may have nothing to do with their thoughtfulness.

When she got home, she put those packages in a small pile under the tree. She'd open them Christmas morning. The child in her has to have a Christmas morning present. And the past sixteen years, it's been gifts from her staff. Family on Christmas Eve; alone on Christmas Day.

As she put the gifts under the tree she thought, "Maybe this will be the last year these will be my only gifts on Christmas morning. It was a rude shock when she realized she had no idea what traditions Hal has for Christmas. Do I know enough about him to marry him? He'll be here tonight - he's already verified that. But what does he usually do on Christmas? Go caroling, parties, hang a stocking?

Hal called just after noon. "Had lunch yet?"

"No, hadn't thought that far yet. I spent the morning at the Library and haven't been home long enough to put the brain into gear."

"Two things - either I pick you up and take you to lunch or I bring takeout home for lunch. Which do you prefer?"

"Oh, takeout. The restaurants are probably busy today."

After she hung up, she realized he said bring takeout home for lunch. This is my home. I never stopped to think it will be his also. In fact, he's taken for granted he'll move in here and I never thought of leaving to move elsewhere with him. Am I even ready to get married again? I just don't seem to be capable of thinking things through anymore. Oh, good gravy, there's just too much to consider. I love him. I'm pretty sure I want to marry him. Why is this a problem? Why wouldn't he think he'd be moving here? He's renting a one-bedroom apartment. It'd be stupid for me to think of moving. Why is this suddenly a problem?

Lyn changed into jeans and a t-shirt before sitting at the kitchen table to make a list of what was for dinner and when to start it. If Hal was helping, a list would be handy. Otherwise everything's in my head and, at the rate I'm thinking these days, I could blow dinner.

Lyn mixed the ingredients for dinner rolls, covered the bowl with a dish towel and set it aside to rise. The ham went into the oven; she mixed the glaze and put it in the fridge until the ham is nearly done. She laid the potatoes on the counter by the mandolin and peeler.

She heard Hal's car pull into the driveway. It took her a month to convince him he didn't have to park at the curb like a visitor. Lyn opened the door just as he came across the stepping stones to the sidewalk. He had a cardboard box filled with little Chinese takeout boxes. She recognized the boxes; they were from the Moon Palace.

"The Moon Palace, how did you know?"

"The night I asked you to marry me we talked a long time and you mentioned that you used to go to the Moon Palace for lunch on Christmas Eve and dinner on New Year's Eve. So I went to the Moon Palace and asked the lady if she knew you. She does indeed. I told her what I wanted to do and she said that she knows exactly what you always ordered for Christmas Eve lunch. And here it is."

As I started opening the boxes, Hal went to the cupboard and got plates, forks, spoons, and napkins. Orange chicken, broccoli beef, fried rice, egg drop soup, and rumaki. I've gotten to be so emotional lately. I cannot believe I am standing over a Chinese lunch and crying. Mae Wong had remembered exactly what Wes and I ordered for lunch every Christmas for twenty years. There was a container with soy sauce, two tea bags, two almond cookies, and two fortune cookies.

Hal saw the tears. "She was sure it was right."

I turned and cried on his shoulder. "It is perfect. It's exactly right."

He handed me his handkerchief and pulled out my chair. "Wonderful. Merry Christmas, Lyn."

As we ate, I asked what were his traditions for Christmas. Did he hang a stocking on Christmas Eve? Go to parties? Sing with a choir? We exchanged stories for quite a while. I looked at the clock and asked if he was ready to go into second cook mode. He was. We cleared the table, washed our hands, and put on our Christmas aprons. I had found two in the indoor box.

Hal is adept at peeling potatoes but wasn't too sure about the mandolin. Once he understood the principle of it, he sliced all the potatoes perfectly. I mixed the cheese sauce and together we had au gratin potatoes ready to go in the oven.

I had apples, one large red, one large green; celery; an orange, pecans on the counter. "What are we making out of this?"

"Waldorf salad."

"Do you want me to peel the apples?"

"No, just wash them well. The skins make the salad pretty." After instructions on how I'd like the fruit and celery cut, Hal set to work while I made the dressing for the salad. Half an hour, the Waldorf was chilling in the fridge. "I can't remember eating a Waldorf salad before. Sure looks interesting."

After I showed him how to apply the glaze to the ham, I worked the dough for the dinner rolls. By 6pm, dinner could be considered ready. The rolls go in the oven and the broccoli in the microwave steamer when Lee and kids arrive. Hal brought a change of clothes and we got ourselves party ready. Setting the dining room table was a breeze; he knows how to do that. There were festive centerpieces from the indoor box and the table was beautiful.

While admiring the tree, Hal said, "Oops, I've got packages in the car." He hurried out and put several packages under the tree before our guests arrived.

The kids had packages in their arms when they came in. They put them under the tree and went to gang up on Hal. Then they realized, there was a tree. Did Hal put that up? Grams has never had a tree before. Hal admitted he helped buy it and decorate it. He said there was all sorts of good stuff in the garage rafters - maybe Grams never put up a tree because she couldn't reach the ornaments. Yeah, that sounded right. "Well, it sure is pretty, Hal. You do good work." They all laughed.

Lee said that her Dad had called about an hour ago. "He figured we'd be here later and thought it best to call us at home. We talked about ten minutes or so. He told the kids it was snowing there."

"He called me last night. It was snowing then so he'll surely have a white Christmas."

"He sounded homesick, Mom."

"Lee, he may be. But he's had a lot of years to build new traditions. Don't feel sorry for him. Just be happy he's alive and well."

I went to the kitchen to handle the dinner rolls and broccoli. Frankly, I was pissed he was trying to rain on my parade. And that is what it sounds like - to me.

Hal excused himself from the pile of grandchildren. "I helped cook dinner and probably should help get it on the table."

"Really, you cook? What did you make?"

I had hot pads in place on the dining table and Hal knew what went where. He went to the warming oven and got out the potatoes. "I peeled and sliced these." He put the dish in place. Then he went to the fridge and got out the Waldorf, "And this too." He put it on the table. The ham was rested sufficiently and I quickly sliced several slices but left them on the platter with the ham. He put that on the table. "And I put the glaze on the ham." The kids are big eyed. Wow. Hal helped Grams make dinner. I took the rolls out of the oven and got down a bread basket. There were dishes of butter and jam on the table already. The broccoli went into a glass dish so its color would add to the table.

Dinner was most enjoyable. The kids pried into Hal's life and asked what he liked best about Christmas when he was a kid and what he likes best now. They talked sports and Wil gave an update on the swim team. They haven't lost a single match this year though they came in second once. I sat and listened. Watching Lee, I could see that she was wishing Larry was here. She enjoyed listening to the kids talk - just as they do with their Dad when he's home.

We had cleared the table and everyone decided dessert should come later because "we ate like oinks". Hal looked at me. He didn't know there was dessert. I made it last night.

Just as we settled in the family room, the telephone rang. Laurie was right next to the phone; she looked at me and I said, "Answer it, please Laurie."

It was Larry. The kids scattered through the house so they each had an extension to talk to their Dad. After several minutes, Laurie handed the phone to Hal after telling her brothers "Hang up, Guys."

Hal and Larry talked about three minutes; Hal laughed a couple times. Then he handed the phone to me. "Good work, Grams. I just warned Hal he'd better take damn good care of you." We spoke a minute and I gave the phone to Lee. She got up and went into the kitchen.

Hal came and sat next to me on the love seat. "Larry didn't know about us until this call. He hasn't been able to get through for a while. Wil and Mike told him. He seems really pleased. He did say that when he asked me to take care of his family, he didn't realize how seriously I took the order." I laughed. "Sounds like Larry."

"I told him this was one thing I probably would've done on my own without orders. Larry laughed and said he was truly happy for us both."

Lee came back to the family room looking happy. The kids were back at the tree. I reminded them that the group in the back was from my staff and I would open them tomorrow. We have the tradition of distributing all the gifts first. Then one by one we each open a gift, and go round until there are no more. The first gift I opened was from Hal. A beautiful stole. I mean beautiful. He said that he thought it would be nice the next time we go out when it's cool but not coat weather. I was quite pleased.

I gave him walking shorts and a polo to match and a book on Beaches of the World. The kids had a funny look at the clothes. I told them Hal came over one Saturday and when I mentioned going to the arboretum, he thought he'd be overdressed. But you know we have emergency clothes in the closet. Hal started laughing. "I wore them that day and wore them home and still haven't returned them. I guess this is a hint." That caused everyone to laugh.

Hal had really put in some thought for his gifts for my grandchildren. The boys each got a video game which they both said, "I've been saving for this game." He gave Laurie a necklace, a thin silver chain with a silver scorpion pendant. But that wasn't the best. He gave each child a jacket, a Marine Corps utility jacket; master sergeant stripes on the sleeve and name tag "BAXTER" over the breast pocket. Right size for each, though he told Laurie hers might be a tad big as he thinks she'll grow more this year. The kids are so excited. They put the jackets on immediately and wore them home. Just like Dad's. This was the first time I saw Lee actually look like she might approve of Hal. She got misty eyed as her children mugged Hal and thanked him a dozen times each.

As usual, I gave each of the kids books, a sweater, their favorite candy, and a book of eight passes for the local theater. Well, the theater passes aren't usual. This is the first year the theater has offered passes this way. Lee was pleased - her gift from Hal was in a handkerchief box. There was a beautiful handkerchief with an A in the corner and under it was a sizable gift card to a department store. "How did you know this is my favorite store, Hal?" He laughed and said, "I pay attention." I have no idea when he heard anything unless it was from the kids.

I gave her the latest kitchen gadget she's been mooning over. The kids gave me earrings and Hal a truly handsome tie and beautiful tie tack. Lee gave us a gift card for the Moon Palace. Everyone was very pleased with their gifts and the way their gifts had been received. I got up to get dessert and Hal said, "Wait there's one more package under the tree. I can see it from here."

Wil looked under the tree. Sure enough a little square package with a big red bow. "It's for Grams."

He handed it to me. It was from Hal. "I'm a bit late with this and ask forgiveness."

A ring. A beautiful ring. He leaned over and took the box from me. He took the ring, got down on one knee and said, "To be sure everyone knows what this is - Madlyn Palmer, will you marry me?" I said, "Yes, yes, I will". I kissed him and he returned the kiss. He slid the ring on my finger. Perfect fit. The kids were actually misty eyed and giggly. Even Lee looked pleased. Mike said, "Boy, I've got to remember to tell Dad about this. What a Christmas!"

Hal and I went to the kitchen to get the dessert ready. Everyone came back to the table. Hal poured milk and the coffee was ready by the time the pie was served. Lemon meringue. Lee took one bite before saying, "You haven't made this for Christmas in a long time, Mom. Thank you."

My family left within an hour of the pie. It was fairly late but it is Christmas Eve. Hal and I stood at the door and waved goodbye until they were out of sight.

My fiancé stood quietly for a few minutes after I closed the door. "Is something wrong, Hal?"

"No, Lyn, things have never been more right. I have never had a family Christmas like this. I am an only child and Christmas was never too important with my parents. Sometimes we had a tree and sometimes we didn't. I guess if one of them thought about it, they'd get one. Both were professionals and I understand now that a child may not have been in their original plans. Neither really knew anything about kids. They did always remember a gift.

On Christmas morning a nicely wrapped package was on the end of my bed when I woke. I never bought them a gift until I was in the Marines. Seriously. I had a wonderful childhood but never a Christmas like this."

We stood together in a warm hug for quite a while. It was amazing to me that he was so pleased. He surprised me with the story of his Christmas as a child. He didn't know better so it was good.

We finished loading the dishwasher and picking up discarded wrappings. I stopped several times to look at the ring. It's a large, square cut diamond set in platinum. I have never owned a ring as exquisite or as large as this. It is beautiful. How he knew the size is a mystery. All he would tell me is that it is a family heirloom. His Mother had it cleaned and sent it to him after he had told her about me. It was his father's great-great-maybe one more great-grandmother's. It's been passed down but there have been no girls on that side of the family for several generations. It was given to his mother by his father as an engagement ring. Once she was married, she didn't wear it daily, or even often, and now that maybe Hal has found his mate, she sent it to him.

For the first time I wished he didn't have to go home. I'm not thinking sex; I'm thinking of seeing him for breakfast in the morning. There's a spare bed, or three, but I don't know how to say something to him. Crazy, huh? Yeah. I just put the kitchen in order.

Hal poured a second cup of coffee and sat at the table. "Lyn, you have a spare room. May I spend the night? I don't want to have breakfast alone tomorrow."

I poured myself a cup of coffee. "I was thinking the same thing but didn't want you to think I was a dirty-minded old lady. I have a spare bed and would be delighted for you to sleep in it. I think there are pajamas in the dresser - if you wear pajamas. And there's leftover ham for breakfast."

He got this look on his face. Happens every time he thinks of something he's never had to think of before. "Oh, but what will your neighbors think?"

I kept from laughing. "Well, all the women will say 'how did she get so lucky'?

He shook his head. "Oh, Lyn, you are just too much. I love that in a person."

CHAPTER FIFTY-FOUR

I checked the room where Laurie stays when she's here. I know there are fresh linens on the bed but wanted to be sure there were towels in the bathroom. I turned down the bed and fluffed the pillow. Hal came in as I straightened up. "There's an alarm clock if you want an alarm. Laurie insists on it but I believe she's never used it. You know where everything is in the bathroom, right?"

"When I used the facilities the night I fell asleep on your couch, I put my toothbrush in the holder. I didn't think to ask what to do with it. So, yes, I'm all set. Thank you very much. There were pajamas in the drawer."

He kissed me soundly and said, "I'll put on the coffee if I'm up first."

"That would be most considerate, Sir. I appreciate it. Would you bring in the newspaper, too?"

He laughed. "Absolutely."

I kissed him goodnight and crossed the hall to my own bed. Once we set a date, I think we should go shopping for a new bed. I'll mention that at breakfast, maybe.

Sleep came quickly. Probably a good thing as there were so many things to think about. Once my brain is in gear, sleep retreats. I woke usual time, about seven, and could smell coffee. I wanted to shower but also wanted to say good morning. I combed my hair to avoid that Medusa look and went to the kitchen. Hal was at the table reading the paper. From the looks of it, he hasn't been reading too long.

"I'm going to shower but wanted to say good morning." An empty cup sat by the coffee pot. I poured coffee.

"Good morning, Lyn. Somehow I knew you looked great in the morning."

That surprised me and I wondered what he expects a person to look like in the morning. "Well, I'm glad you think so as it doesn't get much better as the day progresses."

He laughed and pulled me down to his lap. "I sound really stupid. I know that. But I get speechless around you some times. I can't explain it as I can be quite loquacious when I'm not near you. Harrelson keeps telling me I talk too much."

I laughed. This is the first time he's mentioned his FBI partner in a very long time. "You haven't mentioned Harrelson much lately. I wondered if you were still a team."

"Absolutely. The best team in the Bureau. Oh, by the way, Harrelson's parents host a wallopalooza New Year's Eve party every year. I have gone a couple times. Harrelson asked me Friday if I was coming this year. I asked if I could bring a date and he said sure, haha. With everything going on yesterday, I forgot to ask you."

"Where and how fancy?"

"Upper Arcadia and fairly fancy; ladies wear long dresses type thing."

"Would my Gala dress be appropriate?"

"Oh, yes, it certainly would. Is that a yes?"

I stood up. "Consider it so. I haven't been to an adult party in a long time. You may have to remind me how to behave."

"Very funny. I was counting on you keeping me in line. I'll tell Tom I'll be there with a guest."

"He doesn't know about us, does he? This is going to be a big surprise to him, isn't it?"

"Well, not really. He knows I've been seeing someone. I just never told him who."

"Are you ashamed of me?"

"Lord, no. I just didn't think it was any of his business. I don't inquire as to his love life - he is married and has a little son. I don't ask questions."

"Where in upper Arcadia?"

"Last street east off Santa Anita."

"Arno?"

"Yes, you know the area?"

"I have friends who live on Arno. Well, they considered us friends. They're always one level above me somehow. Sheila calls her house a villa. And, it practically is."

"Sounds like the Harrelson's house. They hire a band, have what they call a great room that houses most of the party but you can wander out onto the patio and the pool area."

"Same set up. I think there are only five houses on Arno. All mini mansions sort of."

"Still want to go?"

"Oh, Lord yes. I have a diamond to flash. I'll fit right in." I laughed and went to shower. I don't take a long shower and was soon dressed in jeans and a Christmas sweatshirt. "Hungry?"

"Yes, ma'am." He paused. "Lyn, I'm sorry if I have offended you. I love you dearly. I am not ashamed of you. I'd take you anywhere. But sometimes Tom Harrelson is nosy. I don't mind telling him where I've been, where I'm going. But it seems like gossip and it's about us. We've been partners about eight years. I was best man at his wedding. I'm his son's godfather. But he's always in my face. When am I going to find someone and settle down? I told him once I was damn near old enough to be his father - back off. He doesn't believe it, but he's only thirty-eight. I just resent his intrusion some times.".

"Hal, did you ever think he doesn't consider it intrusion? You are evidently his best friend. He's married and happy and probably just wants the same for you. He is a different generation and I know they think differently. Look at Lee. Or, are you concerned because we met through an FBI investigation? Do you think he'll judge you for that?"

He looked like I had slapped him. "What?"

"Are you afraid he'll disapprove of me because of how we met?"

Hal sat very still for quite a while. "No. He won't disapprove. He had such empathy for you. He felt the FBI and the whole federal government let you down. Tom thinks you are one of the nicest women we've encountered together. No, he won't disapprove."

"Okay. Then do you want to dress while I start breakfast? Let Tom know that you and a guest will be at his parent's shindig."

Hal started to shuffle off toward the bedroom. Then he turned around and grabbed me and held me very close. "Lyn, just kick me in the ass when I start going afield like this. I love you and am sure than Tom and Linda will be very surprised. Linda said she knows I'm seeing someone as they haven't seen me regularly in quite a while. So she will be delighted to meet you."

The rest of the day went much better and about six, Hal gathered up his belongings and headed home. In a way, I was glad he left early. It is Christmas Day and one would expect to spend it with loved ones. But we had Christmas

Eve with family. I am realizing I don't know enough about him. Maybe I accepted this ring too soon. I do love him but I love only what I know about him and there seems to be very much that I have not touched on.

I didn't know he was godfather to Harrelson's baby. I didn't even know Harrelson was married. If I had a close friend and found myself involved with someone seriously, I would want to take that someone to meet my close friend. Not as a second opinion but so my friend knows what's going on with me. That's how it used to be. Am I so out-of-date that I'm also out-of-touch? I don't have many close friends but I have introduced Hal to my staff - and they're about as close as you can get. I told them I was engaged. I invited him to a very public function; our photograph was in the newspaper. Hal has talked to his parents but apparently no one else. Am I paranoid? Yes, I am.

About eight o'clock the phone rang. It was Jim. "Just called to say Merry Christmas. Did the party go well last night? How old are the grand kids?" "The kids were enthused. They're 13, 14, 16. I put up a tree this year. And, their Dad called just before we opened presents. So it was a special Christmas Eve for them."

He went on to say it had finally quit snowing but it was warm enough he felt it'd be gone in a few days. Work was fine. How was the Library? I told him things were well after the Gala. I didn't bother to mention Mr. Swanson. "Things are great at the Library. We finally have a Board that is reasonable."

I wanted to ask if he had called Lee and the kids but decided not to do that. He would have mentioned it, I'm sure. And I don't want to give him the idea. The kids would certainly relate the ring episode to him. I don't need his BS right now. I thanked him for calling; he wished me a Merry Christmas and that was it.

He sounded a bit more sincere than he has. Of course, it may just be the Christmas spirit - or spirits. It is 11pm in Massachusetts.

Hal had remade the bed; perhaps he plans to spend another night soon. I won't worry about laundry unless the kids want to come for a day or two. I don't see that happening though.

CHAPTER FIFTY-FIVE

Hal called before I went to bed Christmas Day. To thank me for a memorable Christmas. And to apologize for being such an anti-social ass. "Talk to you tomorrow, Lyn. Sleep well."

The Library doesn't close many days of the year so it was really a slow start up that Monday. No one was late to work; but there was more chit-chat than usual. Of course, about half the staff is under thirty so I am sure there was a lot of comparisons being made over gifts and such. I recall doing that when much younger.

I was in before Alice and was at my desk with a cup of coffee when she arrived. She was not late; I was early. She breezed in and asked how my Christmas was. I told her the grand kids were over for Christmas Eve. "Am I now officially engaged, Alice?" I held out my left hand. The ring sparkled and shone brilliantly.

"Oh, Mrs. P, that is beautiful. Yes, I would say you are now officially engaged. Was that your Christmas present from Mr. Tucker?"

"No, he gave me a lovely gift. He said this was late in response to my yes."

The fourteen-year old Alice was very present. She took my hand and tilted it to the right and left. "It is beautiful. I've never seen a diamond that shape before. Wow."

The phone rang and she rushed to her desk to answer it. The front desk doesn't pick up until ten. And Monday was off and running.

The theater staff came in. They had distilled the list patrons made at the Gala down to the top twenty. Top twenty each had more than ten suggestions each to be movies shown at the Library. We usually order for ten weeks at a time so this would be a perfect order. If I agreed with the films, would I order them? They're shipped two at a time, which is perfect as we show two a week. The staff had grouped them by week so there'd be a sense of order. Same actor in the first eight; we've done a certain actor month before. That would be February. Then topic or genre was in pairs for March and April. I prepared the purchase order and gave them a copy. They'll follow up. Alice faxed the purchase order to the film distributor and filed the confirmation with the purchase order.

The nice thing about the survey, we have an idea what people like. Surprisingly, over eighty percent were films over ten years old. I am sure the theater staff will hold on to the survey for future reference.

The day flew by. Or seemed to. Hal called at four; did I care to have dinner with him? He'd pick me up at six. He had reservations at Luigi's. It was a slow Monday at the restaurant and we took our time. He was still in a glow over Christmas Eve. He didn't seem to have any other reason for dinner out. Hal can be so funny. He gets enthused over stuff I take for granted.

Wednesday has been dinner at my house for a couple months now. Hal confirmed, by telephone Wednesday morning, he would be here by 7. Saturday we've always gone out. This Saturday would be a new year's eve party. I am looking forward to it while dreading it. Hal will pick me up around 8:30pm. He said he believes they say 8pm to 1am but he's never gotten there at eight. Okay by me. "Is that what is called fashionably late. Hal?"

"Gosh, I don't know. For a shin-dig like this I have never shown up at the first time quoted."

"Okay. You did confirm with Harrelson Monday?"

"Yes, I did. Told him a guest and I would be there. Do you think I should have told him it is you?"

"No, he'll find out. Might be interesting to see his reaction."

"Yeah, that too." Hal smiled.

And here I am back to wondering about Hal. My Dad always says if it seems too good to be true, it probably isn't. Damn. And the ring is an heirloom, I wouldn't even get to keep it.

Wednesday dinner was a good feeling dinner. We danced a little although the Madlyn School of Dance closed a couple weeks ago. He said, "The Harrelson's usually hire a nice dance band so we can dance Saturday if we get bored."

"Can we dance if we don't get bored, Hal?"

That opposing thought had never entered his mind. I could tell from the momentary blank look on his face. "You fooling with me again, Lyn."

"No, Sweetheart, I'm not. What if we go and actually have a good time? I'd still like to dance a little. You are a really fine dancer."

He sat for a moment and said, "You should've taught English, Mrs. P."

"I minored in Language Arts and could have. I know exactly what you meant but you said it in such a way that we'd have to be bored to dance. Surely that is not what you meant. For an attorney, you mangle the language sometimes, Hal."

"I sat in on four miserable depositions recently and the attorney asked every question at least three ways. He would have said Did you dance when you were bored? Were you bored so you danced? Did you dance because you could? And the witness would look at him and say yes to every question. You're right. There are times I say what I mean without meaning what I say. Do you love me even so?"

"I most certainly do. Forgive me for picking on you. I can't help it. I grew up in a home that spoke sarcasm as a second language. I've gotten away from it a lot - half the Library staff doesn't get it and the other half would be offended if they did. I love you, Hal. I think you're perfect so I pick at stupid stuff. Do you love me even so?" Hugs and kisses must mean yes.

After he left Wednesday I had a long talk with myself. Why am I being petty about little stuff? I haven't done it to him before. What made me do it tonight? Old habits die hard. Was it just a flash to the past? I hope so. I couldn't stand myself if I keep this up. Lord knows how he'd take it.

He called at work Thursday around noon. He was working late tonight. He and Harrelson were trying to tie up loose ends on two cases. He may not have a chance to call before bedtime. I thanked him for the consideration. He does keep in touch everyday usually. Would I have realized tonight that he hadn't called?

I don't like this feeling I'm developing. What the hell is wrong with me? A little voice said, "Madlyn, you're afraid. After more than sixteen years, you're on the verge of no longer being totally self-dependent. You're afraid, Old Girl, of having to be accountable to someone again." I went to sleep with that thought sitting on the top of my mind. Is it true?

I'm more than half afraid it is.

By Saturday, I had pretty much put away feelings other than I was going to a grown-up party. I washed and set my hair in the morning. I used to wear my hair down and let it fall in waves down my back. I have a hair band that looks sparkly - it still does. I cleaned it carefully to be sure it still looks as great as I thought. Wes called it my mini tiara. I guess it really is. With the earrings from my grandchildren, my twentieth anniversary diamond pendant and my Gala dress, I should look grown-up without looking old. And dressed well enough for a party on Arno Drive. Perfect occasion to wear my Christmas stole. I held out my left hand. And this should sparkle up the evening a whole lot.

Saturday mid-afternoon Hal called. Should he wear a dark brown suit or tan? Which will look better with my dress? "The dark brown is what you wore to the Gala. It looks very good with the dress. And with your fair hair, somehow it makes you appear taller. Tall is always good."

"There is always a lot of food around but eat a bit of dinner anyhow. Sorry we won't make Moon Palace this year. But do have a snack."

"Okay. I was wondering."

"Well, I don't like to head for the food trays the minute I walk through the door. Makes it look like that's all I am there for - to eat."

"Smart man. I agree. But I do like a drink soon after getting to a party. I never know what to do with my hands."

He laughed and said, "Are you going to carry a small bag or just put your keys and lipstick in my pocket?"

"Hal, it would be wonderful not to have to worry about an evening bag. I have more than one but your solution is so much simpler. Thank you. See you around 8:30."

About five o'clock I made a grilled cheese sandwich and ate it with a few potato chips. That will definitely hold me until nine or later.

CHAPTER FIFTY-SIX

The Harrelsons had parking valets. I wondered how many cars would fit on that small street. Now I wonder where they're parking cars. Probably on Santa Anita Drive. There's really no other place. We arrived and a young man asked for Hal's name. It was on the list. They gave him a playing card as a token for the car. Hal came around and opened the car door for me. We watched the valet turn the car around and head toward Santa Anita. Hal showed me the playing card.

"How great is this? The King of Hearts?" We both laughed and he put the card in the same pocket as my house key and lipstick. The flagstone walkway was quite wide. We followed it to the house. There were balloons and streamers at the door.

The Harrelsons were within ten feet of the door, evidently waiting for arriving guests. Mr. Harrelson greeted Hal with outstretched hand. "Tommy said you were bringing a guest. He didn't mention how beautiful she was."

Hal shook the old man's hand. "That's because he doesn't know who she is yet." Mrs. Harrelson joined us and spoke to Hal. Hal said, "Mr. and Mrs. Harrelson, this is Madlyn Palmer, my fiancée."

Mrs. Harrelson shook my hand and said, "How wonderful. Fiancée. Are you local, Miss Palmer?"

"I was born and raised in Monrovia and am the Director of the Public Library there."

She stepped back, as if to take a second look. "That's why you look vaguely familiar. Your photo was in the paper a week or so ago." She had a slight snide working there.

I didn't have time to be insulted. And probably a good thing. Just then Tom and Linda came to the foyer. Tom Harrelson did a second take when he saw me. "Hal, you old fox. Lyn, welcome to my parent's home. I can see they're both overwhelmed with your presence and haven't welcomed you yet." He sounded a little off but I've never seen him in a casual setting before. "Lyn, my wife Linda. Without realizing it, I've told her all about you. Linda, this is Madlyn Palmer, Hal's fiancée. He did say that, didn't he?"

"Oh, Tom, you are such a goof." I said that. I couldn't believe it. His parents smiled and Mr. Harrelson said quietly to his wife, 'she knows him. He just didn't know they are engaged.' The elder Harrelsons slipped away and left the four of us standing in the foyer.

Tom suggested we find a waiter and get a drink. He needs to toast this engagement. I felt he was actually pleased about it. He seemed upset with his parents but not with Hal. Perhaps something family was going on.

Within an hour I thought I had figured out Mrs. Harrelson's, the elder, problem. Both the band and the caterer had been hired for the Gala. I found the caterer in the kitchen. "Is this one of those you couldn't believe it calls after the Gala?" "Mrs. P, how are you? You're acquainted with the Harrelsons."

"My fiancee works with their son. Otherwise, I'd never be invited." "Glad you're here. We have some of your favorite foods." "I shouldn't ask but is it usual that someone like Mrs. Harrelson would wait so long to hire a caterer." "Personal opinion, I think she and the last guy argued about something and she lost. I believe she waited around for him to apologize and he never did." "Don't you worry about that?" "Nah, I asked for 90% up front." I smiled and shook my head.

I rejoined Hal, Tom and Linda. We talked about all sorts of things. I asked about their son; how old was he and such. Did I have children? In fact, I have grandchildren. When Hal and I are married, he's immediately a grandfather. Tom asked, "You mean he really is old enough to be my father?" "Well, it would be possible." "Damn, I can't keep up with him. How's he does it?" "The Marine Corps, Tom. I think he didn't age while in the Corps." Everyone laughed.

We laughed and danced. The band leader spoke to me during a short break. "Thanks, Mrs. P. We thought we'd be unemployed this New Year's and then we got this call. We saw your name in the Library ad. Lady said, "The band we had hired has backed out on us." I played kind of hard to get, raised the price a bit, and here we are." "You did get an advance?" "Oh, yeah, always on a last minute deal. We haven't been around a long time as a band but, individually, we've been around a long time. If you want anything special to dance to, let us know."

Hal asked where I had gotten the band for the Gala. "One of my part-time staff plays trombone in this group. When I started looking for a band it was a bit late and he gave me the leader's number. They haven't been playing together long so haven't established a reputation yet."

"Well, this should do it." We danced and danced and danced and never once was bored. The food was good; my friend Shelia and her husband were there. She had the nerve to ask if we ever found out what happened to Wes. I told her that the FBI believes he was put into Witness Protection after helping catch some bad guys. Wow. She was impressed. I told her that it was advised I divorce him as he was probably someone else by now. How long ago was that? Over sixteen years. And you've just found someone? How romantic. I agreed.

It would have been rude to tell her I never looked. Romance found me.

The elder Harrelsons were more than cordial after the little set to at the front door. Perhaps because I actually blended in, knew several of the other guests, looked right; I was okay. I think maybe Hal was always the single, good-looking guy at the party. I doubted he flirted and probably didn't dance but he was single, good-looking and probably good at small talk after a drink or two. I don't know. This is all supposition on my part. I had taken the single, good-looking guy away and brought an engaged, handsome man to their party. The fact that I know their son may or may not be in my favor.

There were little hats, horns, noise makers, and balloons and streamers at midnight. Hal kissed me in front of God and everybody. Tom and Linda were happy that Hal is happy and suggested we get together. I was agreeable; Hal was agreeable; and Tom didn't seem to mind how Hal had met me.

It was a very satisfying New Year's Eve. I hadn't celebrated the new year for a long time. Now I am looking forward to the next one. Maybe a party at home. But a party.

We arrived at my house around two am. Hal asked if he could stay over. He had made the bed. He tried to be a good guest. I told him he could. Would he make the coffee if he was up first? And bring in the Sunday paper? He would.

CHAPTER FIFTY-SEVEN

New Year's morning was a lot better than Christmas morning had been. I was up first. So if there is a disadvantage to sleeping later than your host, it was on him. He came out groggy and looking as though he should go back to bed. I told him so. He poured a cup of coffee and sat down. He didn't reach for the paper, he just drank coffee.

"What time did we get to bed?"

"I was in bed by three. I think you were too. Neither of us had too much to drink. Maybe we're getting old and the late hours are affecting us."

"Oh, come on, Lyn."

"Sweetie, go back to bed. I'll make breakfast whenever you get up. You've been working too hard and a couple late nights can take you down."

"Okay." He finished the coffee in his cup. Set it down and went back to bed.

It was only 7:30. I can't imagine how I was up and feeling so great.

I wrote thank you notes to my staff for the lovely and thoughtful gifts they had given me at Christmas. Funny, cute pins, useful pens, a hair clip, hankies, several boxes of my favorite chocolates, a book of poetry by a new author (we'd discussed whether or not to buy it months ago for the shelves), cubes of note paper, a new mouse pad, a bracelet, two scarves. I have the most thoughtful staff in the world.

I had finished the last and was putting stickers on the flaps when Hal came back into the kitchen. He had showered and was looking wide awake. It was just after 9.

"Feel better?"

"Yes, I can't believe it. I feel absolutely great."

"Good, you look great. Pancakes or toast with your eggs?"

He grinned. "Pancakes. Poached eggs?"

"Sure, if you want."

He poured another cup of coffee and sat down at the kitchen table. I had opened the paper but not read it. I want to take the thank you notes to work tomorrow.

"Haven't you read the paper yet?"

"No, I was working on thank you notes for the staff. Still have others to finish and will write them later."

"Do you always send a thank you?"

"Lord, yes, don't you? I'll even send one to the Harrelson's for the party."

"I have never known someone so dutiful as you are, Lyn."

"Dutiful? Hal, it's manners."

He didn't say anything more and I started breakfast. He reads the paper just the opposite from me. I start at the back and read forward but he reads from the front to the back. This should work well when we are both reading at the same time. There are usually four sections in the paper. I was starting another pot of coffee when Hal's phone rang. It was on the kitchen counter.

"Harold Tucker. ... Good morning, Tom. Great party last night. Thank your folk for me. I am sure that Lyn will send them a note but you know me and notes. ... Okay, okay, I should have told you but you took the surprise quite well. ... I know, she could charm a brass monkey. ... No, we were serious about getting together with you guys. ... We try to go out on Saturdays. Are Saturdays good for you? ... Ah, yes, baby sitters. What kind of criteria does a baby sitter have to have to sit for young Thomas Harold Harrelson? ... At least thirteen, sensible, good grades, live nearby and will sit for five bucks an hour. I just may know someone. You live on Mayflower and Olive, right? May I give your home number to someone who may be interested? What was I doing when you called? I just got up. We old guys have to sleep in once in a while. ... Very funny Tommy. ... We had a great time at the party; truly did. Love to Linda. Sure, I'll tell her. Bye."

Sure wish I could have heard both sides of that conversation. "Do you have someone in mind? How would you know a babysitter, Hal?"

"I have an almost granddaughter who fits the bill. Laurie has babysat a few times around her neighborhood and Tom and Linda could be considered neighborhood - seven or eight blocks."

I am dumb struck. He knows more about my granddaughter than I do, apparently. I didn't say that out loud as I know he's spent hours with the kids in the pool and they talk a lot. "Well, it's not too early. Give her a call. If she's not interested, she'll tell you so."

Between bites of pancakes, Hal called Laurie and asked if she was interested in babysitting once in a while. For who? I am sure that was the question. He explained that his FBI partner and his wife have a baby who is just a year old and how they live at Mayflower and Olive, only pay five bucks an hour, and will take you home. He gave her a number and said, "Mrs. Harrelson's name is Linda; my partner's name is Tom. Tell them you just spoke to your almost grandfather and you're interested in occasional babysitting. That is, if you are." ... "Have your Mom call me. I'll tell her what I've just told you and she can ask your Grams what she thinks of the Harrelsons." ... "Your Grams says your Mom has met Tom. I forgot. She has." ... "Let me know. They need a sitter so we can all go out."

We finished breakfast before Lee called me. She was thrilled that Hal trusts Laurie enough to recommend her to babysit for a close friend. Laurie was working up a resume in case the Harrelsons wanted references other than Hal.

An hour later, Tom called. He and Linda were greatly enthused. Laurie is exactly the type person they want with Tommy. She had called, used the introduction Hal suggested and then said she would like to meet them if possible before deciding. I liked that she was taking control of the situation. Maybe she would be put off by something. Who knows? So she walked to their house. It is seven blocks. She wore her Marine Corps jacket. No doubt who she was. Linda opened the door - she had Tommy on one hip. Linda said Laurie gave her name and Tommy reached for her. So Laurie took him and followed Linda into the house. Doesn't matter what Tom and Linda think, the baby likes Laurie. Tom said he took her resume - a list of five neighbors with children from one to six. Laurie stayed about ten minutes and Linda familiarized her with the house and Tommy's room, where things were kept and such. She left saying she'd be delighted to sit for them. If they were interested in her, just give her a call. She has a cell phone and gave them that number as well as her mother's.

Twenty minutes after that, Laurie called Hal on his cell. She has no clue he's here at my house. He put the call on speaker phone. "Hal, you are so kind to get me babysitting jobs. I went to your friend's house. Mom says she does remember meeting him and thought he was a very nice man. Anyhow, I rang the doorbell and Linda came to the door. Tommy was sort of sitting on her hip. I said, Hi, I'm Laurie Baxter. I spoke to Mr. Harrelson a while ago. And Tommy reached for me. So I took him. He's an adorable baby. Did you know his birthday is two days after ours? Oh, of course you know. Linda says you're his godfather. Well, that made your recommendation even more meaningful to me. This is not just a friend's baby but your godson. Wow. Hal. You are certainly a great person. No wonder my Grams thinks you're made out of gold or something."

She finally came up for air and Hal thanked her for checking out the job. He knows she'll be a super babysitter. And, then he said, "The four of us can go out together sometimes, now. Got to get your Grams back into the social world you know."

"Yes, I know. And I am glad you're the guy who will do it. Love you a whole bunch, almost Gramps. Talk to you later."

He said goodbye and the call terminated. "Almost Gramps?" We both laughed.

CHAPTER FIFTY-EIGHT

School was back in session on January 4th, a Wednesday. On January 5th I got a call at the Library just before noon from my grandson, Wil. He's never called me at the Library.

"What's up, Kiddo?"

"Grams, Mike and I are in Principal Cameron's office. We were on our way to lunch. We brown bag so we can go outside. Anyhow, Principal Cameron stopped us in the hall way and told us we had to remove our jackets. They are considered costumes and are not allowed in school. We told him these were not costumes. Baxter is our name. He said the stripes made it a costume. We told him our dad is a master sergeant in the Marines and these are his stripes. He says too bad. Can you come get us, we refuse to take off our jackets."

"Hold tight. It'll take a few minutes just to get there."

I immediately called Hal's cell. When he answered I asked, "Sweetie, where are you right this minute?"

"I'm standing on the sidewalk waiting for the light to change to go to lunch."

"Yes, but where? You said you wouldn't be downtown today."

"No, I'm not. I'm at Fifth and Foothill in Arcadia. What's up?"

"John Cameron, the high school principal, has Wil and Mike in his office. He says they have to take off their jackets or go home. He says the jackets are costumes."

"I can be there in probably less than ten minutes. It can't be more than three miles to the school. Call Wil back and tell him I'm on my way."

I started to say thank you but he'd already hung up. I called Wil. "Hold tight. Mr. Tucker is on his way. And you know what that means."

I could almost hear his smile. "Yes, I think I do. Okay. We'll wait here in Mr. Cameron's office."

About forty minutes later, Hal called. "The boys are eating their lunch. We have late hall passes for both of them signed by Cameron so they can get back into class. I insisted on this. No way are the kids missing lunch because of a jackass. Cameron said someone complained. I asked who. He'd rather not say. Student, teacher, or someone else. Someone else. If they're not student or teacher, why would he be concerned with what they thought. I told him I gave the boys those jackets for Christmas. Was he aware that their father, Master Sergeant Lawrence Baxter was on his second deployment in two years and has been home less than four weeks of those two years? Does he understand what that can do to a young person's sense of security? How many other students in his school have parents who are deployed? He doesn't even know. How can he possibly believe that wearing their father's stripes is wearing a costume? If he did not rescind his order to them, I will be talking to the School Board as soon as I leave his office. I called him a jackass and unAmerican.

He'd have me know he spent two years in the US Army. Whoopee, I said. Two whole years and you weren't married and didn't have children. You were probably drafted; you're the right age for that. Then he demanded to know who I was. I pulled out my ID and said, "Harold Tucker, Federal Bureau of Investigation". Why would this be of interest to you? Didn't you know? The FBI is constantly on the lookout for unAmericans. This is definitely a slam against patriotism. He kind of shuffled his feet. I said that I could demand to know who had made the accusation. He didn't say anything but finally said they could wear their jackets in school. Then I asked for a late hall pass for each so they could eat lunch. You do understand you kept them from eating? Well, yes, he guessed so but he figured they'd take off the jackets and that would be that. Well, that isn't that. So he wrote them each a hall pass and they're headed for class now.

After they left, I threatened him with his job if he ever harassed any child of military personnel again. Oh, he won't."

"Thank you, my love. Thank you for defending the boys, our country, and their Dad. You've probably endeared yourself forever to them."

"It was the principle of the thing, Lyn. I doubt that anyone complained; he was pulling rank."

"Thank you so much. I could have gone to school but even if I had said the same thing, he wouldn't have paid much attention. I'm just a grandmother. Thank you for pulling rank."

"You are welcome. I hope the boys understand I did it for their Dad as much as for them."

"I am sure they do."

When I got home, Wil and Mike were mowing the lawn. Wearing their jackets, of course. I told them they must realize that Hal feels very strongly about the welfare of the country and their father and he believes you have the right, the privilege, to wear your father's stripes.

"Grams, I told Mr. Cameron he was full of crap when he said get that costume jacket off my school yard. That's probably why we ended up in his office." Mike was still shaken by the event.

"Maybe. But he insisted more than once and then tried to bully Hal."

"Yeah, and you don't bully Hal." Wil was still upset too. His teacher asked why he was late and how he got a hall pass from Cameron. "I told him the whole story. And then he wondered why Cameron backed down. I told him my grandfather works for the FBI and told Cameron he wasn't very patriotic. Was it okay to tell my science teacher that Hal is my grandfather?"

"I'm sure he doesn't mind. Your sister calls him her almost Gramps. He doesn't mind that so I'm sure it's okay."

I hugged both boys; told them I loved them; and reminded them their father was deployed to protect all of our rights, not just Mr. Cameron's. They nodded, blew their noses and finished mowing the lawn. When they finished they came in and we all had ice cream.

They were curious how Hal got their sister a babysitting job and I explained that Mr. Harrelson is Hal's partner at the FBI. We all decided to go to dinner some Saturday but Mr. Harrelson has a little boy. So Hal told your sister and she talked to the Harrelsons and met the baby. Hal told her; she handled it herself then. They thought was just super.

Wil said, "You know Grams, he's a good addition to the family. Dad asked him to watch out for us and he sure does. All of us. I hope Dad calls this week. I'm gonna tell him how great Hal is."

I can hardly wait to tell Hal how impressed they are and, yes, they understand why he did what he did. It wasn't just for them.

Hal asked later why they had called me instead of their Mom and I reminded that she works part-time in Glendora. I was the obvious choice for immediate help. He didn't know Lee worked as she is usually home when they get home from school. I was going to remind him how little the Marines pay but decided he might not realize what the enlisted pay scale is. He's glad I called him.

After this little kerfuffle, life seemed almost too good for the next month. We have gone out twice with the Harrelsons. Both times we picked up Laurie and took her to their house then we went to dinner, frequently a bit of dancing. They are great dancers and Hal feels quite comfortable. We'd take them home, they'd pay Laurie and we drop her off on the way to my house. It was a great routine as we pass her house on the way to theirs. I know Tom always gave Laurie twenty dollars even if we weren't gone four hours.

CHAPTER FIFTY-NINE

About the third week of the year, Hal called me at the Library. "It's time to go see my folk. Dad called last night and asked if we'd be here in February. I guess we did talk about it once."

"We did. The third Monday in January wouldn't work for some reason. I am pretty sure you sort of indicated the Washington's birthday weekend."

"Is the Library open?"

"Yes, we close Christmas, New Year's, Fourth of July and Thanksgiving only."

"Can you get the Friday before and the Monday after the weekend off?"

"Yes. I can do that. But can you?"

"If I apply today, I think so."

"Okay, I'll plan on it. Let me know. Then let me know what to expect weather wise, etc. I've never been to the Florida panhandle."

The next day I called Lee and told her we'd be gone the Washington birthday weekend. "I am being taken home to Mother, Lee. I guess he's really serious."

"Oh, Mom, he's always been really serious. Look at the ring he gave you on Christmas. That's serious business. He's just kicking into high gear so you'll set a date."

I laughed, but I know she's right.

We flew into Tallahassee arriving late afternoon Friday. Hal had a rental car waiting at the airport. It's less than a two-hour drive to Apalachicola. He had talked his parents into staying on shore with us in a suite at the Coombs House. They would meet us there for dinner at seven. Hal registered as the Tucker Family. Sure made it easier, I thought. The suite was very nice. A living room separates two bedrooms. Hal had requested one king size bed and one room with two beds. He says his Mom gets a kick out of a king size bed. She says it's as big as her whole bedroom on the boat. We freshened up and at seven a knock on the door. His parents.

I stood up as they came in. Hal is a younger copy of his father; his mother is beautiful. Very tan and though I believe her hair is naturally white the sun has made sure of it. There is no doubt she is a sun lover. Everything I'm not. His Dad shook my hand, looked me up and down as though he was going to made a bid, then hugged me. "Forgive me for staring. You are exactly as Hal has described, right down to the smile."

His mother didn't bother shaking my hand. She just hugged me, tight. I hugged her. She doesn't feel as frail as she looks. Thank goodness.

She took my left hand. "Did you resize this, Harold?" "No, Mother, it fit perfectly." She smiled at me. "I'm sorry but this reminds me of Cinderella. A perfect fit and it's the right girl."

I laughed and asked, "Have you ever considered writing?"

"Why would you ask such a thing, Madlyn?"

"Because your imagination is sprinkled with fairy dust. Who else would think of Cinderella because a ring fit? I think it's marvelous. And so is the ring." Then I thought - oh nuts, I've known them three minutes and blown it already."

The men were both laughing. "She pegged you, Sarah. I don't know how, but she knows the inner you."

As it is, Hal's mother has written children's short stories for years. She publishes under the non de plume, Sarah Storyteller. "We have every one of your books in our children's section. My grandchildren were raised on Sarah Storyteller. Wait until I tell them I've met you. Bedlam. It'll be pure bedlam. The youngest is thirteen now. She has said so often, "I'd like to be able to write like Sarah Storyteller writes. I understand every single story."

Hal's Dad put his arm around my shoulders. "Well, you've uncovered the family secret. Now if you can convince our son we are starving, I'll be forever indebted to you."

For a brief moment I wondered why Hal had never mentioned that Sarah Storyteller was his mother. Then, I remembered, I'm thinking Hal here. It never crossed his mind. It wasn't important at any time in our relationship for me to know that. Though as a librarian, you'd think he'd want me to know. Well, that's Hal.

Hal's Dad's name is Harold. Surprise. But no nickname, it's Harold. At least that will make the weekend much easier for me. Harold had a small restaurant in mind and we dutifully followed him. It was a small hole in the wall but dinner was great. Hal told them I make a wicked Crab Louie; well, everything I make is superb. There wasn't a Crab Louie on the menu. Maybe a good thing, now as I look back. I don't know how my cooking would compare to a seafood restaurant's.

As expected, before we returned to our suite, the idea of a date came up. "I haven't heard from my Dad yet. I would like to know that he can't make it at all rather than set a date he can't accommodate."

Then I had to explain my Dad is a geologist with the National Geology Society and, as far as I know, he's in Australia. How do you contact him? Overseas cell phone? No. Dad won't carry a cell phone. I write to a post office box maintained by the NGS and they get his mail to him. Primitive, but it's what he prefers now that Mom has passed.

That led to conversation about family in general. Harold thought it pretty amazing that my son-in-law and his son are Marines; that they know a number of the same people; that they've served in the same locations. I told them Larry was on another long deployment only god knows where. He manages to call his wife and children a couple times a month, usually. And I told them about the gifts Hal gave the kids for Christmas, the Marine jacket with stripes and name tag. I didn't mention the dust up with the high school; neither did Hal.

Sarah nodded. "Hal didn't have much in the way of commercial celebrations growing up. So he can catch up with grandchildren. Odd. My son is getting married and without children of his own has grandchildren."

"Does that bother you, Sarah?" I thought it an odd comment.

"No, not in the least. From everything I've heard and experienced, that is definitely the way to go."

I was surprised. But remembering some of Hal's stories about growing up, I sensed that she has always felt that way.

Children are fine but they require so much care. She didn't say that; it was the feeling I took from the comment. And what little Hal has said only enforces the thought.

Hal either was uncomfortable or thought I was. "So. Have you made plans for us for the weekend? Or are we on our own?"

Harold thought it would be nice if we visited his boat and saw where they lived. Sarah has a little desk cubby. And he is a painter. He takes up more room than she does but he does remind her that he paints outside most of the time. I felt there's always been a burr under the saddle about this. But, they've lived on a boat for seven years. Wouldn't you have worked things out by now? I kept my mouth shut. Hal mentioned I was looking forward to seeing their floating home as I'd never been on a ship that doubled as a house. Great. After breakfast, we'll head to the Marina.

The boat was a very nice yacht. Not a huge yacht but larger than the impression I'd been given. The galley is small but it appears there isn't a lot of cooking going on there anyhow. The upper deck is a wonderful place to just lounge, read, or even nap. Harold mentioned that he is sponsoring a small dinner party in our honor this evening. Had he mentioned it before? No, he hadn't. On impulse I had packed a very nice dress, shoes and my Christmas stole. Temperatures range in the mid-sixties this time of year. A stole will be enough.

We got a sandwich from a food cart at the marina while Hal's folk introduced us to their neighbors. They seemed to be enjoying themselves immensely as they showed us off to friends.

Back to the hotel about six. I showered and dressed carefully. I have no idea where we're going or what comes next. Hal felt the same way; he too had packed some good clothes. We met his parents in the living room of the suite. Sarah commented how much she loved that king size bed. Was there one in the other bedroom as well? I told her no. They were too big for me. She laughed. "I can remember vividly preferring to sleep as close to Harold as I could. Good girl."

The look on Hal's face was priceless. Sure wish I had my camera at the moment. I brought the camera but it was in my purse.

"Let's drive to dinner, Hal." His father got into the front seat with him. "I'll point the way."

Sarah and I sat in back. "You look so fine, Madlyn. At ease, even though you're out with two nuts you have just met."

"That comes from working in the Library, Sarah. You'd be surprised the number of nuts we have every day. And each one of them is wonderful."

"Madlyn, maybe you should be the writer. I like the way you speak."

"Thank you. That's a mutual feeling by the way. I feel you mean what you say and you say what you mean. Some people have trouble coordinating the two." I hope Hal hadn't overheard the remark.

The drive was fairly short. We pulled up to a large building that seemed to house a few small businesses. It does. One is Harold's art gallery. There is a large central plaza inside the building. Tonight it is crowded with round tables with white cloths and chairs and a lot of people. It quieted down as Harold and Hal walked in ahead of Sarah and I. Harold held up his hands.

"Thank you all for coming. I know my son is a bit shy about making announcements and so I am doing this for him. This is my son Hal and his fiancée Madlyn. Welcome to their engagement party."

Hal turned and looked at me - shocked. He stepped back and took my hand. There was food and more food. Everyone was dressed to the nines. This was a big event party. I sneaked my camera out and took several photos. We became a receiving line. Sarah or Harold introduced us to their friends. All eighty of them. An hour later a band set up. Harold asked if Hal remembered anything more than the waltz. Hal said, "I've been getting lessons from Lyn. We dance often."

"Good, I wouldn't want you to embarrass me." He laughed and then reminded us we were the guests of honor. No one could dance until we did. Hal took me by the hand. He went to the band leader and talked a minute. I have no idea what he said but we started off with a rumba, to a fox trot, to a tango, to a slow romantic waltz. Then the band stopped as if taking a breath before continuing to play good dance music. The crowd joined us on the floor.

When we got back to the hotel, and in our room, I said, "You could have told me we were going to do an exhibition for your Dad. I could've picked up one of the roses to put between my teeth."

"Are you upset with me?"

"No. Yes. Does your Dad do this competitive challenge often?"

"All the time."

"Quit taking the bait. Someday it'll backfire and I don't want to have to pick up the pieces."

The next morning at breakfast Harold leaned across the table to me. "Madlyn, you must have been a dance instructor in a former life. My god, you two dance so beautifully. You sure shut me down."

I looked him square in the eye. "Good. But it won't happen again."

Sarah clapped her hands like a small child. "Hal, I told you she was the right woman for you. It's too bad you didn't meet her earlier. I really like her."

Hal was fumbling. I could feel it. I put my hand on his. "Sarah, Hal met me at just the right time in both our lives. Neither of us were looking. We were both blindsided. I've had an entirely different up bringing than Hal but he'll come around. My family adores him. They're all competitive but believe it was the Marines that makes Hal competitive. I'm not saying competition is a bad thing to goad your child with, but it can be a killer. Hal was in competition long before the Marine Corps."

Now I've done it. But apparently not. Harold reached across the table. "Madlyn, you really care for my son. It's obvious. I was afraid you were another of those who had their eye on the bottom line but Hal just didn't meet their qualifications. Why does he meet yours?"

"Why? Because he's everything I want in a man. The Marine is all a facade except when he's coaching grand kids in the swimming pool. He's thoughtful, generous, kind, and damn good looking. And, he says he loves me. What else counts?"

"He doesn't make much money with the Bureau."

"I don't make much with the Library. What's money got to do with it? I have a home with no mortgage. I have family. I have a steady job. I like what I do for a living. I don't need Hal for money. I need him for consolation, exhalation, consideration, conversation, someone who likes my cooking; someone who loves my family. If I was looking for money, I would never have given Hal a second glance. His appearance doesn't say money - it says he is a warm, loving human being."

At this point I was ready to ask to go home - to California. I was furious. These may be Hal's parents but they were piss poor parents raising him and don't seem to have improved with age. The engagement party was an extravagant affair which made no sense to me except they wanted to celebrate Hal's happiness. I thought. Maybe it was a show off competitive thing I don't understand. Perhaps he does it with all his friends. I don't know. But my dander is up.

Hal hadn't moved a muscle during my tirade. Maybe I'll be going back to California alone. Well, so be it. His father is a piss ant. His mother may be a known author but she's an enabler. I wanted to bite my lower lip to keep from bawling but either would be a show of weakness. I've gone too far for that. I've actually issued a challenge. Good grief, I'm as bad as Harold.

It is fortunate we were not in the center of the restaurant as I'm sure everyone would have heard my tirade. We were nearly in a corner. I had kept my voice down but also know my voice tends to carry. Oh shit, I am ready to give Hal the ring, pick up my stuff from the hotel, and catch a bus to the airport.

Harold cleared his throat. "Then you're not a gold digger."

"What? There's no mine at this table."

Sarah laughed. "Madlyn, thank you. You're everything I have ever wanted for my son. Let's get the hell out of here. Men, we'll walk back to the hotel while Harold figures out a good apology."

Still no clue to what is happening, I picked up my purse and followed Sarah out of the restaurant. It's a few blocks to the hotel and I am not a slow walker. Neither is she. So if she plans on saying something, now would be a good time. We come to the entrance of the hotel where several stone benches line the walk. Sarah sat down, rather heavily.

"Madlyn, I would sincerely apologize to you for my husband, but I believe every man must apologize for himself. I understand from Hal you have the same philosophy." I nodded. "Do you know who my husband is? Really know?"

"I know that he's Hal's father. I know that he retired as a well-regarded scientist from JPL. I know that he's a very smart man who loves to fish and moved to Florida when he retired - which was only seven years ago. That's all I know. What should I know?"

"He won a large sum of money and that's the reason we retired. A large sum of money. It's in the bank and Hal is the only beneficiary."

"And I am supposed to be loving Hal while hoping his father dies before I get too old to appreciate his money? Are you serious? That is the most obscene thing I have ever heard. I didn't know his Dad had money. Money is money. I have enough to do the things I love. Why would I marry someone and hope his father dies soon? That's what Harold is saying I am doing. As soon as Hal gets here, I'm getting my plane ticket from him and going home."

"No, no, don't do that. It'd break Hal's heart. Madlyn, he's never loved anyone before. He's kind of a nerd who doesn't realize how brilliant he is. You know that and have showed him how to be the kind of nerd who is aware of his life, his surroundings, his needs. He has called me more in the last six months than in the previous six years altogether. He needs you. You've shown him what it is like to live and love and enjoy both. That's why I sent him the ring. He didn't propose until he had it, did he?"

"Actually, he did." I told her the story of the Gala. How he asked me a thousand questions about my childhood, my family, stupid stuff. And then he asked me to marry him. "That was early morning, like 3am, December 11th. He gave me the ring on Christmas Eve, in front of my daughter and grandchildren. He got down on one knee and said to the kids, "This is so you know exactly what this ring means." and he proposed, again. The kids giggled and shouted and were deliriously happy. They love him so much.

"But, I won't put up with a father-in-law that makes everything a competition. I was angry over the first dances last evening, later, when I realized it was a goading competitive move on Harold's part. I was furious." "You do dance well together. Frankly, Harold was amazed. You literally called him out." "Not me, Hal spoke to the band leader. If I had known then what I knew later, it wouldn't have happened. Every Wednesday for several weeks Hal came for dinner and dance lessons as he wanted to be able to dance well at the Gala. He already had the basics down; it was more fine tuning than anything. We danced so well, we ended up on the front page of the Life section of the Sunday paper. He knew we could do it and did it to prove something to his father. I'm not built that way. I'm sorry, Sarah. I think you would have made a great mother-in-law."

Harold and Hal arrived at that moment and Sarah stood up. She faced her husband and said, "I hope to hell you can convince Madlyn you're a jackass and didn't mean a damn thing you said to her. She's planning to go back to California today. Do something. Don't just stand there with your tongue hanging out."

Hal put his hands on my shoulders. "Lyn, please. Let Dad explain why he is the way he is about money. That's the whole problem; money."

"Your father can keep his money. Maybe he should talk to you and tell you he's going to give it to the Humane Society or something. However, if you are waiting for the wind fall, we can call us off. You don't need any more than you have. When you retire, you'll still have income. But if money is so important to you, I need to know. I also need my plane ticket. I'm going home."

I went to the desk and asked for my room key. The clerk looked surprised; I'm sure he could see Hal on the sidewalk out front. He gave me a key.

The rooms had been made up already. I put my suitcase on the end of my bed. Hal came in and turned me around. "Don't leave. Come talk to Dad. He's never met an honest person like you before. And I believe he's sincerely sorry for his behavior. He'll have to apologize for himself but I'm sure he's sorry."

"Why didn't you tell me that your father has money in a trust for you? Why all this hush-hush business and then I get lambasted without being aware why."

"I never think about it. My dad's a competitive piece of work and frankly I figured it was all BS to keep me under control. Of course, it has never worked but I figured that was it. I doubted there is more than a million dollars. I still do, actually. I think it's just another of dad's ploys to stay ahead in a game I never realize I'm playing."

"Your mother says he won an award some time ago - over a million dollars. And finally seven years ago they decided to retire. They were both more than old enough to collect social security. And the award money was just a cushion they figure you'll get sooner or later. Though they did buy the yacht."

"Dad is a well-known artist. His gallery is incredible. Did you see it last night? And Mother still has royalties coming from the first Sarah Storyteller books. They don't need the money either. I don't know why Dad has decided a woman could not see any good in me unless there's a big payday at the end."

"That's because your father has never gotten to know you."

A knock on the door; it was both Tuckers.

"Madlyn," Harold came with a foot of me. "I apologize for being such an ass. It was inconceivable to me that anyone could love Hal for Hal's sake. He's FBI for pete's sake. Other than being fairly good looking, he's just an average guy. I didn't know people still exist that can dig down to find a man's inner core. I apologize. I want you to marry my son. You're the best thing that has ever happened to him. He tried the law, he aced the Marines and now he's a Fibbie. Maybe what he needs is to be a loving husband."

"Maybe if you didn't make everything in his life a competition, he'd be more likable to you. I believe now that you're probably the reason Hal joined the Marines instead of using his education as a private attorney. And basically, you're probably the reason he left the Marines as well. I'm sorry, Mr. Tucker. When I marry someone, I marry their entire family. I don't want my grandchildren to ever know you."

"Don't go home today, Madlyn." Sarah had been crying. "Stay and we'll behave and maybe you can find something in us to love. We did produce this man you love. There must be some good in us. Please stay."

How do you walk away from a plea that sincere? I turned to Hal and cried in his arms. Can I truly give up this man because his father is an ass? Maybe if I never see him again. I don't know. I just cried harder.

Hal politely asked his parents to leave our room. "Lyn, put on your jeans, sneakers and t-shirt. Let's go walk the beach. If you decide you still want to leave, I'll come with you."

CHAPTER SIXTY

The beaches at Apalachicola are nearly as beautiful as Southern California beaches. They aren't as warm and the ocean isn't as blue but they're beautiful all the same. We both changed into jeans. I don't know where his parents disappeared to but they weren't in the suite when we left it. We walked the beach for more than an hour. There is a small stand serving drinks and we stopped for a glass of tea with mint. It was refreshing.

The wooden benches were warm and comfortable. As I finished my tea, Hal begged me to reconsider leaving Florida today. "Our tickets are for tomorrow afternoon; please stay. My Dad's bark is worse than his bite. Honest, Lyn, he is just rough around the edges. As a scientist, he's always been deferred to and he expects that treatment even now. He's quite an artist and has a following. People know one side of him or the other. No one seldom sees the whole man. Unfortunately, you dug him out immediately. I agree - my Dad is a competitive man; always daring someone to be better than he. He's never been bested - until now. I think you called him out and he doesn't know how to handle it. He'll come around, I'm sure. Give him a chance."

I couldn't respond. I don't know how. I want to marry Hal but not if his father is a prominent part of the package. As there won't be any grandchildren, his Dad would have no excuse to visit. For the past seven years, his parents have not returned to California. And it appears to me they never will. They might not even come for the wedding. In fact, I am fairly confident this trip was intended to take the place of their coming to Hal's wedding. The big engagement party. All a part of the plan; this is our contribution to his marriage. Now, we can quit playing parents. I didn't voice this thought to Hal. He thinks they quit playing parents a long time ago. As for the supposed big money - Hal thinks it's a sham; another of his Dad's devices; there is no money. He's never counted on it as he doesn't believe it's real. The yacht cost a lot and Hal thinks that's the money pit. But give Harold a chance? Is that a requirement to marry Hal? Guess that's my question.

"Lyn?" I had forgotten Hal was waiting for an answer of some sort.

"Hal, does our marriage hinge on giving your father a chance? Is this a case of love me love my dog?"

"No. It is not."

"But you're afraid you'll lose your Mom if I don't?"

"Yeah, I guess that's it."

"Don't expect me to be Susie Bright Eyes for the rest of the stay. Let's go back. I need a shower and I have sand in my shoes."

That evening at dinner, Harold apologized again. It actually sounded sincere. I asked him if he really thought Hal would want to marry someone who even vaguely resembled the person he painted me to be. He was quiet for a long while then said, "No. That's why I hope you'll accept my apology. I give Hal a bad time because he's a hell of a lot smarter than I am. I love him; I trust him; please forgive me for being an ass."

He put his hand on my hand. I covered it with my other hand. "Harold, I accept your apology. Please know I'm not really good at giving second chances to asses."

Harold laughed. "That sure puts me in my place. Okay, once, but think hard before being an ass a second time."

I decided, out loud, that Atlantic salmon isn't quite as flavorful as Pacific salmon. Sarah said, "I've been saying that for seven years. However, the shrimp here is the best."

Harold had taken us to a very, very nice restaurant. There was a great dance floor and a good band. Hal asked if I would like to dance. I would. On the floor he thanked me for handling this situation so well. I told him I loved him too much to do anything else. Though I probably could have done better with it. I apologized for my behavior. "Though warranted, it was uncalled for. I am sorry I feel as I do. But, that's me. Better you know now."

When we got back to the table, Harold asked if I would dance with him. I held my breath; had he talked to the band? Was he going to try to show me he was better? Oh, hell, at this point I don't care. I said, "Thank you, yes." I stood up and he swept me onto the dance floor. He's not a bad dancer but not nearly as good as Hal. I didn't say that out loud though. Hal and his Mother danced. She seems to have enjoyed it very much. Probably so; she doesn't have to prove anything to her son.

Sarah excused herself to go to the ladies' room. She looked at me expectantly. I stood up and said, "Me too."

"You're not sleeping with Hal? There are two beds in your room. I noticed they'd both been used."

"Nope. I'm not. He stays over a lot but sleeps in a guest room.".

"For heaven's sake, why?"

"My grandchildren are thirteen, almost fifteen and nearly seventeen. Hal thinks they need every good example of growing up they can get. After he'd stayed over once, my granddaughter popped in as she thought she'd left a book in "her" room. Happened to be the room Hal had slept in and as we were at breakfast, he hadn't made the bed yet. She came out and said, "Grams, someone's been sleeping in my bed."

I nearly laughed but Hal spoke up, "Oh, Baby Bear, how awful." She said, "Does Grams make you sleep in my bed?" He said, "No, but we don't believe you should sleep with someone you aren't married to, even though we are old and decrepit."

"Oh, well, you're engaged."

"That we are but we aren't married."

Laurie said, "Wow, yeah, you're right." It's never been mentioned again. I don't know if she told her brothers or her mother but the point was made."

"And that doesn't bother you?"

"Sarah, my husband went missing about fifteen years before I met Hal. I never thought of fooling around in all that time. Never even dated as I felt I was still married. So I don't miss the physical as much as I could. It's going to be like starting all over again. But it's necessary to set an example - especially as the kids respect Hal so much."

"I'll be damned. Madlyn, that's a hell of a story. Someday when you have nothing else to do, you can tell me the whole story. I can tell 'went missing' barely describes what happened."

"Someday."

We both used the facilities, washed our hands, combed our hair and went back to the table. The men decided we should dance a bit more and then head for the hotel. It is our last night in the beautiful little town of Apalachicola, Florida.

It was sheer delight to land at Ontario Airport the next afternoon and go home.

CHAPTER SIXTY-ONE

We stood on the shuttle island in the middle of airport traffic. Shuttles run every fifteen minutes. We saw one for our lot pull away from the island as we crossed the road.

"Hal, I need to apologize to you. I apologized to your Mother but you're the one I really owe an apology. I sincerely regret being such a jerk with your father. I should have, and could have, handled the whole thing a lot better. But the more I thought about your growing up, the angrier I got. I have the feeling you chose Columbia because your Dad said you'd never get in there. And you took the California bar because you didn't want to stay in New York. But you joined the Marines soon after passing the California bar and it was probably your Dad giving you a bad time somewhere along the line when you mentioned something about lawyering in California. If you want a bad time join the blank-blank Marines or something. So you did. Only he couldn't stand you being rank and file and here comes the Officer Candidate School offer. That takes references and a lot of pull. In the Marines he couldn't harass you anymore. But the longer you stayed in the more you realized the Marine Corps is just one big bully. You banged around for a year or so and your Dad probably goaded you somehow into applying at the Bureau. I know; that's a hell of a lot of supposition on my part but from things you've said and after meeting your Dad, I am sure every move you've made in your career was somehow prompted by your father. He gave you a challenge and you accepted. Where would you be today if your Dad hadn't challenged everything you ever did?"

Me and my big mouth. I think I have really stepped in it this time. Hal has such a look on his face that I can't read. A lot of anger - directed at me or his father? I don't know. The shuttle wasn't in view yet. He sat down on the little metal bench. "I have been wondering that myself this weekend. Your suppositions are pretty right on. I didn't realize it at the time but he did challenge me to do this or do that even when I was doing okay in whatever. I think Mom said maybe I'd make a good attorney. Dad said the best law school is Columbia and no way can Junior get in. Of course, I did. Some of California's laws are a bit archaic and I said so. A Few Good Men was in the theaters, or had just been, and my Dad said if you think the law is archaic, you should try the military. I saw the film and thought I could be a lawyer in the Marines. Without checking that enlisted men seldom rise to any stature in the Marines, I joined. You're right. Dad was furious. If you wanted to join the blank-blank military, you should have said something. I finished basic and found orders to report to OCS. I can't remember how I stumbled on the Bureau. I wasn't living at home; had been trying different jobs after I left the Corps; I don't think Dad had a thing to do with my applying at the Bureau. That may have been my first independent decision in my whole life."

The shuttle for our lot pulled up. It was crowded and we didn't talk. When we got to the car, Hal put our luggage in the trunk. He stood at the back of the car for a while. I thought maybe the car had a flat tire or something. Or maybe he was just mentally reviewing our conversation. He came around and got behind the wheel. He eased onto I-10 and headed home; still silent.

As we got off the freeway, he said, "I have been wondering if he's trying to dissuade you from marrying me because he didn't think of it first."

"What?"

"All this BS talk about money and gold diggers - Lyn, I believe it is all a lie. If my mother believes it, she may be surprised if he dies first. He did win some prestigious award while at JPL - years before he retired at seventy-four. Mom had retired from Cal Tech two years before he retired. I think the bulk of that award went into the yacht. It's not a weekender, it's a pricey ship. Personal opinion is that whatever the remainder is has been his carrot on a stick to get what he wants. I doubt that it's close to a million. I've never been swayed by the money as I've not been in a position for him to manipulate me after he got it. Until now."

He parked in my driveway. I went to unlock the house and he brought in the luggage. What have I stirred up now? My grandmother used to say that whoever stirs the pot should be made to lick the spoon. That's not an exact quote. Have I stirred the pot? Or was it Harold? How accurate is Hal's assessment? Is his Mom really that naive? Or is she at a point where some things no longer matter so she lets Harold do or say whatever? I do believe most of us have a point like that.

It was nearly dinner time. They don't serve peanuts on the airline anymore. They offered a snack box for five bucks but it didn't sound that appetizing to either of us. And I can't think of anything in the house that can be dinner in a short time. This doesn't seem to be a time to ask about dinner, however.

Hal came in. He gathered me closely. My luggage is parked inside the front door. "Lyn, I am sorry we made this trip - in a way. Still, maybe it was a good thing."

Laughing, I said, "The engagement party was stupendous. I'm going to tell the grand kids all about that. I have pictures. I can wow them that I met Sarah Storyteller and the great painter Harold T. I noticed that's how he signs his oils. He is a fantastic artist. I can tell them about the beach; watching the tide come in; that Pacific salmon is better than Atlantic; and the day time temperatures were mid-60s every day. I think that's how I choose to remember this weekend. The fact that I met your parents is kind of a side story. They are two, old, retired people."

"And you're still going to marry me?"

"Yes, I am. Some things don't change with the tide."

CHAPTER SIXTY-TWO

The following week I received a letter from my Dad. He is in New Zealand at the moment. He wrote, "My dearest Madlyn, Your letter was like a soap opera, Daughter. I am glad that you have finally learned what happened all those years ago. I still mourn our Eddy. And frankly, I agree with your assessment of Jim Nolan. He got along fine without you; don't waste time on him now. Meeting someone like Tucker sounds like winning the lottery. One never knows what is around the corner, do they? Speaking of which - you know I am eighty-two now and traveling is not one of the things I do best. Unless your heart will be severely damaged by my absence, I will not come for your wedding. I walked you down the aisle once and thought that would hold forever. Ask that dear son-in-law of yours if he can possibly fill in for me. I will expect photographs however. I will be in New Zealand to the end of June and then am going to London. My health is good. I am as handsome as ever. I love you, Daughter. Do write soon with details - about anything. Missing you sorely, Love, Dad. PS – The newspaper you sent was superb. Well done, my Librarian."

Tears crept down my face. What a great letter. I'll save it for Lee to read. I didn't expect Dad to come for the wedding. A walk down the aisle again seems superfluous for a second wedding. Hal and I haven't discussed a wedding at all, other than there will be one. It's his first. He may have ideas of how it should be. Might be a good idea to talk to him, Lyn.

Hal still comes for dinner on Wednesdays. No more dance lessons but we watch television together. And many Wednesdays, he stays the night. In Baby Bear's bed as he calls it since Laurie found it unmade. This Wednesday after dinner, I handed him Dad's letter. He was very touched by it. Says he'd love to meet a man who realizes he's still handsome at eighty-two. I hope someday he will.

"One reason I am sharing this, Dad has brought up a custom at most weddings. I've been there, done that. But you haven't. Do you have any idea what kind of wedding you want? Formal, informal, destination, family only? Or where you'd like this wedding to be? Or who to invite? Catered, potluck, do-it-ourselves? Music, dancing, just get married at the courthouse? This is your first wedding. Hopefully, your last. You should plan it; or at the very least, have a lot of input."

Hal sat with the letter on his lap. He began to smile. "I guess I always figured the groom's job was to show up."

After I stopped laughing, I got my laptop and sat next to him. "Okay, let's talk wedding. Because it's us and we're old, we probably have particular people we want to invite. Youngsters invite everyone they've ever met - to share their joy and maybe get some nice gifts. We're just into sharing joy. So, who will you invite to your wedding?"

He leaned back and scratched his chin. "The guys I work with. Not the whole office but the ones I actually know,"

"How many? Do you want to do names now or just number guesstimates?"

"There's eight of us and the chief - four are married, chief is in the middle of a divorce. So, thirteen. Maybe by the time we set a date, the chief will have arm candy or something. So say fourteen."

"Work - 14. Then who?"

"A couple of my neighbors. I've been in that complex quite a few years and know everyone but am friendly with four, two are married, two are single, oh and the landlord and his wife. Say eight."

"Work - 14; Neighbors - 8."

"For a few years, I played on a basketball team and have remained friends with three guys. All single. We get together once a month during basketball season and sometimes other times. So - three."

"Work -14, Neighbors - 8, Team guys - 3."

"Right at the moment, I think that's it. Oh, wait. My mechanic. He has bugged me for years to get married and says I damn well better invite him when I do. So John and his wife. She's a real kick. So two more."

"Work -14, Neighbors - 8, Team guys -3, Mechanic - 2."

"That's all the comes to mind right now. How about you?"

"Well, we know Dad won't be here and we aren't sure about Larry, so Family - 4; Library Staff - Hal, I have to invite them all if I invite one. There's thirty-eight and nineteen are married. That's 57. A couple outsiders I work with on other projects - probably 10 total. Total 71 + 25 = 96. Okay, that leaves out having a wedding here at home. The house can't accommodate a hundred people comfortably."

"I don't have a church affiliation but there are a lot of churches that rent out their sanctuary for weddings. Do we want a church wedding? Harrelson and Linda got married at what she called a wedding venue. Big hall, decorated, bar, dinner, pretty impersonal but there was a chapel and the reception was in the same building. I could check what the rental was - of course, that was nearly three years ago but it'd give us an idea."

"I've been to weddings like that. Eddy's girlfriend was married at a wedding venue a few years ago. Really impersonal. I guess we could get permission for one of the City parks. We have some lovely parks and a couple have bandstands if we wanted to use them for the ceremony."

Hal leaned back and pursed his mouth as he often does when he's concentrating. "I know the perfect place. I think we could get permission."

"Great, where?"

"The Library. Maybe we could ask Judge Johannson to officiate at the wedding. You know we have to have somebody. He's on the Library Board; he knows you; he even signed your divorce papers."

All of a sudden he started laughing. And laughing.

"What's so funny?"

"Did I tell you when I met the Judge in the parking lot and asked him to sign your divorce papers he said it was about time you did that. Then he asked if you had finally met someone. And I told him, no sir, I don't believe so. He'll remember that and I'm going to have to be ready to swear I had no intentions at that time. He's a riot, Judge Johannson. But I bet he'd marry us. He's one of the good guys."

I'm sitting remembering how the Judge took on Mr. Swanson in the last Board meeting. Oh, yeah, he's one of the good guys.

"So what do you think? Try for the Library. We know the lobby will hold a hundred people, a band and a bar."

"I just happen to know the Director. But maybe you could ask the Judge if he thinks the Board would approve the usage. Tell him we'll clean up after ourselves. And pay whatever rental they think we should pay. And, you may be surprised to know that a couple weeks ago a few staff members were talking our wedding and they suggested the Library."

"So, the wedding's all planned but the date?" Hal looked relieved.

"Oh, gracious no. Reception - finger food or sit down dinner? Band, bar and dancing? Flowers? How many attendants?"

"Attendants?"

"You were Tom's best man. Did he have groomsmen besides? How many women stood with Linda? Those are attendants. Gift for each attendant. Special theme color? Do I buy a dress for my attendants and you rent tuxes for yours? Or will it be more casual; suits and street length dresses? Of course, the bride still frequently buys the dresses for attendants if she wants something special, color, look, length, etc. Will your attendants just wear a nice dress suit? One color or will you ask them to wear brown, or black, or blue or whatever they have? And then there's the rehearsal dinner. That is usually one of the groom's biggest expenses. Family sometimes, all attendants and the officiate have dinner the night, or two, before the wedding after they have rehearsed the wedding."

Hal sat there for quite a while. "I remember that stuff. We all wore our best suits which happened to be gray. Linda's attendants all wore rose colored long dresses. They were all alike. I remember the rehearsal dinner. One of the restaurants near where Tom was living then has a banquet room and it was held there. The food was okay but not especially great. Good lord, I see why people get married at the courthouse or go to Las Vegas. That's a lot of effort just to get married."

"So, all the groom has to do is show up, huh?"

"So a good deal hinges on how many attendants. How many should we have? I'll ask Tom to be my best man."

"And here is the snag. I don't have a lot of close personal friends to choose from. I had thought of asking Laurie but then the boys would be hurt. A likely choice would be Alice. We've been together for maybe a decade. She's a great assistant. She's a real character and I believe she's never been in a wedding. She was engaged a couple years ago and the guy just bailed. Said she was too immature. I told her she was lucky; guys like that don't last too long. And if they do, they get fat and bald. So, I think I'll ask Alice. I don't need more than one attendant. The attendants sign the marriage license as witness and you only need one witness, I think."

We sat there next to each other thinking our own thoughts for several minutes. "I'll talk to the Judge - ask if he thinks the Board would approve the Library for a wedding; then ask if he would officiate. If he says yes, when, I'll have to say it depends on the Library Board but late summer. That will give us some time. What cha think?"

"Late summer?" I guess I was surprised he was willing to wait so long.

"You will have vacation coming again late summer. And, for some unknown reason, late summer has, in the past, been quieter at my office."

"Okay - so we have six months to put this together. We can do that. Hal, you're a genius. I hadn't even thought of time off. Wow. You can tell it's been a long time since I've gone on a honeymoon. By the way, the honeymoon is also the responsibility of the groom. Rehearsal dinner and honeymoon. And whatever else the bride-to-be asks of you."

He closed my laptop and put an arm around me. "I'll take your word for it, Lyn. Whatever you say." He sounded happy but may have been teasing. That's okay. At least there's been discussion about a wedding. I'm sure once we have something concrete my grandchildren will have some ideas. They probably have quite a few already. They sure like this man.

CHAPTER SIXTY-THREE

Somehow, now that we've had this discussion, life seems simpler. Hal is such a goof. He asked if my passport was valid. Of course, I didn't know. I thought so. But why? Well, what if I decide we should do something wild and foolish on our honeymoon - a cruise, train across Canada, who knows. You'd need a passport and I could have wasted money and a lot of planning if your passport was out dated.

"Let me check. It's in my safe."

"You have a safe here, at home?"

"Of course, doesn't everybody? It's built into the floor in the closet. It was a wedding gift from my Dad." Hal followed me into the bedroom.

"Do you want me to leave so you can open it?"

"Good god no. In fact, it'd be a good idea for you to know the combination. This is easier than a safe deposit box. And I can wear my jewels without having to go to the bank."

He laughed. "You are so funny. But I can see the value for deeds and legal documents and your passport. And, of course, your money and jewels."

"My passport is good for another five years. I don't remember renewing it but here it is."

"Good. Then if I do get crazy, we'll be good to go anywhere."

I put the passport back into the safe and twirled the knob. "All you have to know is the date I married Wesley Palmer. Right 3 times, left, right, left and open. Want to try it?" I was being a smart ass - how could he know the date? But he didn't catch that.

He leaned over the safe and twirled right three times, left to 6, right to 12, left to 80 and he opened it. I didn't ask how he knew. He had read my file so often and this was one date they had to know. "I think that's was a good combination. Your Dad's a smart man. Let's leave it - not reset it. That will make it even harder for people to guess."

He hadn't realized that I thought he didn't know. He also took for granted I'd want to change the combination. No, not so.

"Okay. My passport is good for eight more years so we can get wild and crazy for quite a while before we have to worry about it. Thank you, Lyn, for trusting me with the combination."

"I trust you with everything. You are going to be my husband in a few months."

He hugged me closely. "I love hearing you say that."

The end of March Library Board meeting was scheduled for the second Tuesday of March, 2pm. Alice said she hoped it was going to be a normal meeting for a change. The day before she got a fax with an agenda for the meeting. She made the required number of copies and put them with her note book.

"We have an agenda for tomorrow. That's a good thing, isn't it, Mrs. P?"

"Yes, I think it is. Is it a long agenda?"

"No. Appoint a member as Board Chairman from existing members. And a raise for the Director of the Library. That's it."

"Really? They have a raise on the agenda? Good lord, I can't believe it. It's been a long time. Hope it passes."

"Mrs. P, the current Board is delighted with you. Why wouldn't they give you a raise? Maybe even a good one."

The meeting was short and sweet. Judge Johannson was chosen to complete the term of Chairman of the Board vacated by Mr. Swanson. The board unanimously voted me a raise of six thousand per year. When I heard that, I nearly fainted. It's been more than six years since I've had a raise but five hundred a month? Wow. Alice was super delighted. Yes, she knows it's confidential and won't blab but she's still super delighted.

The first of April came around and I asked Mike what he wanted for his birthday. He hemmed and hawed. "What is it? Just tell me."

"Grams, it's pie in the sky. It's a lot more expensive than the other kids. I'd like to go to a ball game. Dodgers cost a whole lot of money, nosebleed are forty bucks."

"Would the Dodgers' farm team in the California League be an acceptable substitute?"

"The Dodgers have a local farm team?"

"Yes, I have gone many times - well, not much since you were born. But the players are top-notch and your grandpa and I used to go often enough we knew at the end of the season which players were going to be called up to the Dodgers the next season."

"Is it expensive?"

"I think the seats are all under thirty dollars."

"I wouldn't have to take two friends."

"If you want to go, invite your friends as always. Let's check the schedule and see when they're playing at home."

I opened the laptop and entered Rancho Cucamonga Quakes tickets.

We read the schedule and Mike said, "April 11th. That's almost my birthday. It's a Saturday. Are you serious, Grams? I can invite Steve and Donnie too? Can Hal come if I invite them?"

"Honey, you're forgetting. Hal is almost your Grandfather. He's family. Of course, he can come. I am pretty sure since it's a Saturday evening, he'd be available. Let me get my credit card. We'll buy the tickets now. Looks like there aren't that many left. They really don't have nosebleed seats out there. It's not a fancy stadium like Dodger Stadium and when it's full, it's full."

"Maybe I better check with Mom first. Okay?" I nodded. Out came his cell phone. He excitedly told his Mom what he wanted for his birthday and Grams wants to make sure the day is okay before she buys the tickets. "It's early in the season so the tickets are going fast. I know because we've got it on screen right now. Mom, seats like this at Dodger Stadium go for over a hundred bucks each. Grams can't afford that but this is their farm team. Is April 11th okay?" He handed me the phone.

"Lee, we checked the Dodger schedule. The least expensive is so nosebleed, I wouldn't even get to the seat before the second inning ended and they're over forty dollars. No, come on, you and Larry used to go with your Dad and me to watch the Quakes. Sure it's a further drive but so what? It's Saturday and cheaper. Okay. I am ordering the tickets now. Eight for April 11th. Well, count - 2 of Mike's friends and six families. Goodbye Lee. Talk to you later."

Mike put his phone away. "She's worried because it's further." "Well, she doesn't have to drive if that's her problem. My car holds us all, I think. Maybe we'll take two cars. Hal won't mind driving. It's not the end of the earth for pete's sake."

And so at 4:30 on April 11th, Hal drove Lee's big SUV and we went to the Quakes game. They won over Inland Empire 6 to 4. It was a good game. Hal had never been to a farm team game and was impressed with the quality of play. We ate dinner at the ball park as the game began at six. Wil, Donnie and Steve had never been to Rancho Cucamonga either. We got four seats and four directly behind. Even Laurie was happy. It was more costly than the other two kids, but not really, we didn't have dinner at a very nice restaurant later. I made cupcakes to take as it would be too late for cake after the game. No one minded - especially the birthday boy. Mike is now fifteen.

We left Lee's after eleven. Hal half-giggled. "Lee is something else. Did you hear her give me instructions on how to drive her SUV. I'm glad she was amiable to my driving. One car is better in a crowded parking lot. I think she had a good time. She mentioned a couple times that she and Larry had been in that park before."

"A couple summers we went to every weekend home game. There were some really sharp players and the games were fast and good. The good old days when Larry was home regularly and had never been deployed out of the country."

"Mike was in seventh heaven. His buds told him he was lucky to have a grandmother who likes baseball. Otherwise, she'd never know about this place. He said yeah, my Grams knows a lot of stuff." "Do you Grams? Do you know a lot of stuff?"

"I know I'm tired. And I know I love you. Is that enough for now?"

"It certainly is. Okay if I stay over?"

"Of course, if you're up, first, please put on the coffee...."

"I know and bring in the paper. I will."

CHAPTER SIXTY-FOUR

Wednesday Hal called me at the Library. He had just talked to Judge Johannson. "The Judge remembered the divorce paper incident. He said, 'I thought she hadn't found someone, Tucker.' Well, Sir, she hadn't. But I had. She didn't know about us for a couple of months. That set the Judge into gales of laughter. He said, 'So what can I do for you now?' I told him two things; intervene with the Library Board to see if the Library, or part of it, can be rented by a private individual and, if so, would he officiate at my wedding. Judge Johannson said yes to both and asked when. I told him mid-August. I was afraid to set a date until I knew I had a place. 'Getting married at the Library,' he says, 'novel idea. Do you suppose we should consider this as regular thing? A bit of revenue perhaps?' I suggested that we be a test case and he said he'd bring it to the Board at the June meeting. He could see no problem now that Swanson was out of the picture. I congratulated him on being the new Chairman of the Library Board. He said the Library has a director who knows what she's doing. Actually, the Board is superfluous."

"He actually said that?"

"He actually did. So all we have to do is decide when in August and let him know before the Board meeting."

"Let's discuss this after dinner, Hal. Maybe over a celebratory martini."

"I like the way you think, Woman. See you at dinner."

We're in the third week of April. Wil's birthday is the first week of July. I need to set a wedding day in August. Is it possible that I could have the entire month of May without having to think outside the box? I want to say something to Alice; she hasn't asked for vacation time yet and I wonder if I should clue her in before she picks an August date. She did take vacation last August. Oh, how do I get myself into these messes?

During July and August for the last four years, the Library has been open on Sundays from 10am to 2pm. It has worked quite well. We could plan a wedding for a Sunday at 4pm. That was about the only data I had to give Hal that evening but he was pleased I had at least thought about it. I believe he is still concerned that I may change my mind. I don't know why. Well, yes, I do. Taking on his father as I did may be cause of concern for Hal. I was pretty upset and, unfortunately, showed it. I wasn't being very adult and should regret it. But I don't.

Hal said he'd call Judge Johannson with a date as soon as we decided on one. We talked and wavered between the sixteenth and the twenty-third. Finally, Hal said, "I'll ask Judge Johannson which day is best for him. Would that be okay, you think?"

We made another martini and decided the final date would be up to the Judge. Hal will check in with him this week.

And he did. Friday morning Judge Johannson called me at the Library. "Madlyn my dear, I have a young man in my office who says he wants to marry you. Our question is, do you like August 23rd as a wedding date? It sounds good to us both."

"That sounds fine. 4pm August 23rd?"

"Absolutely. And Madlyn..."

"Yes?"

"I approve of this wholeheartedly. I plan to inform the Board that you are being married in the Main Lobby. I am sure no one will dissent."

"Thank you so much. I'll begin making plans. You know how that goes."

He chuckled and hung up. Hal was sitting on my front step when I got home that evening. "Let's go out and celebrate. We have set a date."

It's nearly four months from August 23rd. There goes my peaceful May and June. On Monday morning, I was in before Alice arrived at work. Doesn't happen often and she was surprised to see me. She didn't even put down her purse but came straight into my office.

"Everything okay, Mrs. P? You're early."

"I need to talk to you Alice. Seriously."

The look on her face was shock more than surprise. "Have I done something wrong, Mrs. P?"

"Is that the criteria for speaking to my assistant?"

"Well, no. I guess not."

"Have a seat. I want to ask a personal favor of you and, if you faint or something, you should be closer to the floor."

She gave me that 'huh' look and sat in the chair in front of my desk.

"Alice, how long have you been assistant to the director here?"

"Eleven years, Mrs. P. You know that."

"Do you think we've gotten along well in that time?"

"Yes." She's frowning now.

"Do you think we're as much friends as we are director and assistant?"

"Oh, yes, I do. You're probably my best friend."

"Good. I have this favor to ask but had to be sure you feel about our friendship as I do."

"What? What?"

"This isn't public notice yet. I am marrying Mr. Tucker on August 23rd. The Board is going to allow us to use the main lobby for the wedding. It'll be after the library closes - it's a Sunday." Her eyes are getting bigger and bigger and yet I can tell she's wondering what that has to do with her.

"Will you be my maid of honor?"

She fell back into the chair. "Oh, Mrs. P, are you serious? Me, your maid of honor? Me?"

"That's what best friends are for Alice. Isn't it?"

She's blubbering. "oh my gosh, maid of honor, wow" stuff.

"Sometime in early August we'll take an evening and shop for dresses. It's a four o'clock wedding so they can be street length. I am thinking blue. But that's not set in concrete. If you have a favorite dress shop, let me know. I haven't shopped for dresses much and don't know where to start. It's a long way off but I know you usually take your vacation in August and I don't want to interfere with your vacation plans. Is the 23rd a good date for you?"

She fumbled in her purse. "That's funny." She handed me her vacation request. One week beginning August 9th and her second week in early October.

She stood up and smiled. "I guess I should get my day started, Mrs. P."

"Alice, you haven't said if you will be my maid of honor. Will you?"

She ran around the desk and flung her arms around my neck. "Of course I will. What are best friends for anyhow?"

Later I felt bad. That was a terrible way to ask her. She's at her desk humming so I guess it didn't bother her, but when I run it through my mind, it was almost mean. But it's a detail set and one of the biggest. Hal and I haven't decided what kind of reception yet. I want to call a caterer by the end of May. Between return to school activities and Labor Day, I've been told it's busy at the caterers.

CHAPTER SIXTY-FIVE

By Memorial Day the weather had warmed up and so had the pool. It doesn't have a heater other than the sun. Steve came over a few days before the holiday and cleaned the pool. I thanked him for being on top of it. I had almost forgotten the holiday. I asked if he and his family were doing something special. They were going to their Aunt's in Riverside; big parade and picnic and stuff. I called Lee and asked if they wanted to come for a cookout and swim. They haven't been over a lot lately. I told her the pool was clean and ready.

"You know my kids love to swim. We'll be there. What should I bring?"

I hadn't thought about a menu so the two of us developed one then. When Hal called that evening he suggested this might be the time to inform them we've set a date. He's surprised I hadn't said something to Lee already. I said, "It's still nearly three months off, Hal. I just didn't think of it."

Wrong thing to say. "You still want to marry me, don't you?"

"Of course, why would you think otherwise?"

"I just thought you'd be excited and tell your daughter."

"No. She gets in a frenzy mode too early. I have confirmed my maid of honor though. Alice was thrilled and excited when I asked.".

"Okay, so you are thinking about it?"

"I am. We're thinking blue dresses; hers darker than mine. Street length. Have you talked to Tom yet?"

"Yes, and he's pleased. Then we would look okay in gray suits?"

"That would be a very pleasant contrast - blues and gray."

"Okay, I'll mention it to him. I know he has a gray suit. I'll get mine cleaned."

Memorial Day was a beautiful day. We all swam, even Lee. Sometimes she holds back when other than family is there. So maybe she's accepting Hal as family. The food was great; Wil and Hal handled the grilling. They work well together.

Wil has grown taller this past year. He must be close to six feet now. Still shorter than Hal but impressive. He's bulked up a little. He says swim team has helped him a lot. He'll be a senior this year and so he and Hal have spent a lot of time talking about different colleges and the financial aid he can expect from each. No one is kidding themselves that he can go without aid. Hal is going to contact someone he knows still in the Corps. He's pretty sure there is a program that helps kids with military parents. Hal is encouraging him to apply at more than one school and do it this summer. I think he said get the applications and I'll run through them with you.

The day was nearly over; the sun was slipping down the horizon when we finally got to root beer floats. Everyone was out of the pool and dressed. Hal looked at me and lifted his eyebrows. I nodded ever so slightly.

"By the way, we've set a wedding date."

Four heads swiveled. "Judge Johannson is going to officiate. Sunday, August 23rd at 4 o'clock."

Lee said, "Why so late in the day, Mom?"

Hal fielded the question. "We trying out a new venue. It's not available until four."

Laurie said, "You getting married at the Library, aren't you?"

Hal clapped his hands. "I knew you'd get it. Yes, the Judge says we can use the main lobby and the front reading room and kitchen."

"Why Mom?" Lee looked disturbed.

"Why not? Where else would we have it? We've counted guests and it would be too crowded to get married at home. Though we did think of that."

"You could rent a venue or the Presbyterian Church sanctuary."

"Both would be very impersonal. And may even cost more." I didn't tell her we didn't know how much we will have to pay the Library. "There's ample parking. And we know the Library can handle that few people with no problem."

Mike spoke up. "Mom, people associate Grams with the Library. I think it's a super venue."

"Do you want to be associated with the Library your whole life, Mom?" I hadn't expected this.

"Why not Lee? I love my job. It's a beautiful building. Is there something wrong with being associated with the Library?"

No response. She sat for a few minutes processing. A big sigh. "No, I guess not." That's all she said. Then I remembered she hadn't read my Dad's letter yet. I went to my desk and got it.

"While you're processing, do you want to read a letter from your Grandfather?"

She read it. Then she looked up. "I don't know if Larry can get home in August, Mom."

"Honey, your grandfather was just trying to let me know he hadn't forgotten what he considers a father's duty. I thought it was sweet he thought of Larry. No one needs to walk me down the aisle. We might set up the chairs so there is no aisle."

"Oh Grams, you can't do that." Laurie. "You need an aisle; it's tradition."

I looked at Hal for help. He started this.

"Well, folk, we have nearly three months to work it out. Lee, next time Larry calls will you tell him I would like to talk to him - anytime, day or night?" Hal is finally learning that not all family dynamics are quick, easy, and friendly. He's been lucky so far. Very lucky.

And so, we are into June. Time to discuss invitations and reception. I had forgotten how exhausting it is to get married in a traditional manner.

A week after the Board Meeting, I got a letter. Now, Alice and I were both in the Board meeting but this was official. The Library is available for my wedding. They stated day, time, restrictions. The fee is one hundred dollars. Use of main lobby, front reading room, adjoining restrooms and kitchen; the Library Staff will set up chairs, please notify head of maintenance of requirements. Library liquor license will cover the event.

Alice brought the letter to me and said, "We're in, Mrs. P. We're in." She is getting excited again.

Wil came to talk about his birthday. Could he go to a Quakes game too? Everybody had a great time. I said, "No restaurant dinner?"

"Oh, Grams, we had so much fun at the ball park. The cupcakes were great. The public announcement that they were celebrating Michael Baxter's fifteenth birthday. All that good stuff. He's jazzed they gave him a cap that says Quakes."

"So you want a cap that says Quakes, too?" I could see he was trying to decide if I was serious or poking fun.

Big smile. "Yep! I want a cap too."

"Okay, let's see when they're home close to your birthday." We got on the computer.

"There's no home game on your birthday, but one on the 2nd, a Thursday. There's one the next day on Friday but that's July 3rd. Might be really crowded. They are on an away game on your birthday. It's up to you. Both days still have tickets available."

"I'll call Mom." He explained to Lee what he wanted and the fact that there was no home game on his birthday and the second and third are open but the third's awful close to the holiday. There weren't a lot of good seats left for the Friday game anyhow and he'd rather sit where we had for Mike's birthday and there are seats available there now on the second. She agreed it'd be more fun. I got my credit card and reserved eight seats. He's sure Donnie and Steve can go that night. I didn't ask but I believe they may have already discussed it.

"Lancaster Jethawks. Are they a good team, Grams?"

"They used to be. Guess we'll find out." I put in the birthday announcement request as I had for Mike and printed out the tickets. I hope Hal doesn't mind a late night in the middle of the week. Wil said he'd call Hal tonight and invite him. I said that would be a good thing.

Not married and already I am taking Hal for granted. Got to curb that.

CHAPTER SIXTY-SIX

There was a lot to do at the Library. The last two weeks of June are usually spent selecting books for the rest of the year. We buy all year long but aim for best sellers, what we consider sleepers, new authors in June. We have a regular committee of ten. All have been with the Library for more than five years; all are avid readers. Grandparents, parents, students. A very diverse group. It's not hectic; it's just exacting. Once we select titles, or authors, we have to determine how many of each to purchase. We have a budget. Thanks to the Gala last year, our budget expanded by thirty percent.

Alice has been excited every day since I asked her to stand with me at my wedding. She hasn't told anyone in the Library, yet. She talked to me about it and thought it would be best if it wasn't public knowledge quite yet. I don't know why she feels that way but I told her she knew best.

The baseball game was excellent. Wil also was given a Quakes cap for his birthday after it was announced that we are celebrating Wil Baxter's seventeenth birthday. Hal didn't mind the late night at all. He said it was a welcome relief and he could rest on the weekend. I reminded him it was the Fourth of July Saturday. Would he be present at the family bar-b-q and swim party? Of course. But, of course.

On the Fourth Lee and I spent some time in the pool and then sat down to discuss what kind of food should be served at the wedding reception. Hal hasn't been much use when it comes to reception food. Lee and I decided as it was at four, we should probably have sandwiches, salads, picnic stuff and, of course, the cake. I called the caterer, who did the Gala, in May and promised I'd have a menu by mid-July, a head count by August 1.

Hal and I did a very carefully worded invitation. I did a lot of checking in the etiquette books to properly do a second marriage, or older marriage invitation. I picked up the invitations on July 7 and we spent the next two evenings addressing them. I bought a roll of stamps. We sent an invitation to his parents and to my Dad even though we aren't expecting them. The invitations went into the post office on my way to work on the tenth.

Hal was amazed he hadn't thought about invitations. While we were addressing envelopes, I asked if he wanted a wedding band.

He looked blank. "Hal, I have an engagement ring which should be replaced with a wedding band. If you will wear a wedding ring, I'd like it to match the one you give me."

"Oh, snickle fritz, I haven't bought you a wedding ring."

"Let's go tomorrow after work and see if we can find one we like. We don't have to exchange rings. There's no law that says you have to, I just kind of like the idea."

"Yes, I'd like a wedding ring. And yes, it'd be nice if it matched yours. What will you do with the engagement ring?"

"Many people wear them next to the wedding band. Mine is an heirloom. I'd like to wear just a band and keep it for special occasions. You know, when I really want to flash my diamonds."

"Are you making fun of me, Madlyn?"

"No, Darling, I am serious. Remember the flash of diamonds at the New Year's party?"

He grabbed me around the waist. "I really need a humor tune up, don't I?"

"Hal, you don't need anything. You are perfect just as you are. You have to remember I have an odd sense of humor."

There's Zales and Jareds and a couple other chain jewelry stores close by. But Hal said there is a small store right here in town that seems to have very fine merchandise. Of course, how could I forget? Box has been on the main street of town all my life. Hal met me at the Library at 5:30 and we walked down to the small store.

The jeweler asked good questions. Gold, silver, platinum or something else? With or without stones? Etching outside, engraving inside? When he saw the engagement ring he said, "I have absolutely nothing in the store that could compliment that ring as it should be." I told him I didn't intend to wear it regularly once I was married. He asked to look at it and actually smiled and said, "Oh, yes." Then he called over his shoulder to someone in the back. "Alfred come look at Madlyn Palmer's engagement ring."

Alfred came. He almost swooned. He asked Hal, "Wherever did you get this ring?"

"It was my father's great or great-great grandmother's"

"Do you have it insured? It should be added to your fine art's rider if you keep it at home."

"I have a very secure safe. Why?"

They are passing it back and forth each using a loupe to inspect the ring more closely. "Madlyn, Hal, this ring is so valuable I couldn't even afford to make you an offer on it. I am quite sure it is a Chopard design. Louis-Ulysse Chopard was Swiss. He founded his company in the 1860s. Highest quality diamonds. This is superb quality platinum. The company is privately owned; most are on the exchange, not Chopard. See this little mark right here? Definitely Chopard 1874. So there may be at least three greats in front of that grandmother." He handed me a loupe and pointed to a very small artisan mark.

Hal has more than surprise on his face. I handed him the loupe and the ring.

He said, "This little squiggle actually says Chopard 1874?"

"It does indeed."

"Well, Lyn, put it back on and guard it with your life or whatever they say in times like this. Mr. Hooper, it's a family heirloom and we can't afford anything like it. But we would like a nice set of wedding bands." I slipped it on my right hand hoping to try a band or two.

Mr. Hooper pulled out a couple of trays. Alfred said, "Madlyn, I'll write an appraisal for you. Insure it as soon as your insurance company opens tomorrow. It is beautiful, perfectly made, an unusual design and exquisite materials. This square cut weighs about sixteen grams - that's about eight carats. I will say on the appraisal the stone is estimated at sixteen grams. The color, clarity and cut are superb. The lowest estimate I would make is $450,000."

Hal is looking at wedding rings and I'm looking at an engagement ring worth more than my house. Alfred gave me an official jeweler appraisal. "Please. Insure it." I nodded. Oh I definitely will. I had thought twice about even wearing it as it is rather large and flashy but also very elegant.

Hal had selected two sets. "Lyn, do you like either of these?"

"After this news, I hate to ask but how much are they?"

Everyone laughed and Mr. Hooper handed me one set of bands. Nine hundred dollars, very sophisticated looking, not flashy but beautiful. Definitely perfect. I glanced at the other set and wondered why Mr. Hooper handed me these. Basically, they look the same. I got out my checkbook and asked how much tax on four hundred fifty. The rings were gorgeous. I slipped the women's version on my finger. "How long to resize this?" Hal tried the other ring on. It fit very well. Mr. Hooper made sure it was a good fit.

He sized my finger and said, "I can do it tomorrow. When is the wedding?" Hal told him. "Plenty of time but I believe I can do it tomorrow."

Hal spoke up. "If we were to have something engraved inside, how long would it take?"

"We engrave here. What would you want?" Hal said, "H&M and the date." Mr. Hooper wrote it down on the resize order. He gave Hal a copy of the work order. Hal nodded, that was right.

"Wednesday next week." I said I'd call from the Library on Wednesday before I headed home.

Hal got out his checkbook and paid the balance. Walking back to the parking lot he said, "I intended to pay for the rings, Lyn."

"You don't understand, do you? I want to give you a ring. I want the right to give you a ring because I bought and paid for it." We walked another block. Then he nodded. "Makes sense."

Then we passed the bakery - they were still open. "Hal, do we want a wedding cake?"

"Well, yeah."

I took him by the elbow and made a right turn into the bakery. Everyone greeted me - I used to stop in nearly every morning for a cheese Danish on my way to the Library. "What can we do for you, Mrs. Palmer. Danish is all gone." I thought that was a dumb remark.

"We know Danish is frequently gone by nine am. We'd like to order a small wedding cake." What a surprise! Date was the first thing. Ummm. Sunday. Could it be delivered the day before? No. Where would it be delivered and when? The Library - two blocks north around 3:30 on that date. There seemed to be a disagreement. I know a lot of people get married on Sunday and the cake is delivered that date. Wedding cakes are pretty damn expensive. If you can't get them when you need them, forget it. I have shopped here for twenty years - this was the first indication that they didn't hire knowledgeable help on the front counter.

I said none of that out loud. But when they hadn't come to an agreement and hadn't called the owner (whom I know well) in ten minutes, I said to Hal, "I'll just talk to the caterer." And we left.

I was very disappointed but a cake wasn't going to be a burr at my wedding. I don't know how long it took for them to realize we were gone.

The next morning I called my insurance agent and the caterer. I told the caterer we didn't need a fancy cake with too much frosting on it. Could they possibly make a tiered cake to serve one hundred and maybe decorate it with fresh flowers or something? They certainly could. He'd stop by the house next week and we'd discuss it and review the menu. I thanked him. Didn't even ask how much it would cost. At this point, I don't care.

CHAPTER SIXTY-SEVEN

The insurance company demanded about a dozen photos of the ring from every possible angle and a copy of the appraisal. I took the pictures with my camera, making sure the artisan mark showed, and emailed them with the appraisal as soon as I hung up the phone.

Hal came over about eight - he'd been in the office all day. I asked if he had called the Judge to find out if he wanted a rehearsal and if so, was Saturday at seven okay. No, he hadn't but he would tomorrow. I suggested, "Call him at home. Tonight."

"I don't have his home number."

"I do. He's on the Library Board and I'm friends with Miriam."

So he called and the Judge said as it was a different type venue, a rehearsal might be a good idea. Shouldn't take even half an hour but it would save time at the wedding. Hal said that he'd arrange for a rehearsal dinner after. Please bring Mrs. Johannson, if she feels up to it. Judge said he'd meet us at the Library, Saturday, August 22nd at seven.

"Hal, are you on this side of the County at all the next week or so?"

"Should be next Thursday and Friday unless this case falls apart. Why?"

"We need to get a license."

"Oh, yeah. Damn. Lyn, how do you remember all this stuff?"

"I wrote it down a few months ago. Remember?"

He did.

"Have you decided where to have the rehearsal dinner, Sweetie?"

"No, well yes, how many people will be there?"

"Probably eight. Judge and Miriam, Tom and Linda, Alice and her current beau, you and me."

"Oh, that's not too bad. I'll call Luigi's. Do you think the rehearsal will go much longer than half an hour?"

"Probably not."

"It's a Saturday. Oh, I should have done this two weeks ago."

"Hal, don't sweat it. You know Luigi's. If there's any way in the world they can accommodate us, they will. Tell them it's your wedding rehearsal dinner."

"Okay. I may as well call right now. Right?"

"Hal, is this beginning to sound like a bad idea?"

He looked startled. "Absolutely not. I am just not aware of all the stuff that has to happen."

"The caterer will be over next week to go over the menu and cake. If you want to come, I'll let you know what evening he'll be here. In case there's something you'd like added. Lee and I pretty well made a menu on the Fourth. But maybe you'll want to add or omit something."

"Evening?"

"Yes, either Tuesday or Thursday I think. I'll let you know and if you can make it, great."

The caterer came and went and Hal was satisfied with the picnic theme. That's what the caterer called it. Make it yourself sandwiches on slider buns with lots of fillings. Three salads, good relish tray, a punch bowl. A punch bowl that will be kept filled. And wedding cake. He had drawings of a cake as he thinks I want it but he has never done a fresh flower cake. I like the drawings. I told him that we're sort of going with blues. Are there blue fresh flowers? He thinks so.

The band is the group from the Gala and so are the bartenders. Though there is only one bar and two bartenders. The caterer advised Hal how much of what to buy for the bar and the caterer will furnish ice. He also told Hal where he could buy and then return unopened liquor. Seems like a win-win to us. The caterer told Hal he'd hold on to the liquor until we got back, or if we gave him the receipt he'd return it. He gets down there frequently. I thought this was great as we could select what liquor and what brands.

Hal called me at noon the following Thursday. Could I meet him at the courthouse at one? I said I would be there. I gathered up all the data I would need to get a marriage license. It's much more complicated now than it was thirty years ago.

As we left the courthouse, license in hand, I said, "I hate to bring this up. There is one more thing we should do together before the wedding."

He looked me as if I had two heads. "You're joking, of course."

"No, my dear soon-to-be husband. There's one thing I really want."

"Okay." He looked resigned

"I want to buy a new bed. Maybe an extra-long queen as you're fairly tall. I could do it but I don't know if you like a firm mattress or a soft one or what. So when you have the time, will you come with me to buy a bed?"

He laughed. "That's the neatest thing yet. Sure. I'll pick you up after you're home from work tonight, we'll buy a bed and have some dinner. Deal?

I kissed him. "Deal."

The bed will be delivered on or before the 14th. We bought new linens. It is an extra-long queen size.

July just seemed to vanish. I am down to buying dresses. As soon as Alice gets back from vacation, we're going shopping. I bought her a bracelet as an attendant gift. It's something I'm sure she'll wear. Simple but slightly elegant. And it will look nice at the wedding. I know she'll want to wear it immediately.

Alice called me at home on the fifteenth. She was home from her vacation. How were things at the Library? Did I want to shop today? I told her that was a brilliant idea. Did she have a preference of dress shops? As a matter of fact, she did. At least, a place to start. Like me, Alice has lived in this town her entire life and she knew of a dress shop her mother used to patronize. "Their window display is always work and play clothes, Mrs. P, but in the back of the shop they have the really good stuff."

We looked at perhaps five dresses in the back of the shop before Alice told the clerk we were looking for dresses for a wedding. The clerk said, "Just a minute." The dresses we had seen were all quite nice but Alice said there was no piazza. The clerk brought out a dress in a very pale blue. I asked if she had the same dress in a darker blue.

She started to take the pale blue away. "No, no, we want the same dress in different shades." We tried on the dresses. Alice's fit perfectly. It has a full skirt, knee-length, three quarter sleeves, and is a lovely shade of darker blue. The pale blue was the same design but didn't fit me as well. The clerk went and got the shop owner who said it would be a very minor alteration.

We both really like the dress. How long for the alteration? Oh, it'd be ready Tuesday. She took measurements, marked the dress and asked if I could come in for a fitting Monday. "Is 5:30 too late in the day?" Not at all. I wrote a check for both dresses; the alteration was free.

Alice was 'over the moon', she said. She took her dress home. I took a photo of Alice wearing the dress. Hal was thinking shirts or ties in a blue.

Now he has a color reference. Monday Alice asked what color shoes should we wear? She brought a medium heel white dressy sandal. Would this be okay? She bought the shoes while on vacation. I went shopping to find a pair similar.

The rehearsal went quickly. The Judge made suggestions on how to set up the chairs. Alice took notes as it's her job to have the chairs set up - we have a contract with the Library. That all seems convoluted to me but Alice said not to worry; it's her job.

Rehearsal dinner was superb. Laurie babysat Tommy for the evening. Luigi's outdid themselves for the dinner. Hal had ordered the same entree for everyone. He said he's gone to many dinners and never had to worry what was on the menu. It seems logical to do it this way. It does for many reasons and no one was unhappy about it.

When Hal dropped me off at home at 10:30, I was relieved. One more function and I can relax. I don't remember getting married as this great a hassle in 1980. Of course, my Mother was alive and she must have absorbed most of the worries.

Sunday morning I made my own coffee and brought in the paper. Hal called about ten. He sounded a bit nervous. I was more than a bit nervous. Getting married is a breeze - all the stuff leading up to it is the hard part. I ate a small lunch. Lee came over about two thirty to see if I needed any help. She had promised Hal to bring me to the Library. The grand kids will walk over.

When we arrived at quarter of four, it appeared everyone else was there. We stopped in the kitchen and spoke with the caterer. The cake is outrageously gorgeous. Three tiers and pale blue cornflowers and delphinium cascade down one side of the cake. White roses with blue ribbons adorned the top layer. Lee had her phone and my camera with instructions to take lots of photos for Larry, Hal, and her Grandfather. Hal has been on robopilot all week and may not remember some things.

Alice and I were in the front reading room awaiting our cue. She looked at me and said, "Mrs. P. I have never seen you so beautiful. And your pendant - did Mr. Tucker give that to you? It goes so well with your dress. You wear it every day and said it was from a very dear friend; Mr. Tucker, right? I always wanted to ask and suppose I'm out of line now but it's so romantic."

"Alice, I am an exceptionally lucky woman. Mr. Tucker gave this to me when he asked me to go steady with him. Do people still go steady or just us?"

"People do but they seldom say go steady anymore. I knew it was super romantic. And he's so handsome."

Before I could agree, the music started. "Are you ready, Alice? You lead the way. I'm right behind you."

She smoothed her hair and touched the cascade of white roses on her shoulder. "I'm ready."

The band has a piano that can sound like an organ and the pianist played Mendelssohn. No aisle walks; Alice and I came in from the side. It was still pretty impressive. Hal said later that he held his breath from the moment the music started until I was standing next to him.

Judge Johannson started with the usual "We are gathered here today" and then told a joke that was actually funny about how he had met Hal several years ago. Hal actually grinned. I'm sure he had forgotten the encounter. In twenty minutes, we were husband and wife.

The Judge introduced us as is frequently done. Then he said, "For all of you who have called Mrs. Tucker, Mrs. P for the last couple decades, remember, it's now Mrs. T." Over half the group was from the Library and they all laughed. Hal stood there and beamed.

The reception was a lot of fun. We danced first dance, a rumba and then a slow waltz. Then a lot of people were dancing. The picnic theme went over well. Because the punch bowl was always filled, the bar wasn't always busy. The band quit playing at eight and the crowd gradually left. Our request for no gifts was honored.

Hal and I went home.

CHAPTER SIXTY-EIGHT

Neither of us had any alcohol at the reception. I think we both wanted to enjoy the moment as it truly was. The punch was great. The caterer told Hal that the bartenders had received good tips, there was some unused bottles he would return for us and he gave us the small top cake layer in a box suitable to stick in the freezer.

Hal thought that was the most clever idea ever. We are supposed to eat it on our first anniversary. He'd never the tradition and thought it was really a super idea.

Once home Hal made two martinis. We sat in the living room quietly. Shoes off and feet on the coffee table. I know I was processing the day. Everything had gone off as planned. It was a good party. Every invitation we had issued except two had been there - our parents. I said, "I am glad everyone honored the no gifts request." Hal said, "Well, everyone but two."

"Two? Who?"

"Your Dad and my parents."

"Really? I haven't seen anything from either."

"That because they both came to me." His jacket was over the back of a chair. He got up and reached in to the inside pocket. "Which do you want to read first?"

I shook my head. "I don't know. I am surprised."

"You know I called my Mom after we learned how valuable the ring is. She said that we should consider that our inheritance and I said okay. Does she realize the value? Yes, after you told me, Hal. She said that when she took the ring to have it cleaned she suspected something as the jeweler seemed quite interested in it and said for costume it was attractive and he offered her two hundred dollars. She was sure he was a fraud and a cheat and was half afraid to leave the ring with him. Though she had no idea of it's true value why would he offer two hundred for a piece of costume jewelry? She was sure it was worth a bit more than he let on. Here's her letter."

He handed a fragrant pink envelope to me.

"Your father and I respect your request for no gifts. You're both of an age where you don't need things. We decided however that maybe you want something. When we first married we had nothing - as they used to say not a pot nor a window. You both are satisfied with what you do have but hope you'll accept enclosed check. Maybe open your first joint account - that's not a challenge, Madlyn, just a suggestion. May you have a long and happy marriage. We love you both and appreciate that you love us. Sincerely, Mom and Dad"

The check fluttered into my lap. It was a certified check for five thousand dollars.

I looked at him with utter surprise. "I know, Lyn, I felt the same way. It's a certified check. We should accept it."

"I hadn't thought to reject it if it wasn't certified, Hal. I am just surprised. Evidently my tirade is going to follow me the rest of my life."

"Remember Mom and I both think Dad's tale of a million is just that - a fairy tale. I think the ring and this check are saying, you're right but we don't want to admit it."

I held the check in my hands still shocked. "You may be right. But you were never looking for an inheritance anyhow."

He nodded. "Now for the second letter. I wrote to your Dad several weeks ago after I was sure your passport was valid. He's in London now. I asked if he'd be available to spend some time with us if we came to London on our honeymoon. This is his response." He handed me a letter postmarked London; I recognized my Dad's beautiful handwriting.

"Dear Hal, Apparently everything my darling daughter has said about you is true. What a wonderful honeymoon - to see her dear old Dad. I am not being facetious, Hal. It would be most exciting for me to meet you and see my darling Madlyn. The idea that you would share your honeymoon with me so she can spend time with her Dad says more about you than anything you could write or she could say. The NGS has put me into a little cottage with two bedrooms. A housekeeper comes in weekly for the important stuff. I have arranged for us to tour this part of the United Kingdom; Scotland, Wales and of course Jolly Old England. And Ireland as well. This tour is the wedding gift you did not request. I'll leave it up to you to get here and home again but once you land, the wedding gift kicks in. There is some marvelous geology in this area of the world that I know Madlyn will enjoy and I will enjoy pointing it out to you both. I hope that you will enjoy it also. Let me know what airport and when to meet you. Truthfully, I must admit, this is more a gift to myself. Waiting to meet you - love to my Madlyn, Love Dad."

With tears in my eyes, I looked at my husband. He is seated on the coffee table and watched me read. "You wrote my Dad saying you were taking me to London for a honeymoon was there any way we could see him as well?"

"More or less, I guess that's what I said. I told him you miss him a lot and understand his not coming for the wedding. I also told him I'd like to meet the man that raised a woman like you. I told him we had two weeks and he could pick and choose the time he could spend with us. This is his answer. I hope you don't mind my boldness."

"Mind? I love it. Not only will I spend time with my Dad but I will see country I've never seen. Geology is his life. I have a minor degree in geology so may appreciate this gift more than you. Then again, you surprise me so often, you might be a natural geologist and not know it."

"We should get to bed. Our flight to London leaves at 3:40 tomorrow. Lee et al are taking us to the airport and are picking us up at noon. We arrive at Heathrow at 10am Tuesday. Your Dad says he'll be waiting at the gate."

I rinsed the martini glasses. Surprisingly, the house was in good order. No tidying up needed tonight. Hal locked the front door and turned off the porch light. I turned off lights as I started down the hall.

"Wait. Wait. I forgot to carry you're over the threshold."

"How about the bedroom threshold? Would that do?"

Sometime during the day he had brought over his luggage, already packed, and a change of clothes. I will finish packing in the morning; easier now that I know where I'm going.

The new bed was everything the salesman had said it would be. I've slept on it alone for a week and have enjoyed it. Hal slipped between the sheets, stretched out and said, "You're right. It is a perfect fit." The sun was up before we were. Hal brought in the paper and I made coffee. Lee will be here at here at noon. It'll be a busy morning. And tomorrow this time, we'll be in London.

Milton Keynes UK
Ingram Content Group UK Ltd.
UKHW020625171124
2899UKWH00031B/332/J